A Monstrous World Novel

Sweetling
A Fantasy Fae Romance

S. E. Wendel

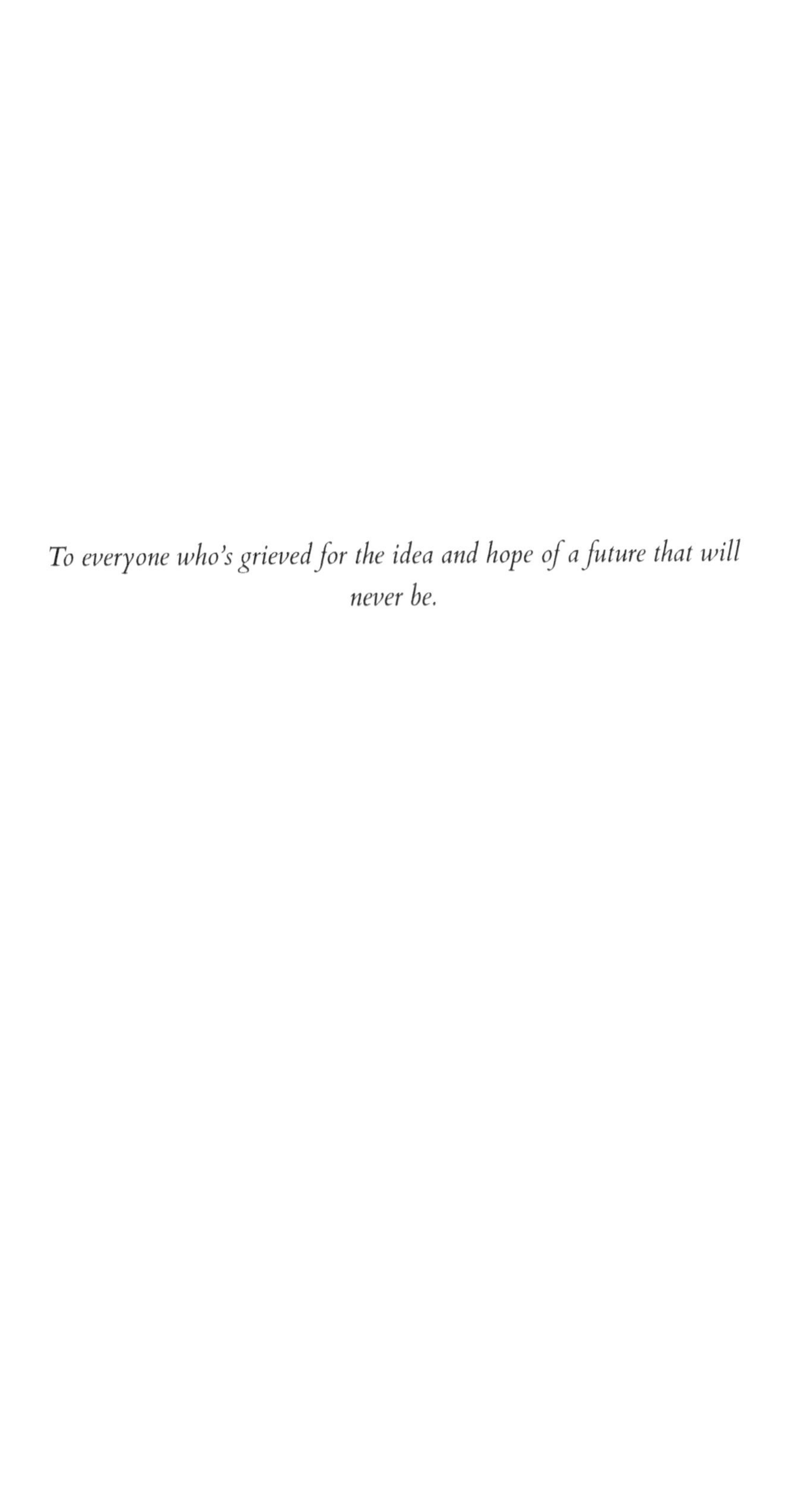

To everyone who's grieved for the idea and hope of a future that will never be.

The Fish
Culda
Larach
Shanago R.
Scar
Northpoint R.
Kilkarach
Bandaraugh R.
Granach
EIREA
Middlerun R.
Calca
Casholl
Rathcaran
Brigga
Southford R.
The Scales
Gray Knolls
FAELANDS
Kinva
Lune R.
Griegen Mountains
FALLORIAN
Kaldebrak
The Twins
Holdur
ORCISH
TERRITORIE
BALMIRRA
Innrinh
DRAGON KINGDOM
The
MONSTROUS
WORLD
HIGHHOME
The Droplets

HD
2024
CALEDON
Glendown
INSLEY
The Gates
Bellbee
Larkspur
Intersea
GLEANNA
Adrigoll
Threepoints
Abbon R.
Kilgaran
GOLD SEA
BORDERLANDS
Birrin
LYCEA
one-Skin
Camp
PYRROS
Irynian
Delta
CONQUERED
CONFEDERATION

Before You Begin...

I hope you're excited for *Sweetling!* A few things before you begin:

This is book 3 of the Monstrous World series. The book stands on its own but will be best enjoyed after book 2, *Ironling*.

A few content/trigger warnings: our heroine Molly has lost her parents in childhood and lives with an emotionally abusive uncle who often uses gaslighting and bullying as a manipulation tactic; there are also subtle themes of domestic abuse. You can check my website for a full list of TW/CW; take care of yourself!

The book includes a glossary of people, places, pronunciation, fae, and medieval terms in the back. Don't be afraid to flip back and forth, but don't spoil anything for yourself.

All righty, here we go!

What's Come Before...

Just a quick refresher for you before you begin! In the first book of the series, *Halfling*, a woman named Sorcha is betrayed to slavers, who kidnap her from her family's estate and sell her on to a splinter camp of orcs, the Stone-Skins. Orek, a half-orc whose own mother was a human slave purchased by the clan decades before, frees Sorcha and agrees to take her home. The two fall in love along the journey, and Orek joins Sorcha's large family.

Upon their arrival, they report what's happened to the liege lord of the land, Merrick Darrow. It is Merrick's son and heir, Jerrod, who sold Sorcha out to the slavers after she rejected his romantic advances. Merrick gives Sorcha the choice of what should happen to Jerrod. She decides he should be banished to the Ward, a castle converted into an infirmary, run by monk wardens. He is also stripped of his inheritance and position as heir, which is given to his older sister and Sorcha's friend Aislinn Darrow.

Orek and Sorcha's story spreads throughout the land, and otherly folk (orcs, fae, dragons, manticores, harpies, and sirens) begin arriving in the Darrowlands hoping to start a new life in peace and find a human mate.

In the second book, *Ironling*, Aislinn grapples with her new responsibilities as heiress, as well as her growing attraction to the new castle blacksmith, a half-orc named Hakon. Their friendship soon grows into more, although they are unsure how they can be together. Aislinn's brother Jerrod reemerges with an army of mercenaries to try taking back his inheritance. Among her own force, many non-human warriors fight on her side, including a fae warrior named Allarion and his unicorn steed, Bellarand. In order to secure his participation, Hakon offered a promise to Allarion, to be named at a later date. Aislinn's forces defeat Jerrod's, who himself is killed in the battle, which secures her place. She and Hakon marry the following spring.

Throughout, Aislinn has sought to help otherly folk settling in the Darrowlands, including Allarion, who purchases an abandoned estate called Scarborough. As a landholder now, Allarion has become a familiar face in Darrows' city of Dundúran, where he visits regularly now, in hope of finding a mate of his own . . .

Prologue

Magic crackled like sparks through the dry tinder of a summertime forest, bursting and popping across the pavilion with the zing of an electric storm. The overwhelming scent of petrichor clutched at Allarion's throat as magic swirled in blue spirals through the marble columns and decorative cypresses.

For one horrible moment, everything stilled—the petals from the many cherry and apple blossoms hung in midair, the magic whorls stopped to sparkle with a macabre gleam, even the stars in the night sky seemed to cease shining.

Then, with all the force and devastation of a thunderclap, a crimson drop of blood fell from the vicious Fae Queen's claws.

Her eyes, darker than a starless night and deeper than the bottomless pits that haunted this world, tracked as Maxim fell to his knees before her, a hole the very size and shape of her clawed hand gaping in his chest. Allarion watched his dearest friend's heart beat one last time, exposed to the air and ripped to shreds by the Queen's claws, then—

A horrid gurgling escaped Maxim's throat, and the Queen swiped her wicked claws across that, too. Blood dribbled down his ruined front, and finally, Maxim slumped back onto the white stone pavers. His final breath was an agonized groan, and with the last of his last strength, he reached out to his human mate, dead already on the ground beside him.

The Queen had begun the day and her cruel plan with Aine, capturing her after years of trying to discover Maxim's secret. The human woman had suffered torment after torment as the Queen's plaything, but she refused to forsake her mate and child. Her bravery was seared across Allarion's soul, having witnessed every terrible moment as the day passed and they waited for Maxim to come for his mate.

He indeed came. Alone.

Maxim stood before their Queen and declared her a traitor and a tyrant.

"You should have passed the crown long ago, crone. No one may say it, but all here know I speak true."

The glamour veiling the Queen's true face trembled, revealing a glimpse of a skeletal, haggard visage. Those perfect red lips had smiled just below sockets sunk deep and a shriveled nose. Black veins stood in relief against papery skin, and eyes gone milky with too much seen glared out.

In that moment, any who may have doubted it knew for certain—Maxim was right. Their Queen was corroded by magic, rotting from the inside.

The fae were the only folk left who could wield magic. It imbued everything, the ground, the trees, the rivers—it wove through the very fabric of the world.

Magic gave dragons and manticores their dual forms. Magic gave orcs their superior strength. Magic gave sirens their songs.

Yet none of them could see it nor even remembered it was magic that made them. Only the fae now could see these threads and harness them.

It was a gift and a burden. They had lived alongside it so long, used it in so many ways, the fae were now inextricably tied to magic. They needed it to sustain not just their long lives but their very existence. They did not drink. They did not eat. Magic and air were the only sustenance they needed.

Yet, this came at a terrible price. Magic would eventually corrode every fae from the inside out, like blades left too long to rust. Even the most powerful among them, their Queen, wasn't immune. Exposed to the many tendrils and tethers that tied every fae to their ancestral lands, the raw power of magic was more dangerous to those who wielded it most.

The magic was shared amongst every fae, a circuit of shared burden that spread the tremendous strength of it. But that circuit needed a center, and that center had to be replenished for the health of them all. A Queen, no matter how powerful, couldn't rule forever.

Century after century, for millennia, each Queen had passed her rule to a daughter or niece before sailing to the Twins, a set of islands off the coast of the faelands. There, she took the stone sleep, returning to the earth and rejoining the magic that threaded the world.

Amaranthe hadn't.

She refused to give up her rule. She slew her own daughters, nieces, and sisters. Allarion had to wonder—had the magic corroded her, or had the rot always existed inside her. In the end, it didn't matter, for the Fae Queen had long since outlasted her rule, festering magic and acidic ambition melding into a toxic sludge that inhabited the throne.

The fae withered as the magic soured within them, but none dared speak against her, the hub of every spoke in the faelands.

Until Maxim and Aine.

Allarion couldn't turn away from their forms, their sightless gazes fixed on each other. Aine's torture had lasted for agonizing hours—Maxim's battle with Queen Amaranthe had lasted perhaps a handful of moments.

He'd known he stood no chance against a Fae Queen, not one as old and ruthless as Amaranthe. Magic oozed from her every glamoured pore, and she didn't hesitate to use it viciously.

Without any to support him and stand against their Queen, Maxim had been dead the moment he entered the pavilion. All of them, a representative of every family residing in Fallorian summoned to witness Aine's destruction, knew it. Still Maxim came for his mate, to be with her in their last moments. It was a sacrifice he'd predicted long ago, and both he and Aine accepted it.

With them would die their most precious secret—the location of their child. A half-fae child who'd foreseen the demise of Amaranthe and her court.

Or so the Fae Queen thought.

It'd been a carefully laid ploy Maxim and Allarion made years ago, one Allarion hadn't liked making or speaking of. Sitting in the kitchen of the seaside home Maxim kept for Aine and their daughter, it hadn't seemed like danger lurked close enough to make such plans. Sitting in that kitchen, listening to the women laugh and the waves crash against the cliffs below, Allarion hadn't wanted to believe anything could touch this little sliver of paradise, even Amaranthe.

That was Allarion's folly.

Maxim had known. Perhaps he always had, or perhaps his daughter had foreseen it.

In the end, Maxim and Aine played their parts, dying so that their daughter might live.

Allarion now had to do his—and it'd begun that morning, watching poor Aine's torment and doing nothing.

The punishment for his foolish hopes lay in pools of crimson blood on the pavilion, a fate far worse than he could have imagined unspooling before him.

Maxim had been his friend for longer than humans had kept histories, for longer than the courses of rivers and the span of forests. They had been boys together, those precious few years when fae were young, scampering through the reeds that lined the Lune River to catch dragonflies. They had trained together, claimed their dreadmounts together, fought the orcish hordes together.

Everything, together.

So when Allarion had discovered Maxim's secret fifty human years ago, the very foundations of his being quaked.

A hidden, veiled house by the sea on the border of the faelands. A human mate, pregnant with their halfling child.

To be trusted with such a secret had honored Allarion, but he'd never been able to completely shed his jealousy and resentment. For the life Maxim had hidden from him. For the life his friend had.

Those died with Maxim.

None of it mattered, not anymore.

Allarion's gaze skittered up from the lifeless bodies of Maxim and Aine, watching as the Fae Queen straightened. Her glamour fell back into place, swathing her in perfect beauty. Long ringlets of hair so white it shone like starlight swept slender shoulders and lissome arms. A graceful neck, delicate swooping collarbones, a rosebud mouth, and glittering eyes of sapphire blue complemented a supple body draped in midnight velvet. And four oval wings, more delicate than stained glass and gleaming like pearls, folded at her back.

If the moon could walk this world, it would look like Amaranthe did then.

But she was nothing but a beetle-bitten acorn, hollow and rotten.

His rage burned hotter and brighter than the sun, pulling him toward collision and violence. The sword strapped at his hip hung heavily, and the magic under his command shuddered and whispered encouragement. *Do it,* said the air, *end this.* All would be better without her.

Oh, he wanted to.

He vowed in that moment that no matter the cost or time, he would be witness to Amaranthe's destruction.

But he remembered his vow to his friend.

This wasn't the end but the beginning. And Amaranthe's end wasn't his to have.

That was now Ravenna's.

It took some days for Allarion to escape the seaside court of Fallorian. The gleaming city was full of winding cobbled streets, juniper and poplar-shaded courtyards, glittering reflection pools and steaming mosaic-tiled baths, and gardens of flowers and crystal—a place of immeasurable beauty that felt every day like a trap closing in around him.

He was watched everywhere he went within the city, the limestone towers and coral arches not hiding him for long from the Queen's spies. The harbor, crowded with white oak ships that hadn't sailed out in centuries, offered no opportunity, nor did the serpentine curtain wall that snaked around the city itself. The five great towers of Fallorian gleamed in the daylight, pink and green with the iridescence of abalone shells, their light seemingly following him at every turn.

Fae did not mark the passage of time like the other folk did—yet, Allarion felt it keenly, a knife in his chest with every day that passed without success.

He kept to his duties, aware that all within the Queen's court watched him and anyone ever associated with Maxim. There were whispers in the courtyards, deep in the shade of the poplars, that even the most distant cousin of Maxim's line was being hunted for information.

Allarion had already been squeezed by the Queen's hand for that information, before Aine was captured, and he hadn't broken. He insisted he knew nothing, and that was what Amaranthe got from him. He might have been kept longer had his mother, Idrisil, the matriarch of House Meringor, one of the oldest aristocratic houses alongside the royal line, not intervened. Ever the politician, despite her retirement, Idrisil had made her veiled threats and half-promises.

For now, Allarion was free. But his name and mother wouldn't spare him from another interrogation should he give Amaranthe any reason to send out the long reach of her arm. His first detainment had been painful enough, and as the Queen continued to go without her ultimate prey, her temper only worsened.

The city seemed to hold its breath, awaiting whatever cruel blow would come. Even before she slaughtered her heirs, Amaranthe's temper was legendary. Many knew to keep indoors and quiet. Those with estates outside the city fled in the night. His mother and older sisters had begged him to return with them to the Meringor estate, but Allarion refused. Doing so would inspire more suspicion, incite further royal animosity toward his family, and ultimately keep him further from his goal.

Escaping the faelands.

For days, the agony of waiting alone in the city—entertaining no guests in his family's villa overlooking the sea, releasing all their staff, writing no letters and talking to not a soul—ate at him like the fevered diseases that befell the humans. In the echoing caverns of the villa, surrounded by luxury and wealth but alone with his own company, Allarion nearly went mad with it.

He dared not even speak with his trusted dread-mount, Bellarand the Black, who awaited him outside the city walls.

Instead, he kept to himself. He walked the city as any other scion of a great house might, talking to no one. Awaiting an opportunity.

The one that found him finally was the barest chance, a change in shift of the border guard. Without needing sustenance, fae could go for long periods without flagging—but the two things that kept them tethered to the mortal world were death and sleep. Even fae needed to sleep.

After observing their rotations, Allarion made his move. Sliding through the murkiness of dusk, Allarion came upon a border guard preparing to leave. A young warrior, he'd likely never known a life without Amaranthe—nor was he a match for Allarion. He took the young warrior easily, forcing his magic down the man's throat, subjugating his magic with sheer force.

The warrior went limp in Allarion's arms, forced into the long sleep they all had to take every so often or when severely wounded. Dead to the world until the sleep ran its course, the young guard lay defenseless before Allarion. The sleep was perhaps their only weakness, like sharks rolled onto their backs, and to use such tactics against another fae was considered the highest offense.

There was a day, not long ago, that Allarion would've been disgusted with the very idea of forcing the sleep on another. Even today, a part of him shuddered with horror at what he'd done and had yet still to do.

But the warrior's honor he'd so prided himself on, which had first called him to a life of warrior's service to the crown over a millennia ago, served no purpose here. He'd given it up when he laid down his sword, as so many had, after Amaranthe's slaying of her kin.

Now, his only duty and honor were to family and friends. His mother and siblings were safely out of the city, and their family name would protect them. Now, his only purpose was his promise to Maxim.

With the guard's helm pulled low over his brow and just enough glamour to trick the glancing gaze, he joined the squadron leaving for the city outskirts.

As they walked, warriors peeled off to their assignment, and Allarion kept pace.

It was how, finally, he ended up alone in the forest outside the curtain wall. With a touch of his magic, he tracked the steps of the others on the forest floor, accounting for each and how far they were.

Then, with the love of his friend hastening his steps, Allarion ran.

By midnight, he'd reunited with Bellarand. Without breaking stride, he leapt onto the stallion's broad back and they galloped north.

It's done? Bellarand asked through their bond, the one shared between every fae rider and his dread-mount. It was forged after a grueling trial of physical exertion and magical stamina, a duel of wills between fae and unicorn, where bonds were tested and decided. Only the strongest and truest warriors were worthy to ride the dangerous, magical beasts, for a dread-mount would never accept a weak rider.

Yes.

I grieve for him, too.

Allarion could hide nothing from Bellarand, not with the bond they shared. The unicorn saw everything, every raw shred of fear and dread. There was no hiding from the truths Bellarand could find, and so Allarion did not hide them, but he did turn away.

It took two days of hard riding to make the northernmost edge of the forest, which he followed for another two days as it rimmed the narrow bay.

As he neared Aine's cottage, the hundreds upon thousands of wards that Maxim had lain over the years passed over Allarion like a cool fall of silk. Maxim had thought of everything so carefully, hiding away his human mate on the western outskirts of the faelands, along the sea. No Fae Queen, no matter how powerful, held any sway over the sea, for its magic was too frenetic, too wild. There, on the borderlands by the sea, Maxim had kept his family safely in a blind spot, guarded with layer after layer of wards.

Passing through the inner sanctum of them, where the thickest layers of magic were, Allarion felt a pleasant hum buzz in his ears, Maxim's remaining magic recognizing him.

Heart aching, Allarion resisted trying to reach out to touch that which couldn't be held.

Inside the wards, past an apple orchard glamoured to look like overgrown brambles, stood the lovely seaside cottage Maxim had built his Aine decades ago.

The sight of it, the tableau of peace as puffy clouds floated in an azure sky above and turquoise waves lapped far below along a narrow strip of beach, nearly broke him. How many times had he come here? How many times had he watched the little family laughing and living in this very place?

The door of the cottage flew open, and out ran Ravenna, her inky black hair flapping like a banner behind her.

Allarion dismounted, the weight in his chest dragging him down.

Ravenna came to a halt before him, her narrow chest heaving, those large purple-blue eyes, Maxim's eyes, staring up at him.

A woman of nearly fifty years, she was a child no longer, not even by fae law. She still had the vitality of youth, and her life would extend far closer to a fae's than her mother's people.

Her cheeks, tanned from days in the sun, colored as she watched him closely. Neither of them moved, save for the gentle, salty breeze that picked up her long waves of black hair. Her four wings flitted at her back nervously, the membranes glinting in purples and pinks in the sun. All female fae had wings, but as a halfling, Ravenna's had always been too small for flight.

She was all dark, moody colors—so like her father. Her control over magic wasn't as strong as a full fae, but it still obeyed her. The only true trait she inherited from Aine was her healthy red blood.

Where she'd gotten her gift of foresight none knew—perhaps from the Twins themselves.

Tears gathered along her lashes, but her face remained rigid, as if she prepared to refuse what he'd come to do.

"It's been *weeks*—" she choked.

"I couldn't come sooner."

Striding past her into the cottage, Allarion quickly found the provisions she'd packed.

Ravenna followed close on his heels. "What's happened?"

The words burned Allarion's throat. "Your father was right."

"Where are they?" Ravenna demanded. "Allarion, where are my parents?"

He paused only long enough to glance at her, unable to hide his grief from her. "They are with you, crow. Always."

Her rosebud mouth parted in shock, and she stood in the middle of the cottage's solar staring at him. She looked so broken in that moment, so young, so alone. She may have been a child no longer, but Allarion only saw the girl he'd watched grow over the years.

The love her parents had for her was achingly apparent—in her every feature, in every nook of the house, in all that they had done.

Allarion suspected it was as much of a cold comfort to her as it was to him.

Ravenna's face cracked, and a sob that ripped at his guts echoed from her chest. He reached out a hand and she took it desperately, clutching it with both of hers. Allarion pulled her into him, sheltering her with his much bigger body.

He took her few things and led her back outside to where Bellarand waited.

Neither of them looked at the house as they mounted and rode away. The lives lived there were over. The memories it held were warm and dear—and all the harder to bear because of it.

Ravenna buried her face between his shoulder blades, her tears wetting his cloak as they rode away from the home Maxim had built.

It took seven days to reach the last part of Maxim's plan. His one last gift to his child.

They left the faelands behind, losing themselves to the forest that was at once in the human kingdom of Eirea but also within orcish territory. The fae could touch all magic that wove through the world, but they had cocooned themselves within the faelands, a hard shell that kept others out—and the fae in. They weren't blind to the outside lands, but their sight was as milky as Amaranthe's true eyes.

The growing distance from the faelands began to nip and gnaw at Allarion, the strain of his bonds to his homeland fraying, but he'd counted on this. He had to cut the ties completely, but first, he had to make Ravenna safe.

Through a grove of trees, beside a clear stream bordered with berry bushes, sat the bower Maxim had made. Built into a shallow hill, timbers insulated with moss formed the outer façade. The size of a bedchamber, it had a door and window to allow fresh air. Within a cavity cut into the hill beside it sat dozens of baskets and amphorae laden with supplies for when Ravenna would need them.

She slid down Bellarand's flank, taking in the bower with puffy, dull eyes.

Allarion came to stand beside her. "This is how it must be for now, crow. I cannot protect you yet."

A wet, shuddering sigh left her. Wrapping her slender arms around herself, she said, "It's preferable to missing them."

Allarion watched as Ravenna inspected the bower, running her fingertips over the baskets and crockery—all of which her mother and father no doubt had made. She touched the mossy rooftop and oak door, a diamond cut into the top.

Beside him, Bellarand's long ears twitched, and the unicorn turned his head toward the forest.

They are here.

Allarion looked to his right to behold more than a dozen unicorns emerging from the trees.

They ranged in color from black to dappled gray, and most were female. The mares were too fierce to ride, and it was they who led the herds of unicorns along the western coasts. They were much like the fae in that way, the fae themselves led by females. The males of their kinds were able to bond to protect both their peoples.

Their untamed energy filled the grove, but Allarion sensed no malice—just a deep, abiding sadness.

One unicorn strode forward. Oberon, Maxim's mount.

The gray stallion touched his horn with Bellarand's before turning to Ravenna, his head bowed low. Ravenna embraced him, burying her face against his neck.

Their shared grief was too much to bear, and Allarion had to look away.

It was Oberon's mother who had led her herd here to watch over

Ravenna in her sleep. Not even orcs were foolish enough to trifle with such a large herd. Under their protection, Ravenna would take the deep sleep, one in between the long and stone sleeps. Not unlike torpor, it would dull and hide away her powers until Allarion could return for her.

Breaking from the faelands would take time and effort, sapping him of his strength and leaving him vulnerable—and unable to completely protect Ravenna from whatever dangers might await them. Maxim had decided Ravenna would take the deep sleep while Allarion recovered and sought a place to establish a new life. He would search the human realms for something suitable, and when the place had been imbued with his magic, free of Amaranthe's taint, Allarion would return for Ravenna.

It'd all seemed logical when Maxim explained it.

Knowing what he had to do, knowing that it was all Maxim's wish, did not make watching his daughter and dread-mount mourn him any easier.

With one last solemn whicker, Oberon pawed the earth, leaving his mark in the dirt and claiming the land for his herd. This place and everything within it were now under their protection.

Ravenna regarded the herd in the trees silently for a long while, and Allarion didn't rush her.

He watched on silently as she slowly went about making up the bower to her liking. She piled it with pillows and blankets, digging through a basket of them until she found a particular one. Allarion easily recognized her baby blanket, a faded blue now, the flowers embroidered on one corner beginning to fray.

Holding it close to her chest, Ravenna settled onto the bed inside the bower, staring back at him with unseeing eyes.

Chest tight, Allarion approached. Kneeling before her, he covered her in blankets.

"Will I dream?" she whispered.

So young, she'd never had reason to take the deep sleep. She asked without fear or nervousness, just a single tear slipping down the bridge of her nose.

"No," he said.

"Good."

Ravenna's eyes slid closed.

It was in this last step, this final moment, that Allarion hesitated. The weeks trying to escape Fallorian had been long, but now everything moved so fast. In a moment, he'd leave her there, hoping she would go undisturbed while protected by unicorns and her father's many wards.

It was time to leave the last remnant of his friend, of his life, behind.

For a moment, Allarion couldn't do it.

The tide of his grief swelled, strangling his conviction. He faltered, tears he'd never let escape gathering in his eyes.

I can't, his heart cried, *I can't, I can't.*

Then Ravenna reached out to take his hand. Her skin was so warm compared to his, and he clutched that hand.

She gave him the strength to complete his dearest friend's final wish.

He reached out with his magic to help guide hers. She struggled for a moment, her mind resisting the unfamiliar task, but with a little nudge from him, she found the ancient path that led the fae into the deep sleep.

It took only a few moments, and when Allarion opened his eyes, Ravenna lay still on the bed. Her chest barely rose with the faintest of breath, and her face went slack with oblivion.

For now, she was free.

For her sake, for Maxim's, he left her there.

Allarion stood, closing the bower door behind him. The herd stood silent witness as he mounted Bellarand. They turned east, toward the rising sun and their fate.

I

Three Years Later

The wedding of Lady Aislinn Darrow to her beloved half-orc was a triumph for all the otherly folk who had come to call the Darrowlands their home, Allarion included. As the happy couple made their wedding vows and sealed them with a kiss, he clapped along with the others, his soul a little lighter to see the obvious joy in their faces.

Maxim and Aine had looked at each other in such a way.

The memory didn't pain him as it once had, though it did stir a familiar ache.

Amongst the humans these past years, Allarion had begun to feel time's passage more acutely than ever before. Time couldn't heal, but it could dull.

Each changing season severed his ties to the faelands. Every fortnight away strengthened his own magic and resolve. Every day longer he took was another day Ravenna slept alone in her bower.

That last thought was a constant prickle beneath his skin.

In the years since leaving Ravenna, Allarion had crossed forests and rivers, fighting the pull of the faelands as he searched for a suitable place. It was mere chance that he heard of a region welcoming otherly folk, and he was one of the first to arrive in the Darrowlands almost a year ago to try establishing himself his own little demesne.

After years with just Bellarand to share the burden of his magic, finding the abandoned estate of Scarborough had been an utter relief. He'd found the dilapidated manor house and wild lands charming and begun imbuing them with his magic even before securing the deed to the property.

Months now he'd been there, reclaiming the land from the forest, tending the neglected house, and warding the borders. Every day a little more of his magic seeped into the land, and the estate was coming to life.

It was all good progress. He should be content.

It took time to bond with the new lands. With just him and Bellarand, the magic quickly grew acidic inside him. He gave it to Scarborough, where it was consumed by the trees and the moss and the stream just west of the house. The circuit gave him a day or two of relief before the magic again turned sour. Two years of pent magic had nearly felled him, and he was still recovering from the schism with the faelands.

In short, he was progressing, but not quickly enough.

Every day it took him to shore up his land and defenses was another Ravenna lay vulnerable.

He still wasn't strong enough to protect her. He wasn't even strong enough to leave his new land for long.

There was a possible solution to this. Something so obvious, it was elegant in its simplicity.

A mate.

In communing with the otherly folk who too wished to make the Darrowlands their home, Allarion had learned that most came with the hope of finding a human mate. More than one half-orc had claimed a human woman, and the manticore pride was growing notorious for sniffing around the skirts of every human woman they saw.

He'd long ago let go of any dream of having an *azai,* a heartmate. No fae stirred his soul and magic as an *azai* was supposed to, and Allarion had lived long enough to search for her throughout the faelands. It hadn't occurred to him that she might exist as a human woman, not even after he met Aine.

Allarion had doubted he could find a true *azai,* the one meant for him, the one who could harmonize with his magic, the one who could match his mind and fill his soul with light. But that was all right. He had learned over his years in the human realms that sometimes life was merely good enough.

A wife didn't have to be his heartmate. He wasn't foolish to hope for perfection, just a good woman to help anchor him to this human realm. Such a connection would surely hasten his bonding to Scarborough and enable him to fetch Ravenna that much sooner.

That was, until just this spring, during a previous visit to Dundúran. His path had been one he'd taken before through the city. There'd been nothing special or different about that day—except for when he heard *her.*

A laugh, the sound so pure it lit him from within, as potent as a burst of magic fresh from the earth. Turning Bellarand, he'd ventured closer to a simple well, unremarkable and similar to all the other wells dotting the dozen other city squares. Yet, it was there that he saw *her.*

And when he saw her, heard her, Allarion *knew.* Finally, the Twins were sending him a little luck.

As the ceremony concluded and the new couple stood to thank their guests, he waited patiently to put his new plan into action.

Some months ago, he'd gotten a favor out of the groom, to be decided later and of his choosing, for helping oppose Lady Aislinn's treacherous brother from seizing the city with an army of sellswords. Allarion planned on doing so anyway, had pledged his loyalty and sword to Lady Aislinn some days before, but he wasn't foolish enough to pass over an opportunity.

Like information, promises were worth far more than metal and gems.

He'd had some inkling of what he was likely to ask of Hakon, but now, his mind was made.

It took over an hour for the crowd to thin around the new couple.

Of course, Allarion could have forced the matter. Curiously, despite having made his home in the region for almost a year, the others, humans especially, gave him a wide berth. He didn't mind, per se, but it was curious.

Still, he minded his manners, those taught to him an age ago by his aristocratic mother. As members of one of the most senior noble fae families, much expectation had been placed upon him and his siblings to succeed. Under his mother's tutelage and kindness, they all flourished—his eldest sister became an accomplished musician, and the younger one of the most famed smiths of Fallorian; his brothers had distinguished themselves in botany and husbandry, and ran one of the most successful farms in the southern regions, harvesting the finest wool and growing the prettiest flowers.

For himself, Allarion had excelled at his warrior's training, alongside Maxim and their other brothers-in-arms. They had earned their armor in the late days of the last Fae Queen and distinguished themselves with honor. They guarded the border and fought a handful of skirmishes against raiding orcs in the early days of the new Queen's rule.

But when Amaranthe began waging war on her own people, Allarion and Maxim both had put down their swords. He'd wandered the faelands without true purpose, pestering his siblings and trying to learn their crafts. Nothing suited him.

It was when he went looking for his old friend Maxim that he'd stumbled across the man's great secret. A human *azai*. A half-fae, half-human child on the way.

He could hardly have believed, finding that seaside cottage on the border of the faelands, how his life and fate were about to change. Now, he had far more purpose than he'd ever dreamed.

As Allarion approached Lady Aislinn and Hakon, he noted a human girl chatting with them. He'd seen her before but not been introduced, though it took little to deduce who she was. The golden circlet round her brow would be tell enough, but her presence at the wedding had been widely announced and applauded before the ceremony began.

Princess Isolde, fourteen-year-old heir to the Eirean throne, had graced today on behalf of the royal family, bringing good tidings and congratulations.

She was a willowy girl, obviously amidst one of her human growth phases, her form slightly out of proportion as some parts grew while others hurried to catch up. Still, she seemed a bouncy girl, her smile wide as she talked with the couple.

Allarion didn't have long to wait for his opening.

"I've heard tell of a unicorn living in the Darrowlands," the princess said. "Is this true?"

"Indeed, Your Grace," answered Lady Aislinn. "His name is Bellarand and he's—"

Allarion stepped forward. "Gossiping in the stables and making a general nuisance of himself."

The humans all looked at him owlishly, the princess's guards twitching at his sudden appearance. Honestly, he was light on his feet, but they should have seen him coming. He wasn't as tall as the orcs milling about the castle courtyard, but he was certainly tall enough to catch attention.

He grinned, trying to put the humans at ease, but this only seemed to make them blink more.

So strange. His grinning often elicited such reactions. Perhaps he ought to give it up.

Composing herself, Lady Aislinn swiftly made introductions. Allarion bit back his amusement watching the princess struggle to keep her mouth from falling open at meeting a fae.

"Grant me a moment with the happy couple, and I will personally introduce you to Bellarand," Allarion promised. "And he'll be on his best behavior."

He didn't miss how Lady Aislinn and Hakon exchanged worried looks, but the princess only giggled and agreed, bobbing her head to Lady Aislinn before heading off in the direction of the stables.

When he had them alone, Allarion bowed, his dark cloak sweeping over the cobblestones. Straightening, he tossed one side over his shoulder, revealing the deep blue velvet of his tunic, a sign of his new allegiance to the Darrows.

"My congratulations," said Allarion. "Weddings are always happy days. I hope you may join the revelry soon."

"I've been promised a few dances," Lady Aislinn quipped, peering up at Hakon with arched brows.

The halfling's ears went ruddy in a blush. *How fascinating.* Truly, humans and orcs were so expressive, changing colors with their moods. Their brows too were always moving, always revealing their innermost thoughts.

And even if they were good at controlling their colors and brows, their scents always gave them away. The acidity of anger, the tang of jealousy, the sweetness of affection, it all touched Allarion's sensitive nose with truth.

He scented nothing but happiness from Lady Aislinn and her groom, though he could tell they were a tad wary of his presence still. It would take time for them to acclimate to him, just as he had much to learn of their kinds.

He hoped a human *azai* would speed his education along.

"I won't keep you long. I only wanted to inform you that I have chosen my promise."

Hakon's expression hardened, and curiously, he pulled his new bride tighter to his side.

Allarion watched dispassionately, unsure what the half-orc found disagreeable. He was the one who made the promise, after all. "Don't worry yourself. It's nothing for you to do. Not yet, at least."

"I hope you mean to stay within the bounds of the law," Lady Aislinn warned him.

"I'll do my utmost," Allarion said, laying his hand over his heart. His own promise. Or at least, as close to one as he was willing to make without actually handing over a precious promise. Fae were governed by their promises, bound to their word by magic. Unable to break them, or to lie, the fae had learned to be guarded with not only their promises but their words.

"What is it you want me to do?" asked Hakon, apparently not assured by Allarion's assurance.

"That remains to be seen. For now, nothing." He smiled again, finding the sudden tension quite amusing. "I have chosen a mate for myself. I have had my eye on her a while now, and weddings have a way of invigorating sentiment. I intend to pursue and claim her."

He turned his gaze to find the object of his new affections, and Hakon and Lady Aislinn followed. At the far side of the courtyard, a handful of barmaids milled about, helping the castle staff serve beer and cider.

There.

He spotted her easily amongst the crowd.

Molly.

A peculiar name.

Everything about her was so totally anathema to a fae, from her brown curls cut short to her shoulders, her warm tanned skin and brown freckles patterning her nose and cheeks, and most especially her buxom figure testing the integrity of her embroidered bodice. Her smiles were often, her colors were warm and intoxicating, and her scent . . .

Allarion first spied her drawing water from a well in one of the city squares. Inexplicably drawn to the way her plush mouth moved as she spoke with other women, he'd discreetly followed her back to a tavern. Nothing distinguished it from other establishments like it throughout the city—but the others didn't have *her.*

Allarion didn't imbibe—he'd no need to. Still, he'd taken to coming at least once a fortnight to sit near the back, an untouched tankard before him, just to see *her*.

He wasn't the only one who came to see her. The tavern crowded full most nights, and Molly kept them laughing and drinking with her wit and liveliness. There was a particular way she tossed her hair . . . and how she twisted her body around chairs and tables so gracefully . . . and how she bent over when delivering the drinks . . .

It stirred something in Allarion he hadn't felt in . . . centuries, probably. He'd partaken in his share of pleasures—one partner, multiple, orgies, as well as years of celibacy. A fae lived so long, they had ample time to explore what pleased them most. Yet, as the magic soured with the lengthening of Amaranthe's reign, desire for anything shriveled inside him.

Molly reignited what had once been dead with a lopsided smile and jaunty sway of her ample backside.

Fae could be known for their avariciousness; he'd never desired wealth nor acclaim, but since seeing her, what he desired above all was Molly.

It was the perfect solution. A human *azai* who awoke his instincts and interest would surely hasten a bond to the land and therefore his ultimate goal. That she incited his black blood to burning only made it sweeter.

The couple didn't seem overly pleased to see that his plan now had a purpose.

Watching them carefully, Allarion said, "Your promise shall be to smooth my way if an opportunity arises—and if not, then to at least not interfere."

A tendon kicked in the half-orc's neck.

"Very well," said Hakon. "I wish you luck in your courting."

That was all he needed.

"Thank you, my friend." Allarion clapped Hakon's shoulder before taking Lady Aislinn's hand and kissing the back. "I look forward to seeing you at the next council meeting, heiress. Hopefully as a mated man."

Lady Aislinn blinked in bemusement but finally nodded.

With a final farewell, Allarion left the couple, satisfied that he had gotten all he wanted.

As he made for the stables to introduce the precocious princess to Bellarand, he couldn't help chuckling to himself, though. For as strange as he found humans and orcs and the others, they seemed to find him infinitely stranger.

How fascinating.

2

The wedding of the Darrowlands heiress was like something out of a fairy tale, the ones they told little children before bedtime. Even a green, half-orc groom didn't ruin the vision—if anything, it only enhanced Molly's wonder at the whole day. He certainly cut a handsome figure up there, beneath the trellis festooned with wisteria blooms, looking down at their heiress like she was everything good and sweet in this world.

Molly and the other barmaids of the city, drafted to help serve the hundreds who'd come to see Lady Aislinn marry her blacksmith betrothed, had sighed with the romance of it all. Lady Aislinn's gown, the crystals dripping from her hair, the way she smiled without reservation up at her groom, all of it made even Molly's heart melt a little.

Now, though, it was time to work.

Opportunities like today didn't come around often. The Darrows were compensating all staff handsomely, even the temporary help like her, and Molly looked forward to adding the handful of coins she was set to make to her secret store of funds.

She'd been growing the little trove since arriving at her uncle

Brom's tavern, knowing that someday, she wanted to start out on her own. No one was going to come and sweep Molly off her feet—fairy tales didn't happen for barmaids. So she saved the coins patrons slipped and flipped her before her uncle could make them disappear, preparing for the day when . . .

Well, when something happened.

As she often had to remind Uncle Brom, she was very grateful for him taking her in. She loved her little cousins—Brom had managed to father five of them between two wives and a mistress—and even loved the tavern itself. Were the patrons loud and handsy? Sure, but they were also lively and often generous. It didn't take more than a wink sometimes to earn a little tip.

But gratitude didn't mean she wanted to stay in that tavern forever. She was six-and-twenty and had spent more than half of her life already overseeing her uncle's tavern and motley brood.

Molly wasn't sure what else was out there for her—nothing, Brom liked to insist—but she wanted the opportunity to find out. And that required money of her own.

Brom had of course protested her leaving the tavern to work the wedding instead.

"Who'll look after this place?" he'd complained.

"No one's going to loiter here when it's the heiress getting married," Molly reminded him as she'd left that morning. *"I'm sure you can manage the one lost soul who wanders in."*

"But the little ones—"

"Already staking out good spots." Probably to then sell on their claimed places for a hefty profit, no doubt. Cherubic as the young ones were, they had the shrewd mind of their father.

She'd left Uncle Brom blustering. That was the way to deal with him, for if he was given an inch, he took a foot, as all the women in his life had found out. It was no accident that all of them had left him and no woman in Dundúran would marry him.

Today, he didn't matter, though.

True, she was working just like any other day, but getting out in the sun, seeing the beautiful ceremony, and taking part in the happiness of the whole city put some jaunt in Molly's steps. She and the other servers kept the thirsty wedding guests happy as the ceremony came to a close and people began to meander through the courtyard or form a queue to congratulate Lady Aislinn and the new Lord Consort.

Molly flashed her best smile—and her fantastic set of tits—as guests walked past. More than a few extra coins landed on the table she manned, and she was sure to wink and bid them come back for more.

It was a game she and a patron played—just enough flirting and flash of skin to keep them enticed but not encourage more. She'd been working tables and serving drinks since she was a girl of thirteen. Her womanly figure had come in much sooner than most, and to survive, she'd had to learn to use it to her advantage.

She still harbored deep insecurities over her body—her tits often garnered too much attention, and her backside had gone round and her belly soft with the thick tavern foods she ate most days. Patrons, *men,* sometimes took her curves as invitation to grab and grope. She'd become adept at dodging or rebuffing, knew when to flirt and when to drop her smile, but that didn't always save her from grasping hands.

It was why, despite her thick thighs, she wore trousers rather than kirtles most days. And why she'd ended up cutting her hair to her shoulders. Not as easy to grab.

Molly didn't like being grabbed.

Still, for the special day, she'd donned her best kirtle and prettiest blouse, with sleeves she'd embroidered herself. The garb was all bright colors, meant to attract attention, and left the top swells of her breasts exposed. She felt safe serving from behind a table, thinking the worst of it would be a sunburn to her tender tits.

She wasn't prepared for her peace of mind to come under threat.

Turning from the last patron to the next, Molly nearly jumped a foot in the air when she saw who stood at her table.

The fae.

There he stood, the ghost of her uncle's tavern. With his impressive height, he positively loomed above her and her table, those dark eyes with their black sclera boring into her with all the intensity of an eclipse.

Fates, something had to be wrong with her, because when he looked down at her like that, something inside her quivered—and not with fear.

Molly didn't know why, but over a month ago, just as suddenly as he appeared before her now, he'd arrived at her uncle's tavern, looking lost.

Every patron had gone utterly silent, as if death itself had entered. The fae looked them over with those unnatural eyes, his thin mouth drawn into a perfectly straight line. Covered from shoulder to toe in a cloak blacker than night that seemed to move like shadow, he'd had mercy on them only after agonizing moments of tense silence, taking a seat at the back.

Molly had been the first to recover, forcing her feet to move and take his order.

"Whatever you recommend," he'd said in a voice smoother than water that made Molly's toes curl in her old boots.

Men weren't supposed to sound like that. Like promises made over pillows, warm amber syrup over griddle cakes, and spicy bonfire smoke, all in one.

He said little else, merely sitting in the back for about an hour before leaving. His mead went untouched, and a neat stack of coins had been left on the tabletop for her.

And so it went, a visit every few days. He said very little, even if Molly wished he'd say more. One word from him could hush a room full of rowdy men, which always gave Molly a thrill.

Seeing him here now . . .

Of course he'd be here, he's friends with the groom. And had fought alongside Lady Aislinn last winter. *And* was now a landholder of the Darrowlands.

Molly wasn't sure how long she stood there gawping at him but hoped it wasn't too long to be rude—or that at least as a fae, he wouldn't know the difference.

Smiling wide to hide how her belly fluttered with that something, she said, "Hello again. I don't have your usual here, that's two tables down."

"Hello," he said in that way of his, not slow but not hurried either. Measured. "Whatever you have is fine."

"Maybe you'll care for cider more than mead," she quipped, a gentle poke at him never seeming to drink much of what she brought him in the tavern.

He reached for the tankard she offered, and Molly couldn't help noticing that his hands were ungloved. She didn't think she'd ever seen his fingers before and noted the scars on his knuckles.

A fighter.

She also couldn't help noticing the faint black pattern just below his pale purple-gray skin. His veins. There were prominent ones tracing up his neck, with fainter, spidery veins spread like a root system across his cheeks and forehead. It'd taken her a few visits to figure out they weren't faded tattoos or markings but veins.

It maybe should have disgusted her, horrified her, even. Just the opposite, though.

His large hand fell over hers to take the tankard, lingering for longer than necessary. Molly knew a lingerer when she felt it, but unlike other times, she didn't efficiently pull her hand away.

She lingered, too.

"What I care for is that you are the one to offer it," he said, those thin lips pulling back into something of a smile. It revealed elongated eyeteeth—*fangs*—which should have been terrifying.

A blush marched up Molly's neck to heat her cheeks.

"Oh . . ."

She'd heard it all, every line and compliment, but somehow, in that voice that was deeper than mountains and oceans, she nearly melted.

Get hold of yourself!

Her fascination with the fae served no purpose—and he was holding up the queue.

But once more, just as quickly as he arrived, the fae bowed his head. "Good day, miss," he said with grave politeness. "Until next time."

"Farewell," she managed through her stupor, just as he turned on his heel to head off in the direction of the large castle stables.

Next time, he'd said. There would be a next time.

Molly's heart fluttered with excitement as she dared to think the most outrageous thing she'd ever thought.

What if . . . he comes to see me?

A sharp elbow caught her in the ribs, and Molly startled, looking up to see a grinning Jennet beside her. Another barmaid, for a tavern down the way, and one of Molly's friends, Jennet waggled her fair eyebrows.

"What was *that?*"

"Nothing," Molly grumbled.

"More importantly, *who* was that?"

"No one."

"That the fae they've been talking all about? With the unicorn?"

"Yes."

Jennet's grin grew insufferable. "And?"

"And nothing. He comes to the tavern sometimes, is all."

"Do they eat?"

Molly opened her mouth to scoff, of course they *ate,* but then . . .

He never had. Not in front of her, anyway. Despite coming to a place where food, and especially drinks, was plentiful.

She blinked, which only made Jennet grin wider. "Uh-huh."

Before she could argue, more of the barmaids hurried over to ask about the fae who'd come to her table, and it was all Molly could do to beat down her incriminating blush.

It didn't matter if the fae ate or drank. It didn't matter at all what he did. It was no concern of hers. She was probably a curiosity to him, *look at the human with enormous tits, how fascinating,* that was all.

He had no reason to give her a second glance, none at all. She wasn't remarkable. She was just Molly, orphan, barmaid, human, with a handful of coins to her name and that was all.

Even the life she dreamed of having, one full of family and home and warmth, didn't rise high enough to warrant notice from someone like a fae. Especially one that carried himself with more elegance and poise than every well-bred noble in the Darrowlands combined. She had no reason to think other fae carried themselves differently, but his perfect manners and precise deportment just screamed aristocrat.

Human nobles hardly looked a barmaid's way, unless they were looking for a fun time while out carousing, so why would a fae?

As the barmaids tittered and gossiped, she began refilling tankards a little too aggressively, cider spilling over the rims. She made herself take a breath, to refocus. Spilled cider didn't get her extra coin.

It didn't matter what the fae thought.

Molly was Molly—granted, one who'd be a little richer after to-day—and that was perfectly all right.

But what if . . .

The stables were a quiet refuge from the crowded courtyard outside. Allarion walked into a haven of sweet-smelling hay and the content whicker of horses.

Drawing the tankard to his nose, he took a curious sniff of the cider Molly had given him. It was a pleasant mix of bitter and sweet, notes of apple and molasses combining with the fermented tang of alcohol.

Allarion couldn't remember the last time he'd drunk something. With magic as their sustenance, the fae had no need. They grew no food, and what animals were reared were used for wool, leather, or milk for soaps and tinctures. He wasn't even sure if he had the internal structures necessary to imbibe. To be sure, his mouth had to go somewhere, but it'd been so long since . . .

A peal of laughter brought him round, and with another sniff of the cider, he left it behind on a haybale. What he'd wanted was a moment with Molly, and he'd gotten that and more. He'd seen the way her pupils dilated when she saw him.

He scared her just like other humans, but with her there was . . . something else. Something tantalizing.

Hope was a painful, dangerous vice pinching his chest.

Perhaps his luck would hold just a little longer to see this last plan fulfilled.

Delving deeper into the stables, Allarion followed the sound of girlish laughter and equine nickering. He wasn't at all surprised to see the princess drawn near the paddock where Bellarand had taken up court.

The unicorn so enjoyed visiting Dundúran for the simple reason that he craved all the castle horses gathering round to treat him like a conquering hero. Unicorns always garnered fear and respect amongst not just *two-leggeds*, as Bellarand called them, but all animals. As the only unicorn for hundreds of miles, it seemed Bellarand enjoyed the more varied company of the castle horses.

Not that Bellarand would ever admit to it, of course.

As he neared, Allarion saw that his dread-mount was performing one of his favorite tricks, drawing symbols in the ground with the sharp tip of his horn.

"I see you are already acquainted," said Allarion.

The princess's four guards jumped, their hands going to their hilts, but Princess Isolde merely turned her smile to Allarion.

"Indeed. I think he's spelling out his name for me." She nodded at the scratches in the paddock dirt.

His incorrigible steed most certainly wasn't spelling his name but something far ruder, not fit for young princesses' ears.

It's funny, the unfunny steed insisted.

It's really not.

Bellarand picked up his head with a huff and shook his long mane of silky black hair. Princess Isolde gasped and sighed with appreciation, which earned her a series of pleased head bobs.

I like this one very much, declared Bellarand through their bond.

You like all females.

They appreciate a fine form and shiny coat.

Allarion resisted rolling his eyes—an entirely human gesture Ravenna had picked up as a youth and passed along to him.

"May I formally introduce the stallion Bellarand the Black, Your Grace. Son of Buecella the Bold, grand-foal of Vortigern the Unmerciful, and dread-mount of the northern reach. He is pleased to meet you."

Bellarand made a show of dipping into a bow, extending his foreleg and bowing his long head.

This one's a princess of two-leggeds?

Yes, so behave yourself.

That earned Allarion an irritated ear flick, but if Princess Isolde suspected the volleying between rider and mount, she didn't let on.

"You have honored the people of the Darrowlands by coming to their heiress's wedding. All I heard was utter delight amongst the crowd when your name was announced."

Princess Isolde smiled fondly, though there was a bright sharpness to her eyes when she turned to consider him.

"My mother has grown quite fond of Lady Aislinn through their correspondence. It was nasty business, that uprising by her brother, and my mother wanted to show her support, even if she couldn't be here herself."

"Do you often travel through Eirea, Your Grace?"

"No, never." Her eyes lit up with delight. "This is my first time outside of Gleanná."

"Ah, I see. A grand adventure, then."

"Not so grand. Dundúran isn't terribly far."

"Perhaps not, but it doesn't take going far from home to have a grand adventure."

The princess smiled wryly. "I suppose not. And I do quite like it here. There are so many interesting things to see and people to talk to." That gaze focused on him again, and Allarion recognized a clever being far older than her years assessing him. "I would've traveled much farther to see a fae and his unicorn."

"I'm glad we could make your journey worthwhile, Your Grace."

"A lone fae—I'm not sure anyone's ever heard of such a thing."

Allarion grinned politely, which just made her guards shudder. "My reasons were quite extraordinary, I assure you. But you need not fear, they have no chance of following me here."

"How mysterious. I hope you will tell me someday."

"Perhaps, princess." He considered her a moment before asking, "Did your mother send you to show her support and perhaps to see these otherlies coming to the Darrowlands?"

"No, but my father did." Another wry grin. "He's fascinated by your arrival. Half-orcs could be expected, I suppose, since they are half-human, too. Even the harpies make some sense, as they never truly left the human kingdoms, just stayed in the fjords of Caledon. But a dragon? A fae? He's understandably curious."

"I see. Well, I hope you will have a long letter to write him with all your news."

"Very long." She turned her smile back to Bellarand. "I'll have to spend a whole page on such a beautiful creature."

Bellarand preened, tossing his glossy mane.

Yes, I like her very much.

You are entirely too susceptible to flattery.

And you are no fun.

Probably not. Although, this little parrying with the princess did give him some pleasure. Her quick mind was evident, and with a little polishing, her skills as a politician and diplomat would be unrivaled.

"He's pleased to hear it, princess. He's glad to have met you."

A look of wonder overtook Princess Isolde's face. "Can you talk to him?"

"Of a sort." He tapped his temple. "We speak through a bond, forged by magic in our minds."

Her mouth opened in awe. "Fascinating! You must tell me all about it."

Allarion smiled. "Someday, princess."

The sound of heavy drums perked his ears, and he turned to listen.

"First, though, I think you'll want to see this." Offering his arm, he led the princess back through the stables after she said her farewells to Bellarand.

"Are those drums?" she asked as the heavy beat began to build.

They made the courtyard, emerging into saturated, late-afternoon sunshine. Much of the crowd in the courtyard gathered near the center, where space had been cleared for dancing.

"It looks like the heiress has had her way." When the princess looked up at him curiously, he explained, "The orcs are doing one of their mating dances."

Her eyes sparkled with interest, and together they rejoined the crowd, eager to see the new lord consort dance for his bride.

3

Some Months Later

Summer came and went, the early autumn harvesttime bringing Molly plenty of busywork. Apple harvests were quickly pouring into Dundúran, and it was the pivotal time of year that all the taverns and alehouses secured the next year's contracts with the cider breweries.

Between that, helping run and serve the tavern, and sewing new clothes for nine-year-old Rory, the penultimate of Uncle Brom's brood, who was in the midst of her third growth spurt of the year, Molly's hand and mind always seemed busy. She enjoyed this time of year, enjoyed haggling with the brewers and conferring with her fellow pub-folk. The air cooled, making the tavern itself less stifling, and she herself preferred the winter selection of brews they carried over summer's.

Lady Aislinn and Lord Hakon had just returned home from visiting his people to the south, in some far-off orc city Molly could hardly imagine it was so distant, and the mood of the city was nearly as jovial as the time around the wedding.

With their heiress returned and the coming harvest festivals,

Dundúran was poised to celebrate. She'd already put her name in at the castle and with Mayor Doherty to work as additional help in several coming events.

The thrill she'd gotten adding her handful of coins from the heiress's wedding had sustained Molly for months. She eagerly awaited more opportunities. A few more days like that and she'd have enough to . . .

Well, she didn't know what yet. But *something*. By next year.

Just the thought of something happening, something that was *hers,* had Molly practically bouncing between tables as she served today's patrons. Not even the boring midday lull could dampen her spirits. That little stash meant a new life, one that was hers.

She would finally be mistress of her own destiny.

Molly's life had been one chaotic spiral after another. She'd lost both parents at the age of ten to the awful wave of plague that hit the surrounding villages of Dundúran hard. Molly too had taken ill, and there were days she wished she'd gone with her parents into the afterworld, for what life was there worth living, left scarred as she was and all alone.

Her Uncle Brom, her mother's younger brother, had taken her in, but it was hardly a kindness. It took a long time for her to adjust to the loudness of the city but especially the tavern. She'd never seen a noisy, drunk man before but witnessed at least six her first night in the city. There were so many people, smells, and noises, she'd hardly slept the first fortnight.

Uncle Brom expected her to work, too. When she'd learned the tavern well enough, he had her fetching things from the back, cleaning up tables, and washing dishes. She hadn't even realized she was supposed to be attending lessons until someone reported Brom to the city council and he was obliged to send her with the other children to school.

She went, hoping to meet friends her own age like she'd had in the village, but she was already far behind. They saw her as a bumpkin and teased her accent. They gawked at the plague scars on her arms and legs and shrieked that she'd spread it to them. Molly quickly came to hate school, but she went, because it got her out of the tavern.

Molly's figure came along earlier than a lot of the other girls. Her breasts grew round and her hips wide and suddenly all the boys wanted to talk to her. At first, she'd liked their attention, and toying with them had taught her how to coax a coin out of the older patrons at the tavern. Watching how she could make the other girls jealous was its own kind of ugly pleasure, and Molly wasn't shy.

What she learned from that time was to find the line she had to toe. It was different for every boy and man, that when crossed, they thought they had invitation to touch. For some it was as simple as a wink or a kind word. She also learned she hated being grabbed and touched. When they tried it, most weren't shy, either. They went for it all, taking as much as they could get until rebuffed. So Molly learned and honed her instinct.

It was that instinct that had her keeping herself awake one night, her suspicions roused. When her door had creaked open during the darkest hours of night, and she recognized the heavy tread of her uncle entering her room, Molly acted. She threw a dagger through the dark, slicing his shirt sleeve.

"Get out and never come again," she'd growled into the shadows.

And he hadn't. Thank the fates, he hadn't.

Her uncle was a coward, down to his very core. It was what she hated most about him. He was a bully, as some cowards were, and enjoyed picking on those littler and lesser than him. Unfortunately, he was blessed with a modicum of charm and, at least when younger, good looks, and those got him far enough.

And five children.

His children were the only thing Molly liked about him. Did she resent that she became another parent to them whenever Brom's wife or lover up and left in disgust with him? Sure. But Bryan, Nora, Merry, Rory, and Oona hadn't chosen their father. And they offered Molly some semblance of a family. They were why, three years ago, she hadn't left Dundúran with the man who'd claimed to love her.

When school ended and she faced the prospect of being in that tavern all day with Uncle Brom, she'd found an older group of youths to join. They welcomed her, and she thought for a while that she had finally found people to accept her. They showed her all the best hidey-holes in the city, even breaking into Castle Dundúran to watch a banquet and sneer at all the rich folk in their finery. They stole, and they had her steal, too, convinced that it was their due—the forgotten youth of the city. She could pick a lock, a pocket, and the winning horse thanks to her years running with them.

That Molly would've done anything for her friends—lied, stolen, harmed. And she had. She'd been one strike away from spending time in gaol, but it hadn't mattered. They were her friends. She thought she was in love with their leader, Finn. He promised her a better life, that they deserved more.

But the cracks had begun to show when she grew a little older. Their wildness began to taste like sour beer. Finn came apologizing after another night with another woman one too many times. Eventually, the law caught up to Finn, and he was exiled from Dundúran. He declared they'd go to the capital of Gleanná, really make it, but Molly couldn't bring herself to go.

Her little cousins, the tavern, they needed her.

The decision felt right, and she hadn't missed Finn and the others as much as she'd once thought she would. Still, three years on, there were times she regretted being left behind.

What would her life look like in Gleanná? Bigger than the tavern walls, that was for sure.

Without her friends, Molly's world had contracted to just the tavern. She loved the place, in its own way, and enjoyed seeing many of the regulars. But the children were growing up. The tavern was becoming rundown, despite her best efforts. Uncle Brom was getting surly in his middle age, not resigned yet to having lost his looks and most of his charm.

A restlessness was growing inside her, a *knowing* that soon, it was time. For what, she didn't know. When, she didn't know either. Just that it was coming and when it did—she'd know.

Grit and big tits could get her places, she well knew, and now she had a tidy little sack of coins to help her with whatever came next.

She practically twirled through the tavern that day, earning her a bemused grunt from Brom. It seemed like the happier she was, the grumpier he became—all the more reason to make herself happy.

When she next turned around to greet a new patron, Molly's heart kicked in her chest.

The fae stood there, looming in the doorway. Late afternoon sunlight filtered in behind him, framing his tall form in an amber-lined silhouette. His dark cloak, draped over impossibly wide shoulders, cascaded behind him as he strode slowly inside.

Molly's breath caught in her throat.

Allarion. That was his name. And his unicorn was Bellarand. He'd told her these things, of course, but only after many visits to the tavern. She'd found out long before, though, asking around at the other alehouses and wells and washing fountains.

Fates, she was stupid to feel this kind of thrill at the sight of him, come like a wraith in the night. Those black eyes and sharp teeth should've terrified her.

She hadn't felt desire for a man since Finn, having decided they weren't worth it. She'd had enough male attention to last a lifetime.

Still, when those inhuman eyes fell on her, Molly *felt it.*

Smiling, she greeted him and waved him on to his usual table in the back.

He was quickly becoming one of the regulars at the tavern, appearing every few days through summer. Each time, Molly tried to coax a little more out of him, even if he seemed perfectly content to lurk in the back and watch.

She didn't know how he didn't get bored, just sitting there with a beverage he never intended to drink, but was grateful for his presence, nevertheless. Other patrons were on their best behavior when he was there, which meant no chair-breaking brawls or shouting matches, and everyone left promptly after last call. Perfection.

"And who'd you like to sit with today?" she asked, smiling at her own joke. "We have a new cider in, and just got a crate of red wine straight from Endelín."

"A mead, please. I enjoy the scent."

Molly bit her cheek to keep from smiling too wide. He almost always got a mead.

"I'll bring that right out," she said with a wink. She'd yet to find a line to toe with the mysterious fae.

I almost wouldn't mind being grabbed by him, she thought as she turned away.

"A moment, please, miss."

Unfailingly polite as always. She made her eyes big as she blinked at him. Fates, she went all breathless, excited to hear what he'd ask.

"I would like to speak with your uncle, when it is convenient for him."

Molly's brows nearly rose to her hairline with surprise. Why should he want to talk with Brom? They'd spoken perhaps once, when Brom was curious about what brought a fae to his establishment, but after gleaning little besides that business didn't slow but actually picked up with Allarion there, he'd retreated back behind the bar, content as always to let Molly do most of the work.

Clearing her throat to hide her shock, Molly said, "Of course. I'll go tell him now."

"Thank you."

She didn't think she imagined the warmth in those dark eyes, and another little thrill zipped down her spine as she headed back for the bar.

What could he want from Brom?

The older male kept Allarion waiting for several hours. From what he'd learned of the man's rather odious character, this made sense—an attempt to prove dominance and gain the upper hand.

Not that Allarion minded or cared. He had time, he had patience. And, most importantly, he had a plan.

Allarion was content to wait as he watched Molly work the tavern and its customers.

He might have been jealous of all the other males there leering at her, yet she was adept at encouraging their attentions only enough to secure more orders and therefore coin. It was subtle, but Allarion had learned her tricks, admiring her strategy. She kept moving; it was a dance she did through the tavern, as graceful as any trained dancer, never bestowing too much attention on any one patron. Still, as Allarion well knew, when her beatific smile fell upon you, it made you feel like the center of the world, the sun in the sky.

His body nearly vibrated with the force of his yearning. As the days and fortnights drew longer, his desire only grew stronger. He had time, yes, and patience, too, but as Allarion continued to dwell with the humans, he felt the dwindling of both acutely.

He *wanted* her. And finally, after months of imbuing his new land with his magic, he had a home to bring her to.

There was still much to be done at the manor, to be sure. But enough rooms were prepared, enough magic infused into the house and land, that he felt secure in bringing an *azai* to it. She would be key to finishing his bonding with the estate, and with every visit to the tavern, Allarion grew ever more impatient to see her on his land, within his home, in his bed.

Watching her that evening only solidified his desire into a heavy knot in his chest.

Her liveliness, her effervescence filled the tavern, making it glow brighter than the sconces and central fire. Imagining her filling his own empty home with such energy made Allarion's fangs ache curiously. His gaze fell to her neck, where he could watch the thick vein there pumping as she danced through the night, balancing heavy trays and carrying multiple tankards in each hand.

He apparently wasn't too old to be taken in by an immaculate set of breasts, and as he did whenever he came to visit her, he was easily enchanted by their gratuitous curves and enticing bounciness. Still, his eyes trailed up to her neck and his fangs ached again and . . . and it was strange. Perhaps even unsettling.

Allarion wanted Molly in all ways—even to bite, it seemed. And while that may have troubled him in the past, he was a fae with few options and too much desire. His course had been decided the day he saw her drawing water from the well.

A tankard landed on his table, amber liquid sloshing over the rim. Allarion looked at it before watching the uncle lever himself into a seat across the table.

He was a large man, who'd once been quite muscular and strong. His shoulders were still broad with strength, but his middle had gone soft and overhung his belt. A thick beard and mop of hair had once been a golden reddish color but now had streaks of white, and the redness of his cheeks nearly obscured the freckles dotting his face. His beard smelled of the ale he'd been indulging in all night as he poured drinks for others, but despite this, his eyes were as blue and clear as a summer sky.

Allarion inclined his head the requisite amount. "Master Dunne."

The man grunted in greeting. "You going to complain about a cup you never drink?"

He didn't bother looking at his untouched tankard of mead. He'd no need or desire to tell the man across from him that the fae didn't need nor want to drink, nor that he only ordered it because it was the closest he could find to Molly's scent. A cup of it near him was almost like scenting her honey-sweet smell.

"No, I have no complaints at all. I wished to speak with you. To make a proposition."

The interest in Dunne's eyes was immediate, though he tried to hide it. "And what is that? Want to be a partner in a tavern, do you?"

"I wish to wed your niece."

Allarion had expected a shocked silence, but Dunne merely chuckled and took a long sip of his ale.

"You and everyone in here," he muttered into his cup.

"Perhaps. But I mean to succeed where they failed."

Dunne's shrewd gaze assessed him over the rim of his cup.

Allarion expected a back-and-forth. From what he understood of humans, it was customary to talk with the head of the family, a person's elder, when a suitor wished to secure a bride. He would have preferred to talk to Molly herself, but Allarion could respect he was in a human land desiring a human, and so would do it their way.

Dunne replaced his cup on the table, catching the nail of his thumb on the handle.

"What makes you so keen?" he asked. "The heiress is taken, to be sure, but there's lots of women between her and my Molly."

"That is for me to tell Molly, but be assured, I have great admiration for her. She is the one I wish for."

"Admiration. Uh-huh." Dunne patted his chest and chuckled to himself, making Allarion seethe at his crude insinuation. Blithely unaware of Allarion's dangerously souring mood, the bartender sat back in his seat, a grin suddenly contorting his beard. "You aren't the first one to come askin' for her."

"I offer her a home, land, comfort. She will be taken care of. I will pledge myself to her and be true."

His words seemed to amuse the man. "An offer from a fae. No one will believe it. But—" here he held up his hands, as if in defeat "—I have to tell you what I told the others. She's indentured to this place. Paying off a debt, you see. Enough for another, oh . . . five years at least, I'd say."

Allarion's nostrils flared. He couldn't smell a lie—at least not over the myriad of other scents in the tavern. Dunne said it with all sincerity and confidence, and . . . it didn't sound so outlandish. An indenture, working to pay off debt, would explain why someone like Molly, vivacious and alive, would tie herself to a rundown tavern like this.

She certainly breathed life into the place, filled it with warmth and cheer, but even her bright smiles couldn't hide the worn legs of the chairs and chipped rims of the cups. There were far better taverns and alehouses in the city, ones where Molly could earn far more coin.

"You would indenture your own kin?"

Dunne shrugged his meaty shoulders. "Had to make her learn. She was a wild girl, you see. Had to teach her to pay her debts."

"How much?"

Dunne's lips twitched. "Now, see, that's difficult. It's not just the indenture. She helps me run the place and looks after the little ones. I've got five, you see, and I'm too old to be running after them. And I'm not blind, I know she's what fills this place up. It'd be too much to find a new girl who filled out a bodice the same and—"

"How much?"

Dunne couldn't hide the small grin this time, no doubt having been waiting for Allarion to interrupt him with that very question.

Allarion let the man think he was winning their . . . negotiation. The truth was Allarion, like all fae, had time—but five years was now a long time to wait. Neither Ravenna nor he himself could delay that long.

He wasn't desperate—not yet. He didn't want to let himself get to that point.

So he was willing to expedite this. Indenture or no, familial bonds or no, one thing mattered to Dunne, and Allarion was willing to offer it.

He'd pay any price for Molly.

Dunne named something expectedly lavish.

"Very well," Allarion agreed. "I will double it, too. To compensate you and your children for her loss."

The uncle sat back in his seat, blinking with disbelief. Allarion had truly shocked him finally.

"You want her that bad? *Her?*" he asked.

Allarion bit back his annoyance. "Yes." From his cloak pocket he pulled a velvet sack of coins. "Half now, half tomorrow, when we are married."

It was fast, but he needed to return to Scarborough—and he didn't intend to leave Dundúran without his bride.

Dunne's eyes went large with the sight of the sack and the clinking sounds it made. He didn't grab for it, which mildly surprised Allarion, but his throat bobbed on a swallow and his pupils dilated.

"Are we agreed?"

The man startled from his stupor. "It'll take time to arrange a marriage. Tomorrow's not—"

"Tomorrow," said Allarion, laying his hand beside the coin purse. "That is my price."

Dunne nodded. "All right. We can at least manage a handfasting. I'll tell her tonight, after we close. Come back tomorrow afternoon."

"Very good."

Allarion stood, and quick as a viper, Dunne snatched up the coins. A sound of disbelief, close to a laugh, escaped his lips.

"I will return anon."

Dunne's graying head bobbed in an absent nod, his attention fully on the sack he weighed in his hands.

Hiding his disgust, Allarion swept from the table. It was time he left, before his triumph got the better of him.

She's mine.

His woman. His *azai.*

Watching a room full of other males leering at her now would be his undoing.

Before he made the door, his gaze tangled with hers. She stood beside the bar, her curious eyes bouncing between him and where he'd left her uncle. A small line of worry drew between her brows, and it took a millennium of training and control not to cross the room and soothe it away with his thumb.

Soon, she would have no need for worry or want. He would give her everything she could ever desire.

Allarion bowed his head, a farewell and show of respect to his future *azai,* as was her due.

Finding her gaze again, his magic reached out despite himself, stretching across the tavern to gently caress her soft cheek. Her lips parted in surprise, and her pulse kicked at her throat.

His fangs ached nearly as badly as his cock.

You're mine.

4

The numbness that gripped Molly when her uncle told her what had happened tightened with every breath, until she could hardly breathe. She didn't sleep at all that night, even desperate as she was to wake up the next morning to find it all a bad dream.

"He's paid for you, dower, everything. Full bride price and more," Uncle Brom had informed her after the final customer left last night.

Molly didn't care one whit what the fae paid—just that he'd paid *for her.*

Bride price.

It was a very old, very outdated custom. Sort of like a dowry noblewomen sometimes had when married off, but this the groom paid the bride's family. It was a contract, a deal between a family and a third party to hand over their daughter. The custom gained popularity again in the tumultuous decades of the wars of succession, when everything had been thrown into chaos and question. Now, though, thirty years on, a bride price was seen as blood money, children sold off by desperate parents. It wasn't strictly legal, especially as Lord Darrow spearheaded the effort to eliminate slaver of all kinds throughout the Darrowlands.

"*You got no right,*" Molly had growled at him. She'd been of age for years now, and she wasn't Brom's child.

"*Just think of it, Moll. A fae's bride. He must have a fortune.*" And he'd held up the clinking sack of coins, everything Molly was apparently worth. "*And this is only half. He's bringing the rest tomorrow.*"

"*He can bring coins made of carrots for all I care. I'm not doing it.*"

Brom's brows drew low in false concern. "*It's unexpected, I grant you. But* think, *Moll. Think what this would mean for us—for the tavern, for the children. I can finally make the repairs this place needs. I can send Merry to the academy in Gleanná. Hells, we can sponsor Bryan's knighthood. Just think, a Dunne knight.*"

His eyes sparkled with a fervent, almost delirious kind of wonder. "*This could make us, Moll.*"

"*Us? Us?*" Her voice went so high the windows shuddered. "*What about me?*"

"*Don't be selfish, Moll. This will change the little ones' lives—you can make it happen for them. And don't be daft, either. How many chances like this will come around for you? No one's come calling for you in years.*"

"*I don't want a suitor. I want—*"

"*I'm not unfeeling, Moll. I got him to agree to a handfasting instead. Just a year and then you could be done. But just think on what you could do in the meantime,*" he'd insisted. "*A fae, Molly girl, a* fae. *Just think!*"

Molly had thought—all night. Brom hadn't left her alone without a tentative promise that she would agree to it. The words slipped out of her numb mouth, mostly to get rid of him so she could hide away in her room.

All night she lay there, staring at the ceiling. She could hardly believe that in the short conversation between Uncle Brom and the fae, they'd haggled over *her*. That her uncle would sell her didn't surprise her—what did, and what hurt most, was knowing that Allarion, her mysterious tavern wraith, had *bought her*.

She hated him for it.

What did they truly know about the fae? Most of the legends and myths about them made their kind out to be scheming and cutthroat. Perhaps Molly should've listened to the fairy tales.

Not all of them ended in beautiful, flower-festooned weddings.

The thought of the wedding, the castle, the heiress, had her sitting up in bed. Without thinking, she'd shoved her feet into boots and hurried to the bedchamber door.

The Darrows won't allow this. They won't let him buy me.

Opening her door revealed Brom sitting just down the hall in a chair he'd brought up from the tavern. He sat whittling by candlelight, his little paring knife catching the glint of the small flame.

He looked at her with his face cast half in shadow. *"You're going with him tomorrow, Moll,"* he'd said in that low, threatening voice he saved for special occasions. *"What you do after, I don't care. Run away, start a new life."*

She'd stared at her uncle's hardened face for a long while, searching it for . . . something. She'd known him longer than her own parents—he'd been the one constant in her life, loathsome as he often was. In the dark, faced with an uncertain dawn, Molly did something she swore she'd never do.

She begged.

"Don't make me go."

Brom's beard twitched. *"You're clever, you'll get on just fine. Do it for the little ones. They'll never want for anything ever again, Moll."*

The weight of the decision was heavy, even if it was no decision at all. They both knew she stood no chance when he spoke of the children. Molly loved her cousins, wanted them to have everything she didn't.

If fae money could buy it . . .

"You swear? The money will be for them?"

"On my life, I swear it."

Molly watched his face a moment longer, unsure if she believed him. Perhaps it was enough money that, even if he indulged himself in whatever he wanted, which she knew he would, there'd at least be plenty left over for Bryan and the girls.

Bryan, who was twenty and had left the tavern as quickly as he could, could quit the apprenticeship he hated and finally have the money to sponsor his training to be a knight. Such a rise would take the whole family with him—they'd be respectable, well thought of. Merry could hone her brilliant mind at an academy in Gleanná, where she'd be challenged and recognized for her gifts. Nora, Rory, and Oona could have dowries or inheritance to build their lives.

"All right," she forced through a throat closed tight in terror.

She'd meant what she said then, even as morning dawned and shed a surreal light upon the situation. Molly seemed to swim through the day, her attention like the sunlight trying to filter through the morning clouds. It was as if she watched herself gather her meager belongings, packing all her worldly possessions and a few provisions into two canvas bags.

All day Brom hovered, reminding her of her promise, of what this would mean for the Dunnes. He darted out to make arrangements but reappeared every hour, ensuring Molly was still there and willing.

At least, as willing as you could make a bought bride.

Her annoyance was what finally broke through her daze, and in a show of the temper she'd been trying to master for years, she shoved him out of her room and slammed the door in his face.

"I said I'd do it!" she yelled at the door.

Brom grumbled on the other side. "I'll go see what's keeping the mayor."

Molly snorted in disgust before turning on her heel to get back to packing.

All four of the girls had crowded into her room, the three youngest—brilliant Merry, boyish Rory, and talkative Oona—piled on her narrow bed while the eldest, Nora, sixteen and haughty, made a nuisance of herself by the window. She ostensibly was picking through the things Molly had decided not to bring with her, even though Nora had scoffed she wouldn't like any of her things.

Really, Nora wasn't ever to be left out of anything. Aloof as she might be, she dreaded missing out.

Nonplussed by Molly's outburst, the three younger girls got back to wondering aloud what the fae and his house would be like.

"Do you think it glows with magic?" said Merry.

"I think he lives in a tree," quipped Rory. "Aren't they into nature and trees and the like?"

"That's stupid," sneered Nora, "nobody would live in a tree."

"Plenty of things live in trees," Rory argued back.

"Squirrels, raccoons, birds . . ." Oona began to list all the creatures she knew.

"Those are *animals,*" Nora insisted with disgust. "He's a man. A fae. And where would his unicorn go in this tree house of his?"

"In his own tree, *obviously,*" said Rory, just to rile their sister.

Nora, always so sensitive and easy to rile, pinched her lips together in a sour expression. "This is a stupid thing to talk about. Everyone knows he bought the old Scarborough estate, so it's probably just an old moldering house."

Oona gasped in delight. "You get to live in a big house?"

Molly did her best to smile. "So it seems."

"An *old* one," Nora interjected. "Probably doesn't have any floors anymore and no furniture."

"Enchanting, Nora, thank you."

Nora rolled her eyes. "Let's talk about something else. What are we going to do with this room? It has the best window. I think I might want it. I'm oldest, so I should get to have it."

She looked up when none of her sisters responded. Molly too glanced up, expecting at least one argument, for argument's sake.

The three younger girls were staring at Molly, their faces gone downcast.

"Do you really have to go?" asked Oona in a little voice.

Molly's heart lurched, and she quickly knelt on the floor before them. The girls threw their arms around her neck, and Oona began to cry.

"Hey now," Molly soothed. "It's all right. Things will be just fine. You'll hardly miss me at all."

Oona shook her head, rubbing her tears and leaky nose into Molly's neck. "No, we won't! We won't forget you!"

"I know you won't, love. And I'll be sure to visit. It's not forever."

"Did the fae say that?" Nora asked. She didn't sound malicious, but Molly still threw her a dark frown over Oona's head.

"I haven't spoken with him yet, but it doesn't matter. I say I'll visit, and so I will."

"You haven't spoken with him?" Nora repeated suspiciously. "Didn't you last night—"

"Never mind. I'll speak with him."

That seemed to placate the girls, and Molly spent the next few moments mopping up tears, even as her own heart cried out.

She didn't want to leave them.

Sure, she'd been making plans to leave. She had her stash of coins—now packed safely in one of her canvas bags. But she didn't think she would've gone far—maybe a different neighborhood, establish herself somewhere new. And maybe the girls could have come with her after a time, the younger ones at least.

All her plans, vague as they'd been, had come to nothing. They hadn't been much, but they'd been hers—and now they were less than a puff of smoke.

Her life was careening out of her control again, and Molly had to swallow back her panic.

That terror lodged in her throat when a brusque knock came at the door, and on the other side, Brom said, "They're here—the mayor and the fae. It's time."

Heart racing, Molly ushered her cousins from her room. "Go on, now. I've got to change into something nice."

The girls threw her uncertain looks, but Molly closed the door on them, too. She couldn't bear their forlorn faces. It made her impending departure that much more real, even as she stood in her bedchamber in her last few moments of freedom.

This can't be happening, her heart moaned as she went through the motions of donning her finest clothes.

She couldn't help a grimace that her best bodice and kirtle were what she'd worn to serve drinks at the heiress's wedding. She'd done all the embroidery on the brown bodice and white sleeves and butter yellow kirtle herself, and it was some of her best work, but a little bit of her withered to know she'd be handfasted in her barmaid clothes.

He'd seen her in them. He'd know.

Well, if he didn't want a barmaid, he shouldn't have bought one.

Righteous tears burned her eyes as she finished dressing. She didn't bother with her hair—*he gets what he gets*—and made quick work of her best pair of boots. Hauling the bags over her shoulders, she trudged down the steps to the tavern below, not letting herself think.

It wasn't until she'd set everything down that she realized a small crowd had gathered inside.

The fae was there, but she couldn't bear to look at him. A few of their neighbors, a few of Brom's friends, a few other tavern owners, the mayor. Jennet and a few other barmaids she was friendly with poked their heads through the windows, but none dared come to her and pass by the fae.

Other than the mayor. Seeing her, Mayor Doherty quickly approached. Thom Doherty was beloved throughout Dundúran, a wise, moderating voice for the people. He worked well with the Darrows and oversaw city business fairly. He was also spry for a man who'd gone white and wrinkled long ago, hurrying over to draw her aside.

Giving her hands a sympathetic pat, the mayor said, "Miss Molly, this is all very sudden and strange. I'd heard Lord Allarion visited this tavern, but I hadn't thought . . ."

That he'd ever stop to look at a woman like you.

Molly bit her cheek.

"The fae can be strange," was all Molly could think to say.

"So I gather." When Doherty looked over his shoulder at the small crowd, it was at her uncle, not the fae, that he leveled a considering frown. "Is this what you want, Miss Molly? Your uncle isn't doing something . . . untoward?"

Molly sucked in a breath, the truth on the tip of her tongue. She glanced over the mayor's shoulder at her uncle to find him boring into her with a desperate stare.

Then, unwillingly but drawn there as surely as an avalanche rolled down the mountain, her gaze flicked to the fae.

He stood on his own, a silent, looming presence. He too was staring at her, his gaze unwavering and intense in its own right. She stared back, weighing her next words.

I can end this. I don't have to go through with it.

The mayor had enough power to stop whatever this was. He could appeal directly to the Darrows, maybe even bring her to the castle immediately.

But . . .

The money would be gone. And worse, what would the fae do in retribution?

She hadn't ever sensed violence from him, and in her fantasies, he wasn't capable of harming her or her family. But then, she'd never imagined he'd buy her.

Looking at him then, every nerve shook in trepidation but . . . not fear. She didn't fear this fae.

He wanted her. Like so many men before him, he wanted something from her. It lessened him in her eyes—he was just like all the rest. More powerful, richer, to be sure, but the same, nevertheless. He didn't use violence but money to get his way, to manipulate and force.

Molly had seen his type before. She knew how to handle men like him.

The realization gave her some comfort, as did her promise to herself that she would take this man for everything he was worth. Whatever he held dear, whatever he loved, she would find and take. Brom was right at least in that she didn't have to stay with him. A handfasting was a year and a day; after that, if neither cried off, the couple was considered married. But until then, until that year and a day, it could be called off at any point.

Molly intended to make this a short handfasting. She would take her freedom back and the life she wanted. No man, not even a fae, was allowed to take it from her.

So she told the mayor, "It's all right. I want to," because she meant to make the fae regret it.

The mayor gave her another concerned look, as if trying to determine if she lied.

Squeezing his dry hands, Molly whispered, "I'd appreciate if you kept an eye on the girls, though. Make sure they go to school. My uncle is often too busy."

Doherty made an uncharitable noise. "Indeed. Rest assured, Miss Molly, I'll look after the little ones. Everyone will attend school as they should."

"Good. That makes my heart lighter."

Doherty nodded, patting her hand one more time before releasing her.

Together, they approached the fae.

He was in his standard long dark cloak, but both sides had been folded back over his shoulders, revealing the strong, lithe form of him. Broad shoulders narrowed into a trim waist and lean but powerful thighs. A rich doublet of claret red molded to his form, a silver belt cinched at his waist, and his black leather boots had been polished to a high shine.

He looked like a groom in his finest, arrived for his wedding day.

Heat crept up Molly's cheeks, and she couldn't help picking at a stray thread on her skirt.

The others gathered nearer, and Doherty began the handfasting.

The fae held out his large hands with their dark blue nails and tapered fingers. Molly stared at them for a long moment before remembering to slide her hands into his. She thought perhaps his hands would be cold—he had the color of someone nearly gone to hypothermia—but found the opposite. His skin was smooth and warm, not unpleasant at all.

Molly's nostrils flared, her pulse beginning to throb. She couldn't keep his gaze but instead stared at the fae's throat. It was after a few long moments that she realized with a start that no pulse of his own beat in his neck. She didn't feel one in his hands, either.

Does . . . does he not . . .?

The mayor produced a red ribbon, snagging Molly's attention. She said the requisite things when prompted as Doherty twined the ribbon around their hands, tying them together. The fae's voice was deep and resonant as he repeated the promises back, and Molly couldn't help it, her insides quivered to hear that tone of his.

The promises of a handfasting were simple enough, to love and be true. In her fantasies late into the night, Molly often dreamed of hearing the words. She'd never quite seen the face saying them to her, and as they were said now, she refused to look at his face.

The heat continued to rise in her, the witnesses and tavern itself seeming to bend near as the ceremony finished. A hush fell over all of them, Doherty falling silent.

It wasn't until a long moment of silence passed that Molly dared glace up. The fae looked down at her . . . softly, expectantly.

Oh.

Handfastings ended with a kiss.

Molly bit her cheek. If he wanted a kiss, he'd have to come down and get it, and he wouldn't be getting a good one.

He remained perfectly still, those dark eyes searching hers, before finally he bent at the waist. Molly held her breath as he descended to her, locks of starlight hair slipping over his shoulders as he dipped his head.

His lips hovered over hers, but Molly made no move to meet him. She kept her eyes open wide and forward. Within the red ribbon, her hand trembled.

She felt his lashes, silvery like his hair, flutter against her cheek. His head dipped lower, and her belly swooped. She thought he meant to kiss her on the cheek, and to the others that's what it must have looked like, but no, he—

His warm mouth pressed gently into the side of her neck, near where her pulse beat rapidly at her throat. The heat of him exploded through her, and if she hadn't been clutching his hand with her own, she would've sworn he ran them down her sides to her waist and hips.

For one prolonged moment, they stayed like that, bound together, his mouth on her skin.

Molly's breath burst from her aching lungs when he finally pulled back an inch.

Low enough so only she could hear, he murmured into her skin, "*Azai.*"

Her breath shuddered out of her, and Molly stared wide-eyed at her groom as he straightened. Even with his black sclera and violet irises, she thought he looked at her . . . warmly.

"Thank you, sweetling," he whispered to her. "I treasure the gift you give me."

Molly's lips parted in surprise, but she didn't know what to say.

A few of the crowd around them began to clap, but it didn't quite catch on. Mayor Doherty looked between Molly and the fae, as if to see if either would suddenly renounce the handfast.

Stuck again in a daze, she followed when the fae went to pick up both of her bags and lead her outside. There would be no celebration nor wedding dinner. They wouldn't stand to greet guests and well-wishers.

They were pledged and that was that.

Outside, a much larger crowd of curious neighbors had gathered in the street. The fae's black unicorn stood proudly just outside, and everyone gave him a wide berth. When they appeared, a curious hum of chatter began.

"Congratulations to the happy couple," called Brom from behind them.

More awkward clapping followed, making Molly's cheeks burn. She might as well have been naked for how exposed and vulnerable she felt then. Tears pricked her eyes to think of herself, hair unkempt and dress worn, standing beside this ethereal being.

What we must look like.

Molly followed without a word as he walked to the unicorn. No saddle sat on his back, just a finely woven blanket and a pair of stirrups. The fae slung her bags across the unicorn's broad back before offering his unbound hand to help her up.

Her cheeks burned. "I don't know how." She'd never learned to ride.

Without a word, the fae took her by the waist and hauled her up. With an *oof,* Molly clutched at the strap of her bags as she flung a leg over the unicorn's back. It was difficult, one of her hands still bound to his, and she had to scramble to right herself. Her skirts rode up higher than her boots, exposing her knee and pockmarked lower thigh.

She'd barely gotten her seat when the fae mounted up behind her, graceful as could be. He curled his arm around her to rest their bound hands in her lap. With nowhere else to put her other hand, she laid it on the lump their hands made.

The crowd tittered and murmured, gawking as the unicorn turned to head down the street.

And that was how Molly finally left her uncle's home—on the back of a unicorn, handfasted to a fae, and utterly humiliated.

5

Allarion thought the day went rather well—the ceremony was efficient and to the point, Molly had looked lovely in all her warm colors, and even better, she'd come to him willingly. Now he rode for home with his new bride safe in his arms and under his protection.

And she's mine now. Mine.

All in all, certainly not a bad day.

Despite the triumph he felt, though, he couldn't help a nagging feeling that something wasn't right. Even for Bellarand, far swifter than a mere horse, the ride back to Scarborough took hours, especially laden with two riders and two full bags. His bride hadn't said a word to him throughout those long hours.

He'd asked multiple times as the sun began to sink across the sky if she needed to stop, but all he received for his courtesy was a stiff shake of her head. She held herself rigidly in front of him, always looking ahead. Her cheeks had gone pink with the wind rushing past them, but otherwise her coloring was abnormally pale.

He didn't like that. She should be flushed with warmth and high spirits. He didn't like that she'd only had two bags, either. When he'd asked if she had nothing else to bring or would like to stop somewhere to purchase more, that had only gotten him a terse shake of the head.

When they lost the sun, Allarion could feel how her limbs went cold, even if she shook her head to that, too. Resisting the desire to roll his eyes, and not wanting to be the fae who let his new bride go cold, he slipped his cloak from his shoulders onto hers, wrapping her up in the fine cloth. It almost swallowed her, but Allarion didn't miss how her tight shoulders loosened a little under the warmth.

He liked seeing her in something of his. Soon, she would begin to smell of him—and even better, her scent would permeate the house, sink through the floorboards and touch the rafters above.

Having the cloak between them was for the best, as thinking of her in his house, filling it with her laughter and scent and presence, had his cock twitching with interest. Holding her against him had his black blood running hot, and it was all he could do to focus on the ride rather than the warm, alluring female practically in his lap.

He'd known about her sumptuous curves, of course. They drew his eye every time, the heavy slopes of her breasts and rounded globes of her backside, the thick plushness of her thighs and enticing nip of her waist. It was one thing to know—it was another entirely to feel.

He didn't let himself explore, not without her permission and not in the gathering darkness as they neared Scarborough, but *oh,* it was more than just his fangs aching to feel every curve and contour of her.

But because his magic was concentrated inside him after being away from the estate, and because his instinct rode him hard to take and claim and *bite,* horrifying and baffling as that might be, Allarion did allow himself to duck his head and take a deep pull from her hair.

He filled his lungs with her, a pleasure not unlike wielding magic running sweet through his veins. It was as sweet as she was, that hint of honey and vanilla underlying her scent of woman. He didn't know what about her scent drove him to such madness—whether it was the humanness of her, the thrill of something new, or neither at all.

Whatever drew him to her, he was ensnared, with no desire to be free.

His plans so far had borne fruit, and he just needed his luck to hold a little longer.

As they neared the estate, his anticipation grew. It was already an inky dark, the moon climbing above the trees and the stars glittering in a clear, velveteen sky. Perhaps they should have camped for the night, but Allarion trusted Bellarand and the unicorn's sight implicitly.

They were so close—and Allarion wanted her to see her new home.

It wasn't finished and certainly wasn't perfect, but now, with her, he hoped to complete his work very soon. Imbuing magic into the house and surrounding land took time, allowing the native magic and his own to accustom and acclimate to each other. Over time, it began to act as a sort of circuit like that in the faelands, sharing the burden of the magic.

Allarion hoped to one day soon include Molly in that circuit. As a human, born of this land, he suspected she would ease the bond. She would likely never wield magic like a fae, but on his land, bonded to him and Bellarand through magic, she would still be part of their circuit. Someday, he hoped to have Ravenna too within the circuit, and together, they could build a safe little haven away from the faelands.

Imbuing his magic into the house had had some interesting consequences. The house itself was gaining its own sentience. Some structures in the faelands, as well as trees and even lakes, had been known to grow such sentience. As he added his magic and made the necessary repairs to the house, it surprised him how quickly the formerly abandoned manor awoke and took to its new state, but it wasn't unwelcome.

Another being for their circuit.

He very much wished for Molly to like the house and his repairs to it—and for the house to welcome her.

Allarion knew the moment they passed onto the estate. They crossed over his thick layer of wards, the magic flowing over them like the finest gossamer. Molly shuddered in his arms, her head turning this way and that for the first time.

"Be at ease," he soothed, "it was only my wards. We are now on my estate."

Her head jerked in a short nod, and although it wasn't much improvement from a shake of her head, it was still an improvement.

The moments passed quickly as Bellarand found the familiar path through the forest deeper into the estate. The trees and ferns rustled sleepily, welcoming them home.

Summoning his magic, Allarion lit the lamps that lined the main drive up to the manor. A soft glow emanated between the trees ahead, and as they neared, he felt Molly straighten just as the trees thinned and the path evened. Soft blue light from the lamps puddled in circles on the ground, lighting their way home.

Bellarand's hooves crunched on the gravel as he trotted up the slight incline to the manor itself. The house loomed above them, and with a thought, Allarion lit a few of the lamps and sconces within the finished wing. Light burned in the windows, a sentinel in the night calling them in from the wilderness.

Molly's head tilted back as she looked up at the four-storied house, with its two turreted south and east towers and grand staircase leading up to the second level front doors. Her human eyes likely couldn't discern much in the darkness, even with the light from the lamps, but Allarion still awaited her noises of delight, or at least approval.

Such noises never came.

She said nothing as Bellarand trotted past the grand staircase and around the side of the manor, to the back where a side door into the kitchen stood.

Allarion could feel the house waking from its slumber, shutters rattling and shingles twitching. It was as if the house leaned over to get a good look at them, holding its breath with anticipation.

Molly held perfectly still, and Allarion watched in surprise as the skin at the back of her neck prickled.

Off you get, grumbled Bellarand, *I'm tired.*

Yes, yes.

Allarion slipped off, turning to help Molly down, too. She reluctantly put her hand on his shoulder as he caught her waist with his free hand. He lifted her, only to have her slide down his front.

He just barely caught the groan in his throat.

She peered up at him with those big brown eyes, and for a moment, all Allarion could think of was how good she smelled and how soft her skin had been when he kissed her in her uncle's tavern.

Twins take him, he wanted to do that again. Soon. Many times. All over her body.

As soon as they were dismounted and the bags relieved from his back, Bellarand shook out his mane with a great huff and headed off into the darkness, sliding through the shadows to find the meadow of clover he preferred to bed down in.

Molly watched Bellarand disappear amongst the shadows, her lips drawn thin.

"Shall we?"

She looked at him then at the house. "It's just us here?"

He frowned, not quite understanding her meaning. "There's the house." He would explain its sentience to her soon. Now, he suspected she needed rest after that long ride.

When she nodded slowly, Allarion took the encouragement and led her into the house.

The kitchen was cold and quiet, slumbering as it waited for her to breathe new life into it. Allarion had neglected the room at first, as fae had no need of kitchens, but when he'd determined to bring a human bride home, the kitchen was his next project. It now gleamed with clean countertops, a new oven and stove, and an array of pots, pans, and utensils. Unsure what she'd need, Allarion got her everything. He considered lingering, to point out all his repairs and refurbishments, but decided that could wait.

He took her up the most direct path through the house, choosing the sturdiest floorboards. Lamps lit to guide their way, helping him point out where she needed to tread carefully or where she should refrain from going until he'd made it safer.

They passed through corridors with wallpaper faded from the sun and the ghostly squares of where paintings once hung. Many of the original sconces had gone missing, so he made do with lanterns. He'd cleared most of the rooms of the moldering furniture and tattered curtains, so it was empty rooms that greeted them.

Ready for her to fill.

She followed him in silence, her big eyes skittering over everything as if she dared not miss a thing. Allarion hoped to hear a noise or word of interest, but her lips remained tightly sealed.

Too soon, they reached the bedchamber he'd prepared for her. It was near his own, where he took his needed long sleeps. He hoped one day to share a bedchamber, a *bed,* with her, but even in the throes of lust, he knew he had to give her her space in these first days.

Setting down her bags, he inclined his head at the door just ahead, left ajar. "That shall be your room."

A lamp illuminated the inside, and she'd just be able to see the fine canopied bed and cedar chest awaiting her. He'd filled the room with things he hoped she'd like, things that were a pleasure to touch and see. As his mate, she would have only the finest things—if she didn't like something, he'd procure her something else. Now that she was here, he would undertake the rest of the repairs to her taste, and one day soon, the house would be just as she wanted it.

"Mine?" she asked softly.

Allarion didn't like the wariness in her gaze when she turned it on him, like she was asking far more with that one word.

"Yours. My bedchamber is just there." He pointed out his door, not far down the corridor.

"We're not . . .?" Her lips twisted with alarm.

"Not yet. But I hope, when you are ready, we may share a space."

Whatever he'd hoped for in her response, it was more than the brusque nod he received.

In terse movements, she pulled the cloak from her shoulders and threw it over one of his. When she made to move away, their bound hands pulled her back.

Molly stared at the ribbon tying them together before pulling a small knife from her pocket. With a quick flick of her wrist, she cut the ties, freeing her hand and leaving him clutching the ruined ribbon.

Without a word or glance, she ducked to pick up her bags and hurried into her chamber. The door closed swiftly, with a resounding *thud,* behind her. Then the lock scraped into place, echoing through the empty house.

Allarion stared at it, befuddled.

That . . . wasn't what he'd expected. Or wanted.

Did he expect her to want to or even insist that they share a bed-chamber? That he join her in bed or that he stay with her through the night? No. But . . . it was a pleasant thought.

Faced with a shut and locked door instead, the disappointment couldn't be helped.

Peering down at the ribbon in his hand, he brought it to his nose to catch the waning scent of her before stowing it away in a pocket.

He lingered at her door, listening to her quietly move about the room. It sounded as if she opened every drawer and upended every cushion. For what purpose he couldn't guess.

What's wrong? asked Bellarand through the bond, no doubt feeling his disquiet.

She's retreated into the bedchamber and locked the door.

A distinctly equine whinny of laughter echoed in his head.

You're no help.

Oh, bah, huffed the unicorn. *Tomorrow, we'll find the biggest human male we can, then you'll fight him for dominance and prove you're a suitable sire.*

Allarion couldn't help it—he rolled his eyes.

Finally, after another long moment of staring at the closed door barring him from his bride, Allarion decided to quit the field for the night, a little disheartened but certainly not displeased. He had her here, with him. She was his bride, his *azai,* and every day she spent here would be another closer to his goals.

One day soon, she would open her door to him.

Hopefully morning would shed new light on how to further his cause.

6

The day, however, brought no celestial inspiration—nor even a peek of Molly. He found himself perpetually drifting to the residential wing of the house, where the finished bedchambers were, multiple times a day. Only to find that her door was still shut and locked. None of the fine particles he left on the floor had been disturbed, proving no one had emerged.

She hadn't even opened the door to inspect the corridor.

Finally, in the late afternoon, Allarion couldn't resist. He rapped his knuckles against the oak paneling, wishing for even a morsel of her attention.

"Molly? Are you all right?" he called after his polite knock.

After a long, tense pause—

"I'm *fine,*" she called back, even if . . . Allarion didn't think she sounded so. He vaguely remembered the half-orc Orek warning the other halflings and manticores gathered in the growing otherly village that *fine* was the most dangerous thing a human woman could say. A multifaceted word, it meant many things, none of which were obvious to an unsuspecting male.

Allarion prided himself on being a fairly fluent interpreter of the female language—he had older sisters, past lovers, many sisters-in-arms, and had watched Ravenna grow from girl to youth to woman. Still, as he stood outside Molly's locked door, he couldn't help feeling a sensation not unlike drowning.

At the very least, he wished she'd emerge long enough to let him show her the kitchen he'd stocked full in preparation. He hadn't known her tastes, so he'd purchased a bit of everything, allowing the kind merchants in the nearby market town to guide him.

The idea of preparing her a meal—even though he never had before—piqued his hope.

He tried once more. "Would you like me to—?"

"I want you to go away!"

Allarion blinked at the closed door. "Are you well?"

A snort, dripping with derision, echoed from the other side. "I'm *fine.*"

I don't think she's fine, Bellarand offered unhelpfully.

Allarion scowled over his shoulder at the unicorn. *Beasts of burden belong outside.*

Bellarand blew a puff of hot breath in his face. *Good thing I'm not burdened by much.*

Turning back to the door, Allarion laid his hand on its face. A tendril of his magic worked under the door—he didn't mean to intrude, just to ensure she was as fine as she claimed. He couldn't *see* with his magic extended, only really sense. The house creaked in question, as if it too waited to learn how their new mistress fared.

Easy, easy, he told it. *We must wait for her to become comfortable.*

The shudders rattled, as if the house sighed with impatience.

Through the tendril, Allarion sensed she lay in the bed, a lump under the mountain of blankets he'd left there. It gave him some encouragement—at least she hadn't tried to make a rope of bedding to climb out the bay windows. He'd have sensed her, of course, and the house would have told him, but still. That wouldn't have been an auspicious start to their courtship.

When nothing further came from her room, Allarion departed, Bellarand clopping behind him.

She has a strong will, Bellarand noted, *that's desirable in a female.*

Allarion agreed—a strong-willed matriarch was exactly what a house needed to succeed. He just had to be patient. It wasn't for males to rush females—they were the ones who decided when a courtship was to happen. He knew in the human kingdoms that things might be different, but he intended to treat his human *azai* with just as much respect and reverence as he would a fae woman.

Their union would be all the sweeter for his waiting, he was sure.

That night and the following morning brought no further interaction with his new *azai,* but Allarion didn't despair. It was early days yet, and while he already missed her smiles and scent, he could be patient. No matter how his fangs ached and lips wished to taste her again. He *could* be patient.

He spent his day on the roof, repairing slate shingles. The residential wing's roof had taken him many days to repair and it had been in better condition than the south wing. He'd kept steady business with the market town an hour's ride from the estate, needing a constant supply of timber, shingles, tiles, nails, and fabrics.

It was from his vantage point on the roof that he watched a cart bounce up the drive. The perimeter ward had alerted him to the presence of coming guests, and he let them pass without issue—even if annoyance prickled under his skin at their uninvited presence.

Once the two halflings came to a stop at the front of the house, Allarion leapt down from the roof to greet them. The horse pulling their cart startled and Orek twitched, slapping his hand over his heart.

"Good day to you," Allarion said, nodding at the two half-orcs.

Orek, who had mated a horse trainer named Sorcha and begun this small migration of otherly folk to the Darrowlands, offered a wary nod but Hakon, the new lord consort of the Darrowlands, was look-ing up at the roof from where he'd leapt, tracing his quick path down to the ground. He shook his head absently.

"What occasion brings the lord consort to my door?"

Hakon finally looked at him and sighed. "You know why, Allar-ion."

"You've come to congratulate me."

"No."

A visible shudder ran through both large males, and they turned to watch warily as Bellarand emerged from the forest. The unicorn made a show of slowly, deliberately circling their horse and cart.

They are very rude for males quaking in their boots.

Bellarand, try to behave.

Why?

Allarion waited to give an answer, considering the men. They hadn't come down off their cart. There were no congratulatory slaps on his shoulder or handshakes as he'd seen given to Hakon when he wed Lady Aislinn.

His annoyance bled through his tone. "Why are you here?"

"Mayor Doherty came to Aislinn yesterday," Hakon explained. "He was worried that you forced the hand of a barmaid, Molly Dunne."

His face cracked with a frown, and the house behind him creaked with foreboding.

"You think I've stolen the woman."

So what if I had?

He wanted her more fiercely than he had anything before, even keeping Ravenna safe. He had yet to find a limit to what he'd do for her.

Allarion would have liked to ask Molly directly, of course, but he respected tradition. And, he couldn't believe her uncle would *force* her. Her coming to him, going through with the handfasting, had to mean she wanted this, at least in some small way.

Orek held up his big hands. "We aren't accusing you of anything,

Allarion. We just wanted to get to the bottom of this and assure Lady Aislinn and the mayor."

"Everything we did was legal. The mayor performed the handfast himself. It was all by human tradition, and she came willingly."

"Willingly and enthusiastically are two different things," Hakon said.

Allarion turned a withering glare on the lord consort. He liked the halfling, they were friends, but the reminder was an arrow to Allarion's pride. He was painfully aware of the difference—and the lack of enthusiasm Molly had thus far shown. His mind filled with the image of her closed, locked door.

Bellarand pawed the earth, feeling Allarion's growing frustration. *Shall I run them off?*

I'm not sure we have to start a war yet.

Oh, please? It will be fun.

You already have your war with the squirrels and badgers.

The house creaked again and then—a new noise. Allarion looked up as a third-floor window opened, and out leaned Molly herself.

"Hello!" she called down.

All of them stared at her in surprise.

"Are you Molly Dunne?" Orek eventually called out.

"Yes! I'm sorry for the confusion and for worrying the mayor. He's kind for thinking of me, but I came willingly."

Willingly.

Allarion stared up at his new bride, her hair a little mussed from the down pillows of her bed. Even from the ground, he could see the strain around her eyes, the tightness of her smile.

She wasn't lying, but she wasn't being truthful, either.

His wounded pride took another kick. Twins take him, he just needed more time. She would see—she would come to love this place as much as he did. He just needed a chance.

"You swore you wouldn't interfere," Allarion reminded Hakon, too low for Molly to hear.

"I did," Hakon agreed, "but Orek didn't. He drove us here, and he's the one asking the questions."

Allarion grinned, despite himself. "Indeed."

He allowed his anger to deflate, his magic seeping back down into the ground. These were his friends, and in truth, it spoke well of them that they would care to check on Molly's welfare. He hoped it meant he could rely on such consideration in the future, but for now, he didn't need their meddling.

Looking back up at Molly and her forced smile, he said, loud enough for her to hear, "Our beginning was unorthodox, but I intend to woo her properly. This I promise—to her, with both of you as witness."

Molly's smile faltered as she stared down at him, her big eyes gone even wider with surprise.

Better she understood his intentions fully and upfront.

"But did you need to spirit her away to do it?" asked Orek.

Allarion smiled back at him, showing his fangs. "I seem to recall your orcish ancestors having something of a similar tradition?"

She'd gone mad. That was the only reason she could think of as she smiled and waved from her window while the two half-orcs made their farewells and she let them go—without her in tow.

Maybe the fae's magic was so potent, especially here in his creaking house and dark forest, that she was already being influenced by it. That was the only thing that made sense, really, or offered any explanation for why she didn't take her chance at escape.

The deeper truth, though, was that Molly feared two nights wouldn't be enough. What would the fae do if she cried foul to the lord consort and his friend? What would he do if they brought her back, humiliating an ancient being and disrupting whatever his strange plans were?

Molly feared it'd be far worse than demanding the money back from her uncle.

And Brom . . . he'd beat her blue if the fae came calling for his money.

As Molly watched the two halflings retreat down the drive, she told herself just a few more days. He'd so far let her be, ensconced in the relative safety of her room. She doubted a lock would do much good against him if he truly meant her harm, but for now, she could hunker down in her chamber. Even if the apprehension had her wanting to tear through the rations she'd packed for something to do and the comfort of a full stomach.

Give it a few more days. Let him grow sick of me.

Maybe then Brom would have spent or squirreled away the money and there'd be nothing to return anyhow.

I'm not going back there, Molly decided. No one said she had to go back to Dundúran. So, maybe she gave it a few days and then, when he'd indeed lost whatever notion attracted him to her, she'd call off the handfast, as was her right.

The fae's promise echoed in her ears.

Before departing, the lord consort had asked, *"And if she rescinds the handfast? Will you let her go?"*

The fae had looked up at her, in her window, when he said, "Yes. *On my honor, she may leave whenever she wishes."*

Molly had stared down at those inhuman eyes, dark even from three stories away, and wondered if she could believe it. Surely, he wouldn't go to such trouble, such expense, just to let her walk away.

She didn't know if she could believe his earlier promise, either, that he meant to woo her properly. It all seemed absurd, ridiculousness of the highest order. Nobody made a fuss over her, including Molly herself. This all had to be some elaborate plot, some scheme to get . . . something from her.

Molly had no wealth nor title, and where her skills lay weren't with housekeeping nor carpentry, as a house like this required. So that only left one thing.

Once again, her tits seemed to have gotten her into a bit of trouble. The question was whether she used them to get herself out again.

As she gazed down at the fae again, her heart beat a rapid rhythm in her chest. She wasn't sure she could risk it—her opponent was an ancient being, powerful and wily. Best to bide a little more time and make her escape before anything else happened.

Still, she couldn't pull her attention away as the fae continued to stand by the front of the house, peering up at her.

As she watched, her breath left her in a rush when he bowed low to her.

A sign of respect? Or was he mocking her somehow?

Molly pulled herself back into her room and closed the window, latching it tight.

The room was quiet again, a stillness to it she didn't trust.

There was something *off* about this house.

She'd felt it as they rode up the other night. Even through the darkness, illuminated only by eerie blue light burning in the lamps lining the drive, Molly felt as if the house . . . *anticipated* their arrival. It loomed above the forest like some great bird of prey, ghostly in the light of the will-o'-wisp glow. It creaked and shuddered though no wind blew, and she swore as he walked her through the empty, dilapidated corridors that doors had opened and closed on their own.

Even in her bedchamber, there were things she just couldn't explain. Although she'd forced herself to stay awake late into the first night, clutching the knife she'd secreted in one of her bags and not afraid to throw it at a fae as she'd done to her own uncle, Molly eventually succumbed to the sheer exhaustion of the day. It was only a few hours, but when she woke again, the doors of the lacquered armoire in one corner had been flung wide and the drawers pulled out, and the ornate chest at the foot of the bed had its lid open.

As if . . . *waiting* for her to put her things in them. To make the room her own.

Molly had paced around the room that morning, wondering how the fae had gotten in without her hearing. She'd become a light sleeper over the years, necessary when unwanted intruders came bumping around in the night.

Nothing looked disturbed. There was no dust to unsettle, the room immaculately clean, so she had no true way to know. Still, it didn't *feel* like he'd been inside her bedchamber.

Molly did a circuit around the room, checking the windows and doors and nooks and crannies to ensure nothing had changed. Satisfied it hadn't, she went to sit on the bed again.

It was a thing of beauty, this bed. Softer than any she'd ever touched, let alone slept on, and four times the size of her small one back at the tavern. The thick coverlet was somehow both airy and warm, and the down pillows cradled her head, inviting her into their softness. Despite herself, the second night, she'd slept like a lamb, too comfortable to worry about opening drawers and trunk lids.

Unable to resist the softness and without much else to do, she lay down. Molly wasn't one to lollygag, but it'd been an age since she'd last had the chance to laze about and rest. So she'd take the opportunity but stay on her guard.

She half expected the fae to come knocking on her door again, demanding to know why she'd lied to the halflings—Molly wanted to know herself.

But he didn't come knocking.

And it wasn't truly as much of a mystery to her as she wanted to believe.

The deepest of truths was, even holed up in her sumptuous bedchamber, Molly got a bit of a thrill from all this. It was . . . an adventure. One she wasn't quite ready to end. What waited for her back in Dundúran? Nothing but an angry uncle and gossiping neighbors.

Oh, she still intended to play it safe. Stay in her room, ensure the fae got bored of her, and then break off the handfast.

In the meantime, she'd sleep on the softest bed in the kingdom and form her plan. She had her wits about her, her trove of coins she'd saved, her trusty knife, and her big pair of tits—more than a lot of women could say. Give her a few days and she'd figure something out.

When she did emerge, the fae wouldn't know what hit him. He'd find his time and his coin wasted.

Not her problem.

Laying back on the soft bed, Molly got comfortable and began to think.

Could the unicorn be bribed? With carrots, maybe?

7

Her grand plan, however, never quite came together—especially when she ran out of food and her stomach began to rumble. Molly had managed to bring some sustenance with her, but a few apples, half a loaf of bread, and some nuts only went so far.

After a day of listening to her stomach complain and squeezing the last drops of water from her canteen, she decided it was finally time to brave outside her chamber. She was also growing desperate to figure out how the chamber pot was changed and cleaned and a bucket of fresh water brought in each morning before she woke. She never saw him, and she didn't drink the water, of course, but she had to know how he did it.

And quiet her stomach. Molly had promised herself, as a ten-year-old newly orphaned and skeletal from hunger, that she'd never starve again.

That was first and foremost on her mind when she cracked the door of her bedchamber open, her head woozy and her stomach painfully empty.

She peered up and down the corridor to find it unoccupied. Squinting at the door he'd indicated was his that first night, Molly slowly stepped from her room. Only a layer of dust greeted her.

She stared down at that dust suspiciously. He'd been here at least once, and she suspected many more times than that. No boot prints had been left behind to prove it, though.

What, can he fly now, too?

She wouldn't put it past the fae. What little she'd managed to learn about him was that he wasn't human. She knew that already, of course, but glimpsing him work at his tasks tirelessly—literally, *tirelessly,* for days on end—only underscored his strangeness. He didn't seem to rest. He could hammer at the roof all day. He'd practiced archery from dawn to dusk one day. Another, he hauled buckets all morning without signs of exhaustion.

Molly grew tired just watching him.

His strength and endurance were inhuman—*superhuman.*

Today, though, the house was quiet. No hammering, no whizzing arrows. Maybe he truly did need to rest eventually.

After a morning of listening to only the complaints of her stomach, she decided to try her luck—which had been abominable up to now, but she had to keep up hope it'd change soon.

Careful to keep her footfalls light and soundless, Molly eased down the corridor.

Although a little dusty, the corridor was nevertheless grander than any place she'd lived before. The walls had once had some sort of wallpaper but had been stripped and cleaned, though they still bore faint traces of hung paintings and paper glue. Scratches on the floor indicated where decorative tables had once stood and slightly darker areas where carpets had once lain.

To her right, the wall was lined with tall leaded windows that rose nearly to the corniced ceiling. Light streamed inside, and the wall of glass offered a stunning view of the forest beyond. In the daylight, it wasn't so foreboding as that first night. Still, she didn't think it was entirely her hunger that made her think the trees whispered to each other.

That was *his* forest. This was *his* house.

They were probably whispering to him, reporting back on everything. Including her.

A prickle of unease ran up Molly's neck at the thought.

Much as she'd loved the tavern, it was her uncle's, and he reminded her of that whenever he could. She'd felt Brom in every panel and floorboard. Always looking over her shoulder in what was supposed to be her home made existence exhausting, and she'd promised herself life would be different when she made a home of her own.

Food first, and then, with a full belly, she was sure a better plan than making a rope of bedsheets would come to her. That new life of hers was only a few days and one good plan away.

The corridor spilled out to a shallow set of steps that led down to a landing with four doors. Holding onto the banister, Molly took the stairs a step at a time, careful not to make the floorboards groan.

Still, a loud *creak* reverberated through the empty stairwell when her foot touched the landing. Cringing, Molly hurried to the first door and threw herself through the threshold.

The other side was far darker than the last corridor. Tattered curtains hung limply from grimy windows, and dust carpeted the chipped floor. A hideous wallpaper that'd once been robin's egg blue peeled from the walls, and desiccated flowers just a breath from crumbling to nothing drooped in cracked porcelain vases.

It was an eerie space, a reminder of the family that had once lived here. Molly didn't know much, just that whatever family had once owned Scarborough had lost it and then their lives in the bloody wars of succession that nearly tore Eirea apart. Although it'd been thirty years ago now, the scars were still present—and so were the ghosts of that time. Everyone knew Scarborough was haunted.

Holding her breath, Molly ventured deeper into the gloom to test the first door. The room inside was bright, and she couldn't resist a closer look. The fae had obviously done work in here, and she could see why.

The first door led into a beautiful library. Rich bookcases of cherry-wood were stuffed full of gilded tomes, their shelves sagging beneath the weight of the pages and bronze devices and dried up inkwells. The walls were lined in burgundy velvet wallpaper, and a plush carpet had been cleaned and laid before the stone fireplace. A set of leather armchairs had been recently oiled, the scent of it tickling her nose.

An expansive desk stood to one side, beneath a pool of light from the set of four windows on the east wall, a framed, faded map of Eirea laid out on its face. Molly peeked and found old borders still dotting through the landscape. A few books also sat on the desk, as well as abandoned papers, quills, and what looked to be a fresh crystal inkwell.

He uses this.

Pulse picking up, she hurried from the room via the nearest door. It was a small one tucked into the back of the library, leading into the adjoining room.

What she found was an empty room, dark save a single shaft of light streaming in from the drooping corner of the heavy curtains. It'd been a solar, perhaps, somewhere to meet and chat with guests. The walls had been stripped, the floors cleaned, but the emptiness of it tugged at her, filling her with dread.

The door out to the corridor opened.

Molly gasped, jumping back, and watched as . . .

The door opened, but—no one stood on the other side of it.

The wind, she told herself, even though she felt no breeze and nothing disturbed the curtains.

Breath caught in her throat, Molly crossed the empty space to use the other door, tucked into the back of the room. She found another chamber just like the last, although this one still had its wallpaper.

Her heart beat fast as she hurried across this room, a headache pounding behind her hairline and her head itself swirling with wooziness. *That's all this is, I'm just—*

The door at the back of the room opened before she could reach it. Again, no one was there.

She couldn't help it—Molly yelped in alarm and jumped back.

The door she'd been about to open slammed shut only to open again, again, again, the sound pounding against her already throbbing head.

Molly raced to the other door, throwing it open and herself into the corridor beyond.

Which way did I come?

She didn't remember.

The doors on each side of her rattled and creaked, their old hinges scraping as the doors shut and slammed closed in a macabre harmony.

Molly turned and ran.

The doors chattered at her, then the curtains began to rustle and the decorative tables to shudder. A moldering curtain flapped, trying to get in her way.

Molly batted it away, feet pounding.

Get me out, get me out, get out!

Panic numbed her fingers, and her ears rang with the litany of doors. Tables crashed to the floor in her way, and the curtains reached for her like arms. Molly threw her hands up to protect her face and jumped over the shards of wood and porcelain.

The doors—so many doors—they just kept going and going and—

There—there was one that didn't slam and laugh at her. That one had to be right. That one—

Wouldn't open.

Molly screeched and threw her weight into the door, forcing it open. The latch gave with a scream, and her momentum carried her over the threshold—

And right into a gaping maw of darkness.

No floor waited for her foot, the floorboards completely gone.

The scream caught in Molly's throat as she began to fall.

Her breath punched out of her lungs when something hard and unforgiving wrapped around her middle. An indelicate noise wrenched from her throat as her momentum suddenly stopped. Even as her limbs went flailing in front of her, something pulled her back, away from the hole that fell three floors.

Wheeling her legs, Molly stumbled backwards and clutched at whatever pulled her away.

Her fingers dug into a fine brocade sleeve.

She was pulled back, away from the danger, and into a hard wall of—chest. Heart hammering, it was a moment before she realized her nose filled with the scent of man and magic, spicy and deep like cloves and pepper and leather oil.

Allarion.

The tip of a sharp nose parted her hair to run behind her ear and down her neck. Molly trembled to feel his skin against hers.

"This is why I warned you not to come to this wing of the house," he rumbled, voice richer than the brocade she clutched.

A puff of disbelief was what came out of her.

With utmost gentleness, he ushered her further back into the corridor. The door to the floorless room closed on its own, while all the other doors opened slowly.

She wasn't too proud to admit a little whimper escaped her.

"What's *happening?*" Her voice sounded screechy even to her own ears.

"Please don't be afraid, sweetling. It's only the house."

Molly turned her incredulous gaze on him. "*What?*"

Allarion pulled her even closer and rested his other hand on her hip, as if she was a spooked horse in need of soothing.

"You must forgive me, Molly. I haven't had the chance to explain. I am bonding with this estate—the land and the house both. My magic is having . . . interesting effects on the house. It's growing sentient."

Her mouth opened and closed like a fish, nothing intelligible making it up her throat.

He took the chance to turn her to face him, and in her shock, she was more amenable. His hands ghosted down her arms to hold them out as he ran a quick, assessing look over her. Whatever he saw, he nodded once and, so fluidly she didn't think to stop it, turned them down the corridor to begin walking. He kept stride with her as he tucked her hand into the crook of his elbow, as if they were some fancy folk on a stroll.

Molly blinked at him, at her hand caught in the folds of his sleeve, at his hand coming to cover hers with its finely tapered fingers. How . . . had he managed all this so smoothly?

They were passing the library again when she finally found her tongue.

"You mean this house is *alive?*"

"Indeed. I find that most homes have a life to them, but the magic imbuing it now has given this house a greater sentience. A consciousness."

"It . . . *knows* we're here?"

"I should hope so," he said with a chuckle. "We are living inside it."

Molly looked around in wonder, only to realize they were back at the landing.

"It's fortunate the house has a mind of its own—it warned me of your little adventure."

The bottom fell out of her stomach. "The doors . . . that was the house?" She stared at the walls as if they would suddenly grow faces. "That scared me nearly to death!"

A mournful creak echoed down the stairwell.

"I assure you, the house means you no harm. I suspect it was trying to lead you away from danger, not towards it."

Molly opened her mouth to argue, the cadence of the slamming doors still rattling her bones, but then . . . she remembered how the last door didn't want to open.

Allarion patted her hand. "Be at ease, sweetling. The house likes you very much. It's curious about you. For months now, it's only been me and Bellarand, and before that, there was no one for many years. It wants people living within its walls."

The thought should have scared her—and it did. Sort of. But through her deflating terror, Molly also couldn't help being a little . . . charmed. She supposed it made sense; a home would want to have people.

With a little effort, Molly caught her breath and calmed her nerves. Focusing on the prospect of a sentient house seemed less daunting than acknowledging the strange man standing beside her, whose hand on hers sent a little thrill down her spine.

"I didn't mean to go jumping through floors—I was just looking for the kitchen."

A sudden smile broke across the fae's face. "Marvelous. I was hoping to give you a tour. Luncheon first, though, I think."

And easy as that, hand still tucked into his elbow, Allarion led her down through the house to the kitchen. He pointed out salient places along the way, his pride in the home practically oozing from him.

There was the front solar, which got the best light. And here was the sitting room, just waiting for a set of plush furniture. Here was the grand atrium, the wooden staircase with its ornate banister and curved steps oiled to a high shine. Every place they stopped on their way, the doors opened on their own, as if the house too was proud to show off.

Molly followed along, struck a bit dumb with the grandeur of it. To be sure, there was so much work to be done; most of the rooms were stripped and completely empty. But there were *so many* rooms, and the craftsmanship of the home spoke to its builder's wealth. It was in the cornices and doorknobs, the arching banisters and parquet floors. The faint outlines and stains of former furniture and decoration were a ghostly reminder of just how opulent this house had once been.

Even dusty, sun-bleached, and moldering, Molly still felt the place was far too fancy for her.

The kitchen, though. The kitchen she took to immediately. Lined in stone, it was noticeably warmer and cozier. A fire already burned in the large oven, and fragrant herb fronds hung from the rafters to dry. It too was sparsely furnished, just a few utensils and pots, but they were things she recognized. It was probably the nicest kitchen she'd ever been in, but there was a familiarity to it that put her a little more at ease.

Enough that, when Allarion finally released her to fetch some food from the cold box, she was brave enough to ask more questions.

"Did you mean what you said to the lord consort?"

He didn't answer immediately, but when he returned to set a block of cheese, a loaf of bread, apples, carrots, and other vegetables on the block before her, his expression was gentle and open.

"I did," he said.

"So you mean to go through with this handfasting?"

"My intentions are to take a wife, yes. I very much want her to be you, Molly Dunne."

"And what if it's not? What if I don't like it here?"

That gentleness faded from his face, but while Molly tensed, awaiting anger or frustration, instead it was a profound sadness that darkened his brow.

"Do you not like your chamber? I had hoped . . ."

Molly shrugged. "It's a lot better than being kept in the cellar, I suppose. The room's nice. But that's not really what I'm asking."

His frown grew troubled, and for a moment, it looked as though he was trying to parse out meaning from her words. What he didn't understand she didn't know, but she wasn't going to thank him for not keeping her tied up somewhere dark and dank after *buying her.*

Finally, slowly, he said, "You aren't my prisoner here, Molly. I wish to woo you, to court you." He came around the butcher block, his movements deliberate.

Molly held her ground, watching him come, as graceful and silent as a predator. When he stood before her, he loomed tall, making her crane her neck to keep his gaze. One purple-gray hand rose to gently touch her cheek with his fingertips.

"I wish to show you what it is to be a fae's mate. We cherish our females, you see. You would be the air I breathe. The ground I walk upon. Nothing would please me more than giving you everything you deserve, *azai*."

Molly's mouth twisted in a sardonic grin. *What I deserve, huh?*

She'd heard flowery words before. Sure, his made her belly flutter with excitement, and she couldn't ignore how she suddenly ached between her thighs. Something about the way he looked at her, those amethyst eyes set in darkness, promised her everything he'd said and much more. A life of comfort and luxury, and nights of softness and passion.

His back bowed slightly, as if to curl himself around her, and she knew without a single word, he'd kiss her.

Instead, Molly turned to the butcher block to start sorting through the vegetables. A stew was in order—*that's* what she deserved.

"We'll see," she told him, because fairy tales and fae promises weren't for barmaids.

8

For all that the looming fae and brooding unicorn mystified and terrified her, respectively, Molly had little trouble learning to love a sentient house. Her first evening knowing the situation, she stayed up late into the night, testing out ideas of how to communicate.

She figured out it was the one who'd brought her water and changed the chamber pot. Through a few more halting conversations with Allarion, she learned the house laughed by rattling its shutters and pouted by creaking. There were all sorts of noises it made—Molly just had to listen.

Soon, she had a system—one drawer or door opening was yes, nothing was no. This way, she was able to at least have something of a conversation, odd as it was, with the house itself.

"Did you like your first family? The one who built you?" she asked, feeling brave and vulnerable as they sat talking in the deepest hours of the night, awash in soft candlelight.

The armoire drawer opened and closed many times. An emphatic *yes!*

Molly smiled. "You must miss them."

It wasn't a question, but the drawer again opened and closed, much more softly this time.

Her heart hurt for the house. Absolutely mad as it might be, she felt its sadness in that one action, could feel how the very walls mourned the loss of its former family.

"Do you like having people living with you, then?"

The drawer opened and closed in rapid succession.

"More than just the bats in the attic, anyway."

The shutters rattled and the house groaned as if it too laughed along with her. She wasn't sure the house actually minded the bats in the attic or the raccoon family in the east tower or even the bee hives in the rafters of the north wing. They were all little friends, little inhabitants for the house to take care of.

And that was what the house liked most, Molly came to find. Taking care of its inhabitants. It was always finding ways of being helpful—opening doors for her, turning off the spigot when she forgot, and even having the kettle already going by the time she got down to the kitchen to make tea. The house anticipated her needs before she even knew them herself.

Although, there was one thing that was a bit of a sore spot between them.

Every evening, the house opened the armoire and the large trunk at the foot of her massive canopied bed. Every night, Molly refrained from storing her things inside them. Her clothes were getting wrinkled and she'd made a bit of a mess on the far side of the bed laying out what she didn't bother putting back in the bags.

The house would creak at her, drawers opening and closing to emphasize that her things belonged there.

But they didn't.

Something about putting her things in those drawers would mean . . . they were now part of the house. *She* was part of it.

But she wasn't.

No matter how the house rattled at her. No matter how its master looked longingly at her over the butcher block.

Molly didn't intend to stay.

That didn't mean, however, that she wasn't amenable to making friends. She got on well with the house, and felt, within a few days, that although she couldn't count on its loyalty to her over Allarion, she could at least trust that it would tell her the truth.

Strange as it was to think, Molly found the house guileless.

It was comforting to sit cross-legged on her bed and chat with the house. Knowing she could ask it questions and get a truthful answer.

"Is it strange being inhabited by a fae and unicorn?" Molly asked it. She tried to camouflage her curiosity by picking at her cuticles, but she didn't know if the subterfuge worked—or was even necessary.

She waited a long time, but nothing happened. It took her a moment to remember that nothing meant *no*. The house hadn't responded in the negative in a long while.

"Not strange . . ." she muttered to herself. "Do you like Allarion?"

The drawers opened and shut three times, and Molly couldn't help her grin.

"That's a yes. But . . . would you like him even if it meant you weren't sentient?"

Without even the shortest pause, another series of opening and closing drawers.

Yes yes yes, it told her.

Molly's heart lurched in her chest. The answer was so earnest, so forthright.

Wetting her lips, she forced out the question she'd been dreading. "Can I trust him?"

This time there was a pause. The house creaked, and Molly held her breath.

The room seemed to bend, as if the house held its own breath as it leaned in closer to her. Molly clutched the pillow in her lap, trying to stay still.

The drawer opened and closed twice.

Yes.

"Are you sure?"

Opened and closed.

"Does he mean me any harm?"

Nothing. *No.*

The breath hissed out of her.

Well, fates. That was a relief, except . . . could she trust the house?

Although talking with a sentient house was fascinating, Molly eventually grew bored of keeping to her bedchamber. Over the ensuing days, she dared more ventures beyond her door, careful now to mind the house's warnings when something was unsafe.

Allarion seized the opportunity to give her the tour he'd been waiting to take her on. With obvious pride, he took her through the grand atrium that led to the ornate curving staircase; the ballroom with an inlaid parquet floor; the conservatory with its mullioned windows and humid air; the vast wine cellars where dozens of casks and hundreds of green-glass bottles still lay; and the cold box, pantries, and buttery where food was stored.

The south wing was almost entirely servants' quarters, and Molly marveled at the number of people who must have once lived here—to support one noble family. It didn't rival the staff of Dundúran Castle, but it still would've been a force unto itself. With so many people moving about . . . it was no wonder the house enjoyed having inhabitants again, even if it was only a human, a fae, and a unicorn.

Allarion took her through his many projects, detailing how he was fixing the roof shingles now but would then move onto the floor of the second-level study—or rather, would create a floor to the study.

"I can't have any more beautiful women falling through the floor. It's just not in good taste," he said with what she took for good humor.

He even smiled through a chuckle. While it did warm the cool pallor of his skin and severe contours of his face, a smile could only do so much—especially when it flashed those wicked fangs.

Molly couldn't help staring at them before remembering her manners. She offered a lukewarm grin in return, her stomach still knotted with anxiety as he led her here, there, and everywhere.

It wasn't that he felt threatening or that she entirely disliked the way he insisted they walk arm-in-arm—it was more that she half-expected that every door he opened would reveal some new horror. The corpses of the former family. A dungeon of other barmaids he'd bought. Even a bevy of more crimson-eyed unicorns.

Despite the kindliness of the house, it couldn't help that the areas he'd yet to fix or renovate still bore the scars of abandonment and general air of doom and dread. The air was dank and stale in places he hadn't gotten to yet, and he didn't have to tell her to avoid them— she'd no desire to linger in such forgotten places.

Still, as he took her through the house, she made sure to remember all the routes and where each door led to. She'd every intention of running far away from this place someday soon, and she'd like to take something for her troubles. Yet, other than her bedchamber and the kitchen, none of the rooms had much if any furniture. While her room was sumptuously furnished, it wasn't decorated. Not even a pretty vase to filch.

Not that she *really* thought he was storing all his valuables in some kind of hoard. He was a fae, not a dragon.

As the days began to pass, though, Molly came to understand that the house not being decorated was something Allarion fully intended to rectify. He just . . . wanted her opinion first.

It started out simply, asking if she'd like flowers in the kitchen.

"Of course," she said as she stirred that day's stew, "flowers brighten up any room."

He left immediately, as if she'd asked him to go slay some great beast for her favor, and returned a while later with a literal armload of larkspurs. He arranged the blue and purple spears in deliberate, artful bunches, filling pewter pitchers and ceramic cups.

Molly silently watched him work as she ate her luncheon, deeply curious. He approached flower arranging with the same focus as he did repairing the roof or practicing his sword forms or any other task. Gaze unflinching, mind totally consumed, it was as if placing each flower perfectly was his only concern.

Just think what a focus like that could do.

Molly hooked one knee over the other and squeezed her thighs together.

Fates, she couldn't start having thoughts like those.

Still, she couldn't help noticing the strong column of his throat, bared to the air for once in his downright casual attire of the day. Although his trou were still stiff and tight, his boots still high and shiny, and his jerkin still laced and form-fitting, the top three buttons of his black shirt had been left undone, revealing the long, pale line of his throat and winging arches of his collarbones.

He'd tied the top half of his silvery fall of hair back into a tail with a strip of leather, ensuring the inhumanly sharp cut of his cheeks, nose, and jaw were on full display as he filled the kitchen with flowers. She'd never seen a man arrange flowers before, but when the fae did it, it was beautiful, almost . . . sensual.

Molly nearly choked on a piece of carrot.

She waved him away when he would have come to her aid—she doubted she'd survive a powerful fae smacking her back to clear her airway.

He still hovered with concern for a while before returning to his task.

Thereafter, she always found flowers adorning the kitchen. And after another few days, she opened her bedchamber door each morning to find a new bouquet awaiting her. Her room slowly filled with flowers, none of which were in bloom but somehow he'd found, and fine porcelain and glass vases.

After the flowers came colors. Without much else to do, Molly would sometimes follow Allarion along on his projects. In the big solar on the second level, he asked her more than once what color she thought would be best.

Molly blinked in bafflement for a long while, not understanding why he asked. Uncle Brom certainly never let her change the tavern—even for the better—and hadn't even let her repaint her own bedchamber. The most she'd ever been allowed was a few of her own baubles and some garlands for festivals.

Allarion wasn't satisfied with *It's your house,* nor *I don't know, white?*

"The library I did to my own tastes," he said, as if having one room to his own taste was enough. And she could definitely see him in the room—all the rich fabrics and dark colors were exactly what the fae seemed to favor. But . . . it was his house.

Molly shrugged and avoided his question and gaze by wandering through the empty room. When she came to the large set of windows that looked out onto the forest, she turned.

Soaked in light, Molly truly looked at the room.

White is too plain. Gray too dour. Red would overwhelm the room, and gold would wash it out.

"Green," she whispered more than said.

A slow smile spread across Allarion's face, and Molly swore those dark eyes watched her with an avaricious sort of . . . pride.

"Sage?" he asked. "Seafoam?"

Molly shook her head. "No, a dark green. Like the forest outside."

The shutters rattled, widening Allarion's smile.

Without so much as a blink, all that fae focus directed at her, and as though she had passed some sort of test, he said softly, "Perfect."

Why he cared so much about her opinion, Molly couldn't quite figure out. If she let herself think about it, she supposed it might be good that he was asking for the opinion of the person he wanted to share the house with. It was another point to his being serious about the hand-fasting, making it permanent.

He was trying to make the house to *both* of their tastes.

The revelation was a terrifying one, which was why Molly didn't let herself think of these things much. That way lay danger, and she'd had far too much danger in her life already.

She just had to wait for the right vase.

Molly wanted to take something with her when she left—ideally something to sell in the next town for some pocket money to get her where she wanted to go. Wherever that was. There just hadn't been the right vase yet. All of them were either too large or too heavy porcelain, colored glass, smooth marble, they'd all fetch a pretty price, but they'd all slow her escape down. She needed just the right one, not too big, not too delicate, not too heavy. Something nice but not *too* nice—nothing that would make a shopkeeper think she'd stolen it. Even if she had.

Until then, she supposed she just had to content herself with watching Allarion in his strange renovation of his sentient house.

Yet, when she unlocked and opened her bedchamber door on that seventh morning, she found no flowers nor vase. The corridor was empty save the shafts of light filtering in from the wall of windows.

The house itself was quieter than Molly had ever heard it.

Strange.

Molly crept from her room, wondering if something had happened. Nothing looked amiss, but it felt . . . different.

The kitchen yielded no clues, nor did the library or study, with its newly finished floor. After a quiet breakfast, Molly ventured outside, skirting the house to see if she could spot him on the roof.

Peering up, she tried multiple angles but couldn't see him. She didn't always when he was up there replacing shingles, but she certainly *heard* him, and today, the estate was quiet. Quiet but not exactly peaceful. She couldn't quite put her finger on it, but even outside, the wrongness of something lingered in the crisp autumn air.

A shiver skated up Molly's spine, leaving an eruption of gooseflesh in its wake.

A threatening nicker echoed behind her.

Turning slowly, carefully, Molly came face to face with the unicorn. Bellarand.

He stood not five paces away, his great head lowered so those crimson eyes were level with her own. The wicked point of his long horn bobbed in the air, only a single lunge away from piercing her vulnerable throat.

Molly swallowed hard and held up her hands.

"I don't suppose you've seen the master of the house."

A low rumble emanated from the unicorn's thick neck, and he flicked his black tail.

She didn't know why she felt defensive all of a sudden, nor why she felt the need to insist, "I wasn't running away, I was looking for Allarion."

The unicorn shook his mane, waving that horn at her menacingly, and began to paw the earth. He flicked his head at the house.

"Fine, fine," she grumbled, "I'm going back in."

Scowling at the overgrown guard pony, Molly retreated into the kitchen, careful to keep the unicorn in her sight until she was back inside. Although she liked the fresh air and view of the estate, she shut and locked the split door, just for good measure.

Rubbing a hand on her chest, over where her heart wanted to race right out of her ribs, Molly paced around the kitchen. When that didn't settle her nervous energy, she threw herself into making a meal with the last of the food in the larder. She kept back crusts and peels and rinds, her uncertainty over when Allarion would return making nervous knots out of her guts.

Molly knew what it was to go hungry, and she'd promised herself never to be in that situation again.

As the day passed without hide nor hair of the fae, that anxiety and fear in her grew into anger. The fire in her belly was a relief—she'd much rather be angry. And fed.

Before she lost the sunlight altogether, she went looking for him again. All throughout the house, up to all the levels and back down again.

Nowhere.

She called his name, told him to call out and tell her where he was, if he was hurt.

Nothing.

Fuming and tired from her hike through the house, Molly stomped back toward her bedchamber.

She could make what food there was stretch another two days, three if she took only one meal. The thought of having to do so only brought painful memories, of scraping moldering bowls and gnawing rotten apple cores during the long days of plague that took her parents. Sequestered in their house by the town council for fear of spread, they weren't allowed out until the fever had passed or everyone inside was dead.

Molly spent nearly a month raiding her family's meager stores, eating the weeds growing in the flowerboxes and boiling leather strips from their shoes. Sometimes she didn't have an appetite from the smells emanating out of her parents' room, where she'd left them prone in their bed weeks before. But most of the time, her hunger ate at her, and she spent her days finding things to put in her belly.

When she'd finally emerged from that house, pockmarked, bony, orphaned, she'd vowed to never know hunger like that again.

Molly indulged in food whenever she could, the comfort of a full belly something she couldn't resist. Her uncle may have scolded and berated her for it, Nora may have made snide comments about her figure because of it, but Molly didn't care. A rumbling, empty stomach brought her to that house of death, a place she refused to go back to.

Planting her hands on her hips, she didn't immediately go into her room. Instead, she scowled at the door he'd pointed out as his.

It was the one place she hadn't checked yet.

As if it could sense her question, his door opened a crack.

He didn't walk out to flash that sharp smile, even though Molly stood glaring at the door long enough to wait him out.

When he still didn't appear, she stole down the corridor, easing her angry stomps to instead creep silently to the cracked open door. She grasped the handle but held still just outside, listening.

Nothing.

No moving, no breathing.

Utterly confused and more than a little frustrated, Molly opened the door and entered his bedchamber.

Inside was as rich and sumptuous as the library. Heavy curtains draped from the windows across the room, and an expansive rug shot through with red and gold thread covered the floor. The drapes had been pulled closed on two sides of the massive four-post, canopied bed, creating a cave of velvet and silk.

Within the darkness of the room, laying motionless on the bed, was Allarion.

He lay supine, hands folded neatly on his abdomen.

Molly crept closer, daring to whisper his name. "Allarion?"

Nothing.

The closer she drew, the more she could discern from the meager light of the corridor. His long hair spilled across his pillow, falling over the side of the bed. His sharp nose and proud chin jutted up at the canopy. He was clothed in a loose shirt and linen braies, leaving his lower legs and feet bare.

He had no body hair—not on his chest, not on his legs.

And she'd never seen his feet before. She didn't know what she'd expected—hooves? Claws? That they were fairly ordinary in shape—perhaps a little large, with prominent bones like the rest of him—was more shocking than if he'd had taloned bird feet.

Her gaze skated up his body to his chest and—

He wasn't breathing.

Molly lurched forward, just catching herself on the edge of the bed. Her fingers sank into a plush silk coverlet, the softest she'd ever touched. It was dark, but she thought it was perhaps an amethyst purple.

Like his eyes.

This close, she could tell for certain he didn't breathe. His chest didn't rise and fall. His eyes didn't twitch behind their closed lids. He just . . . lay there.

Her guts knotted tighter.

Had he died in his sleep?

Did fae die?

Did they die in their sleep?

She didn't know, and not knowing had frustrated tears pricking her eyes.

Hand trembling, she reached out to just barely touch his neck. When she felt nothing, she pressed a little harder to his skin.

Molly felt no pulse.

Yet, he was as warm as he usually was.

If he'd died, he'd only just done so.

Muttering a curse, Molly held her breath as she prodded his cheek and then his temple. His head rocked to the side and then straightened.

He didn't move. Not even a twitch.

What in all the hells is this?

All this scheming and effort to get her here and he just goes and *dies—*

I'm watching you, vermin. You think you are safe up there, but I watch.

The bottom fell out of Molly's stomach, and she gasped, rearing away from the dead fae.

That voice—it was in her head! And it wasn't hers!

You can run run run, but I will chase.

It wasn't Allarion's voice, either.

A whimper fell from her lips.

The house creaked at her noise of distress.

With a yelp, Molly ran from the dark bedchamber, feet pounding on the floorboards.

That's right, run run run—

The door of her room opened for her, and Molly careened inside.

I like it when you run, when you beg—

"Stop it!"

Tears streamed down Molly's face as she turned in circles in the center of her room. The house creaked, the shingles rattling.

Molly grabbed for her nearest bag and began shoving clothes into it.

She had to get out. Whatever this was, whatever spoke to her, it was evil. Wrong. Something was *wrong* with this place, with everything, and she needed—

Molly skidded to a stop before the window.

In the haze of dusk, she watched a large form skirt the edge of the forest.

Bellarand.

The unicorn patrolled the estate, his red eyes casting a glow in the growing darkness.

Molly dropped to the ground when she thought his head swung toward her window. Clutching the bag to her chest, she crammed herself into a corner, putting her back to the wall.

Come out, come out, come play, the voice taunted.

Trapped. Molly was trapped, in a haunted house that spoke, with a dead fae and murderous unicorn. Without food.

Another whimper escaped her, and Molly buried her head in her hands. "No, no, no," she groaned.

Oh, yes.

9

In the long sleep, he dreamt of Molly.

The long sleep was an odd sort of place, outside of temporality, full of wisps of memory and tendrils of ideas. Dreams usually played no part, a fae mind so closed off and shut down that there was little happening beyond the barest of senses.

Still, through the purple clouds and knitted hopes, Allarion dreamed of her, or if not dreamed then thought of. Dreamed in the allusive sense— dreamed of her lying beside him in this big bed, the silk sheets gathered at her waist. He dreamed of what she would feel like, tucked into his side, safe and warm and just where she belonged.

What would it be to be held in her arms? To feel the weight of her limbs and beat of her human heart? What would the puff of her breath feel like against his skin, or the fine silk of her hair through his fingers?

What would it feel like to slide into the wet heat of her body, to be welcomed inside her, a needy moan on her lips?

He longed to know, so desperately, the ache found him even in the long sleep.

He'd never be free of her now, if she haunted even his sleep.

Good. He never wanted to be free of her.

Allarion woke from his long sleep refreshed—and with a stiff cock. The sight was almost amusing, though the fierce, hard ache tempered any humor. It'd been a long while since he'd woken with a demanding cock, and his hand was out of practice.

It took several exploratory pumps to get the right rhythm and grip, but once he did, it wasn't long before he spilled into his own hand.

He was left with an empty sort of relief—not satisfaction, just the absence of immediate discomfort.

It's not her.

Indeed not. And although he'd had the privilege of her company over the past days, he feared he was still quite a ways from earning a place as her bedfellow. The thought of how, even after days at Scarborough, she still looked at him askance, wariness lining her eyes, cooled any of the residual ardor lingering in his blood.

Hauling himself from the bed, Allarion cleaned himself up and slipped into his attire for the day. Although it was far less than he'd wear in the faelands, forgoing a tunic or coat to cover his shirtsleeves, he was growing more comfortable with the less formal customs of everyday human life. Even the Darrows didn't stand on ceremony that often.

And, it's my own house. I should dress as I like.

Feeling more at ease in his informal layers of clothing, like a second skin, he swept from his chamber. On the narrow table he'd placed by his door, he found the vase and bouquet he'd asked the house to make up before taking his long sleep. It pleased him to see the bursting yellow sunflowers, and even more to leave it before her door.

It gave him great pleasure to give her beautiful things.

His Molly was more reticent than he'd expected. Still, she was slowly beginning to accept his gifts. Flowers were nothing to what he could and would give her, but it was a start.

Filling her room with bright, beautiful flowers, taking care of her, offering her a fine home—well, a home that would be fine one day soon—fulfilled his most basic needs as a male fae.

Although the males of his kind were large and physically imposing compared to the females, it was the latter who led them. Blessed with a magic more intrinsic than the males, it was female fae who ruled and governed—they were the monarchs, the scholars, the healers, the politicians. To be sure, there were male academics and male physicians. Males outnumbered females almost two to one, so there were many roles they had to fill.

For the fae, though, it was a matriarchal society. Females were to be cherished, valued, worshipped even. They were life-bringers, magic-singers. If a male desired a female and was blessed with her favor, it was his duty and his honor to take care of her every need, to protect her with life and limb, and to ensure she knew only comfort and happiness.

It was what he wanted to give Molly, if only she'd let him.

Finding his way down into the kitchen, the house creaked as if waking itself from slumber.

"Yes, good morning," he greeted. "Nothing of note happened while I was asleep?"

The top half of the split kitchen door opened with an ominous creak.

Allarion's attention snapped, his senses sharpening. "What's happened?"

The house fell silent, so that Allarion could clearly hear the pounding stomps of his *azai* coming downstairs to join them.

Although the house's warning unnerved him, he donned a smile to hide it, expecting a wary greeting from Molly.

What he got was an angry hellcat.

Molly burst into the kitchen in a plume of petals and snapping, angry eyes. She slammed the vase of flowers down on the butcher block, turning that glare onto him. The force of it nearly sent Allarion back a step.

"You!" she shrieked.

"Good—"

"What in *all the hells* is this?"

Allarion looked between her and the flowers, now missing many of their petals. "Sunflowers. I'm the one who has left you flowers in the mornings."

He knew immediately that wasn't what she wanted to hear, the red of her cheeks deepening to an alarming shade and her eyes flashing dangerously.

"I *know that,* Allarion. What I mean is—where were you?"

Ah. He'd failed to warn her of his upcoming sleep. In his defense, he was unsure, given her wariness of him still, just how much to tell her of his nature. He worried one misplaced fact would have her barricading herself in her bedchamber again.

"You must forgive me, Molly, I—"

"I don't have to do anything—you're the one who needs to explain!"

"Yes, I'm trying. Fae do not sleep every night like humans. Instead, every few days, we take the long sleep."

"The long sleep," she repeated, her voice rising to a rather unpleasant pitch. "And in this long sleep, you just, what, are dead to the world for a whole day?"

"That is what it looks like to those not sleeping, yes. Depending on what has occurred, the sleep can last longer than that. We need the restorative time. Little can wake us."

Something like horror passed over her expressive human face, and Allarion hurried to reassure her. "I take it you must have seen me in my sleep. Please don't worry yourself, I didn't wake because I sensed no threat from you." He would have intrinsically known her to be his *azai,* even *dead to the world,* as she put it.

Once again that morning, he was proven utterly wrong. What

was meant to comfort and soothe her only elicited another screech of frustration.

"*Allarion—*" He wanted to enjoy it when she said his name, but honestly, he didn't in that tone, scolding and furious "—you can't just do that to me! We're almost out of food. I didn't know when you would—I thought you were *dead!* I thought I was going to starve. And *him—*"

She pointed an accusing finger at the kitchen door. Bellarand had put his head through the open top half, peering inside with interest.

Now what's she yelling about?

Allarion frowned, now doubly confused. *She was yelling before?*

All last night, his steed confirmed, *it kept all of us awake.*

Dread began to trickle through his veins. Goddesses, what trap had he left for himself?

"Your overgrown guard pony wouldn't let me leave! He would have made me rot in here. There's only food enough for another day or two. After that—after—" Emotion clogged her voice, and Allarion's chest lurched seeing the obvious pain in Molly's face.

Pony? Bellarand repeated, offended.

Never mind that, she's upset.

The moment you were asleep, she looked to leave. If it wasn't for me, she'd be a hundred miles from here.

Bellarand—

The unicorn shook his mane. *She will not speak of me so. I am a dread-mount of the northern—*

Molly gasped. "It's here—it's here again!" She looked around wildly, a hand on her head.

Allarion approached her, hands up in placation. She was truly beginning to worry him with her anger and raving, having never seen this from her, never even suspected it.

"Sweetling, please be calm. There's no one—"

"In my head," she moaned, grinding her palm into her temple, "a voice, not yours and not mine. It taunted me last night, and I . . ."

Allarion's brows rose in surprise. *Think something to her,* he instructed Bellarand.

He knew it was possible, but to happen so soon . . .

Bellarand huffed, never liking being bossed about.

Finally, after a moment of agitated ear flicks, Bellarand thought loudly, *You are a very loud creature, stomping here and there. The birds hide their faces under their wings to get some peace. The trees shake as you clomp down the stairs.*

Allarion glared at his steed, but the unicorn was unrepentant.

Molly gaped at them. "It's . . . it's the unicorn?"

"It would seem so, yes. Bellarand and I share a bond—every fae warrior and his mount can communicate in their minds. It is the way of the magic and the bond. Sometimes bonded mates can hear the unicorn speaking, too."

He stared in wonder at her. *It's working. Her just being here—she's bonding to the estate, the magic. It's working!*

But just as the elation began to expand his chest, Molly let out another vicious shriek. Grabbing the bunch of abused sunflowers, she flew at the kitchen door.

Bellarand was quick enough to pull his head away and retreat, but Molly charged after him. Allarion watched in stunned astonishment as she hurled sunflowers at the unicorn, catching him on the flank.

"Don't you ever threaten me again, pony!" Molly cried. "I didn't ask to be here!"

Bellarand reared around in affront. He pawed the earth menacingly, shaking his mane and swiping his horn through the air, only to catch another sunflower in the face.

His red eyes narrowed.

Don't—!

The unicorn didn't heed the warning, a great war whinny ringing through the air before he charged.

Allarion raced out the door.

Molly, clutching the last sunflower, stood her ground, glaring.

Bellarand's great hooves carved up the soft dirt as he slid to a stop, the tip of his horn just catching on the fabric of Molly's shirt at her shoulder. He puffed a great waft of hot air into her face and bared his big teeth at her.

"Stop it," Allarion spat, coming up alongside Molly.

My words yesterday were for the squirrels who torment me, but mark my words, insult me again and you will face far worse, human.

A tear spilled from Molly's eye and her lower lip trembled, but she kept her back straight, not giving in to the unicorn's threat.

"I'm rooting for the squirrels," she growled.

Bellarand huffed again before tossing his mane and turning to leave.

Allarion grabbed Molly's hand, clutching another sunflower, before she could raise it to throw.

Yanking out of his grip, Molly turned in the opposite direction to stalk away.

Allarion stood there, unsure how the morning had turned so.

She doesn't understand, he entreated his steed.

Then make her understand, was the haughty reply.

Would that he could.

He turned to find Molly but saw she had come to a stop only a few paces away, her back to him. His insides twisted with self-reproach as she knelt down, putting her head between her knees, and the unmistakable sound of a sob drifted up to him.

Allarion didn't understand what had happened, but he knew, as surely as he knew Molly was his mate and Bellarand his trusted friend, that this was his fault.

He went to kneel beside her. When he placed a gentle hand on her shoulder, she didn't pull away, which gave him a little hope. Not that he deserved any.

His *azai* cried, her tears watering the dirt.

He was lower than that dirt, lower than the worms there and the roots below.

"What can I do, sweetling? How do I make this better?"

He thought his very soul would crack and break if she shed just one more tear. Her sobs tore at him more than her anger confounded him. He could bear her anger, never her tears.

"We need food," she said in a voice so little, it pained him. "I won't starve again. I won't."

"Never," he growled. "You will never want for anything again, *azai.* This I vow to you."

Her words unnerved him. *Starve again.* As though she . . . had before. His mind reeled at the thought, and a new anger for her circumstances, for her uncle, began to burn inside him.

Just what had his Molly gone through?

He'd thought it didn't matter, not when he meant to give her anything and everything.

But he now saw that was wrong. What she had gone through made Molly who she was, and Allarion had to learn that side of her, too.

Gentling himself for her, he said softly, "I'm sorry, Molly. I should have told you of my coming sleep, as well as the possibility of hearing Bellarand. There is much I have to explain, and when you are ready, I should like to tell you."

For a long moment, he didn't know if she would respond or even acknowledge his words.

Finally, she picked her head up. He ached to see her damp cheeks and puffy eyes. The unhappiness in her was so stark . . .

"I shouldn't have yelled like that. I hate that I have this temper. I was scared and it got the better of me."

Allarion carefully reached out to take one of her hands in his. He stood and gently pulled her up after him. Bringing her hand to his lips, he kissed each knuckle.

"The fault is mine. I never meant for you to feel afraid or ill-prepared. Your needs are different from my own, and I must anticipate them better. There is a market town not far from here, two hours' ride. I will take you—today if you like."

You're on your own, huffed Bellarand.

Well, then, a few hours' walk. He'd go much further for his Molly.

As he watched, Molly composed herself. Allarion was struck with a sort of pride seeing her gather her wits and courage. He squeezed her hand, hoping she could feel his admiration for her.

"Can we go tomorrow?"

"Of course. Name the time."

IO

When Molly saw how Allarion intended to walk with her to the market town, she couldn't help it. A peal of laughter burst out of her at the sight of him, in all his black finery, but with a huge wicker basket strapped to his back. It was big enough for her to fit in and was triple his own width.

Allarion blinked at her, obviously bemused, which only made her giggle more.

It was a fine change from her mood yesterday.

Fates, her outburst had just . . . burst out of her. Seeing the flowers there that morning, as if nothing had happened or changed, snapped something inside. All her anxiety from the day before and the broken fears she still harbored from her girlhood surged to the fore, uncontrollable and devastating.

Seeing him standing there in the kitchen, casual as could be—casual as he ever was, that is—only infuriated her more.

Part of her still couldn't believe she wasn't locked away somewhere dark in punishment. Or at least confined to her chamber. She'd yelled right in his face and thrown his gifted sunflowers at the *unicorn*.

Only someone stupid or with no regard for their own life made so many lethal mistakes, one after the other.

And yet, here she was, trundling down a quaint country lane, a sprawling meadow to one side of her, the forest on the other, and her fae companion with his big basket keeping pace.

Molly snorted every time she saw the ridiculous thing, as if he meant to buy every loaf of bread and celery stalk and bolt of fabric. That bemused look never quite left his face, but he smiled amiably whenever she giggled. Those fangs of his made an appearance, but they weren't so daunting when the rest of his expression was so . . . soft.

After her flare of temper, she'd spent most of the day embarrassed. She shouldn't be, she told herself—she had plenty of reasons to be angry, especially at *him,* and he was lucky he'd gotten off so easily up till now. While she rationally knew all that, it was hard not to burn with shame at letting herself boil over.

Her temper was her worst feature, everyone told her so, even her beloved parents. She'd worked hard to get it under control, to learn to breathe through her initial spark of anger. Sure, it sometimes helped to rebuke a handsy tavern patron, but let loose too much and she not only lost their business but all tips for the night.

Customers wanted someone jolly, lively. Even a little sassy. But combative? No.

So Molly learned her dance, of not only how to tease men to earn a little more coin but finding her own limits, too. How far could she be pushed until her temper took hold—it was a delicate dance, but one she'd been mastering the past years.

Having such an explosion of emotion rattled her—and she'd certainly shocked Allarion.

Honestly, it wasn't a bad thing if he was a little scared of her now.

The exhaustion after such an outburst, though, always left her feeling tired and vulnerable. Not something she wanted to be in front of a fae she still hadn't figured out.

She peeked at him from the corner of her eye, forcing herself not to look at the basket on his back and start giggling again.

He'd been gentle with her, defended her against the unicorn. At every turn, Allarion had done the opposite of what she expected.

Yet, there was plenty more he could do to put her at ease. He insisted that's what he wanted, for her to feel comfortable and to be happy, so Molly determined to test his resolve. Away from the living house and grumpy unicorn, she felt a little more confident about daring to test him.

She started simply, about the estate and village they walked to.

"I thought Scarborough didn't have any associated villages."

Allarion's head bobbed in assent. "That's correct. Mullon, where we head now, was once attached to Scarborough, as well as several other townships. However, when the previous line was extinguished and the estate abandoned, they shifted allegiance to the Burgoyne family in Kindley, I believe."

Mullon, Molly mouthed. *What a terrible name for a town.*

"You've been to Mullon before?"

"Oh yes, many times now. I don't believe they consider me a friendly face, but a familiar one now at least."

Molly couldn't help a snort. "I reckon you're right. A fae and his unicorn riding into town to buy sugar would be something to see."

"Indeed, especially since I don't eat sugar."

Another surprised snort. "You don't eat anything."

"No, I do not. Fae have no need."

"But still you'd order mead."

Allarion's gaze slid to her as they walked. Under the bright autumn sun and wide azure sky, he didn't seem so terribly otherworldly. Oh, he was still pale and unnerving with his black sclera and veins, but in the bright light of day, he wasn't so imposing.

The sun glinted off pieces of his starlight hair, glistening like spider silk. His eyes, too, the irises at least, sparkled in the sunshine, as brightly as the gems they resembled. Without all the shadows carving him up into stark lines, he looked like . . . just a man.

A tall, purple-gray man, yes, but a man.

"I like the smell. The sweetness. It reminds me of you."

The humor drained from her, and she felt her cheeks heat in a furious blush. Molly looked away, unhappy to seem a coward, but unable to hold that intense amethyst gaze.

Fates, when he says things like that . . .

She hadn't determined if he knew what he did when he said things like that, romantic things that would make most women swoon. Sometimes she thought yes, surely he must; the fae were known for their cleverness, and Allarion hadn't disappointed. Yet, there was another side to him, something almost as guileless as the house.

Part of her wanted to believe he meant what he said.

The other was quick to remind her, *He bought you.*

Yes, there was that. A thorn in her boot and not something she could forgive.

They lapsed into silence, the green countryside rolling around them.

Molly had never been out this way. In truth, the furthest she'd ever traveled was from her village in the far north of the Darrowlands down south to Dundúran. Since living with Uncle Brom, she'd hardly ever left the city.

It was a much different experience, strolling the packed-earth country lane as opposed to walking the cobblestone streets of Dundúran. This place was so vast yet so quiet. She was used to the hustle and bustle of the city.

When she wanted to escape the noise of the tavern up in her room, she still opened the window to listen to the street performers or chatter of their neighborhood. Many a night Molly spent embroidering, keeping her fingers and mind busy as she listened to snatches of gossip and song. Those quiet moments to herself hadn't truly been *quiet*—she hadn't known the meaning of the word until coming to Scarborough.

There was a stillness to the land, even with the breeze rustling through the leaves and grass. The clouds rolled overhead silently, and the flowers unfurled and followed the sun in quiet.

As she listened, though, she began to hear more. Birdsong, mostly. And the quietness of it wasn't bad—she actually rather enjoyed it.

Although, not when it gave her mind time to wander—and wonder about the fae walking alongside her.

Finally, she pushed her question past her lips. "What truly brought you here, to the Darrowlands?"

He made a considering noise. "That's a deceptively simple question. There are many reasons. For protection. To fulfill a promise. To escape the reach of our Queen. And of course, to find a mate." He looked over his shoulder to grin mildly at her. "Many of the otherly folk who came to the Darrowlands for a new life began talking of finding a human mate, and after seeing their success, I began to consider it for myself."

Molly cleared her throat and chose to pursue the much less dangerous line of questioning—a potential magical despot. Even humans had stories of enigmatic, all-powerful Fae Queens, but their names had long been lost to history.

"Was your queen very bad?"

His face returned to that grim set she'd become used to, and Molly almost regretted her question.

"She is cruel, yes. A disgrace to her foremothers and her people, who suffer under her rule."

Molly's brows rose to hear the vehement, almost vicious way he described Amaranthe, the current Fae Queen. She listened with interest to hundreds of years of fae history. How they were the last magic-wielding folk and took this responsibility with an ingrained sense of duty. How the women of their kind led them, headed by a powerful queen who oversaw the health of the faelands, its people, and its magic.

"But fae are not immortal, even a Queen. Amaranthe should have chosen a successor centuries ago," Allarion said, and it obviously pained him to speak of how his land began to fall into turmoil as the cycle of queenship was broken. Molly listened with horror to how Amaranthe slew her daughters, sisters, and nieces to prevent any from usurping her.

"She keeps a cadre of loyal courtiers near, so none can get close. That some *want* to be taken into her harem . . ." He actually shuddered with disgust. "I had to leave there—I couldn't bear it any longer."

It was much to take in, so much history and horror both, yet Molly got the feeling that wasn't everything. Not knowing how to ask him to explain something she couldn't articulate, her mind caught on something else he said.

"Her harem? Fae women take multiple husbands?"

"Some do. There are twice the number of men than women of our kind." He called back to how their women held the most powerful positions, explaining that theirs was a more matriarchal society.

It wasn't totally unlike how kinship and inheritance used to be decided in Eirea. Children usually took their mother's family name, and lands often went to eldest daughters. It was a tradition that held all the way until the wars of succession, when part of the royal family married into a branch of the Pyrrossi royal family to help their cause. Pyrros kept much more patrilineal customs, and these had begun to trickle down among the common folk from the royal and noble houses.

Not that Molly had much of a family name and certainly no inheritance, but she liked the old way of doing things, on principle. This fae way didn't sound so bad, either.

"So your women are heads of the house?"

"Often, yes."

"Even though they're smaller?"

"Indeed. Although smaller, fae women possess a stronger control of magic—as well as their wings. But it isn't about one dominating the other. Our women are the knowledge-bearers and the life-bringers. Without them, our links to magic would wither, and our kind itself would die out."

They came across a babbling brook that cut through the lane, no doubt left over from the heavy rains they'd had in the region over spring. The crystalline water shimmered in the sunshine, and spindly legged bugs skated across the surface.

Allarion easily stepped over it with his long legs, but he turned to hold out his hand for her.

Swallowing hard, Molly took it and let him help her jump across.

Without dropping her hand nor her gaze, Allarion said, "It is a male's duty and honor to protect that which is dearest. To be a man is to protect, to serve, and to cherish."

Throat gone dry, she croaked, "So you, what, came here to have your own lands and lord over a human wife?"

His brows snapped together, and for a moment, Molly was afraid. For a moment, he looked like the terrible fae the stories spoke of, the ones that threw lightning bolts and trampled their enemies to dust.

"Absolutely not," he said, his voice gone dangerously low. "My greatest hope is to build a home where I and my mate are safe. Where she can be comfortable and protected." His grip on her hand tightened, pulling her a little closer into the curve of his looming form. "I want a queen of my own, sweetling. One who is generous and kind, strong and willful, who will help lead our house, however small that may be."

Molly lit up like a paper lantern, glowing with warmth not just from a blush but a throb between her thighs.

Fates, the words he said, the way he spoke, the intensity of his gaze . . .

There was little else for a human woman like her to do but turn pink under all that fae focus.

Burning up, Molly cleared her throat again and slipped her hand out of his. Unable to keep that intense gaze, she looked out at the rolling hills as she began to walk again.

"That's quite a lot to hope for," she said, sounding breathless even to herself.

"I am all and only hopes."

She couldn't help it—her gaze cut back to his in surprise, her eyes gone wide. His face had gentled again, that small grin spreading his thin lips a bit wider.

He seemed to take mercy on her, letting her drop her attention back to her footfalls for a while. He filled their walk with more innocuous facts about the fae, such as their journey to the faelands long before his time, sailing from the west to settle in the highlands adjoining what was now Eirea.

He even spoke of his bonding to Bellarand and how fae warriors worked for years, sometimes centuries, to hone their skills enough to earn a place atop a unicorn. Molly didn't quite understand all the intricacies of it, just that the bond formed through magic, forged when the fae first came to these lands and found themselves in need of allies. Magic-wielders themselves, the unicorns gradually became much-trusted allies and symbiotic partners.

Much like the fae, the unicorns too were ruled by fearsome mares. Female unicorns were often too dangerous to ride, and so it was they who remained wild and raised foals while the stallions joined the fae to patrol and protect the lands. Molly could hardly imagine anything more terrifying than Bellarand, a stallion, so to hear the mares were even fiercer made her shiver with terror.

They walked for hours even if it didn't feel much like it, Allarion weaving interesting tales to pass the time. When the first thatch roofs came into sight, though, he turned to her, a curiosity in his eyes.

Molly braced herself.

"I wish to tell you all I can and will answer whatever you ask. I want you to feel confident and comfortable with me." He waited for her to nod before continuing, "But I hope you will permit me a question of my own."

"Seems only fair," she allowed.

Allarion nodded gravely. "I've wanted to ask before—is Molly your full name?"

She stared at him, waiting for more, and then blinked in surprise at the banality of his question.

"Yes. Well, my family name is Dunne, but Molly is my whole given name, yes."

He made a noise—almost like he was disappointed.

A surprised laugh escaped her. "Why?"

"I—it's only . . . fae have long names. Many humans do as well. I merely wondered if Molly was perhaps short for something longer."

"Afraid not, it's just plain Molly."

"Never plain," he insisted. "Just . . . succinct."

"I'm almost scared to ask, but—what's your full name?"

He perked up, shoulders straightening, as if he enjoyed this question. "I am Allarion Salingar Undori Bar-sil Meringor, first son and third child of my mother Idrisil, rider of Bellarand the Black, betrothed of . . . Molly Dunne."

She snorted with laughter at how ridiculous his names were—and how ridiculous hers were compared to them. Then could only laugh harder to see how her having such a short name truly did seem to vex him.

"That's the short of it, yes," she giggled. "If you wanted, since you're in human lands now, I could shorten your name. Call you . . . Larry?"

His disgust was potent, his mouth pulling down as if he'd tasted something intensely sour.

"Not Larry? All right, what about—"

"Allarion will do fine."

"Are you sure? I thought you wanted to integrate with us humans."

"*Yes,* I'm sure."

"Fine, Allarion, then." She snapped her fingers. "What would we call Bellarand? Randy?"

An evil grin overtook his fine fae face. "Now *that* would be amusing."

For all that Mullon was a terrible name, the town itself was quaint. Orderly rows of stone cottages and multilevel wattle and daub homes spread out from the town center, where a permanent marketplace had been erected on the cobblestone square.

It was a bustling place—of course much smaller than Dundúran but still bigger than the village Molly had first lived in with her parents. Children and dogs scampered about, people gathered at the well to fetch water for washing, merchants haggled over their stall counters, and shopkeepers stood in their doors chatting with passersby. Colorful garlands and flags had been strewn across the square from tall poles, and a few old linden trees offered plenty of shade for those taking their luncheon.

Despite the hubbub, the town itself nearly went still at the sight of the fae.

Molly had hoped that without Bellarand, perhaps they might not make too much of a sight, but she'd been wrong. Most everyone within eyesight stopped what they were doing to gawk at the fae— and her beside him.

For his part, Allarion didn't miss a step, nodding and greeting people he seemed to know. Molly trotted behind, anxious all of a sudden with so many eyes fastened on her. It was almost like . . . they were more curious about her.

She stuck close to Allarion, though not so close that she couldn't make a run for it if the crowd turned.

To her surprise, one of the first shopkeepers they walked past, an older man with a graying beard, smiled cheekily at them, revealing his missing front tooth.

"Good day to you, master fae," said the shopkeeper.

"To you as well, master soap-maker."

"What brings you to town today?"

"A bit of everything."

"Well, now. That's what every shopkeeper loves to hear!"

After promising to stop by his soap shop on their way out, Allarion led her deeper into the market. Molly watched on, surprised and eventually . . . delighted, to see that the townsfolk greeted their fae visitor with politeness if not always warmth. He'd clearly been here before, and was a good customer at that, if every shopkeeper trying their mightiest to lure him inside was any indication.

Most of the other townsfolk were shy or cautious, but they couldn't hide their curiosity. It didn't take long to attract a curious crowd as they began wandering the stalls of food.

Molly tried to ignore it as she picked out vegetables.

Allarion stayed with her, asking questions about her preferences and how best to choose produce.

"It's all good!" complained the cabbage vendor.

Molly arched a brow. "You want one that's heavy in the hand and compact," she explained, weighing the cabbage before selecting the one she wanted.

The seller harrumphed. "And who's this, then, master fae?"

"Forgive me. This is Molly Dunne from Dundúran. She is to be my wife."

This drew a few gasps, and interested murmurs began to buzz behind hands. Molly's cheeks heated as she scanned the crowd, feeling every set of eyes on her.

"Is she now. Well, congratulations, then!"

"Thank you."

"What else can I get the happy couple?"

Allarion turned to bestow that unnerving smile upon her. "We're here for whatever she wants."

Oh, fates.

Molly barely held in her groan as every vendor and shopkeeper's eyes lit up and turned toward her. A few even began putting the more expensive things in the back out on their counters and tables, just to make sure she saw.

She tried to be good and sensible, but despite them coming for supplies for her, Molly wasn't the problem.

It became painfully obvious by the second stall that Allarion had never haggled before. Whatever price the shopkeeper named, he paid. Molly felt sick to her stomach watching so many gold coins disappear.

The further into the market they went, the more there was to buy. Vendors came to them, afraid they'd be passed up. Even though his basket was ridiculously large, they were quickly filling it up with dried meats and beans, flour and sugar, a cheese round, honey, jugs of mead and bottles of wine, bags of cherries and cashews and dates, cloth-wrapped butter, a crate of apples, a sack of potatoes, carrots, onions, garlic, turnips—all of it and more went into the basket.

She didn't know how he managed to carry all of it—nor how she'd be expected to eat all of it by herself.

"You really don't eat anything?" she asked again at the bakery. There was a deal on rosemary loaves, and she wanted to make at least a few bargains.

"Magic sustains us fae," he said. "But don't worry, the house will help keep and prepare whatever you buy."

That made her feel a little better—Molly hated wasting food.

She did her best to haggle for better prices, but Allarion only smiled and paid the merchants what they asked. Even for expensive items like oil and berries and wine.

Her head went light with all the top-price purchases, and although it pained a part of her to watch him pay the full prices, something of a thrill began to build. He insisted she get whatever she wanted. When her eye strayed over something pretty—a necklace or bauble—he took notice. Molly wasn't the type for that, though, and refused to let him buy her needless sparkly bits—much to the chagrin of their vendors.

Still, when they passed the dressmaker's shop, she couldn't quite resist.

Allarion peered down at her as she stared up in wonder at all the pretty fabrics and threads displayed in the window, and then back at the shop. With a gentle hand at the small of her back, he ushered her inside.

The shopkeeper, a kindly looking woman with tight, spiraling blonde curls pulled up in a cloth fillet, was of course there to greet them at the door.

"I was hoping you might pay me a visit, master fae," she said, bobbing her head. "And this is Mistress Molly, I presume?"

Fates, word traveled so fast.

"Indeed. She's to have whatever she wants. If her eye lingers on anything, wrap it up for us."

"That won't be necessary," Molly croaked.

"We have some fine new gown patterns in from Dundúran, if mistress would care to see."

Molly had absolutely no need for gown patterns—what was she supposed to do, run around a half-decrepit, moldering manor in three layers of silk?

"No, thank you."

The dressmaker's smile went tight, and Molly bit down on her grimace as the woman tried to figure out what she wanted.

"I'd like to look at your threads, please."

The woman brightened and showed her over to a whole wall of color threads, displayed on wooden spools.

"If you need anything else, my name is Lorna and I'll be happy to help you find it."

Content to pick through colors, Molly took no offense when Lorna the dressmaker set her sights on Allarion, guiding him over to some new bolts of velvet and brocade she'd just gotten.

Molly couldn't help grinning as the dressmaker expertly talked Allarion into several bolts of black velvet. She supposed she too had benefited from the fae's generosity in the tavern, when he'd lay out many more coins than necessary for his untouched mead. If he single-handedly wanted to make the shopkeepers here rich, well . . . that was his business.

Although, she had and would continue to make sure he wasn't robbed blind. There was a good price and there was greediness.

It didn't take long for her to select a whole handful of threads—sturdy black and workhorse brown and white, but also soft pink and lilac, vibrant emerald and saffron, even elegant blue and violet. She enjoyed embroidering, and at least it'd be something to do with her time as she chatted with the house.

As Allarion cut his bolts of fabric, Molly took her thread to the dressmaker. It didn't take much for her to be persuaded to look over some more practical cotton and flannel bolts, and Lorna smiled to have figured out Molly was the more reasonable sort than her fae companion.

With the two of them carding through cotton on one side of the shop and the fae on the other, Molly decided to ask. "Does he come into town a lot?"

The dressmaker smiled warmly. "Indeed. Perhaps a little less so the past month, but he's a regular sight, ordering supplies to repair that great house."

Molly blinked in surprise. She hadn't even thought about all the supplies he needed to do his repairs. She just sort of assumed he magicked them into existence.

"So the town has been supplying everything?"

"Yes, he puts in many orders. I hear he keeps the lumberyard quite busy, and the potters haven't stopped talking about the size of his last order of shingles."

"The town doesn't mind having a fae for a neighbor?"

"It's taken quite a while to get used to him—and that unicorn is something else. But he's polite and pays all his bills upfront, so few complain."

Molly nodded, turning back to the fabrics. That was . . . good to hear. Although Scarborough was no longer a noble seat and the town no longer held any allegiance to it, that the people here would welcome such a strange neighbor was heartening.

"I'm surprised to know he's taking a wife—a human woman, anyway," continued Lorna. "To be honest with you, there are more than a few women here purple with envy for you."

Which begged the ever-important question—*why did he choose me?* Molly asked herself this many times a day and could never come up with a good answer. Surely there were many poor women he could have bought off their families—and she was sure her uncle hadn't asked a small sum. He could have easily found one close to home for cheaper.

The fae truly was a poor shopper.

Molly demurred, only smiling politely at the comment. Understanding she wouldn't get anymore from her, the dressmaker helped her choose and cut several bolts of practical blue cotton for embroidering and a few blouses, as well as Molly's one concession to vanity—a soft cream muslin. She supposed she may need a dress—one that she hadn't served patrons in.

When it was all said and done, the price almost made Molly choke, but she tried to cover the sound of horror with a cough.

"Oh," said Lorna as she wrapped their purchases, "I nearly forgot. This was a canceled order and within the parameters of what you asked for."

Crossing to a sturdy armoire, the woman pulled out a breathtaking gown of red velvet. Molly's heart pitter-pattered to see the delicate black lace at the sleeves and the glisten of the expensive fabric.

The gown was far too small for her, though. Much more suitable to someone with a willowy figure—not her soft belly and thick thighs. She'd spill right out of that low, narrow neckline.

Allarion reached out to touch the gown and made a sound of approval. "Yes, very good. I'll take it."

Red suffused her cheeks and her brows rose, though Molly quickly looked away when Allarion rejoined her.

The gown wasn't sized properly for a woman like Molly—and although beautiful, perhaps not her style, either. Inexplicable anger sparked in her chest, and she was horrified to feel tears gathering at her lashes.

Why would he buy her something like that?

All day, he'd at least asked if she wanted something. He'd never presumed or forced the issue if she truly put up resistance.

It wouldn't fit her, no matter how it was altered. There wasn't enough fabric.

Confused and embarrassed and disliking both feelings, Molly was quick to flee the shop once everything was safely packed in his ridiculous basket.

The market was still busy, but it seemed the crowd had grown bored with how long they'd spent in the dress shop. Molly was grateful for fewer eyes as she blinked back more frustrated tears and fewer bodies to dodge as she headed back the way they'd come.

Allarion soon caught up to her. "Have you found everything you wanted?"

"Yes," she said sullenly, not wanting to seem ungrateful but also not wanting to be there any longer.

"We did promise to stop at the soap-maker's."

"*You* promised," she reminded him, and pushed on.

II

As dusk fell on their eventful day, Allarion knocked before poking his head into Molly's chamber to see how she was getting on with all her new things. The trek home had taken far longer than the one to Mullon, as it was done in relative silence. Upon returning home, Molly quickly made herself busy sorting through the foodstuffs purchased, ensuring everything went where it needed to.

She seemed disinclined to chat as they had that morning, and so Allarion left her to her business. Something had changed amidst their shopping. Allarion couldn't pinpoint when it happened nor why, and he spent the better part of the late afternoon pondering it as he hung the heavy green curtains he'd bought for her solar.

When he returned to the kitchen, hoping to find her in a better mood, he found it smelling of savory things, but she had obviously already organized the foodstuffs, prepared herself a meal, and eaten. The countertops were immaculate, as she always left them in the evenings. Although he'd insisted the house could see to it, Molly had a habit of cleaning.

He found it endearing—until he realized it almost made it seem as though she'd never been there at all.

To ease his troubled spirit, he sought her out. He'd vowed never to enter her space without permission, so his head was the only thing he allowed past the threshold.

His smile of greeting fell from his face to see the state of her room. All of the things they'd purchased had been laid across her bed—there seemed to be some method to the chaos, but he couldn't find it. What truly troubled him was that nothing, not even the belongings she'd brought from Dundúran, seemed to be stored away properly.

Her clothes erupted in a geyser of fabric from her bags; small items like a hairbrush and mirror had been crowded onto the side table adjoining the bed. The drawers of the armoire and lid of the chest were open, ready to receive her things, but both lay empty.

She . . . never unpacked.

That troubled knot in his chest tightened.

When his gaze returned to Molly, it was to find her staring warily at him. Frustration had him grinding his back teeth.

He'd no inkling why she looked at him so—this morning, she'd been almost friendly, asking her questions and even joking with him.

Larry indeed.

The memory of her laughter set his soul to longing. Her laughter he craved above almost all else—second only to her happiness. Although . . . his fangs ached to sink into her sweet flesh nearly as much as his cock into her warm cunt.

That she teased him, laughed at him, had given him such hope. She seemed to warm up to shopping after accepting that he would pay any price for her to receive whatever she wanted.

What changed?

Molly cleared her throat. Her expression had gone mild, hiding that wariness away, but he could still see it in the set of her shoulders.

He forced a pleasant smile. "Have you found everything to your liking still, now that we're home?"

"Yes, thank you." Her prim politeness raked down his soul like the sharpest claws.

When she said nothing else, there was naught for him to do but nod and let her be.

Pulling himself back into the corridor, Allarion stood before her door, wishing for something smart or interesting to say—but nothing came. Her sudden shift in mood left him on the back foot.

Was this truly who she was, someone who oscillated between warm and cool? If so, he had to learn to better handle the shifts.

Unsatisfied with that answer but having little else, Allarion stepped away from her door and down two more, to the third bedchamber he'd prepared. Opening the door, he walked into a room as finely furnished as Molly's, but the air here was stale and cold. Even if she hadn't added her things to the room, Molly's bedchamber held a warmth to it, a vitality that this one lacked.

He hoped one day soon to remedy that.

With great care, Allarion hung the gown he'd purchased in the armoire. It joined several others similar in size to it, all awaiting Ravenna. She would prefer to choose her own things, of course, but he knew, after so many traumatic changes, it would be good for her to start anew, with things she could enjoy. Once she'd settled and healed, she could choose her own things, start making decisions for herself.

Until then, Allarion would make the house ready to welcome and support Ravenna until she was strong enough to stand on her own.

That frustration inside him wouldn't leave, a stitch in his side that reminded him time was running thin. Every day Ravenna was left out there was another chance for her discovery. Amaranthe wasn't the only enemy—she could be discovered by hostile humans, or worse, orcs. Prone like that, weak and disoriented from the deep sleep, she would be terribly vulnerable.

Everything had gone so well to this point. The land was absorbing his magic, helping siphon off the excess he gathered. The house grew more alive every day, and one day soon, it would be repaired. Although still somewhat empty, it was for all of them, him, Molly, Bellarand, and Ravenna, to fill this home together. Their home and house would be small, but it was theirs. Away from Amaranthe's influence.

Patience. He just had to have patience. It'd served him well so far. The Twins had guided his path, he was sure of it. That he happened to be in Dundúran that day, that he should happen to see Molly at that very spot . . . it was far more than coincidence. As goddesses of destruction and rebirth, war and love, sun and moon, the Twins knew all and saw all. Duality was in their nature, and so they blessed worthy fae with an *azai,* their perfect match to magic, soul, and spirit.

After waiting so long, feeling how the magic of the faelands was turning rancid, Allarion had had little hope of such a match. He could still hardly believe he'd found his *azai,* his fated one, in a human, nor that she was here, in his home.

He just had to convince her she wanted to be there. To be with him.

There was that frustration, gnawing at him again.

Goddesses, guide me just a little more. How do I win her heart?

He would never let the stores go low again. He would tell her next time when he had to take a long sleep. He would convince Bellarand to apologize . . . somehow.

Allarion's head turned at the sound of approaching feet, his brows lifting in surprise to see Molly push open the door to the chamber. She looked about the space, her gaze finally falling on the armoire full of gowns.

A frown cracked her face, and she folded her arms beneath her impressive bust.

His gaze fell to her chest, admiring how the movement pushed up her pretty breasts. So distracted was he with the sight and his aching fangs, he hardly understood her question.

"Is there another bride I should know about?"

With effort, he peeled his attention back to her face, her expression there growing more dangerous by the moment.

"Of course not," he said.

What a ridiculous thing to ask. He'd made himself very clear that he wanted *her,* that he intended to wed and mate *her.*

Has she not heard me?

Or worse . . .

Does she not believe me?

Closing the armoire door, he strode toward Molly. She watched him come, holding her ground. Desperate for any hope, frustration goading him, Allarion set his forearm on the doorframe to loom above her, caging her in with his larger form.

Her pupils widened and the pulse at her throat jumped.

Yes, he thought, *that's it, sweetling. You aren't as unaffected as you pretend.*

"Then what is all this?" she asked. Her voice clung to her affront, but it'd gone throaty to his ears, and those breasts, goddesses those breasts, they rose ever higher with her deepening breaths.

"I hope one day to welcome a friend to Scarborough. This room is for her, when she comes."

Molly's brows rose in two perfect skeptical arches. "A friend, is it? And who is this friend? When can we expect her?"

"I don't know. Soon, I hope. Her plight is more dire than mine, and it is my wish to offer her a safe haven."

Those expressive eyes searched him, some of that ferocity banking. He'd caught her curiosity, but he couldn't reveal more.

"I will tell you when it's time, sweetling. It's not my secret alone."

And . . . first he needed to know if he could truly win her heart. That she would stay here with him and be his queen. Ravenna's secret was so dire, Maxim and Aine's sacrifice so great, that Allarion couldn't risk them without complete surety. Even from his own reluctant *azai.*

"I see." That wariness had returned to her, but she didn't pull away.

Allarion met her curious gaze, wishing there were no secrets between them—wishing there was nothing between them at all.

Dipping his head even lower, he drew deeply of her scent, filling himself up with it to gird his patience.

"I wouldn't presume to buy you gowns, Molly. Not yet, at least.

One day I hope to know you well enough to do so."

Surprise replaced all else in her big brown eyes.

Does she truly not understand? Does she not feel how I long for her?

I'm not sure she cares.

Go away, Bellarand.

You're the one thinking LOUDLY.

Quieting the bond between them, Allarion returned his focus to his *azai*. She still hadn't moved out from under his arm, defiant little thing that she was.

"I am curious to see what you create with all that you bought." Daring her and his luck, he traced a finger up the strap of her stays, feeling the texture of the embroidered vines there. "You are talented with a needle."

"I'm talented with a lot of things."

Allarion's gaze snapped to hers then down, to that plush, pouting mouth.

Goddesses, was she flirting?

"I hope to learn of every one," he murmured.

Daring a little more, he took the curve of her cheek into his palm, feeling the velveteen textures of her, the soft warmth. Running the pad of his thumb across her skin, he couldn't help teasing the corner of her mouth.

She allowed it, although she gave him no other signals—she didn't lean forward nor part her lips in invitation. Allarion doubted she'd permit many more liberties from him, but while he had her, there was something else he wished to discuss.

Finally stepping back, Allarion straightened to hold out his bent arm for her. She peered at it before his face, her gaze questioning.

"If you would be so good, I wish to show you something before you turn in."

Molly stood there for another long moment, no doubt considering what he might show her. He very much doubted she would guess—but there again, that was his fault.

When she finally nodded and slipped her hand into the crook of his elbow, Allarion bit back his grin of triumph. Her touch was most welcome, even more so her trust. Even if both were only the barest taste.

He led her back down the corridor to descend the staircase. The house lit their way, banishing the deepest shadows with orbs of yellow light from the oil lamps and mounted sconces. A quiet night had befallen the estate as they spoke in Ravenna's bedchamber, and Allarion ensured his pace was suitably slow and cautious to ensure his human *azai* didn't turn an ankle.

Her safety and comfort came first—which was why he took her down to the cellar.

Well, what looked like the cellar to all who didn't know how to look.

All afternoon, the memories of how troubled Molly seemed to be by all the goods they purchased nipped at him. Not only that, but the things she'd uttered about not starving again—Allarion would know the history behind all of it, but for now, until she was ready to tell him, he had to infer.

He'd suspected her life before had been one of lack and absence. He noticed that she lived with her uncle, cared for her cousins. There were no parents nor siblings, nor children of her own, though Allarion would have cared for them, too. She didn't hoard lovers nor trinkets nor the sparkly bits so many others coveted.

His Molly was practical, unassuming. The idea of spending so much money had seemed to truly bother her, and his assurances that she could have anything she wanted inspired tension rather than happiness.

For now, Allarion could only guess as to the roots of her anxieties over this, but he hoped, when she saw the cellar, she would understand and *believe* when he promised that she'd never go without ever again.

He sensed her confusion growing as they delved down beyond the ground level of the house, descending past the wine cellar to the very lowest, coolest point of the house.

Molly stood tensely beside him, her eyes blown wide in the murkiness of the dark stairwell. He could hear how rapidly her heart beat, and to ease her fears of the dimness, he created a will-o'-wisp of magic. Blue light illuminated the landing, glinting off the large ring door handles.

"The cellar," she said in a strangely high voice.

"Yes. But also no."

She looked up at him with those big eyes. He patted her hand in comfort before reaching out to trace a few figures on the circular doors. The figures burned blue against the wood before sinking into the grain. Molly gasped when the left door popped open.

Allarion opened it wide, and with a wave of his hand, created a dozen more will-o'-wisps throughout the cavernous false cellar.

He led his *azai* inside their house's hoard.

Chests full of gems; piles of coins; cabinets of fine silver plate and delicate porcelain; copper, bronze, silver, and gold ingots; a collection of irreplaceable silk-thread tapestries; sets of finely tooled filigree; and sets of rings, diadems, torques, necklaces, and bracelets set with precious jewels—all of it and more lined the stone walls of the false cellar.

Leading her further inside, he plucked a few gems from the ground to place in her hand.

Molly stared at the sparkling uncut jewels in her palm, her mouth hanging open.

"My mother is from an ancient line, one that was on the ships that sailed here from the westlands. The House of Meringor has done well for itself. This is but a fraction of my share."

To bring more in his flight from the faelands would have been too difficult. Thankfully, what he'd managed to bring was more than sufficient. Within a year, he hoped to have the manor repaired and operating in the production of something that would generate revenue for the estate. Orchards, perhaps. He'd learned several tricks from his brothers while he stayed with them—and Eirean humans seemed particularly fond of apples.

He'd brought his hoard via a handy magical sack his great-grand-mother had devised. The inside lining had been imbued with so much magic, it created a pocket of pure magic that existed outside the limits of space and reality. He'd stored all sorts of things there over his long life, and it made fleeing Amaranthe one step simpler.

In his first days at the estate, he'd used a great deal of his own magic to expand the bag until it lined the cellar itself. Now, it was a pocket as large as the cellar but vastly more infinite—and only acces-sible to those who knew how to open it. He liked to think he'd made his great-grandmother proud.

Turning to his *azai,* he watched as she took in the wealth of their house. He hoped she saw it as a comfort, an assurance that she would be cared for. There was no need to scrimp and haggle. She would never go without. Their stores would never run out.

"I hope this puts your mind at ease, sweetling. I have every inten-tion of taking care of you, of providing the life you want."

Allarion waited for a response—for a long while. Longer than he thought strictly necessary.

Her eyes kept roving the false cellar, reflecting the blue light of the will-o'-wisps. Those plush lips had parted upon their entry but not closed, as if she still couldn't believe her eyes.

Finally, Allarion couldn't bear it. "Molly . . ." he asked gently, "do you . . . like it?"

A strange sound emanated from her throat—almost as if she choked. Allarion watched her in alarm, looking for signs of distress.

Her lips parted further, and a high-pitched laugh escaped. It was an unpleasant noise, one that sent a shudder of unease down his spine. He wanted her laughter, but this wasn't the warm sound of the morn-ing.

Another echoed in the false cellar, and Allarion watched in horror as she dropped the gems to press her hands to her cheeks. Tears began to slide down her face.

"Molly, sweetling—" he groaned.

"All this . . ." she breathed. "No wonder you could afford to buy me." Another unnerving laugh split her lips. "Uncle Brom should've asked for double."

Allarion's chest went cold and tight at her words. He stared at her, trying to glean any meaning from her ramblings and fidgety movements, but Molly had worked herself into a state.

"Molly, you are my *azai*. I would have paid any price for you."

Her curls bounced as she shook her head, her eyes glassy and dazed. Did the air in here affect her? The magic?

Frustration roiled through him. Somehow, despite his best intentions, he seemed to have erred again. Twins take him, why could he do nothing right—with his own *azai?*

Suddenly, she turned on him. She bared her teeth in a sneer, her face an ugly contortion of rage.

"You may have bought me, but you won't own me! You'll *never* own me."

The cold grip of panic wrapped its fingers around Allarion.

She . . .

She truly thought . . .

Horror opened its black maw inside him, sucking at his innards. *By all that is good and beautiful, let her not think . . .*

"I didn't—" It was him who choked, the words clogging in his throat. "I paid your indenture. And a dower. I never—"

Disgust burned his throat. This was what she thought of him? That he considered her as easily bought as the *things* they procured that very day?

Every odd thing she'd said, every wary glance and awkward silence . . . it was because of this? Because she thought he'd tried to *buy* her?

"Indenture?" she repeated. "I'm not indentured."

They stared at one another, the truth seeming to dawn on them in the same moment.

Brom Dunne had had the better of both of them.

Rage like Allarion had never known licked up his neck. "I would never, *never* buy someone," he hissed. "And never my own *azai*. My fated one, my heart. I cannot—"

He bit back the words, as they grew in volume and ferocity, and the balls of blue light trembled with his anger. It wasn't her he was angry with, but her uncle.

No, that wasn't entirely true. His frustration burned alongside his rage—that she would think him capable of such cruelty and degradation, of thinking so little of her and another's life and dignity. His honor recoiled at the thought.

"How could he . . ." Another tear rolled down Molly's face, piercing Allarion's very soul. Her face contorted again around an angry grimace. "No, of course he did. Just to be cruel. He told me you'd paid a bride price."

"I did only as I thought proper. I was told you had an indenture, so I paid it."

That horrified glare fixed on him. "You *bought me!*"

"*No,*" he insisted, "I spoke to your elder, the head of your house. It is your kind's way." At least, so he'd believed. Or wanted to believe.

"You should've talked to me—asked *me!* Instead, you went behind my back and forced my hand!"

Allarion's spine stiffened, a curiously nauseous feeling rising in his gullet. "I forced nothing," he said through numb lips. "You agreed to the handfasting."

"Because I thought you'd rescind the offer! That you'd take the money away. I didn't think I had a choice!"

"You came willingly." Even to his own ears, his voice sounded faraway.

"As willingly as a prisoner being led to the gallows," she spat.

She may as well have sunk a dagger into his chest, the pain of her words radiating out as devastating as a quake, shaking all in its path.

"I won't apologize for wanting you. You are my *azai*." He'd yet to explain the meaning to her, of course, but only because she'd been so shy, so wary of him.

"What about what I want, Allarion? Did you ever consider I might not want to be in a sentient house guarded by a terrifying unicorn? That maybe I wouldn't want to be locked away with a fae I don't know?"

No, he hadn't. The stark truth of it must have been plain to see on his shocked face, for Molly sneered at him. But Allarion wasn't ready to quit the field—there had to be a way to salvage this, surely. *If only I can make her see . . .*

"I have offered to give you whatever you want. Have I not said that since the beginning? For days now? What was today if not that?"

"You can't buy me, not again. Those are *things*, Allarion."

"They are things you wanted and needed, things I can provide! I offer you everything—a life of comfort, of position. This house, my magic, all of it is yours. You have only to accept it."

"Do I want any of those things?" she demanded. "You came in with money and used it to get your way. Don't you dare say I should be grateful for that."

"You put words in my mouth! I do not want your gratitude, I want your happiness! Why is that such a bad thing?"

"Because you don't know what will make me happy. You've never asked!"

"I'm trying to learn!" he insisted. The blue light of the will-o'-wisps flickered and expanded with his growing agitation. "I want to know everything about you, but you refuse me the smallest chance! You refuse to open your mind to the possibilities!"

"Don't you dare yell at me! I didn't want any of this. I didn't ask to be here."

"Is it truly so terrible?" He spread his arms wide. "All this, all for you, and yet I am the villain?"

"This isn't for me. This is for you and Bellarand and your mysterious friend who may or may not come. None of this is for me, so don't you dare try to make me feel guilty. I had a life, Allarion. It may not have been much, but it was *mine*."

"And now that life could be here. Was that life in the tavern truly so wonderful? Was it really what you wanted?"

"No, but I wanted the chance to find out! And you *took that away!*"

To his horror, fresh tears dripped from her eyes, which gazed upon him with all the hurt and betrayal in the world. The cold hand of failure gripped him in a vice, snuffing the heat of his anger into a tight ball of regret.

"Molly . . ." He couldn't help it, he reached for her.

"No!" she yelped. "Just leave me alone!"

He watched in despair as she fled the false cellar, leaving him alone in the dying glow of the will-o'-wisps.

Allarion stood perfectly still, the sound of cracking filling his ears. His chest ached with a hollowness, as if everything inside him had followed her out.

A mate in tears, a beginning built on a lie . . .

His assumptions and predictions had wrought possible ruin—and it was all his own fault. He feared the loss might cost him dearly, a mortal blow he couldn't weather. If he'd lost, if he couldn't woo her nor sway her . . . what more could he do?

He'd promised Hakon but more importantly Molly that if she wanted to leave, she could.

If she did, if he truly lost this fight, he would have to honor that promise. Doing so would cleave him in two.

Allarion may have initially gotten what he wanted, handing over that bag of gold to Brom Dunne, but really, he hadn't at all.

12

Molly did the only thing she felt she could—she holed up in her room and didn't come out. It was childish, certainly, but in this strange place, full of magic and mystery, she considered it the only place that was hers.

It was a silly notion, of course. Inside a sentient house under the fae's command, no place was truly safe from him. But as the night and finally the next morning began to pass and he didn't darken her door, she took what reprieve she could.

Curled up in the window seat of her room, Molly watched with tired, bleary eyes as the sun rose over the trees. A shadow occasionally moved within the first rows of trees, and she knew it was Bellarand. Patrolling, no doubt.

She hadn't heard him since the other day—she supposed he'd figured out how to block her from hearing his thoughts. That was just fine with her, she'd no wish to be privy to whatever deranged things that beast thought.

That left only herself in her head, and it was a crowded place already.

Yet again, Molly berated herself in the aftermath of another outburst. It wasn't so bad this time around—a righteous indignation burned in her belly. At the trick Brom played on her. At the arrogance of Allarion, assuming he knew best in all things.

She couldn't stand the thought of either of them.

Another wave of tears pricked at her eyes, but Molly held them back. She was so sick of crying—and of letting men push her about. Since the age of ten, Molly had lived her life trying to please or placate or avoid men. They grabbed at her, wanted things from her, cajoled and teased and demanded.

Well, enough was enough.

Allarion may have been fae but he was still a man. And right then, Molly hated all men.

He may have that ethereal fae beauty and all the money in the world, his words may be sweet and his promises tender, but in the end, what did they amount to? Nothing. For all his magic and money and mystery, he was just like any other man. Doing whatever he wanted for his own ends.

Molly was sick of being collateral.

What she could actually do about it was another question entirely. Despite the hours she sat up staring out the window, she hadn't come closer to any sort of plan that would get her out of here. If the house didn't stop her, the unicorn surely would. What hope was there?

Though her legs had long since gone numb and stiff, Molly curled into herself even tighter. Sequestered away in her room, she'd never felt smaller.

And she *hated* him for that.

Yet, she also hated herself some, too. For letting this all happen. For not seeing through her uncle's scheme. Of course he'd tell her whatever he had to, to get her out the door with Allarion—Molly had seen the sack of money, and that was apparently only half of what'd been promised.

If she didn't find it all so disgusting, she might've been flattered by the small fortune he'd paid.

Which only made her angrier with herself. She should be worth more than two sacks of coins—to her uncle, to a potential husband, to *herself*. The problem was . . . Molly wasn't always so sure. And if she wasn't sure herself, it was no wonder everyone around her paid that or less.

Her mind ran circles round itself all morning, a filmy sort of haze settling over her. Her eyes stung with exhaustion and her tongue stuck to the roof of her mouth for want of water. She'd give herself a proper headache if this went on any longer, but Molly just couldn't summon the will to move.

She was still there when the knock came in the early afternoon.

Molly didn't answer, but Allarion still opened the door. A brief glance revealed that he'd brought a tray laden with an eclectic variety of foods. Apples and cheeses and turnips and what looked like un-soaked oats. It might've been amusing, his attempt at putting together a plate when he didn't eat himself, had she anything inside her but apathy and self-pity.

"I learned from the house that you haven't eaten today," he said gently.

Molly scowled at the ceiling. "Tattletale."

"Don't be too angry with it." With measured steps, he walked across the room to place the tray on the lid of the trunk. "It worries for you—as do I."

"*I* worry. Do you know how scary it is, thinking the house itself spies on me? That everything here is working against me to keep me here?"

His lips pressed together with unhappiness. "I can imagine the feel-ing, yes. But please, don't be afraid, sweetling. For all the magic here and the unicorn outside, it is you who are most powerful within the estate."

Molly snorted. "Right. Forgive me if I don't believe you."

"The house adores you—I think it likes you even more than me.

You talk to it. Bellarand will come around. And I . . . there is nothing you could not ask of me."

"There's *plenty* I can't ask of you," Molly retorted. "Or have you already forgotten your mysterious friend?"

"I have not. It isn't my secret to share, not yet at least. But even that won't be denied you, given time. That is the only secret I keep—all else is yours to know. You have but to ask."

"And why should I trust that anything you tell me is the truth?"

A tendon jumped in his neck and at his temple, a sign Molly recognized from yesterday of his growing frustration. "I have worked every day to prove this to you. I have shown you who I am—if you would only stop to look."

Biting her cheek, Molly turned away. He sounded too much like being right, and she didn't like it.

"I don't want to argue again," she sighed, leaning her head against the windowpane.

"I haven't come here to argue. I only wish to speak with you, to make clear what has been obscured between us."

"Figured you'd be sick of me by now." It was fairly clear her bursts of temper unsettled him. She'd gotten some satisfaction last night from knowing that whatever he'd thought of her before, he hadn't bargained on someone who would yell back.

Now, though, she was just tired.

"Never. You are my *azai*."

"You keep saying that."

"It's the truth. I realize now it is something I should have explained long ago. But I'm getting ahead of myself."

Molly turned to watch in amazement as Allarion bowed low to her, his long fall of silvery hair nearly hitting the floor. The sight stunned her almost as much as it left her squirming in discomfort—to see a being as tall and proud as him stooping like that . . . it didn't sit right, for some reason.

"Please, I beg forgiveness of you, Molly. I'm ashamed to have raised my voice to a woman, but *you* of all people. I spoke to you in anger, and that is not acceptable."

It was a flowery apology if Molly ever heard one, but the fact that he made it at all, and he said it so earnestly . . .

"This is all . . . a lot," she muttered, unable to think of anything better to say.

"I understand this. We are from different worlds, you and I, but I like to think the goddesses had a hand in bringing us together. That they knew we would need each other."

He straightened to his full height, those dark eyes of his somber. The purple had gone dull, not sparkling like jewels but faded like a bruise.

"Like some other folk, the fae believe in a fated one, a perfect mate. Such a union is considered devised and blessed by the goddesses and coveted above all else. The bond between *azai* is sacred, said to be stronger than those between the fae and their magic. I had not found mine amongst my own kind and long despaired that such a blessing would never be bestowed. And then I saw you."

Slowly, he closed the distance between them, but rather than loom over her, he bent to kneel before her on one knee. Molly's heart lurched in her chest, and all the blood that'd gone sluggish in her unmoving body gathered at her cheeks in a blush.

"I will be honest—it'd entered my mind to find a human mate as many of the others hoped to in the otherly village. Bonding to an Eirean woman would help secure my foothold in the native magic and hasten my own in creating the circuit I require to live."

"So you thought, ah, I'll just get a poor woman and take her away to my house," she said, though without any heat. She couldn't say she was overly surprised—how many times had she seen much the same happen to other women, especially those who didn't have the safety of a home or business or family. They easily became prey or playthings to more powerful people.

So no, she wasn't surprised, but she was disappointed to hear that

Allarion too would do this.

She'd been beginning to hope he was different.

His wince of shame was telling. "Not quite like that, but yes, I sought an expedient option. I needed to like the woman, of course. It had to be a true union. Then, one day, I saw you—and I knew. I felt it, here." He laid his hand over where, for a human, a heart would be. "That pull to you. I soon realized what it was—the goddesses led me to you, for you are my *azai*. My fated one."

Unease clenched in her middle. "But I'm human."

"It can happen between a fae and a human. I've seen it."

"But . . ." Molly just couldn't swallow this fated lover business. It was too easy. "Why me? I'm no one special. If it's a human you wanted, Lady Aislinn could've introduced you to many who'd gladly be the lady of this manor."

"I didn't want a lady or a noblewoman or any other barmaid." The corners of his mouth lifted, as if he tried for humor, but quickly fell. "I wanted *you,* Molly. Since the moment I saw you. Your liveliness, your vitality—it filled up the room, and I was in awe. I knew within a moment why the goddesses led me to you."

Molly shook her head. "Allarion, that person serving in the tavern isn't me, not really. It's an act, a persona. All barmaids do it. Patrons want a jolly serving girl. But that's not who I am."

His lips drew thin, and despite his strange features, she could tell this truth troubled him.

Fates, what a mess. All this because she wanted a few tips and her uncle wanted a payout. Maybe her and Brom weren't so different, after all.

"Then who are you, Molly?"

His voice was gentle, his question soft, but it struck her with all the devastation of a killing blow. A fat tear escaped her lashes, leaving a hot trail down her cheek. That hollowness in her chest expanded wider, threatening to suck all that she was, whatever she was, down into it.

"I don't know," she whispered.

And how pathetic was that? Separated from the tavern, she didn't know who Molly Dunne truly was.

A pained sound escaped his throat, and Allarion reached out to lay a comforting hand on hers. She didn't push him away—the weight of his hand felt like it was the only thing keeping her from breaking apart.

"I first saw you in a square, fetching water and speaking with other women. You were laughing. You had a brown fillet in your hair. I don't know what you said to them, but I stood and watched, unable to look away. When you left, I followed and found the tavern."

"Allarion," she groaned, "you can't just follow women back to their homes."

"It's too late now," he said, a sad sort of humor to his voice. "It wasn't in the tavern I first saw you. That Molly at the well is part of you, too, as is the Molly at the tavern. I wanted all of you, and I didn't care what stood in my way. Another lover, your uncle . . . not even your own wishes." His grimace was pained and heartfelt. "I see now that that was a mistake. I should have spoken to you first, announced my intentions. As I am now."

He took both her hands in his, claiming her gaze with his own. "You are my *azai,* Molly Dunne. The goddesses have declared it so. But I wish to earn that blessing, and your trust. I cannot go back, but we can go forward. Please, I beg of you, consider what I offer."

"Allarion . . ."

He shook his head once, that silvery hair sliding over his shoulder. "I would love you, Molly, if given the chance. I have loved the Molly at the well and the Molly in the tavern. I want to love the Molly I see before me, too. I hope that this can be a safe place where you can discover who it is you are. I should like to get to know her, too."

Allarion's gaze fell to their joined hands, where they sat in her lap, knitted together not unlike their handfasting. His throat bobbed, as if getting out his next words pained him.

"If, however, this cannot be done, I swear to you, I shall return you to your uncle's door. Nothing will be expected of you. You can return to your life as if this never was."

Molly's lips parted in surprise. "You would do that? Take me back?"

"Yes," he said, although it was evident he struggled with the word. "I would ask only that you consider, now that you know the truth. That is all I wish." And, never dropping her gaze, he dipped his head to press a single, soft kiss to the back of her hand.

Molly sucked in a breath, unprepared for how his lips on her skin made her every nerve alight. Was that his magic, or just him?

"Please, sweetling, tell me you will at least consider staying?"

Fates, did she dare? Did she even want to?

Those questions were hard to answer in her fuzzy, dazed mind. She still held onto her anger, but her insides twisted with indecision. He gazed up at her with so much longing, his words so gentle and loving, it was hard to deny him outright. Yet, she didn't have any answers, for him or for herself.

He's not asking for an answer, he's asking for time.

She was in no state to make a decision, that was certain. So maybe . . .

Maybe she should take that time he asked for. Not for him or anyone else. For Molly.

Slowly, Molly nodded, her heart racing with a baffling kind of excitement.

A great rush of air left him, and he bowed his head in relief. "Thank you," he whispered against her skin.

He lingered there another moment, but neither said a word. Shocked into silence with all he'd told her and what she'd agreed to, Molly watched as he finally stood, bowed to her again, and made his exit.

She stared at the door long after he'd closed it behind him.

Without thinking, mind still fuzzy, Molly drew her hand to her mouth and pressed her lips to where he had, imagining she caught his lingering warmth.

Fates, what will I do?

13

Allarion had done and said all he could. Now there was nothing for it but to wait and hope.

Every hour that ticked by seemed an eternal agony. Never before had he so acutely felt the passage of time, nor had it slowed so to a trickle for him. His mind could grasp onto nothing; no matter the task he set himself, he started it halfheartedly, only to abandon it soon after. He tried to keep near the house, for fear that she would decide and wish to speak with him but be unable to find him.

No answer came, though, and he spent most of his time alone.

Without a task to focus on and his mind a mess, the magic that gathered in him had little release. Usually, he went to give over excess to the forest every few days, but as he awaited Molly's answer, Allarion found himself wandering into the trees each morning and night, needing to purge away the roiling, unhappy magic. He even thought he might be affecting the local weather, and so gave over more than he might have otherwise to the forest, for fear of creating a tempest with his unease.

Two full days passed thusly. He didn't think he exaggerated to consider them the longest of his long life. In that span, he saw her a handful of times. She nodded politely but didn't invite conversation, and so he let her be, his hope withering that much more.

By the third day, Allarion fled the house, unable to stand having four walls surrounding him. The house had grown somber, moaning and creaking as it felt the upset of its inhabitants. The whole estate grew quiet and dour, sensing that they all stood on the edge of a precipice.

Hemmed in by the waiting, her decision, his decisions . . . outside was the only place capable of containing his frustration.

Splitting wood was an excellent task for taking out aggression, and Allarion wielded the axe mercilessly. His newest order of timber and other supplies had been left at the border of the estate nearest Mullon, and the forest had helpfully carted it along on a bed of moss. Organizing the supplies should have been a menial task that took him a day, but instead, he still hadn't completed it.

The best he could do was split some of the timbers he knew to be too long. And, if he was honest with himself, the swing of the axe and the way it split the wood apart felt good.

It made the waiting bearable, if not better.

If Molly had any sympathy for his agony, he didn't see her enough to mark it. He had none for himself, as their revelations had revealed the true depth of his miscalculations.

His disgust over what she had thought of him, of what she likely *still* thought, was hard to shake. What stuck in his craw most, though, was knowing that he'd have done nothing differently. He still would've paid any price for her. Oh, to be sure, he wished dearly that he'd spoken to her rather than her uncle, but if she'd refused him or hesitated, Allarion knew he'd have resorted to similar tactics as he did.

As the son of a old noble house, he prided himself on being an honorable warrior and a good man. Deep down, though, when it came to Molly, he was neither.

So, he had no sympathy for himself, for it was his own mess he'd created, and given another chance, he'd have created a similar one.

If she chose to return to Dundúran, he would take her—whether he would leave her there was another question entirely.

But perhaps the one with the least sympathy was Bellarand.

The unicorn trotted out of the forest to inspect the new supplies, feigning interest when really, Allarion knew the beast wanted to gloat.

Still you chase her tail?

Don't be crass.

Then you shouldn't be stupid. Her silence is answer enough.

It was a truth he'd no interest in hearing. Throwing Bellarand a glare, he resumed his chopping.

A hot huff of breath washed over him, and Bellarand nudged his shoulder with his muzzle. *Much as it amuses me, I don't actually enjoy seeing you like this. Why do you not give this one up? There are other females.*

Not for me.

Another huff, this time ruffling his hair. *The forest is vast. To say it is not is folly.*

She is my azai. *My fated one. A gift given by the goddesses.*

Bellarand snorted. *Some gift.*

That earned him another glare.

It is a dread-mount's duty to point out when the rider chooses a perilous path, is it not?

Allarion sunk the axe into the tree trunk he used as an anchor. *It is. But this path is not perilous, merely rocky.*

You behave sillier than a foal over her—and for what? She has shown no interest, nor made you any promises. It is time to cut our losses.

Shaking his head, Allarion turned to walk away, needing to leave the conversation. He didn't enjoy how much like truth it seemed.

But Bellarand wasn't done with him. Easily keeping stride, the unicorn bobbed his head, pointing his horn at the manor.

This is supposed to be about Ravenna. Everything we've done, it's been for her. This human delays you. Do your promises not matter anymore?

"Of course they do!" Allarion shouted. "But an *azai* changes everything. I would not ask you to leave a mate—do not ask me to give mine up."

A deeply sardonic nicker vibrated in Bellarand's long throat. Pawing the earth, his voice came deadly quiet in Allarion's mind. *Haven't I, though? Have I not left all my kind behind, to aid you in your promise?*

Allarion bared his teeth. "You promised Maxim as much as I."

I did. Yet I am the only one keeping that vow.

He clenched his fists, resisting again how much his mount's words sounded like truth. If he let it, the words would rend him in two.

Allarion was a fae of his word, and he would fight to his last breath to fulfill Maxim's vision. Ravenna would live her life free of Amaranthe's tyranny; her parents' sacrifice would be avenged. But no fae could resist the pull of an *azai*—they were fated, destined. To give up Molly entirely would be to abandon all that was good inside him.

His honor or his mate.

It cannot come to that.

Bellarand blew out an irritated breath. Whipping Allarion's flank with an indignant tail flick, the unicorn headed back toward the forest.

We don't need her. The estate accepts you, and your magic will soon finish bonding with the land. She is hindering us. Give her up, Allarion.

He watched his mount and one of his oldest friends walk off, aggravation rubbing his soul raw.

I can't.

Molly couldn't decide what to do, and the indecision ate at her. She hated this uncertain person she'd become over the last few days, but crawling out of the hole she'd found herself in proved more difficult with each passing day.

The easiest thing to do would be to leave. Not even have Allarion take her back to Dundúran but just pack up her things and strike out on her own. She at least knew she could walk to Mullon within a day—there were inns there where she could stay for the night, or perhaps even find work.

However, her face was known there, and the thought of all the gossip passing behind cupped hands made her skin crawl. She could bear it for a night, she supposed, but after that . . .

Where did she go from there?

The answer didn't immediately come to her.

She spent her time uninterested in much of anything, although she did put effort into avoiding Allarion. He gave her her space, which she appreciated, but still, whenever they crossed paths, Molly had to contend with the despair that positively radiated from him. A kicked dog or hungry kitten couldn't have looked sadder, and she hated knowing that she'd made him feel so.

Her indignation and righteous anger might have sustained her had he not given her back her choice. It was one thing to rail against oppression and coercion—it was entirely another to fight against indecision.

One afternoon, growing despondent over the sounds of Allarion chopping wood, Molly found herself wandering down through the house. She hated the little mournful sounds the house made, and guilt tugged at her heart when it opened every door before she came to it, trying to anticipate where she headed.

The one door it didn't open was the only one she wanted.

Molly approached the cellar door holding her breath. When it didn't open on its own, and doing so herself revealed a plain cellar of old barrels and unused equipment, she closed the door and thought a moment.

Heart in her throat, she traced the symbols she remembered Allarion making when he brought her here. In amazement, she watched the places she'd traced burn with a blue glow before sinking into the grain.

With a *pop,* the door clicked unlocked.

Molly cracked it open to reveal the cellar of wonders.

Without Allarion's magical spheres of light, it felt more like a cave, a hoard buried deep underground. Molly lifted the lantern she'd brought, and the light caught in all the thousands of gems and jewels and coins. Nearer ones sparkled in the light, while those further away almost glowed.

Drawing in a deep breath, Molly sat on the threshold stoop and just . . . stared.

No one she'd known in her whole life could ever have imagined such a fortune. And he said this was only part of his wealth. The idea was staggering.

Leaning forward, Molly plucked a coin from the floor and turned it over in her hands. It carried a bit of heft to it, being solid gold, and had motifs stamped into the faces she didn't recognize but thought the words looked Pyrrossi.

Choosing another, she found coins of all kinds, stamped with different rulers and legendary heroes from all three human kingdoms. There were even some older than Caledon itself, from before it'd split from Eirea hundreds of years before.

Some of the pieces of jewelry looked old-fashioned as well, and some not in any human-made shape or style.

Where these could have come from she couldn't fathom, but then, if the fae lived as long as believed, perhaps it wasn't surprising that this wealth tracked through the ages.

And there was another thing for her to worry about—if Allarion truly was immortal, or at least ancient, what could that mean for them? Would he remain the same even as she wrinkled and grayed? The span of a human lifetime must have seemed so fleeting to a fae—

no wonder they hardly interacted with other folk.

But that was a worry for if she decided to stay—which she hadn't.

Molly very much hadn't forgotten her promise to herself, to take the fae for all he was worth and leave him. A small handful from this hoard would be worth far more than a vase and get her further through the world.

Taking all she could carry would set her up for life.

No need to stay at an inn or find work in Mullon—she could buy her own place and business. Added to her own stash of savings, she could do anything she wanted anywhere in the world.

A part of her, not so little, thought she certainly deserved it after everything she'd gone through in her life and short time with the fae.

She worked hard, she tried to be a decent enough person, and she'd sacrificed for her family.

As Molly turned the coins over in her hands, she knew she could take as much as she wanted and walk out the door. Something inside her suspected Allarion wouldn't stop her. Bellarand was another matter, but at least the gold and gems would hurt more than sunflowers if she threw them at him.

Molly suspected Allarion would let her have them, and knowing that only soured her stomach.

She took a handful of coins and gems, but only enough to halfway fill her pocket. She didn't know what she'd do with them, but it gave her some relief, to know they were there.

When she left the cellar, closing the door behind her, the house creaked in its despondent way.

"I don't know," she told it, "I just . . . want to know it's there."

Late that day, as the sunset painted the sky with brilliant peaches and lilacs, Molly stood in the bedchamber two doors down from hers.

Opening the door to the armoire, she stared at the small collection of fine gowns hanging there. She ran her fingers over the rich fabrics, admiring how the vibrant light of sunset caught on the gold threads and created shadows over the elegant draping and tight seams.

Whoever his friend was, she seemed the type of lady who he should want to run this house. A fine lady, who wore gowns and jewels and an iron will. Molly felt downright dowdy compared to the imaginary woman who could wear these gowns, the one who seemed a better match for a fae and his plans.

Molly was just a barmaid. Nothing special.

She knew dozens, hundreds of young women just like her. It didn't make sense that out of all of them, even just the women who'd been at the well doing the washing that day, that she should be the one he chose.

Molly didn't know if she believed his claim about fated mates and goddess gifts and destiny. Sure, she knew plenty of otherly folk believed in it, and that was fine for them, perhaps it worked that way for fae and dragons and orcs—but humans? *Her?*

Surely not.

No destiny, no goddess had ever turned to look at Molly.

And that was all right—she didn't need fate or destiny to forge a life for herself. She knew better than anyone that nothing was just handed to people like her.

Handsome men riding up on a noble steed to save the day was for fairy tales.

And his steed was more of a pain in the ass than noble.

She didn't need saving, nor fae magic, nor divine intervention. She didn't need anything or anyone.

Then what do I need?

And . . . what do I want?

Those were the questions she kept leading herself back to. She didn't know the answers.

If Allarion was to be believed, she could have anything she wanted; she need only ask. What that could be was a far more difficult question. Without the feeling of being coerced into this situation, of knowing the truth of her uncle's treachery and her chance to set things back to the way they were, Molly found herself . . . reluctant.

She'd never disliked it here, per se. The house was an interesting, if strange companion. The same could even be said for Allarion.

Molly was comfortable, fed, doted on, even. Many others would be perfectly content with that.

Why can't I be?

Rubbing the red velvet of the gown he'd bought, Molly still couldn't help feeling . . . none of this was meant for someone like her. The woman who could occupy this bedchamber and wear those gowns would feel it her due, no doubt, that this was the life she was meant to have. For Molly, though . . . she'd be waiting for it all to be taken away.

It'd happened before, why not again.

And she wasn't sure she could live like that.

Morning brought no further answers, and Molly's uncertainty had grown into a frustrated restlessness. Pulling her arms through the sleeves of her coat, she made her way down through the house.

It was quiet, as if it held its breath for her. Outside, fog had rolled in across the estate, keeping the birds in their beds and blocking out the meager dawn light. Burying her hands deep into her pockets, Molly set off down the drive, hoping to work some of the jitters out of her legs.

The fine gravel crunched beneath her boots as she walked, and the damp of the fog kissed her cheeks. The cool air had a thickness to it from the fog, smelling of water and rich earth.

She kept to the path, not willing to delve into the darkness of the forest that lingered just two trees deep. What light there was struggled to penetrate the fog, let alone the foliage. No doubt something watched her from the shadows, but she put it from her mind. Strange things happened in strange places, and this estate was the strangest of all.

Molly watched her footfalls, for there wasn't much to see through the fog. The drive eventually gave way to a simple rutted path that followed the gentle curve of a shallow hill. She hadn't seen how the land of the estate rolled and undulated with hills on their journey here, but then, it'd been night and Molly had been stiff and tired from the ride.

She followed the path up the hill, stopping near the top. The fog hadn't cleared, but it was a bit thinner higher up, and below, she could spot the tall spires of trees rising out of the gray mist.

Something inside, something innate, told her that not far that way lay the border of the estate.

Molly couldn't explain it—it was just a kind of *knowing*, like when the house creaked and she knew if it was a happy or sad creak.

Was that the magic? Had she been here long enough for it to start affecting her?

Changing her?

The thought lodged in her chest, though not entirely unpleasantly. She wasn't scared of the idea, but it did make her worry—if she left, would there be repercussions? Like a person who'd had their drink taken away or those whose families sent them to Wards when their love of poppy milk grew too much.

Before her was the way to Dundúran. To the north lay Mullon.

But . . . did she want to go to either place?

What if . . . she didn't leave?

The thought caught in her guts and pulled. Again, not unpleasantly. The idea of remaining on the estate didn't cause dread or fear, not when she knew she wasn't being kept against her will. It was just . . . Molly had survived this long knowing the rules of the world she lived in.

It'd taken years after moving to the city to learn its rules. Those of the tavern and neighborhood also took many experiences to understand. Once she'd learned the rules of how the place worked, Molly was better able to navigate it.

Here, in Scarborough, though, there didn't seem to be any rules. Or at least, none written in a language she understood.

Go on, then.

Molly jumped, spinning in a circle to find who'd spoken.

From below, the shadows of the forest began to move. Molly wrapped her arms around herself as she watched the unicorn emerge from between the trees, moving seamlessly between light and shadow. Those glowing red eyes pierced her as surely as the tip of his horn speared through the air as he mounted the slope.

There is your path, he thought loudly at her. *Go. Leave this place, and don't turn back.*

"So eager to be rid of me?" she couldn't help sniping.

A low, rumbling nicker echoed through the fog. *Yes. You have done enough here. Be the coward that you are and go.*

"I'm not a coward," she growled.

No? Then decide. Put Allarion out of his misery and let him lance the wound.

Her temper dissipated as quickly as it'd formed at the mention of Allarion. His sadness haunted her, even here, far from the house.

Do the right thing and leave him, said the unicorn.

No! her soul cried, but she didn't know if the unicorn could hear.

Tears sprang to Molly's eyes, and she turned to glare at him, but Bellarand had already moved back toward the forest. He flicked his tail at her as if to bat her away like a bothersome fly.

Biting her cheek, the pinch of pain helped her contain her tears.

She hated that the overgrown pony was right.

She needed to decide.

But knowing and doing were two very different things. And what if she chose wrong?

Closing her eyes, Molly breathed in the damp air of the morning, trying to clear her mind and make herself think.

In that quietness, one truth became clear—her heart didn't want to leave.

Her freedom and independence meant much to her, so if she could maintain it here . . .

If she could come to understand or even establish rules for this place . . .

She supposed there was no true reason to leave.

There was nothing for her back in Dundúran.

What if she gave this a chance? What if she stayed?

She liked the house. She liked the promises the fae made her. She even liked him, with his strange ways. He took a little getting used to, but she often found him oddly compelling. There was something to the set of his shoulders and the jut of his chin . . . even with his black eyes and sharp fangs, there was a gentleness to him she couldn't deny.

No man had treated her as well as he had—paying for her or not. No man had looked at her the way he did.

He'd told her all along he meant only to please her. He'd spent their days together being patient and gentle.

Perhaps . . . she could do the same.

I4

olly's walk back to the house was slow and meandering. Although the fog had mostly burned off by the time she turned back, she still watched her footfalls. With each right step she listed a potential problem with staying—*he could be lying, he could change his mind, this is all a trap, if he's willing to buy he may be willing to sell,* and more—and with each left step, she counted the possible boons of staying—*away from Uncle Brom, comfortable bed, not having to wait tables, only one man to contend with, wanting to see that fae-man smile again, a friendly sentient house,* and much more.

Before she knew it, she had all her arguments for and against arranged in her mind. She stared at the kitchen door, realizing with a start the possible boons far outnumbered the potential problems.

Of course, she realized that many of the boons were creature comforts. Most of the problems hinged on the fae-man in question, who she found sitting on a stool in the kitchen.

His brows rose almost as quickly as he did from his seat when she entered. They stood there blinking at each other for a long moment before Allarion cleared his throat and bowed his head.

"Forgive me, I will leave you."

Before he could turn to go, Molly yelped, "Wait!"

His gaze flicked back to hers, and the small glimmer of hope there had her stomach doing flips.

Through her furious blush, she said, "You don't have to go. I wanted to speak with you, actually. Let me just make some tea . . ."

With a small roar, the stove burst to life, fire licking up the side of the kettle she kept there. They both watched as within a few moments, the water began to steam.

The house was apparently eager to have them speak, too.

Hiding her blush behind the motions of making tea, Molly gathered the leaves to steep and poured the water, all the while feeling Allarion's intensely curious gaze on her back.

Bringing her steeping cup to the butcher block, she faced him. It would've been easy to stare at something more innocuous, like his throat or nose or left ear, but she made herself look him in the eye.

"I think . . . I will stay."

She watched in astonishment as his broad shoulders sank and a heavy breath rushed out of him. The floorboards beneath them shook, and the house rattled its shutters.

A smile burst onto Molly's lips, uncontrollable.

Leaning against the butcher block for support, Allarion placed his other hand over his heart. "You do me the greatest honor, Molly. I swear, I shall earn this honor and your trust."

Her grin widened, making her cheeks ache. Fates, who said things like that? Only him.

Still, though—"But I do have questions. I need a few things answered—for my peace of mind."

His gray face grew serious, although he didn't shed that new animation upon hearing her news. Gone was his dour, stiff demeanor, as if he stood waiting for a blow. Instead, although he sat still on his stool, he regarded her with intensity, his brows and mouth moving and twitching as he thought.

Taking a sip of tea, Molly dove in.

"I know you said it's not your secret to tell, but I need to know as much as you can tell me about why you're here. And whether I'll be safe staying with you."

To his credit, he didn't guffaw and regale her with manly bravado. He nodded seriously, and when he spoke, his voice was thoughtful.

"As I have spoken of before, the Fae Queen has long outlived her reign. She is a poison in our very blood. I laid down my sword after she slew her kin, as I couldn't stomach serving someone so cruel and unjust. I'm sorry to say, though, that I did not leave."

Those purple eyes, sharp as cut gems, turned to look out the kitchen window as he considered his next words.

"I wandered, aimless, for a long while. It seemed my conscience was satisfied with my protest. I did not serve Amaranthe and therefore my honor wasn't in question."

"But what could you have done?" she found herself asking. It tugged on her heart to see him so ready to condemn himself.

"Something," he said. "But that opportunity is in the past. I tell you this, though, to explain that if given the chance, I will oppose Amaranthe and lend my aid in restoring the faelands."

That hot sip of tea burned in her belly. "So you're going to leave?"

"Perhaps. But I doubt any time soon. And—" he leaned forward, placing a hand on the butcher block as if he would reach for her "—I would have every intention of returning. You are here, so this is my home."

Her grip on her mug tightened, but she made herself breathe through the weight of his admission.

"When will you go?"

"I don't know. What that path looks like and how long it wends, I cannot say. I just know that, someday, Amaranthe will meet her end, and I intend to see it with my own eyes. I tell you this to be honest. It isn't something I foresee happening for a while yet, and I will do everything in my power to ensure it doesn't affect you. The Fae Queen has a long reach, it is true, but so deep into human lands, we are safe here."

Molly nodded cautiously. "All right. That's good to hear."

"Your staying here also strengthens the estate and makes it that much safer."

"What do you mean?"

He'd made comments or mentioned something like this before, but Molly needed to know, in clear language, what this meant—and what it would require from her.

She listened with no small amount of amazement as he explained how magic flowed through the fae, how its raw power was so great that they needed a community of them, working as a sort of circuit or cycle, to handle the magic. The faelands was so ancient and so imbued with their magic now that young fae knew how to do it intrinsically from birth, like breathing or blinking.

Away from the faelands, though, Allarion needed his own smaller circuit. Between him, Bellarand, and the estate, he was creating such a little community. He imbued his magic into the land, and over time, it was knitting with the magic of Eirea.

"Just like every land has creatures that are native to it, the weave of magic changes across landscapes," he explained.

To create the circuit he needed to sustain himself and the estate, having a human mate would tie him to the land that much quicker and more wholly. What might have taken a year or more could now possibly take months.

"So, *I* would become part of your circuit?"

"Yes, the most important part," he said gently. "It would imbue you as surely as it has the house and the land. I suspect it already has, given that you can hear Bellarand."

Molly took another deep breath, working to swallow such a revelation. Her, magical. Unimportant Molly Dunne, orphaned barmaid— imbued with magic.

"We would be bound in the human way and in the fae tradition.

Given enough time, you would come to influence the estate nearly as much as I can."

Blood rushed in her ears. *Incredible. And terrifying.*

The house creaked happily, breaking through her stunned silence.

Allarion looked up at the rafters, grinning. "Although, I think you already influence the house a great deal. It likes you very much."

"I like it, too."

Their smiles for the happy house turned on each other, and Molly's stomach flipped again.

"When you say bound in those ways, you mean married. Mated, like Lady Aislinn is."

"Mated. Yes." He leaned forward again, those dark eyes boring into her with an intensity that made a shiver run down her spine and straight between her thighs. "I want you in all ways, Molly, but I am a patient man. Or at least, I can be. We will go as quickly or as slowly as you wish."

She swallowed hard, trying to wet a throat that'd gone dry at the thought of performing marital activities with the fae. Fates, she should find it abhorrent—but then, if she did, she wouldn't be staying, now would she? Molly could admit, at least to herself, now that she had thought past her indignation, that getting to see everything beneath all that formal clothing of his was of *marked* interest to her.

"What about the circuit?" she croaked.

"It may take more time, but I am willing to wait. The bond isn't simply about the carnal. To forge a strong one requires trust. That is my aim, above all."

"And what about your friend?" Molly asked. "Will all this delay her coming here?"

"It may," he admitted. "But she . . . she is secure. And creating this bond with you, it will only make this land safer for her and for you."

Nodding, Molly said, "All right. I suppose that's acceptable. But, I want to know for certain that this is what you want, too." Those dark eyes tightened with confusion, and Molly hurried to explain, "What

I mean is, I wouldn't want this to happen just because it's convenient for you. If we do this, it'll be for true. A woman wants to be wanted, you see. So, if it's to be a real marriage, a bonding as you say, you need to want me for me, for Molly."

She made herself stop, to suck in a much-needed breath. Unsure how much sense that made, she watched him carefully, her words hanging above with the drying fronds suspended from the rafters.

Those dark eyes took her in, and a sort of uncanny understanding flickered there.

With care, he laid his arm across the butcher block, offering her his open hand. That simple act of reaching for her had Molly's pulse fluttering in her throat. Breathless, she tentatively reached to lay her hand in his.

His long, elegant fingers wrapped around her hand, his purple-gray skin such a contrast to her freckled, tanned tone. His blue-black nailbeds were still an otherworldly sight, but they didn't alarm her like they once had. His were just hands, like any others.

Well, that wasn't entirely true, and not just because of their color.

No other hand had had Molly breaking out into a riot of goose-flesh from her neck to her toes. Not even Finn, and Finn, like all good cons, had had a way with words.

"Oh, sweetling," he said in that voice, the one as smooth as warm honey, "there is nothing in this world or the next that I want more than to have you in all ways. Not just because you are my *azai,* but because you are you. Since that day at the well, it has only and always been *you.*"

Molly dared to look into his amethyst eyes, and what she saw there stole the breath from her lungs. She wasn't ready to name all that she saw, only a hunger so deep, it went beyond lust or a need for sustenance. He looked at her as if one word from her could have him across that countertop, devouring her in all the best ways.

His lips curved with the slightest smile as he said, "There isn't a male alive who will be more devoted a mate than I. When you are ready, I look forward to proving it."

His promise left her steaming hotter than her mug, and for a moment, Molly really had nothing coherent to say.

She thought he might be enjoying her befuddlement, if his enigmatic little grin was anything, but he patiently waited for her to find her final question.

"The only other thing I want to know is that I'm free," she said, giving his hand an experimental squeeze. "That if I want to go somewhere, I can. I don't need your permission, and that big guard pony outside won't stop me."

His horrified frown calmed her nerves almost as much as his answer. "Of course, sweetling. You have never been a prisoner here. This house, the estate, I mean for it to be as much yours as it is mine, which means you may leave it whenever you choose."

"So I could go to Mullon on my own? Or back to Dundúran to see my family?"

"Yes, of course. I'm not your keeper. I hope to be your friend and soon your mate, but that will never mean I dictate where you go or what you do." He paused, his lips scrunching into something of a troubled moue. "Unless it is a question of your safety. Then, I might make a few vehement suggestions."

She didn't know why, but *vehement suggestions* had a giggle bouncing up her throat.

"Good. That's what I wanted to know."

Feeling a bit braver, she let go of her mug and extended her other hand across the countertop to him. The small smile that came to his lips upon seeing it almost broke her heart. He connected them together as if she offered the most precious gift, his touch gentle and his gaze reverent.

Him looking at me like that could go right to my head.

"I will stay and give this a try," she said, for her own benefit as much as his. "If it's to work, I think we shouldn't have secrets."

When his look grew troubled, she said, "You can have the one.

I respect that it's not yours to share yet. But otherwise, we're honest with each other."

He squeezed her hands, and his thumbs began to make little teasing circles on the delicate, sensitive insides of her wrists.

"You are as wise as you are brave, my Molly. Whatever you need, you shall have—you need only ask."

She truly listened and heard when he said it this time and nodded her agreement. She'd be sure to test him on it soon.

"That goes for you, too. No more assumptions."

He had the decency to look embarrassed, those pale cheeks purpling in an endearing fae blush.

"I agree to your terms. To honor our pact, I shall tell you a truth—we fae cannot lie. We may omit, we may obfuscate, but a baldfaced lie, we cannot tell."

Molly's brows nearly arched up to her hairline. She supposed she'd have to trust him on that, too.

"All right, then. I'll endeavor to be as honest, too."

They shared a smile, and though it was but a moment, it lingered for Molly. Like laying tinder for a new fire or filling an empty pitcher, there was something about it that made Molly think of changes, or renewals.

His lips parted, and he searched her gaze with his when he said, "We go at your pace, like I said, but this once, may I embrace you?"

Molly blinked in astonishment. All this talk of mating and he just wanted a hug?

"Yes, that's fine." With the way her body seemed to vibrate, like it needed to be closer to his, she suspected it was more than fine.

He rose with the grace and fluidity of a great wildcat, that predator's hungry gaze focused on her. Keeping one of her hands, he gently pulled her toward him once he'd come around the butcher block.

Molly stepped into his space, heart thundering in her chest.

Given how tall he was, she fit neatly under his chin. Tucked into his chest, she wrapped her arms around his narrow waist and laid her cheek on the slab of muscle over where his heart would be. Nothing beat below her ear, but he was warm to the touch.

His arms came around her, securing her to him, and she felt his lips fall to the crown of her head. He breathed deeply there, a contented sound rumbling through him.

Those big, tapered hands held onto her, and for a fleeting moment, Molly imagined this was what feeling safe and secure felt like. It'd been a figment of her imagination for so long, she didn't trust it to be real. But the glimpse was nice—and so was holding onto him, bony as he might've been.

He felt . . . *good* in her arms. Molly wasn't the most tactile person, but she could appreciate a good hug, and this one was excellent. She almost wanted to burrow her face into his chest.

Warm lips teased at her temple, and in that honeyed voice, he murmured, "Welcome home, Molly."

15

Molly awoke to a new day with a hopeful glimmer in her heart. Going to sleep the night before, she'd decided, for her own sake and Allarion's, she would close the chapter on her first fortnight here fresh—not start over but anew. They would move forward, as he'd said.

Stretching under the luxurious bedding, she rolled around in a happy little wiggle. Without the burden of dread, she practically floated from the bed to her things.

It was as she laced her stays that she took a long look at her things. Still strewn about the far side of the room, her clothing, a few keepsakes, and what she'd gotten from Mullon sat in unkempt piles. Things were getting wrinkled and a bit rank, if she was honest. She'd need to do laundry soon, but she could get a little more life out of a few things if she finally . . .

Drawing in a deep breath, she looked over at the armoire.

"All right," she said.

She opened one of the doors before the other went flying open and the drawers began to open one after the other, making a harmony. The house opened and closed the cedar trunk lid as if it clapped. *Finally,* it seemed to say.

"I know, I know," she laughed. "I just do things in my own time is all."

The house rattled the shutters in what sounded like laughter to her. Molly laughed along, folding and hanging her things.

She couldn't help a smidge of trepidation as her things disappeared into drawers and the trunk lid shut. The room almost looked bare once she finished—or at least, she could see the floorboards. There was still a line of vases full of bouquets atop the dresser. The flowers Allarion left never seemed to wilt or die.

With more space freed up, she redistributed the bouquets around the room.

Pleased with the bursts of color, Molly planted her hands on her hips and nodded. All of Allarion's pestering about this wallpaper and those curtains made a bit more sense now; he wanted her opinion on fixing up the house, and he'd gotten her thinking about where things would look best.

Decorating wasn't something she had much experience with, but given the chance, she thought she could come to quite like it.

A vase full of foxgloves sat waiting for her when she opened her bedchamber door. Her smile was uncontrollable as she bent to retrieve it, and she took the gift with her down to the kitchen.

Allarion began to smile when she entered the kitchen, but the sight of the flowers had him looking suddenly serious.

"Are the flowers not to your liking?"

"I like them a lot. So much, I want to look at them today." She positioned the flowers behind the kitchen sink, in the window that looked out at the forest beyond. The growing morning sunshine caught in the blue and purple cones, giving them a velveteen quality.

That smile took flight on his face, although Molly suspected he contained the full scope of his happiness at her liking his gift. Charmed, she went about preparing her breakfast as they made light chatter, talking of the weather and the work for the day.

"And what am I to do?" she asked as her oats boiled.

"Whatever you want to do," was his sweet but unhelpful answer.

"I've already laid in bed and wandered aimlessly for days. What if I helped you with your project today?"

"Absolutely not."

She looked up in surprise to hear his vehemence.

Allarion shook his head, quickly amending, "Forgive me, sweetling. It's only, I'll be finishing the roof today and under no circumstances will I have you up there. It's dangerous." He lowered his head, looking at her from beneath his rigid brows. "This is one of those matters of safety I spoke of."

Molly nodded in agreement. "All right. I don't really relish the idea of getting on the roof anyways."

His shoulders sagged in relief, making her notice how stiffly he'd been holding himself in anticipation of her answer.

"I could keep you company, then?"

She glanced up to see his reaction as she poured her steaming oats into a bowl. A blush crept onto her cheeks to see the way his expression went soft at her suggestion.

"I would like that very much."

Decided, Molly made quick work of her breakfast and then followed Allarion to see about his project. He showed her the dwindling pile of blue-gray shingles, already loaded onto a pulley. Pushing his sleeves to his elbows, he took one end of the rope and began to pull, hoisting the heavy load up, up, up the four stories to the roof.

Molly marveled, watching how his forearms tensed with strength, his sinews and tendons pulled taut. She bit back her grin to think he did it on purpose, to show off. Well, that was all right, she supposed. They were betrothed—and he had very fine forearms.

When the load neared a balcony, he secured the rope and led her up, up, up to where the shingles waited. She watched as he leapt onto the sloped side of a nearby gable, clambering gracefully up onto the roof.

Those long, pointed ears cast a shadow on her as he leaned over the side to grin at her.

"You should be safe there, and I can hear you."

"You're sure you wouldn't prefer the birds for company?" she teased, watching a handful of pigeons gather on a cylindrical ceramic chimney.

His look soured. "Honestly, no. They have defecated on me once too often."

Molly bent in half laughing, startling the pigeons and Allarion, too. It was a while before she got her humor under control.

As Allarion began his work, Molly called up, "Why do you have to do this manually? Why can the house not . . . fix itself?"

The questions felt so silly in her mouth, the words in a ridiculous order and pairing, but Allarion's shadow nodded as if she made perfect sense.

"The house is an entity unto itself and can only control what makes it up. Its rooms are like its limbs, and everything inside it makes up the body. It has no control over what is not part of it, so until new materials are added to it, it cannot, say, replace shingles."

Molly's brows rose, surprised over how much sense that actually made.

"So, once it's added to the house, it becomes part of the house?"

"Exactly that."

"So . . . all my things I put away this morning are now part of the house?"

His hammering stopped abruptly, and his pale face appeared again over the eaves. Those dark eyes bore down on her. Molly held still, her heart fluttering with an excited little thrill.

"Did you?" he asked softly.

"I did. Does that mean my things are now the house's?"

"They are still yours," he assured her.

Indeed, when Molly went to her bedchamber to fetch her embroidery project, she found that the clothes she'd stored away in the armoire and trunk were freshly washed and ironed for her.

"How . . .?"

The shutters rattled in a happy cacophony, and Molly couldn't help laughing along.

"Well, thank you! That saves me some chafed fingers."

She headed back to the fourth level in awe. No laundry! Other than feeding herself, she had so few chores to keep busy. She truly would need to find something to occupy herself, which was why she'd retrieved her project.

Setting up a stool, Molly sat on the balcony, enjoying the cool autumn afternoon, a shawl around her shoulders and her embroidery in her lap as she chatted with Allarion on the roof.

They talked about a little of everything. She learned he was one of five siblings, with two elder sisters and two younger brothers. In his years after leaving service, he went to each of his siblings, hoping to find purpose and inspiration in what they did. While he learned a great deal from each that proved useful, none of it was a true calling like that of being a warrior had been when he was young.

"Now, though," he said, peering down at her to flash those fangs in a toothy grin, "I feel it all over again."

"Found a passion for home renovation, have you?"

He chuckled at her joke. "Indeed, all the human nobles will glow with envy to see my skill."

Molly laughed as she bit off her green thread. It was time to start with the red.

She took breaks to eat and stretch her legs, yet she was still amazed when the sun began to set over the trees. Allarion inserted the final few shingles as the sky, shot through with violet and saffron, deepened with impeding night.

They'd spent the whole day chatting while working on their projects. Molly had nearly finished her sleeve, impressed with her progress. It was amazing what having the time to devote to something could do.

Allarion levered himself back onto the balcony, looking as pleased as a cat who'd swallowed a bird. His silvery hair had been mussed and stuck to his skull with sweat in places, and his pale face was smudged with grime.

Grinning, Molly pulled out a kerchief to wipe his face.

It wasn't until she'd placed the cloth to his cheek that she noticed how positively still he'd gone. Her eyes snapped to his, and they stared at each other as she finished cleaning him off.

Her hand lingered on his cheek, the contour so sharp and inhuman. She almost wished . . . the cloth didn't separate them.

Keeping her gaze, Allarion bowed his head to press his lips to the inside of her wrist.

"Thank you, sweetling," he rumbled against her skin.

"For what?" she said, tucking her kerchief and hand back into her pocket.

"For today. For your company. I hope you weren't too bored."

"Not at all."

Offering his arm, she slid her hand into the crook of his elbow and let him lead her back down into the kitchen. In the better light, he asked to see her embroidery and spent a good few moments tracing the patterns and colors with a fingertip.

As Molly began preparing her dinner, she stole glances at him from under her lashes, anticipation stringing her tight.

"This is beautiful work," he extolled. "You have an artist's eye, my love."

Blushing with pleasure, she made the necessary refutations, *she wasn't that good* and *her lines could be neater,* even though she practically glowed with the praise.

They'd spent the lion's share of the day talking about him and his life in the faelands, which Molly was perfectly content with, curious as she was about all things magic and fae now, but as he continued to admire her work, he managed to shift conversation to her. Molly was far less content to talk about herself, but she supposed, if he took the time to ask, she may as well answer.

"My mother taught me, initially," she said, "and I kept at it."

Allarion nodded gravely. "And where is your mother now?"

It took effort, but Molly told him her story. All of it. From life in the village with her parents to the plague to going to live with Uncle Brom. Allarion sat quietly, absorbing what she said.

When she dared look up at him to see what he thought, she was relieved to find not pity but empathy shining through those dark eyes. It was strange . . . he wasn't the most expressive person, yet she knew from looking at him that he hurt *for* her. It was the angle of his mouth, the somber turn of his shoulders. And it was how he asked her questions she never thought of—and listened to the answers.

Did she remember the sound of her mother's voice? What was her favorite thing her father would say? He asked her all sorts of things—her favorite scent of Dundúran or color of the sunset. All things Molly knew but had to think about. And while some of the answers were painful, that pain was easier to bear when she knew she confided in someone who cared to hear.

And so their days went, Molly joining Allarion in his work, or if she couldn't, finding things for herself to do.

With the roof complete, Allarion turned his focus to the solar next to the library. He insisted it would be her solar, where she could work on her own projects and fill the room with whatever she wanted. Molly hadn't known what to say other than, "Thank you."

Growing serious, Allarion closed the distance between them. With a crooked finger, he lifted her chin so she met his gaze when he said, "There is no thanks needed here, sweetling. It is your *due*."

Throat running dry, Molly could only nod.

That was much easier said than done for someone who'd had to earn or take or steal every scrap she'd ever had.

Still, even if she couldn't quite wrap her mind around his sentiment, it gave her a thrill to hear it. Her due. Imagine.

Between the solar and the unused room beside it, Molly became an expert in hanging wallpaper. Used to physical labor but not so much the skilled labor it took to redecorate a great house, she endeavored to learn quickly and came to enjoy the work.

When they next went to Mullon—this time with Bellarand pulling a cart after a ferocious argument over it—they sought furniture to fill the rooms. That was how she found herself with a beautiful set of armchairs for under the bay windows of her solar, a little table to sit in between them, a long worktable, and a chest of drawers for all her supplies. Allarion hunted for a table and chairs to put in the conservatory, so they could sit there in the evenings and watch the stars.

This time, he let her haggle to her heart's content, and Molly enjoyed showing how ruthless she could be when it came to a discount. She wasn't ashamed or afraid to use Bellarand for effect if it meant more money off, either.

Before her eyes, the solar became a dreamy green escape, where she could tuck into a cozy chair and sew. The rich green drapes and sage green walls, with the tall windows looking out into the forest beyond, made the room feel like an extension of the sylvan scene just outside. Molly even pulled a few of her small keepsakes from her room to display on the fireplace mantel, making the room hers with a touch of old and new.

On more than one occasion, they settled after dinner in their respective spaces, Molly in an armchair with her sewing, Allarion at his large desk in the library. With the connecting door open, she had but to look up to see him scratching away at his ledgers and maps.

She . . . liked it. That they could spend their days together in companionable chatter but then also be close in the evenings in equally pleasant quiet.

Molly had sometimes stolen up to her room above the tavern with her sewing, opening her window to hear the bustle of the city at night. She listened to the vendors come home for the day, the street performers play their sets, and the congenial chatter of the neighborhood. Here, it was forest noises and Allarion rustling paper, but she still enjoyed the quiet serenity of it.

She also liked stealing glances at him as he worked at his desk. Molly wasn't a strong reader or writer, but she appreciated how his hand moved across the page, quill held masterfully in his fingers. The angle of his brow and curve of his neck as he bent his head over a ledger, how his lips parted as he traced a finger over a map . . . Molly felt it as if it was her skin he pored over.

Fates, there was something wrong with her, that she was starting to find those pointed ears charming and his sharp fangs endearing. With every day, his otherness inspired admiration, even . . . lust rather than aversion.

As she watched him work, whether on his books or on a wall or chopping wood, she grew to appreciate the sharp lines of his body and the fluid grace of his movements. He was all coiled strength, skin stretched taut over densely packed muscle. A wildcat, beautiful and dangerous, and Molly liked him all the more for that danger.

Definitely something wrong with me.

Except, nothing about it, about *him,* truly felt wrong. Quite the opposite.

As well as helping on projects, Molly decided to take up hobbies or skills she'd been meaning to. She set herself to improving her reading, she endeavored to keep the garden alive, and she even tried her hand at drawing. Her cooking and baking got more creative, too. Even if he didn't eat, Allarion seemed to enjoy hanging around the kitchen as she cooked, watching her chop and knead and stir.

Eventually, she put him to work.

She couldn't help laughing at his abysmal chopping skills, although his determination to see it through had her smiling.

"It's nothing like stabbing an enemy," he remarked as he butchered a radish.

"No, it's not," she choked on her laugh.

He held the knives awkwardly—and it was more than being a rich scion from a great house, it was the untried movements of someone who'd truly never prepared food nor even watched someone do it. Still, he tried his best—and covered in seasoning and sauce, his ugly cutting made little difference.

Even better, Molly discovered he could sing.

They stood preparing the night's dinner, chopping vegetables, when Allarion asked if there was truly nothing she liked about serving at the tavern.

"Oh, there were things I enjoyed."

"What was your favorite?"

That was easy. "The songs."

He looked up in curiosity, and Molly explained the nights when singing would take over the tavern. Bawdy ballads and sea shanties, she loved leading or joining in with the patrons in a round of singing. No one cared if they harmonized or sounded halfway decent—most were drunk, after all—it was only about the camaraderie and good cheer.

"Would you sing for me?" he asked.

Molly's stomach flipped with nerves. Her first instinct was to deny him, that she couldn't possibly sing by herself just for him—but then, she loved to sing. She'd never be someone who gathered an audience, but she thought her voice was fair enough.

"All right," she agreed.

She used her chopping to set a beat and began a ballad familiar to anyone in Eirea, a sweet song about loving their rolling hills and vast forests. Molly couldn't quite look at him as she sang, but soon enough, she swayed her hips in time and her voice filled the kitchen as they worked.

It didn't take long for a deep hum to accompany her voice. She looked up in surprise to find that, after two verses, he'd picked up the tune. He added a deep, guttural hum to her song, using his voice as an instrument.

Breathless with pleasure, they soon forgot about dinner and cooking. Molly sang song after song to his accompaniment; sometimes he hummed and others, when he picked up the words, he'd harmonize with her.

It shouldn't have surprised her that his singing was as beautiful as his speaking voice, rich and syrupy like molasses.

She remembered him saying his eldest sister was a musician and how he'd enjoyed playing with her, but Molly hadn't realized that meant he sang, as well.

They spent most of the evening trading favorite songs, and he even had her singing in broken faethling, his language, as he taught her some of their favorite ballads. Molly loved how his eyes went bright and his face soft as he sang, the long column of his throat vibrating with his baritone. His pitch was perfect, his harmony a thing of beauty.

To her amazement and utter pleasure, it didn't take him long to procure a harpsichord.

One morning, she watched it slowly roll up the drive, the gravel beneath moving it along in gentle little waves. Molly couldn't help but laugh and shake her head at the strangeness—it was to be expected by now.

Once up the front steps, the house took care of moving the instrument. By the time they entered her solar, the house was just moving the harpsichord into place.

With a flourish, Allarion sat at the bench, tossing his cloak over the back. The rich fabric pooled around his feet, a waterfall of glistening black velvet. Those tapered fingers moved seamlessly over the keys, testing the sound.

Molly sat on the bench beside him, returning his grin when he leaned down to see how she liked it.

"Needs a little tuning," he said as his fingers moved almost too quickly to track. "Do you know this one?"

The music changed to a familiar song, and Molly bounced on her seat. Together, they sang about bonny lasses and forlorn love, filling the house with out-of-tune music and their harmonized duet.

To Molly's surprise, even Bellarand, after another fortnight of her presence at the manor and seeing that she meant to stay, seemed to be coming around. Not that she necessarily sought or needed the unicorn's esteem, but it was nice to know she wouldn't be stabbed in the back whenever she went to tend the garden Allarion established for her.

Molly liked to think of herself as adaptable, sometimes even clever, and she wasn't above bribery to get her way. She'd started a subtle campaign of flirting with Allarion, mostly to see where the line for him was. How much could she push—for she wanted to know if what he said was true.

As for Bellarand, as a glorified horse with a superiority complex, Molly figured the way to win his—if not affection, then at least approval would be through his stomach.

Most males were similar that way. The ones that ate, at least.

As she tended to the garden, she got in the habit of pulling up a carrot for him. They weren't ready yet, but the unicorn seemed to take delight in the small roots.

The young ones are the sweetest, he said without a hint of remorse.

Molly swallowed her horror and continued her campaign, making sure to procure additional large carrots when next they went to Mullon.

The large carrots were quickly a favorite. Soon, Molly had herself an enormous household pest.

One that enjoyed scaring the daylights out of her.

With the split door open on top to catch the afternoon breeze, it was easy for Bellarand to stick his head into the kitchen, and he loved to do it suddenly, never giving her warning he was coming.

He bared his teeth in an equine laugh whenever she dropped or spilled something.

This time, though, she merely jumped when he stuck that big black head through the door.

I require more carrots, human.

Molly didn't bother looking up from where she stood at the stove, stirring that day's stew. "May I please have another carrot, Molly?"

A snort of derision blew through the kitchen. *Dread-mounts do not beg.*

"Being polite isn't begging," she sing-songed. "It's having good manners."

Another great huff, and Molly did her best not to look at the looming unicorn taking up one side of the kitchen. She kept to her business, chopping her vegetables and stirring her stew.

Finally, when Bellarand saw she meant it when she ignored him, he stamped a front hoof on the packed earth outside.

Fine! A carrot, please.

It sounded more insulting than polite, but Molly figured they had to start somewhere. Pulling one from her pile, she approached where his head hung over the open half-door, but she didn't give it to him immediately.

"Please, who?"

His hot, irritated breath threw her hair back with its velocity. *Please, Molly,* he grumbled.

Content, Molly handed over the carrot to his grasping horsey lips. And nearly had her fingers chomped off for her trouble.

"Watch it!" she yelped.

Carrot faster next time, then, he chortled, and she swore the unicorn *winked* at her.

Unsettling. There was no other word for the unicorn.

Molly glared as she returned to her stew, but she didn't rat out the big pony to Allarion when the fae came trotting down the steps. She wanted to be amicable cohabitants with Bellarand, if nothing more, and Molly had never been one to snitch.

Allarion sat himself on a stool, and he and his mount seemed perfectly happy to watch her cook. Bellarand laughed his braying laugh when she set Allarion the task of stringing green beans, but quickly turned to goading the fae into throwing him pods to crunch on.

"I'd like some of those for my dinner," she groused as another green bean went sailing into the unicorn's wide-open mouth.

Allarion bit down on his laughter, schooling his features into something contrite as he did as his *azai* bid and kept back her green beans.

Coward, bullied Bellarand.

"I heard that," Molly sang from the stove.

Bellarand had the decency to swing his ears back, abashed.

She'd set him to stringing green beans enough times that Allarion didn't have to watch his hands as he worked. Instead, he had the much more enjoyable view of his lovely *azai* standing at the stove. He didn't know if she realized, but a little smile adorned her plush mouth as she listened to Bellarand gripe.

These past weeks had been some of the happiest of Allarion's long life. Having a companion like Molly filled his days with joy. The work around the manor wasn't work when she was there with him, either lending a hand or sewing in an out-of-the-way corner.

She'd warned him that the happy, vivacious barmaid wasn't her true self, but Allarion had his doubts. Perhaps her smiles weren't always so wide, but now that he'd seen more of her true smiles, he realized how often in the tavern she had forced the expression. He understood now what to look for—not just the widening of her mouth but how her eyes crinkled at the corners and a dimple appeared in her right cheek.

He was learning, and that gave him hope.

Allarion knew himself to have a fierce acquisitiveness, even for a fae. Collecting the parts of his Molly, discovering all the bits and hidden layers of her, satisfied him in a way nothing else ever had. Learning her, sating his curiosity over what she thought and liked and savored, offered him the very thing he'd longed for all his life—purpose.

The only thing missing was Molly in his bed.

But he had hope there, too. She'd never been totally immune to him, even when she was angriest with him. With his sensitive senses, he'd tasted on the back of his tongue how, every once in a while, her body quickened for his. Over the intervening weeks, he'd come to suspect she was flirting with him.

Her big doe eyes, ensuring her generous breasts pressed or brushed against him when they were close, finding excuses to gently lay her hand on his arm—all of it spoke to growing interest. He dared not acknowledge it too much for fear that his desperation for her might scare her.

The last thing he wanted was her locking herself away again in her bedchamber.

As he learned Molly and she grew into her place here at Scarborough, Allarion knew he just had to keep his wits and his patience about him. *Just a little longer,* he told himself as he stroked his cock to thoughts of her every morning and every night.

His hunger for her grew with each day, a writhing, boundless thing that gnawed at his ribs. More than once, he hadn't been able to keep himself from her, creeping into her bedchamber to watch as she slept.

His cock had ached and his hand twitched to stroke it, but he had a few remaining shreds of honor. He waited to do that after he left the sanctity of her room. Still, however much this *little longer* was, he feared it'd be too much for the desperate thing inside that wanted to *devour* her.

Polite and gentle as he forced himself to be, Allarion dreaded the day when his patience, that ancient thing that had kept him alive for centuries, finally gave under the enormity of his need for her. It would happen, someday soon, and he could only hope Molly was ready.

When she tossed him happy little looks over her shoulder, as she did then from the stove, his hopes soared almost as quickly as his blood to his cock.

The minx winked at him before saying, "You can add those to the water now."

Allarion gritted his back teeth, hoping his tunic hid the worst of his bulging trou. Holding the green beans in his hands out in front of him, he crossed to his mate to deposit them in the pot of boiling water.

This cooking business fascinated him—why some foods were cooked and others weren't offered an endless puzzle. Some foods could be enjoyed either way, and there were so many methods of cooking. His favorite was baking—it filled the kitchen with sweet, sugary smells and his Molly always looked a treat bending over to pull them from the brick oven.

She seemed distracted enough by the added beans that his cock went unnoticed, but now that he was near, Allarion had no desire to leave her side.

She'd laughed before, asking why he liked to hover at her elbow while she moved about the kitchen.

The answer was simple. *"To be near you."*

That was his greatest desire of all, even above finally indulging in the pleasure of her body. Despite her misgivings, Molly exuded warmth. She may not see it, but her presence breathed new life into the estate. The house hung on her every word—almost as much as him—and she filled their days with music and song. Even Bellarand had been less cranky of late.

As Molly tended her cooking, Allarion couldn't help lifting his fingers to twirl around one of her brown curls.

"Your hair has grown," he said. When they handfasted, her hair had fallen to just past her ears, but now it nearly swept her shoulders, the hair trying to turn for one more curl.

Molly reached back to feel the ends of her hair. "I suppose it has. I hadn't thought about it much, honestly."

"If you prefer it short, I could cut it." He'd trimmed Bellarand's mane before and he had a hard time seeing Molly as a more exacting client than the unicorn.

She made a considering noise. "I think I'd like to grow it some. The only reason I kept it so short was so it couldn't be grabbed easily."

Allarion went perfectly still. Sensing his shift, Molly looked up at him, those brown eyes of hers wide.

It took two tries to force the words from his throat. "Grab you?" Even he heard how his voice had dropped low in his throat.

Her lips thinned with displeasure. "Yes. Drunk men often get braver. And handsy."

Rage licked up his spine. He'd certainly seen some rowdy behavior for himself in the tavern, and Molly had told him a few anecdotes of her serving there, but he hadn't imagined her having to make a sacrifice like cutting her hair in order to keep safe. That she hadn't been safe in that tavern, her home, burned like molten lead in his guts.

Allarion didn't realize he'd lost himself to his rageful thoughts until one of her small, gentle hands came to rest on his chest.

"It's all right," she soothed. "I know how to handle myself."

He cracked his jaw, trying to loosen the hold his anger had on him. It did nothing but make Molly uncomfortable—he could save it for a more deserving recipient.

Steadying his breathing, he covered her hand with his and cupped the side of her dear face in his other. Sliding his fingers through her hair, he marveled at the softness. What would she look like with a heavy curtain of chestnut curls? He hoped one day to find out.

"You need never make such alterations again. You are safe here, sweetling. Always."

"I know," she whispered, her words arrowing through him.

Something thudded painfully in his chest, shaking his ribs. His throat went tight as she looked up at him with eyes that crinkled at the corners. A soft smile touched her lips as she turned her cheek into his hand to nuzzle his palm.

He could hardly believe his eyes, watching her little show of affection. For *him.*

His mind ceased to work for several moments.

Allarion's gaze fell to how her throat elongated when she turned her head. A tendon in her neck pressed against her skin, and he could just see the faint beat of her pulse there.

His fangs *ached.*

Staring at her throat, Allarion had the distinct desire to *bite* her. To draw her blood, her very essence into himself. She would be *his.* In the most visceral, primeval way.

Saliva pooled on his tongue to taste her.

Noises dulled, his vision narrowed. The pulse at her throat matched the thud in his chest, a quake that shook him in his boots.

Let me, he wanted to beg her, *let me taste you.*

"Allarion?"

The sound of her voice—his name—he blinked, trying to put her face into focus.

Molly still looked up at him, but concern had wrinkled her brow. "Your eyes . . ."

He turned his face away, needing to take a steadying breath. On looking around the kitchen, he realized all the spoons and pots and herb fronds had lifted in the air from his wayward magic.

He'd need to siphon some off soon, even though it was far sooner than his usual interval. His indomitable desire for his *azai* had stirred more than just his lust inside him, it seemed.

Goddesses, what had he been thinking? Drink her blood . . .

There were old rites, more ancient than the fae in these lands, that spoke of *azai* biting each other. There were even still fae women who enjoyed scoring their partners with their fangs, and more than a few fae men wore their scars like a badge of pride.

He remembered Maxim had spoken of blood before, Aine's blood but was vague, even with Allarion. He'd wondered if Aine's blood was the reason for Maxim's transformation.

Gone was the spiderweb of black veins beneath his skin. Instead, Maxim bled red. His sclera had gone white, his tongue pink. Allarion thought it had to do with Aine being human. That Maxim spoke of her blood metaphorically, like the heart or spirit.

What if . . . what if . . .

He didn't know if he dared touch the thought too firmly.

Allarion tried to soften his features and hide his whirring thoughts.

"Forgive me, sweetling. I lost my way in my thoughts."

Molly blinked up at him, her expression skeptical, but let him make his retreat. "All right. I'd tell you to sit down and eat something, but you don't do that."

"No," he said numbly, although he did take her advice to sit.

Bellarand was less gentle. *What's wrong with you?*

Allarion stared at his friend, feeling dazed. *I'm not sure.*

16

It was a quiet morning for Molly, which made her suspicious. Allar-Iion wasn't due for his next long sleep today, but even then, some-times his projects were so quiet or so far away that she didn't hear. Bel-larand too could sometimes disappear and not be heard from all day.

But that *both* of them were so quiet had her a little worried.

So when Bellarand stuck his big head in the open top of the split door, she was more relieved than startled. She didn't even mind when he nickered with disappointment that she hadn't jumped with fright.

"And where have you been?" she asked.

Come, human. I need your thumbs, was his answer.

Quick as he'd come, his head disappeared back outside.

Baffled, Molly untied her apron, trading it on the peg by the door for her overcoat. Sliding her arms into the warm brown wool, she opened the bottom half of the door to follow Bellarand to the back of the manor, where a shed kept some ancient-looking hardware mostly dry.

Using his horn, Bellarand snagged a beaten tin bucket by the han-dle to give over to her. Inside lay a hammer and a collection of old nails. *Take this,* he told her, *and grab that, too.* He pointed his horn at an old set of folding steps.

"This won't help," she warned him, "I've hidden the carrots where you'll never find them."

That's impossible, he retorted, tail swishing. *I have but to plumb the depths of your mind, and depending on my mood, I may not be gentle about it. But carrots are for later. For now, bring that and follow me.*

Molly didn't know if he was joking, lying, both, or neither. Heart in her throat, she picked up the stepstool and hauled it with the jangling bucket behind the unicorn. She kept her grumbling to a bare minimum, too, just because she didn't feel like chancing having the overgrown pony hoofing through her mind.

She paused at the tree line, worrying her bottom lip between her teeth. Molly had never ventured deeper than a few trees; all her time here, she'd kept to the drive or lawns surrounding the house. The wood was so vast, so *different* . . . she couldn't help a quiver of trepidation.

Come along, prodded Bellarand, *keep up.*

Molly pursed her lips and followed the unicorn, not wanting to seem a coward.

She shivered as they delved between the trees, leaving behind the meager warmth of the late-autumn sun. The air within the forest was cool and dense, rich with the scent of earth and decay. Browned leaves crunched underfoot, and Molly had to watch her steps for fear of catching a hidden root with her boot.

Bellarand led her with confidence, never deigning to inform her *why* she was hauling the supplies through the forest.

It became immediately clear, though, when they came to a towering oak tree littered with holes in the bark.

"Oh, no," she groaned. This was about the squirrels.

I asked for your help, not your commentary, he huffed.

"You didn't ask at all," she reminded him. Plopping the supplies on the ground, she planted her fists on her hips.

Please, Molly, help me?

She snorted. She was already here.

Unfolding the stool, she set it where he pointed and then hammered nails to attach it to the tree. All the while, the furry residents of the tree poked their little heads from their dens, angrily chattering and shrieking down at them.

Oh, yes, I'm coming for you now. Run, run while you can, Bellarand taunted.

More than a few acorns and twigs came sailing at them from above. Molly yelped when the sharp end of an acorn poked her head.

"All right, that's it!" Covering her head, she retreated away from the line of fire.

You see? Menaces, all of them.

Molly would've said something about the squirrels just defending their homes, but all her thoughts were wiped away at the sight of Bellarand climbing the stepstool. It creaked under his weight, but still he climbed, gaining ground.

Acorns came flying in vicious volleys, but he didn't stop, his red eyes burning as more and more squirrels gathered in the branches above.

The tip of his horn had just reached the first den when an ominous *crack* echoed through the forest.

From one moment to the next, the stepstool collapsed under his weight, splintering into a hundred small pieces. Bellarand whinnied in outrage as his horn scraped down the bark then sank into the tree.

He landed on his front hooves, but when he went to shake his mane, his horn stuck in the tree.

The squirrels barked in triumph as Bellarand bucked and pulled, trying to free his horn.

Molly pinched herself to make sure she wasn't hallucinating.

"D-do you need help?" she called, trying to contain her giggling.

No, he grumbled. *Leave me.*

"Are you sure—"

YES, he bit out, twisting his head to start working the horn loose.

Biting her lips together, Molly did as she was told, her peal of laughter joining the squirrels'. She wiped at her eyes, wet with how hard she laughed.

But as her boots crunched leaves and the breeze rustled her unbound hair, Molly's laughter slowly died in her throat.

Coming to a stop, she realized she'd been watching her feet, not the way, as she followed Bellarand here. They'd gone deep enough that she couldn't see the house beyond the trees—only more forest.

Her laughter turned to trepidation as she turned in a circle. She could faintly hear the chatter of the squirrels, but the trees cut the sound. Turning, turning, she couldn't tell which direction Bellarand was, nor where the house would be.

Molly was a creature of the city and house—she'd never spent any real time in the wilderness. Give her crowded buildings and overpopulated city squares, that she could handle. As she stood alone in the forest, the trees seemed to lean nearer, the ferns rustling with the wind as if they whispered to her.

The cool dampness of the air clogged Molly's nose as her heart nearly beat out of her chest. The exposed nape of her neck prickled with awareness of dozens, if not hundreds of eyes, watching her, waiting . . .

She was about to open her mouth and call for Bellarand when the ferns parted. Molly stared as the leafy fronds created a pathway for her between the trees.

A warm weight settled at her back, as if to push her along.

Was it . . . the house? The estate?

Allarion.

Sucking in a breath, Molly tried to be smarter and chipped off bark from trees she passed, marking the way she'd come. Not that her previous spot hadn't been entirely lost, but at least she knew it was somewhat close to where Bellarand and the squirrels did battle.

As Molly went, heart caught in her throat, the dense foliage continued to part, easing her way. That feeling of assurance didn't leave her, a gentle press on her shoulder that seemed to say, *that's the way.*

When the trees began to thin and the forest lightened, Molly quickened her pace. For a hopeful moment, she thought the forest had led her back out to the house.

Instead, Molly found herself walking into a clearing—a meadow, blanketed in soft grass and bordered on two sides by moss-covered boulders. Berry bushes crowded round what sounded like a babbling stream on another side. And at the center lay a figure covered in roots and vines.

The bottom fell out of Molly's stomach.

She knew that silvery hair.

"Allarion!" she gasped, running for him.

Molly stared at his prone form, his eyes closed, as roots and vines crawled over him. Little brown and white tendrils slithered up his arms and legs, and clusters of mushrooms pushed through the dirt by his head and feet. Ivy reached green fingers from the forest beyond, wrapping around his fingers and hair, and three great tree roots had erupted from the ground to secure him in a wooden vice at the hip. Wherever they touched him, a faint blue glow emanated from him, and his black veins stood in even starker relief against his skin, gone bone white.

They're eating him!

With a yelp, Molly fell on him, ripping at the roots and vines. She dug her nails into the dirt and pulled, plant matter snapping in her fists. The smell of sap and dirt filled the meadow as she frantically clawed at the plants, desperate to free him.

"Allarion! Allarion, wake up!" she cried.

Still the roots came, and Molly threw her weight behind pulling off one of the large woody roots. It clung to him tight, refusing to budge. She pulled and pulled, knees dragging through the dirt, but she couldn't free him.

"No!" she cried, flinging off roots and leaves. "You can't have him!"

Something curled around her wrist, and Molly screamed. Throwing herself backward, she struggled to free her arm, yanking with all her strength to get away, shoulder burning under the strain.

"Molly."

She gasped at the sound of her name.

Only then did she look at what had taken hold of her.

A hand. With purple-gray skin and long, tapered fingers.

Panting, Molly looked up the macabre form of Allarion covered in wriggling roots to see his eyes open and focused on her.

A sound of alarm buzzing in her throat, Molly crawled toward him, putting her hands on his shoulders to try helping him sit up.

"What are they doing?" she demanded. "Help me get them off you!"

"Please, don't worry for me, sweetling. This is all perfectly normal."

Another sound, this time a shriek of utter disbelief, escaped her. "This is *not normal!*"

He had the decency to wince. "I must ask for forgiveness again, my Molly. I'm afraid I failed to explain how it is I share my magic with the land."

Molly fell back onto her bum gracelessly.

"They're *eating* your magic?"

"Of a sort. They are certainly absorbing it. I come here to give over my excess magic."

"To help strengthen the circuit," she said, remembering how he explained the fae and their relationship to the magic inherent in the world.

Allarion smiled softly. "Just so."

Ever so carefully, Molly laid her hand on his chest. "So . . . they aren't hurting you?"

"No," he said, his hand coming to lay atop hers. "The opposite, in fact. I rest and they take what the forest needs. It binds us together."

Molly had a hard time swallowing back her gorge as it tried to rise in her throat—the sight of him there, roped to the ground by earthly bonds, was difficult to reconcile.

They lapsed into quiet, and before her eyes, the flora began to creep over him again. Her skin crawled and tingled when tendrils began to poke and flutter at her hand, and Molly bit her lips together, catching the scream in her mouth.

It was an odd feeling, but not . . . bad.

Strange. Not her favorite. But not *bad*.

Allarion chuckled softly. "Breathe," he reminded her.

She pulled in a breath, her discomfort slowly giving way to interest. The plants were ever so gentle with her, and they seemed just as careful with Allarion. Even the woody roots of the trees held him loosely, never putting their weight on his middle.

Before her eyes, more roots began creating intricate webs over him, rebuilding what she'd broken. Soon, he was almost cocooned in foliage, her hand with him.

Molly laid down in the grass beside him, marveling as moss sprung from the earth to pillow her head. Allarion watched her with a gentle gaze, his face one of the only places free of plant life.

"How long have you been doing this?" she asked in wonder.

"Today, about two hours. Before, every few days since I've been at the estate."

"This is how you gave the house life?"

"For the house, it was more a matter of working on it. Everything I touched to repair it was imbued with my magic."

She couldn't help a smile at that. "You brought it to life, piece by piece."

"I suppose I did, yes. But the estate itself, the forest, is different. It is already alive—sentient. It will never listen to me the way the house does."

"I'd think not. It's a *forest*." If it did obey him, she doubted its woodland creatures would be harassing Bellarand so. Or . . . perhaps it would, if Bellarand annoyed the fae enough.

"How long do you lay here for?"

"Usually a few hours. I think they'll be done with me soon."

"Bored of your taste?"

"Indeed," he laughed. Beneath the mat of foliage, his hand squeezed hers on his chest. "I will admit, it was a . . . harrowing experience the first time I came here. I wasn't sure if the forest would accept me and my foreign magic. The earth could have swallowed me up as easily as it took the magic."

Molly tried not to think about that. "You didn't do this back in the faelands?"

"No, there wasn't a need. My kind's bond to the faelands was already forged in ancient times. Between that and my people, the circuit was strong. At least until . . ."

"Amaranthe," she finished. Molly had found he didn't even like speaking her name.

"Indeed. Although, the first centuries of her reign weren't so polluted. It was only when the end was in sight that she usurped the order of succession."

First centuries. Molly chewed her cheek; she'd willfully not thought much about how truly old Allarion was—and it went far beyond the gap between their own ages. Everyone knew fae were nigh immortal. Did that mean, even for all his talk of fate and mates, he would live well beyond her mortal years?

A jealous heat burned in her belly to think of him moving another human woman into the house after the appropriate mourning period for her.

"Allarion . . . how old are you?"

Whatever she thought his response would be, it wasn't the hearty chuckle he gave. He smiled at her, showing off those fangs, and Molly couldn't help sidling a little closer, drawn inextricably by his pull.

"Now that is a complicated question for most fae."

"What, do you stop keeping track?" she joked half-heartedly.

Her stomach swooped when he nodded in assent.

"In your human years, it is many, I think. I remember a time when your kingdom was not a kingdom at all, but many small lands, with their own chiefs."

Molly swallowed hard. "That was over a thousand years ago."

"Truly? Well, over a thousand, then." He rolled his head to the side to regard her with those unnatural eyes, the roots folding and twisting with him. "It doesn't feel like a thousand years, if that makes sense. Time passes differently for fae, particularly in the faelands, surrounded by our magic. Life is simply . . . life."

Molly struggled with the idea, turning it over in her mind. "I suppose . . . life doesn't feel fast to the mouse who only lives a few years. It's just their time allotted."

One side of his mouth ticked up. "Indeed. Just their time." His face took a familiarly serious mien as he said, "But I must tell you, connected to me, your human life would be much longer. Not that of a fae, but not human, either."

Her mouth fell open in shock. "H-how long?"

"That I cannot say. Only that with our lives intertwined, yours shall lengthen and mine shall shorten."

"What?" she gasped. "You'll die?"

"We all do, someday. Even fae. My end shall just come a little sooner now."

"But . . ." Guilt gnawed at her to know that being tied to her was somehow a death sentence for this strange, incredible man.

His hand squeezed hers under the roots, offering his comfort. Molly held on tighter as the world spun.

"Don't despair," he said gently. "It isn't about the number of years but how they are lived."

She clung to him and those words. The prospect of having so many years—of outliving everyone and everything she'd ever known—expanded before her mind's eye, an incomprehensible journey she couldn't fathom. Like trying to see the path through the trees, her mind pushed against thinking in such lengths and temporality.

Molly rubbed at her temple. "That's . . . going to take a while to accept."

His mouth lifted in a wry grin. "We have the time, sweetling."

Despite herself, Molly guffawed. Snorting with a laugh, she propped herself up on her elbow, the worries of living for more years than she could count left in the grass for now.

There was something far more pressing, right in front of her.

Tucking her hair behind her ear, Molly leaned over Allarion to kiss him.

His lips went perfectly still under hers, but that was all right. She kissed him gently, a slow introduction, savoring the feel of him.

She heard his sharp intake of breath, and then his warm hand cupped the side of her face.

Molly pulled back at his touch, looking just in time to see the smallest roots disappearing back into the earth and the large tree roots sliding away from his middle.

"Molly."

She met his kiss with a smile as he pushed up to capture her mouth again. Free of the plant life, Molly framed his dear face in her hands, holding him at just the right angle.

Molly loved kissing. It'd always been her favorite part of flirting and even fucking. Too few of her past lovers hadn't kissed beyond a cursory duty to get into bed. Even Finn, who'd preferred to use his mouth to talk too much during sex. It was a shame, because a good kiss could make Molly amenable to quite a lot.

And now she knew—she loved kissing Allarion.

"Show me," he murmured against her lips, those purple eyes sparkling.

So she did. Molly showed him just how she liked to be kissed with teasing strokes and playful nips. He followed her lead, chasing her tongue when she coaxed his into her mouth to tease and circle.

His taste sparked on her tongue like his magic, electric. He tasted of spring water and ancient rites and somehow, the color purple. He was warm as cinnamon and cloves, smoky as a bonfire, and rich as the earth beneath them. This fae might have been the best thing she'd ever tasted, and she couldn't get enough.

Those big hands gripped her waist, his fingertips somehow so gentle but piercing with their need as he pulled her down to him. She laid over him as surely as the roots and vines had, cocooning him in her.

As the birds chirped and the forest distributed Allarion's magic, they lay in that meadow, kissing. Molly nearly melted with his sweetness, how every moment he learned and acted. He seemed to delight in pleasing her, and soon it was him delivering nips and laves, sparking a needy heat between her thighs.

Molly moaned into his mouth in encouragement, fusing their mouths together in something a little deeper, a little hotter. His hands roamed her back, kneading the wool of her coat in desperate circles. She gasped his name, needing air, but he gave her no quarter, those warm lips trailing down her neck to suck at her pulse point.

"Molly," he groaned, "tell me not to."

She was beyond words, mind too fuzzy with pleasure to make sense of what he said. Molly caught his mouth with hers again, sinking into his kiss. She needed less thinking, less *talking*, and more of him.

Fates, I should've been kissing him this whole time.

A hissing sound slithered against her lips, and Molly shuddered to feel those fangs. She traced each with her tongue, her cunt throbbing at their sharpness.

His fingers sank into her sides, and a needy sound escaped her throat.

"*Azai—*"

Ah, there you are. Without care or shame, Bellarand clomped into the meadow, stalking right up to hang his long face over them. He unceremoniously nudged Molly with his muzzle. *Come along, I need more thumbs.*

"We're busy," Allarion grumbled.

No, you're not. You're laying there playing with your mouths. You can do that any time. Quit lazing about and come be helpful.

"I told you before, I'm not helping you murder woodland creatures," said Allarion.

Molly laughed, rolling off him onto her back. She wouldn't be riding her fae in front of the unicorn. She didn't need to hear how two-leggeds were disgusting or a critique of her form or whatever other asinine thing Bellarand thought.

Allarion's face scrunched into nothing less than a pout to have her retreat, and it was Bellarand who got the brunt of his displeasure.

"You need to give up this pointless feud with the squirrels," he told the unicorn.

Me? They are the ones who started it. War criminals, all of them.

"If you would simply parley with them . . ."

Molly lay in the soft grass of the meadow, chuckling under her breath and watching the branches and leaves sway in a soft breeze as her fae and his stubborn pony argued over the merits of eradicating every squirrel on the estate.

Just another day at Scarborough, where strangeness was the norm.

Touching her lips, still tingling from his fervent kisses, Molly smiled to herself. Maybe not just another day. Maybe a very special day. A beginnings sort of day.

17

olly should have known that once she started, she wouldn't want to stop. That was the dangerous thing about kissing Allarion—now that she had, she wanted to again and again. And she did.

It was the most pleasurable kind of game, finding little ways to sneak a kiss. Molly enjoyed the surprise that always met her ambush, as if he was equal parts shocked and grateful that she'd kiss him again. If she was honest, that sense of gratitude went straight to her head—and her cunt.

Molly had been known to like a little forceful bed play; she enjoyed a partner who took charge and knew what they were about. Still, something about being the instigator had her pulse thrumming at her neck and between her legs all day. To know she was wanted so badly . . . there was no other feeling like it.

Her favorite was thanking him for another of his kind gestures by pulling him down to her by his stiff collar. She loved sliding her lips against his surprised smile, tasting his pleasure and devotion.

She also liked how he'd come to hover near as she cooked, wrapping his arms around her middle. Sometimes he hooked his chin over her shoulder to watch—unless she was cutting an onion, then she was on her own—or even balanced it on the crown of her head. Sometimes he hummed or sang as her meal boiled or sizzled, and he rocked them to the tune as Molly giggled and stirred.

Or perhaps her favorite had been the night they sat at the harpsichord, singing another lovelorn ballad of parted lovers, when he suddenly stood from the bench and held his hand out to her. Between the house and his magic, the instrument continued to play while she slid her hand into his and followed him to the center of the room.

Facing each other and holding hands, he led her through a popular jig, the harpsichord plinking merrily as they danced. His footwork was impeccable, and Molly laughed breathlessly as they twirled and stomped their feet. He even knew when to lift, taking her by the waist to hoist her high. Molly squealed, balancing on his shoulders as the music crescendoed.

Flushed with delight, Molly kissed him senseless after that dance. They swayed in the center of the room for a long while that night, her body tucked tightly to his, the music softening to a gentle melody.

That night was . . . perfect.

Another to add to her growing collection of perfect moments here with him.

When she stopped to think about all that had happened, Molly realized that maybe Allarion's fae sense of time had begun to rub off on her a little. Other than the deepening browns of late autumn, there were no other indications of the passage of time alone as they were out on the estate.

For all that Allarion had his goals to establish the estate and bring his friend here, Molly never felt rushed or the need to decide anything urgently. She filled her days however she pleased, happy with nurturing what was between them with lively chatter and gentle kisses.

She loved that his idea of grubby work clothes still included immaculately polished boots and a tailored jerkin and that showing off shirt sleeves somehow counted as casual. She loved how when he was confused, the top of his nose wrinkled in a charming little frown. She loved how often she saw his fangs, for he only showed them when he smiled. She loved that he endeavored to learn food and cooking despite not eating himself, and that he could wiggle his pointed ears, and that she could scandalize him with the simplest swears.

Molly didn't think she'd made a lover wait this long for sex before. She usually enjoyed sex and wasn't overly picky about the circumstances, but as with everything else about the fae, sex with Allarion would be different.

She knew it would be spectacular—if he was half as good at it as he was at kissing, she'd enjoy herself. Molly also knew that they were betrothed and therefore it'd be expected for them to *test those waters*, as it were. There was no true reason not to take him to bed if she wanted him.

And with each passing day, Molly became surer that, yes, she did want him. Badly.

Deciding to stay on the estate with him had implications that she meant to be his wife in all ways. She intended to give it her best consideration, and taking her fae betrothed to bed wouldn't be a chore. Still, crossing that threshold with him had implications of its own. A finality.

But with each passing day, Molly was coming to understand that that wasn't something to fear or dread. Indeed, as they spun and danced around that room to the music, her mind finally caught up to what her heart had been trying to tell her.

She wanted more than just kisses.

Old habits died hard, though. First, she needed to know if there was a line she couldn't cross. In her experience, every man could only be pushed so far. Molly needed to know where Allarion's was, for although he'd been nothing but patient, of any man she'd ever known, he had the most power to hurt her.

So as much as she enjoyed their kissing and dancing and cuddling, Molly had to be practical—at least this one last time—for her own peace of mind. But nothing said she couldn't have fun while doing it.

Allarion sat in his library, a late autumn storm blowing outside. Loose detritus clinked against the walls and windows, and the wind howled through the trees just beyond. All their activities had been housebound today, and even Bellarand had sought shelter inside—much to Molly's chagrin.

He couldn't help a grin remembering the ferocious argument as the unicorn went rooting around the kitchen looking for food as Molly tried to push him out the door. Allarion finally intervened when someone threatened to defecate on the clean kitchen floor and then someone else threatened to make horse jerky.

After dinner, Molly shooed him from the kitchen, and so Allarion wandered into the library. He hadn't found anything overly productive to do yet, instead consumed by staring at the missive that had arrived yesterday from Dundúran. He almost wished it'd been delayed a day, for if the words were washed away with the day's storm, he couldn't be faulted for missing the message.

With the end of autumn fast approaching, it would soon be time to leave for Dundúran to attend the seasonal council meeting. As a landholder, Allarion was beholden to attend at least twice a year. He'd been dutiful, attending at every opportunity.

That had been before Molly, though. An excuse to be in Dundúran was an opportunity to search for a possible human wife. He also enjoyed the company of Lady Aislinn and her blacksmith-turned-lord husband.

Allarion hadn't mentioned the message to Molly, nor their impending departure, for he wished neither to be so. The truth was, he didn't want to leave the estate. Everything had been going so well, *finally.* Every day with her was a boon as she found new little ways to surprise and delight him. Each day revealed a new aspect of his *azai* he savored, and he could feel the bonds between them strengthening.

He couldn't predict what a trip back to Dundúran might mean for their delicate courtship.

Allarion might have thought to forgo it altogether—he'd already attended his two council meetings this year—were it not for the underscored last line of Lady Aislinn's letter.

<u>Your presence is required, as requested by Princess Isolde Monaghan.</u>

Even with the seriousness of the message, Allarion stalled. He'd given himself the day to come up with an excuse, but alas, had found none. He couldn't deny, either, that his curiosity was piqued over what could be so important that the princess required him.

Still, upsetting the balance of his growing rapport with Molly wasn't something he relished. His reluctance to cause any more obstacles to their strengthening bond had led to his prevarication, yet he knew . . . he had to tell her. She'd asked for total honesty from him, and although fae never lied, omittance could still be a falsehood.

Slumping in his wingback chair, Allarion brooded on the letter. It sat on the desk, deceptively innocuous. He wanted to believe that such a trip away would mean nothing to their bond. He knew, rationally, that for the bond to have any hope of being truly set and strong, they would need to be away from the estate sometimes.

He'd assured her she wasn't his prisoner, and that had to be true even when he was receiving her kisses.

As if his thoughts summoned her, the door opened a moment before Molly breezed into the library. Straightening, Allarion smiled to see her coming to him.

His skin prickled with awareness that something was *different.*

Her hips swayed hypnotically as she walked, and her lids had fallen low over her sultry eyes. She still wore her customary billowy linen shirt and cotton trou, but rather than tucked under her embroidered stays and waistband of the trou, her shirt hung loose to her thighs.

Allarion's gaze snapped to her heavy breasts, his mouth running dry to see how they swayed with her gait, unbound. The smallest crescents of shadow curled beneath where the soft peaks of her nipples pressed against the fabric.

His breathing deepened, and he could feel his pupils dilating.

"Good evening, sweetling," he said.

"Good evening," she replied, not stopping until she'd come to stand beside him on the far side of the desk.

He gazed up at her hungrily, marking how her growing curls framed her heart-shaped face. Those brown eyes held a seductive glint in the warmth of the fire- and candlelight as she looked upon him. Allarion's palms itched to reach out and grab hold of her flanks, draw her between his spread knees, but he waited.

His little minx of a mate was testing him. Had been for days now. Perhaps she always had been, in different ways, but he recognized her subtle seductions. Finding ways to touch him, brushing her breasts against his arm or back, rounding those doe eyes at him, plumping her plush lips for a kiss.

He was immune to none of it, of course. She hardly needed to put effort into seducing him. One word would be enough.

But until that word was *yes,* he would play her game.

Still, she hadn't been quite so bold before. The sight of her there, her clothing loose, her gaze soft and sultry, battered at his iron resolve. His fangs ached with the temptation of her; she looked good enough to gobble up.

It took monumental will, but he forced himself to say, "There's news I must share with you."

Rather than growing serious or worried like he thought she would, Molly merely arched one of her brows. "All right," she breathed, then put her hand on his shoulder.

He watched in desperate delight as she climbed into the chair with him, straddling his lap. Unable to help himself, Allarion filled his hands with her hips, fingers digging into the generous flesh of her backside. Goddesses, how often had he thought of doing just this, sinking his fingers into her. Fingers, then cock, then finally, *fangs.*

Pulling her close, a groan escaped him as her soft, unbound breasts pressed against his chest. He could feel the hardness of her nipples through his own shirt, little points of warmth he wanted to suck and roll between his tongue and teeth.

With one of her small hands, Molly gripped his jaw and held him just as she wanted as she lowered her head to his. Allarion thrilled at the show of confidence, welcoming her tongue as it invaded his mouth.

That's it, take what's yours, azai.

He let her lead them in a dance of nipping teeth and swirling tongues, breathless to see what she'd demand next. Allarion was content to be the instigator in passion play, and there were many delights to take in being the dominant partner. One day soon, he very much hoped to take charge of his Molly's every pleasure and show her just how well a fae could sate his *azai.*

Still, witnessing this burst of confidence and power from her, who'd been so wary of him in their first days, pleased him to the very core. He wanted more of her demands and control. He wanted her to be the queen he knew she was.

Daring, he slid his hands up under her loose shirt, the pads of his fingers finding the warm burn of her skin. The breath shuddered out of him to feel how silky soft she was, and he knew immediately hers was his favorite texture. Nothing would compare to her now.

She rewarded him with a little moan into his mouth, and her hips levered down to give his lap a little of her weight. His abused, impatient cock throbbed at her nearness, begging for just another inch. He wanted to feel the kiss of her cunt there, even if it was through layers of fabric.

He felt the grin spread across her lips.

"Vixen," he accused.

"Mmhmm," she hummed, her hips beginning to rock in sweet little motions that teased his cock, straining against the seam of his trou.

When he remained still, receiving her teasing without reprisal, her grin widened into a smile. He rumbled to see her approval, and he hungrily accepted her praise as it rained down on him in kisses.

He wasn't above a little retribution, though. Hands seeking higher, they spanned her ribs, fingers tracing the dip of her spine. He ran his thumbs in teasing, testing circles at the undersides of her breasts, feeling how she burned here. Her flesh was somehow both firm and giving, a temptation he needed more of for fear of perishing without it.

Her scent bloomed through the library, a sweet, musky scent that tantalized the back of his tongue. Her hips began to work faster, snapping and rolling as she sought her pleasure.

Her kisses grew frantic, sucking friction that had his blood pounding through his veins. His hands grew greedier, needing to feel the full weight of her breasts.

But no sooner had he slid his hand around to take her in his palm than she broke her kiss and sat back on his knees.

Allarion stared at her, dazed, as she looked back. Her eyes had glazed with lust, and he took vicious pleasure at seeing how her lips were swollen and pink from his attentions.

Sucking in a deep breath, Molly asked, "What did you want to tell me?"

He blinked at her.

His head fell back against the chair, and a single laugh escaped his throat. "Ah, sweetling, you rob me of words and sense."

Her answering chuckle was a sound he knew would haunt his dreams in his next long sleep, low and lush. The minx kissed his cheek before leaning back to smile saucily at him.

Replacing his hands on her hips, he quirked a brow at her before lifting her up to deposit on the table. Stepping between her spread legs, taking up her vision, he planted his hands on either side of her.

He watched her pupils expand, and her enchanting pulse fluttered at the hollow of her throat. Allarion hovered over her for a long moment, regaining those words and senses. It was imperative he pass her test, win her challenge.

When the time came, he would lay her on the nearest surface and not let either of them up for days. He would have every part of her, again and again. He'd taste and indulge and *devour*—although, he was starting to suspect he'd never be truly sated.

Not with how badly she left him *aching*.

Snagging the letter from his desk, he lifted it to her eye line.

"We are summoned to Dundúran."

The playfulness fell from her face as she reached to take the letter. Her eyes skimmed over the lines, a frown gathering at her brow.

Allarion regretted being the one to ruin their play, and he disliked how she looked back at him with uncertainty, not quite meeting his eyes.

"You . . . want me to come with you?"

"Yes. You are mistress of this estate as much as I am master. We will stay a few nights in the castle."

"With Lady Aislinn?" Her eyes widened with astonishment.

"Indeed. All landholders are welcome to stay at the castle while the council is convened."

He didn't miss the excitement that sparkled in her eyes, but still she seemed hesitant.

"And . . . you're sure you want me to come?"

"Very much." With a crooked finger, he lifted her chin to make her meet his steadfast gaze. "This changes nothing, sweetling."

Slowly, Molly nodded, and Allarion decided he'd have to be content with that. She would just have to see for herself how proud he was to have her as his *azai*.

"Now, do you have questions, or shall I lay you back on this desk and show you just how a fae prefers to please his mate?"

Color bloomed on her cheeks, and Molly rediscovered her sultry smile.

Placing her hand on the center of his chest, she slipped off the desk, her body sliding down his. Allarion bit back his groan.

Minx.

"If we're leaving for the city soon, then I should probably get some sleep," she said, those big brown eyes batting up at him, daring him.

But he wouldn't break. She would come to him, tell him when she was truly ready. Not with teases or tests but with acceptance and enthusiasm.

"Good night, then, sweetling. May your dreams be of me."

Molly entered her bedchamber and shut the door behind her, her mind tumbling over the last hour. She wanted to ponder the prospect of going to Dundúran, of staying in the castle itself, but she couldn't think past how much she *throbbed* between her thighs.

She couldn't decide if she was pleased with the night and still not finding Allarion's line. Fates, she'd pushed him so far, she'd found her own breaking point.

Grumbling with interrupted lust that was entirely her own fault, Molly paced the room for a few tense moments before finally barking, "House, ignore me for an hour, please!"

The drawers of the armoire opened and closed before falling silent. Everything went quiet, so that the only sound was the howling wind outside and her own agitated breathing.

"House?"

When nothing rattled or creaked, Molly decided she'd have to trust that the house had turned its attention elsewhere.

Muttering under her breath, Molly ripped off her trou and climbed into her big, soft, empty bed. Flopping onto her back, she spread her legs and got to work.

A moan slipped past her lips to feel just how hot and slick she was. Fates, she'd gotten carried away with him in the library. She stroked herself to the memories of rocking on his lap, teasing the hard bar of a cock she could feel trapped beneath his trou. The way he rumbled and groaned into her greedy mouth had her cunt clenching, and Molly had no choice but to use both hands, sliding two fingers inside her while she circled her clitoris.

Never usually one for delayed gratification, she prodded and pinched the sensitive nub, shocks of pleasure shooting down her legs and up her belly.

His eyes, fates, she'd never had a man look at her the way Allarion did. As if he wanted to eat her up. That gaze spoke of endless nights of good, hard fucking, yet his touch had been so gentle. Her skin broke out in gooseflesh and her nipples tightened almost painfully remembering the skating glance of his thumbs on the undersides of her tits.

If she hadn't pulled back when she did, she'd be riding that fae cock even now.

Why aren't I? Her thought was grumpier than she'd anticipated, and a whimper burst from her lips.

It'd all made sense to her earlier, when she'd come back to her room to divest of her stays and outer layers. Seduce him, test him—it was a good plan, until it wasn't.

As her soaked fingers shuttled in and out of her dripping cunt, Molly wasn't sure if she'd passed her own challenge. Playing with fire often got you burned, and she felt like she might combust with how much she needed his touch.

Her tits ached for attention, but her hands were too busy. It was all too much, and with a growl, she finished herself off with a trusty stroke of her callused thumb over her clitoris.

Molly heaved as her cunt clenched down on her fingers, trying to grasp and suck at what wasn't there. She stroked and stroked herself, prolonging her pleasure, until finally, she collapsed back on the bed, spent.

As she lay there, sleep blurring the corners of her vision, Molly drifted on errant, unlinked thoughts.

Need to finish the dress so I have something to wear.

And, *Need to truly seduce him.*

Allarion's shoulders hunched as he bent over himself, straining the seams of his tunic. Teeth exposed to the air in a vicious snarl, he leaned his weight against the doorframe of Molly's bedchamber, his other hand manhandling his angry cock.

He strained his ears to hear Molly's small sounds of pleasure over the cacophony of his breath sawing in and out of his lungs. Although feeling a beast looming there at her door, he couldn't help himself. Couldn't help following her as she'd fled back to her room, nor listening as she began to pleasure herself.

One day very soon, those sounds would be *his.* He would know their very taste as she made them into his mouth while his cock slid inside her wet heat, taking what he knew to be his.

There was a brutal pleasure in knowing that even as she tested and teased him, she wasn't immune. Her body knew what it wanted, no doubt sensed the pleasures he could give. Very soon, her heart and mind would understand it, too.

And when that day came, Allarion would *feast.*

A mewling little moan emanated from under her door, and he shuddered with orgasm at the sound. He painted the door with his spend, unable to stop as his hips thrust home, seeking a warmth that wasn't yet there.

His mouth hung open as he panted with release, his body shaking from the force.

Yet, his blasted fangs still ached something fierce.

From the darkness, a bucket and rag came sliding down the hall to clean his mess. Pushing back from the door, Allarion tucked himself away.

He might have been embarrassed at the sight of his spend all over her door, proof of his beastly, desperate need for her, if it didn't satisfy some deep, primeval part of him. Marking his territory was a base, animalistic need—no doubt one Bellarand would approve of. Still, Allarion couldn't say he regretted it.

Soon, sweetling. Soon you will be mine in all ways.

18

Molly found it bittersweet saying farewell to the house as they prepared to leave for Dundúran. Turning to wave one more time, she called, "We'll be home soon, house!"

She didn't miss the goofy little grin that brought to Allarion's face. Molly hadn't missed his growing worries over returning to the city and what it might mean for them, either. While she did intend to visit her family and see how they were getting on with their new fortune, she also intended to stay with Allarion—both in Dundúran and coming back to Scarborough.

She'd promised herself a seduction of her stoic fae, and she wouldn't be denied.

Preparing for their trip had taken most of Molly's time, leaving her too tired by evening to enact any of her seductive plans. Still, she was happy she made the effort as she stood in the cold morning with a brand-new gown, every seam straight and the embroidery some of her best work. Having a pretty new garment gave her a little more confidence to ride into Dundúran Castle alongside her fae.

Molly watched as Allarion kitted Bellarand with his riding blanket, a set of stirrups, and their bags.

Careful, the unicorn complained, *I'm not some common pack mule.*

"And yet you're still an ass to me," Molly quipped, grinning evilly when the unicorn shot her a glare.

"Don't start," laughed Allarion. "We haven't even gotten on the road yet."

Snickering, Molly allowed Allarion to hoist her up onto Bellarand's back.

NOTHING FUNNY, NOW, she thought, focusing on the back of his head.

Bellarand grunted, ears twitching. *No need to shout.*

Allarion swung up behind her, arms going round her to take hold of the loose reins looped around Bellarand's head. They were more for something to hold onto rather than to lead—the unicorn went where he pleased.

Molly settled back into Allarion's wide chest, humming contentedly to feel his firm form. She might've entertained ideas of a little seduction if she didn't know the surly unicorn would buck her off immediately for it.

Bellarand started forward, and Molly leaned around Allarion to wave one last time at the house. All the shutters on the front façade swung in farewell.

"Do you think the house will be terribly lonely?" she asked.

"Most likely."

Allarion got a pouting frown for that. She already felt terrible for leaving the house all alone. As she'd sat embroidering, Molly made sure to explain at length to the house that they weren't leaving for good like its last family had, that it was only for a few days.

I think it will enjoy the time alone, Bellarand mused. *Finally, it will have some peace and quiet.*

Molly knew exactly where this was going. "I *don't* sound like an orc going to battle stomping down the stairs! I don't stomp at all!"

Those of us with sensitive ears would disagree.

"Overgrown pony."
Tone-deaf titmouse.
Allarion sighed mightily.

Her second ride through the countryside was far more pleasant than her first. Without the weight of dread and the night descending on her, Molly was able to enjoy the rolling landscapes of the Darrowlands. She admired the grassy knolls and shimmering brooks. It was too late in the season for wildflowers, but a few trees still had their autumn colors.

"They are your colors," Allarion remarked as she gushed over a handful of orange, yellow, and red leaves.

Molly blushed. "A little less dramatic than red and purple, to be sure."

"Less severe," he amended, "and warmer."

Oddly charmed by the strange compliment, Molly tipped her face up and got the kiss she wanted. And she only yelled at Bellarand a little bit for jostling them when the kissing went on awhile.

They stopped a few times to allow her to stretch her legs and get a bite to eat, but Molly didn't want to be the one to make them late and so hurried through her stretching and snacking.

Allarion smiled gently from atop the unicorn as she shook to get the blood back to her lower extremities. "You will grow used to it," he assured her.

Molly decided not to argue—or point out that practice would require cooperation from Bellarand. Allarion pulled her up onto the unicorn's back when she was ready, and they set off again as the morning eased into afternoon.

When she realized she recognized the path and nearby hills, nerves began to pinch her middle. Not long after, they rounded a hillock to find the grand silhouette of Dundúran spread out before them on the banks of the Shanago River.

Molly couldn't help how her breath hitched to see the city again. She hadn't been away terribly long, but it still felt like a lifetime. So much had changed. It was a new perspective, to approach the city from the north, on the back of a big unicorn.

They entered from the north gate, passing beneath the teeth of the drawn portcullis. Bellarand's hooves clipped on the paved streets as they climbed toward the castle, nestled in the heart of the city.

Through it all, curious eyes followed them, the hubbub of the city shushing at the sight of the fae and unicorn—and woman riding with them. She was suddenly grateful she'd taken Allarion up on borrowing one of his cloaks; the fur collar provided warmth on their ride while the draping velvet and silk suited Bellarand far more than her brown wool coat.

At least in the cloak, she looked a little less like the odd one out.

Molly tried to keep her head high and her gaze forward, but she didn't think she imagined hearing her name as they rode past. Folk flocked from the squares and public houses to see the sight of a fae and unicorn. Although Allarion and Bellarand weren't strangers to the city, before their coming to the Darrowlands, the sight of any otherly folk had been exceedingly rare.

She couldn't truly blame the crowd—Allarion did cut a regal figure.

She would've been proud to see so many gawking at him in awe had those eyes not then turned onto her. Confused frowns darkened the wonder at seeing a fae and unicorn as people puzzled out who rode with them.

Her stomach churned the longer they rode, so when the castle gates came into view, Molly sucked in a breath of relief. They passed under another portcullis, the guards on either side bowing their heads in respect to Allarion.

The wide courtyard of the castle spread before them, not nearly as full as the day of Lady Aislinn's wedding, but still plenty crowded. Many of the demesne's landholders had come, and most had brought a retinue. The decorative poplars, flowerbeds, and statuary were almost hidden behind the crowds of servants, officials, and knights. Some stood chatting while others hurried about on business.

At the grand entrance of the castle—a pair of arched wooden doors at the top of a set of curved shallow steps—a line of horses and carriages had queued to unload their noble passengers.

Bellarand, of course, had no care for protocol or politeness and brought them right to the front step of the castle. Nobody protested, though a few disgruntled rumbles came from the carriages two or three back.

The courtyard went silent as the unicorn stopped. Allarion dismounted with a great swish of his cloak onto the polished white limestone steps.

Molly's gaze clung to him, her nerves growing to a buzzing hive in her chest. When he reached up for her, her hands trembled as she laid them on his shoulders. Taking her by the waist, he lifted her off Bellarand's back to stand beside him.

She locked her knees and stared at his chest, afraid if she looked anywhere else—like behind her, at all the noble people staring at them— she'd faint. Or worse, vomit.

Allarion made quick work of pulling off their bags, hefting the straps onto one shoulder before offering her his free arm. Molly grabbed hold, clutching his forearm with her other hand. His gaze turned concerned when he looked down at her, but she could only shake her head.

Not here.

She just needed to get inside.

Allarion regarded her another moment before leaning down to place a gentle kiss on her forehead. The crowd behind them murmured as they turned to ascend the steps.

Enjoy playing politics, was Bellarand's farewell, but Molly didn't dare look back.

Two stairs up, she had to let go with one hand to gather his voluminous cloak before she tripped and broke her nose on the castle steps. She watched her footfalls, each thudding in her head like a thunderclap.

Tension gathered behind her left eye, and she had to remind herself to breathe.

She focused so much on her steps that it was almost startling when they came to the top. Molly looked up just in time to see them through the arched threshold of the castle.

Inside was a richly tapestried atrium with a grand staircase leading up to the second level. The sight reminded her of the one back at Scarborough, and she welcomed the distraction of the thought.

They hadn't gotten more than three steps inside when two staff stepped forward to take their baggage and outerwear. Molly pulled off the cloak by rote but immediately wished it back on. Her neck was cold without the collar, and, much worse, she realized her new dress was hardly better than the uniforms the staff wore.

The woman who took their cloaks bobbed a polite curtsey and hurried off, but the man with their bags couldn't help a long look at Molly in her white muslin dress.

Allarion took her hand and tucked it back at his elbow, but that only drew her attention to the luxurious fabric of his tunic, with its silver threads, silver buttons, and embroidered cuffs. A flush of embarrassment stained her cheeks—she didn't even look a peahen beside her peacock but a drab little wren.

The feeling only grew stronger as they ascended this second staircase and entered the great hall.

It was a beautiful room, with dark wood beams that resembled the boning of a ship's hull. Banners of all colors, boasting the heraldry of the many Darrowlands families, hung from them, as well as six circular brass chandeliers studded with flickering candles. Narrow, arched windows set into the thick stone wall allowed in the afternoon light.

That light glittered off the gold and jewels adorning the hundred or so people already gathered in the hall. Satin, silk, and velvet gleamed in the warm light, and more than a few women positively glittered with how the light caught in their jewels and refracted back on the stone walls.

Allarion walked into the room with confidence, practically dragging Molly behind him. She forgot to breathe again when those nearest the entrance turned to mark their arrival.

Many bowed their heads to Allarion, murmuring greetings, but then their curious gazes turned on Molly. None seemed to know what to do about the woman standing beside the fae, and she wished desperately to melt into Allarion's side and disappear.

She swore the chatter of the crowd quieted as more and more heads turned to behold the new, strange arrivals. Everywhere Molly looked, she found a pair of eyes staring back at her, some shadowed by a frown, others punctuated by imperiously arched brows.

Who is this? those gazes said. *Who's brought this into our midst?*

Allarion crossed through the hall, acknowledging those who greeted him but not stopping to strike up a conversation. Molly was grateful, unable to bear so many eyes, and when her fae came to a far wall and decided to take up residence with it at his back, she found a sliver of relief.

Yet, standing there clinging to him made them an easier target of all those gazes. Her stomach sank watching hands come up to cover mouths as heads bent together.

Molly had never been looked at so much. Sure, she was used to getting some attention at the tavern, but to be the focus of so many, to know that the words whispered behind decorated fans and delicate hands were about her and Allarion . . .

When a servant walked past bearing a tray of goblets, Molly took one just for something to hold onto other than Allarion's arm. As she took the goblet, she and the serving woman locked gazes. The woman opened her mouth to ask something—*aren't you needed in the kitchen?*—when another couple approached.

Molly could hardly hear them introduce themselves over the buzzing in her ears, and the wine in her goblet came dangerously close to sloshing over the rim with how badly her hand trembled. The man and woman executed elegant bows, and she could feel Allarion nod, but Molly stood frozen, cheeks aflame and heart beating right out of her chest.

"And who is this with you, my lord?" asked the woman, her smile all teeth.

Allarion laid his hand on Molly's where it clutched at his sleeve. "She is Molly Dunne, my betrothed."

More arched brows.

"Betrothed?" repeated the noblewoman, her pearl earrings bobbing as she looked to her companion.

"Dunne," said the man, "I'm not familiar with the name."

Both looked to Molly as if she could spout some rich estate or noble line to sate their curiosity and make sense of her beside Allarion.

Her throat seized. She didn't dare open her mouth for fear of croaking.

The couple asked more questions—*wherever did you meet, how long have you been engaged, why hadn't their handfasting been announced*—which Allarion answered in the fewest syllables possible. If she could think beyond her own panic, she might've thought him annoyed with their questions, but she couldn't do much beyond forcing her stinging eyes from unleashing her embarrassed tears.

"And your gown . . ." said the woman.

Molly's gaze snapped to hers, and she bit her cheek.

Don't, don't, don't.

"Forgive me, but who are you?" Allarion asked suddenly.

The question took all the humans aback.

The woman recovered first, trying to smooth the awkwardness with a tinkling laugh that grated on Molly's nerves.

"As I said, we are the Braithwaites of Longmere." She bobbed her head. "I am Fiona and this is my brother, Dougal."

"Have we met before?"

The brother and sister exchanged looks of growing alarm. "No," said Dougal, "we haven't."

"Which is why we made introductions."

"You ask many questions of those you haven't met before," was Allarion's observation.

Color bloomed on Fiona's cheeks. "Well . . . how are we to get to know one another without questions?"

"Are we neighbors? Do our lands share a border?"

"No . . ." answered Dougal.

"Do you wish to present business prospects?"

"No, we . . ."

"Then why should I want to get to know you? I will allow yours aren't my customs, and I am still unfamiliar with your Eirean ways, but for my kind, your questions are presumptuous."

Fiona's mouth opened and closed like a fish on a hook.

It was Dougal who had the sense to bow and apologize. He drew his sister away by her elbow, and they disappeared back into the crowd.

Molly might've laughed at their retreat had her insides not been twisted in so many knots.

"They are very strange people," Allarion muttered.

Something between a laugh and a relieved huff of air erupted from Molly, and she turned to drop her forehead onto Allarion's arm, hiding her manic giggles.

She didn't look up again until she'd gotten herself under control. When she straightened, she found Allarion's concerned gaze upon her again.

"I'll be all right," she assured him. "This is just . . . very new to me."

He nodded slowly. "I don't understand it myself. But I will never abide rudeness, especially not at your expense."

More tears pricked her eyes. Molly hugged his arm to her and rested her cheek on his bicep. Somehow, she felt a little better despite the horrifically awkward encounter with the Braithwaites. The room had stopped spinning, at least.

Of course, as soon as she had the thought, a familiar golden head appeared nearby.

Molly just barely contained her gasp to see Lady Aislinn approaching with her half-orc husband, Lord Hakon. It was surreal to see them stop before her and Allarion, even more so to have the noble couple nod in acknowledgement to them when they bowed in respect.

Allarion greeted Lady Aislinn and Lord Hakon warmly, a stark contrast to the Braithwaites. And when Lady Aislinn looked over at Molly, asking without words for an introduction, Allarion seemed to stand straighter and taller as he said, "My lady, it pleases me to introduce you to my betrothed, Molly Dunne."

"It's a pleasure to meet you, Molly," said Lady Aislinn, every bit as beautiful and graceful as Molly believed her to be, having only ever seen her from a distance.

"The pleasure is mine, my lady. Thank you for having us here."

"You are doing well, Miss Dunne?" asked Lord Hakon.

She blinked up at the hulking halfling, and it took a moment to remember—"Yes," she hurried to assure him, "I meant it that day. I . . . I'm happy with Allarion."

Molly smiled up at her fae, realizing the truth of her words.

Surreal as it all was, she'd never had happier days than those at Scarborough.

"Thank you for worrying over me, though," Molly said. "You were kind to come after me."

Lady Aislinn smiled in good humor. "I wanted assurance that Allarion hadn't kidnapped one of my citizens."

Another manic little giggle burst out of her, and Molly was quick to slap her hand over her mouth.

Conversation eased into Allarion's progress with Scarborough, and Molly was content to let her fae lead. Still, Lady Aislinn and Lord Hakon asked her gentle questions, no doubt trying to suss out anything worrisome or false in Allarion's account. It warmed her to know that the Darrow heiress cared over a common barmaid's welfare, but she made more assurances that she was comfortable and settled at Scarborough.

"I hope you will join us at the high table for dinner," said Lady Aislinn. "I'd love to hear all about how you two found each other."

"Of course, my lady," Allarion said, ignorant of how Molly's heart skipped at the thought, "and hopefully we will learn why the princess herself requires my presence specifically."

Lady Aislinn seemed to deflate. "Yes, that. I believe she carries letters from her parents, the king and queen. I have arranged a meeting for the both of you in the front solar the day after tomorrow."

"It's nothing bad, I hope."

Lady Aislinn could only shrug. "Verbose as the princess is, she's been silent on the matter to me. She says her business is between the two of you.

"Then I shall endeavor to live with the mystery another night," said Allarion.

The couple agreed, and once dinner arrangements had been confirmed, farewells were said. Before they turned to leave, though, Lady Aislinn's gaze snagged on Molly's sleeve.

"Oh, Molly, that embroidering is absolutely beautiful!"

19

When they were finally shown to their room after an event-ful dinner—Molly still couldn't quite believe she'd conversed with the Crown Princess of Eirea, who was staying on in Dundúran through the winter—it took all of her willpower not to slump into the bed, gown, shoes, and all. Her back ached from all the standing still and her face ached from all the forced smiling.

But no, she couldn't risk wrinkling her gown. It was the only good thing she had, and she'd need it for tomorrow's council meeting. Molly ate that night's dinner so slowly and carefully, knowing she couldn't afford to stain her dress—nor slop in front of Lady Aislinn and Princess Isolde.

Still, she couldn't help wilting onto the cushioned seat at the foot of the four-post bed. Their room was lovely, the walls covered in richly stained wood paneling, several small tables laid about the room covered in candelabras, and a warm fire crackled in the small hearth. The room was all rich browns, reds, and greens and sumptuously fur-nished—yet, so tired was she that it could've been a haybale and she'd have sunk into it gratefully.

Her overwrought mind snagged on the sight of Allarion unbuckling an obscene number of daggers from his belt. Where had he been hiding them all?

"Are you supposed to have so many weapons in the castle?" She couldn't remember them being searched, but he'd left his sword strapped to Bellarand, and no one else carried weapons other than the guards. Molly had heard that since the threat of Lady Aislinn's brother and the condemned Lord Bayard the previous winter, security had been quite tight within the castle walls.

He looked up, seemingly surprised by the question. "I don't know." Then, with a frown, he amended, "I don't really care, either. Most of my magic is tied up at the estate, so these are my best means of defending you."

"Are you expecting to need to defend me?" she wondered.

"No, of course not. I wouldn't have brought you had I thought otherwise." Stepping closer, Allarion brushed her cheek with the backs of his fingers. "Your safety is paramount to me, sweetling."

Blushing, she nodded her understanding. Honestly, it did feel good to know that her fae warrior was armed and knew what to do with the business end of a blade. She'd never seen him in a fight, of course, but he'd regaled her with plenty of stories from his days as a warrior in the Fae Queen's service, and she'd seen for herself how he could train for hours without relenting. She'd witnessed her share of bar brawls, enough to know that her fae would be quick and deadly in a fight.

Allarion went about turning down the bed as Molly cracked her neck and knuckles.

"Is the room to your liking?" he asked.

"It's wonderful," she said, biting back a yawn.

"It's the one I prefer when I stay here."

That piqued her interest. "Do you usually keep a room when you come here? Even though you don't sleep?"

"Indeed," he said. "I've found that the people of Dundúran find my walking about at night discomfiting, so I keep inside. Usually I just read."

Molly grinned despite her tiredness, imagining how harrowing it'd be to run into him in the wee hours. Especially if he wore his customary cloak.

"I can find somewhere else to spend the night, though, if you prefer."

Molly frowned up at him, not quite understanding why he'd offer. Rubbing her eyes, she tried to work some of the stinging tiredness from them so she could have an intelligible conversation.

Before her blurry eyes, Allarion knelt on the ground at her feet. "However," he said, gently picking her foot up by the ankle to balance her heel on his knee, "I would much prefer to stay with you."

Her lips parted, but no words managed to come out as she watched him tenderly unlace her boot and pull it and then her sock from her foot. Molly's head fell back on the bed, a lusty moan erupting from her lips when he began to massage her foot, starting with the arch.

"Whatever you want," she gasped, "just keep doing that!"

A low chuckle filled the room, making parts of Molly stir despite her frayed nerves and exhaustion.

He worked methodically, just as she knew he would. There was always a method to whatever Allarion did—he approached each task with a warrior's mind, intent on performing his work effectively.

Molly admired his effectiveness.

By the time he finished with one foot and moved onto the next, her leg flopped as if boneless, her toes curling with delight.

He'd managed to work most of the tension from her legs when he went and ruined it by asking, "What did you think of today?"

Sighing, Molly sat up straight. "It was . . . a lot. Lady Aislinn is lovely, and the princess is obviously smart as a whip. But I just . . ."

Her gaze fell to her lap, and she had to stop herself from picking at the threads of her gown.

"Just what?" His hands stopped moving as he looked at her in concern, but a poke with her toe got that wonderful massage restarted.

"I didn't like how much they looked at me," she admitted, not quite able to keep his gaze when she said it.

"They admired your beauty," he said, and Molly's heart ached to hear the sincerity in his voice. He truly believed that.

Molly leaned forward to kiss his cheek. "You're sweet for saying so. But that's absolutely not what they were doing. Everyone was wondering why you'd brought a nobody in from the street."

Allarion's eyes went wide with shock. "Why should they think such a thing?"

Molly shrugged. "What were they supposed to think?"

"That you are my *azai,* the new Lady Scarborough."

She did like the sound of that, but still. "Why should they know that? There you are, looking handsome in your finery." She traced a finger down the exquisite threading on his sapphire blue tunic. "And there's me beside you, a nobody in a plain dress."

The words brought a sudden sob, but Molly kept it in her throat. It was silly to cry over not having the prettiest gown—especially when she hardly wore them. Allarion didn't seem to mind or notice what she wore around the estate, and Molly had always preferred a pair of trou over skirts.

Still, it was a sharp, feminine sort of pain to know that everyone had looked at her and found her lacking. All the hours she'd poured into the embroidery hadn't mattered one whit to the likes of Fiona Braithwaite; they saw her unfashionably short hair and simple dress and found her wanting.

While Molly did cling to Lady Aislinn's compliment and her knowledge that she was skilled in a way that Lady Fiona could never be, such gifts and her plain, common clothes were flimsy armor against that stare.

Allarion knelt in silence for a long while, that fae gaze of his intense as he regarded her. Molly bit her tongue for fear of saying something else to make herself feel even smaller. It all may have been a silly thing to be hurt over, but that didn't stop the bruise to her pride.

When Allarion did speak, it was low and serious, making her lean forward to hear him properly.

Voice thick, he said, "I fear I must ask for your forgiveness again, sweetling. I sent you into battle without proper kit." His mouth pulled down in a grave line. "I've failed you."

Molly gasped, hurrying to cup his cheek in her hand. "You've done nothing wrong," she assured him, "you didn't know."

"But I did. I understand the importance of presentation and how courts are full of jackals hunting for any weaknesses. Dress is far more than vanity, it is a statement."

Drawing her hands to his lips, he kissed her knuckles. "I will make this right, sweetling."

"Allarion, it's all right. I can make do."

"You absolutely cannot. Whatever you need, you shall have."

"What, are we going to beat down the door of a dressmaker first thing tomorrow? The council meeting starts soon after breakfast."

But by the determined set of his sharp jaw, Molly suspected yes, that's exactly what they were going to do.

Relief fluttered in her belly, even as she sent whatever unfortunate dressmaker they found tomorrow her well-wishes for a restful night's sleep.

"We will find you whatever will make you happiest. If we miss the council meeting—well, I was summoned to speak with the princess, not attend the meeting."

"That's true . . ."

Nodding, the matter no doubt settled in his mind, Allarion stood and pulled Molly up with him.

"Now, will you let me make my amends?"

"You have nothing—"

With a crooked finger, Allarion lifted her chin. "Sweetling, I want to make you feel good, to show you how beautiful you are to me. Will you let me?"

A flush of heat cascaded through Molly so quickly, her head spun. Arousal dulled her exhaustion as she plucked at the buttons of his tunic.

Looking up at him from under her lashes, she asked, "What did you have in mind?"

That hungry gaze swept over her, his hands coming to frame her hips. "I'm going to strip you down and finally look my fill of you. Then I will lay you back on that bed and please you until you beg me to stop."

Her breath stuttered in her lungs. "Is that all?"

"For now, yes. When I sink my cock inside you for the first time, we will be in our home, in your bed. Until then, my mouth will have to suffice."

"I suppose that depends on how well you use your mouth," she teased.

One of his fine brows arched with her challenge, and a cocky grin, the likes of which she'd never seen on him before, unspooled on his lips to make her tingle *everywhere*.

She ate up the sight of that grin as he set about undressing her. First were the laces of her gown, and he helped her step out of the pool of fabric. He laid it with infinite care on the armchair by the fire, ensuring it wouldn't wrinkle overnight.

His nostrils flared to see her thin stockings and good set of stays, a pretty concoction of soft cotton and silk that molded to her breasts and middle and had cost her months of tips. She'd known it was worth the price for the comfort, as well as the look of any man who saw her in it. Allarion didn't disappoint.

Those amethyst eyes sparkled as they roved over her curves, and his hands soon followed. With gentle fingertips, he traced down her arms and then up again, leaving gooseflesh in his wake. She could feel the puff of his breath on the tops of her breasts as he loomed above her, and she was flattered by how his breathing had gone deeper.

Molly wasn't a stranger to having her body admired and lusted after. Even with her soft middle and pockmarks, men always loved a big pair of tits. Yet, having Allarion look at her like that—like she was better and more precious than velvet and jewels and magic—brought a novel thrill.

Despite the day, under his gaze, Molly did feel beautiful.

More damn tears pricked at her eyes, but they were happy this time.

Fates, she wanted him to never stop looking at her like that.

Like with everything he did, Allarion unlaced her stays and stockings with methodical precision, his attention never wavering. Molly's own breathing deepened as she felt her clothing loosen from her body, and by the time he pulled away her stays, her nipples had hardened, eager for his attention.

Allarion's lips parted on a needy groan, and Molly stood a little taller, arching her back.

He didn't immediately grab for her tits, which both impressed and disappointed her, but instead knelt again to unlace her stockings. The knotted strings were nothing to his questing fingers, and he kept her gaze as he gathered them down her legs. She used a hand on his shoulder for balance to step out of them and then, finally, for the first time, she was completely bare in front of her fae.

A shuddering breath fanned her middle as he did as he'd said he would and looked his fill.

He'd barely touched her skin, and yet she burned. When he reached out to touch one of the deeper pockmarks on her upper thigh, Molly nearly jumped.

His eyes softened with tenderness. She'd told him of her beginnings in the village with her parents, and how the plague had taken that all away. Molly had spent many years being ashamed of the marks left behind and often resented the reminder. There were many days she hated the sight of them.

"I have many of them," she warned him. She'd been lucky at least to avoid scars on her face and neck, but there were still many spots and marks across her lower half.

His fingers were so gentle, his gaze so tender as he said, "Every leopard has her spots. These are yours."

He kissed the pockmark, and then one at her hip, and another on her other thigh.

Molly carded her fingers through that silvery hair, loving the silky glide under her palm almost as much as his easy acceptance. Yet again, he took her breath away with the boundlessness of his devotion. Sure, he could be sweettalking her into bed—he wouldn't have to work hard to do it. But as she dug her fingers into his scalp when he turned a kiss onto her lower belly, Molly knew, deep down inside where all her deepest hurts lurked, that he meant it.

Fae don't lie.

Smiling up at her, he rose suddenly and brought her with him, picking her up only to lay her down on the bed. Molly scooted up to lay on the fluffy pillows, biting her lip in delight to see him looming over the side of the bed.

When he went to plant a knee in the bed, though, she stopped him with a foot on his chest. He looked down at it as she toed a button on his tunic.

"Off," she said. "It's only fair."

He arched his brow at her again, wrapping his hand around her foot. Her ankle got a nipping kiss before he stepped back to undress himself. Molly watched greedily as he shed layer after layer, revealing a little more of his true form beneath. Her pulse quickened when his undershirt was peeled away, revealing pale purple-gray skin pulled taut over densely packed muscle.

He was all coiled strength, not a shred of fat on him. He almost seemed too skinny, his ribs prominent over an etched abdomen. No hair decorated his finely wrought chest, although he did have flat, dusky purple nipples. His shoulders were rounded with muscle, his arms lanky and lean. He looked every bit the fae warrior, stripped down to his most elemental.

His boots and socks went next, but when he tried again to join her on the bed with his trou still in place, Molly stopped him with her foot.

"Those too." He'd said he meant to focus on her, but Molly wanted all of him.

"Not tonight, sweetling. I need the reminder."

Molly pouted, opening her mouth to argue, but he was quicker. Levering onto the bed, he was suddenly above her, his starlight hair falling around them. Molly fell back into the pillows, her hands coming up to run over his flanks and feel all that hard strength for herself.

She was easily distracted, his mouth taking hers in a searing kiss.

Molly didn't know who had the upper hand anymore as his mouth made love to her, confident tongue swirling around hers, teasing lips coaxing her to chase and claim. She wasn't sure it mattered, not truly, not when he kissed all her thoughts and cares away.

Those kisses moved down to her chin then neck and throat. He lingered there, his body trembling beneath her hands. Her pulse kicked below his hovering lips.

With a sigh, Allarion delved lower. Fluttering kisses rained down on the tops of her breasts, the tip of his nose teasing her sensitive skin.

"The way I have *dreamed* about these," he said reverently, plumping one in his big hand.

Molly chuckled as he groaned in ecstasy, his fingers sinking into the plush give of her flesh.

"What have you dreamed?" she breathed, hips already beginning to rock needily.

His purple eyes cut to her, bright and dancing like an aurora. He said nothing but kept her gaze as he swooped down to fill his mouth with her. Molly gasped and arched as the hot burn of his tongue seared her. He caught the nipple between teeth and tongue, rolling it over a fang for a burst of pleasure-pain that throbbed deep in her cunt.

Molly writhed on the bed, reduced to only sensation as his expert hand plucked and plumped her breast and his lips played the other like an instrument. She dug her nails into his flanks, not sure if she meant to push him away or pull him closer.

He released her captive breast with a wet *pop* before turning his attention to the other. Molly could hardly track all the feelings and sensations, but it wasn't her imagination when something teased at her well-loved breast other than his hand.

His magic.

As his hand trailed down her middle, his magic pooled on her skin, bubbling like champagne. It teased the underside and circled her nipple, leaving a swathe of sparking sensations in its wake. It was almost too much to bear, especially when—

Those long fingers found their way down her lower belly, past her mons, to delve into her warm heat. Molly parted her trembling thighs, greedy for his touch there.

Another groan buzzed on her skin. "You burn for me," he growled, the pleasure vicious in his voice.

"Don't stop," she demanded, hips rolling as his fingers explored.

"*Never.*" His mouth latched over her breast again, teeth biting down just enough to shred her sanity. Between his mouth and his magic, Molly could hardly breathe, but then those fingers found her clitoris and everything else ceased.

Molly came apart under his care, all of him working to push her up the peak and over. She fell from that precipice into a pleasure so consuming, she forgot who and where she was. She was but a string pulled taut, strummed masterfully to create the perfect note.

She cried out and mewled and made other sounds she'd never made before, hips snapping, chasing every touch and stroke of his fingers. When she fell back onto the bed, forehead damp and chest heaving, though, he didn't relent.

He buried his face between her breasts, his magic pushing them against his cheeks. "Again," he said, although Molly wasn't coherent enough to understand.

But she did when those fingers stroked deeper into her gushing heat, finding her aching cunt and spreading her wide. Her breath stuttered in her lungs—what did he—

Another tendril of magic curled over her lower belly, snaking down over her spread folds and between his fingers. Molly choked on a gasp as the magic swirled around her entrance before pushing inside.

Allarion shuddered above her. His arm pushed beneath her and wrapped around to capture a breast, freeing his mouth to press kisses up her chest to her neck, where he set his fangs at her throat.

Molly couldn't pay attention to any one thing, her senses overwrought. She filled her fist with his silky hair and scratched her nails at his scalp. With her other hand, she hooked behind her knee to open herself wider to the magic. Her mouth fell open in wonder at the feeling of being filled—her eyes saw nothing more than the air around them wavering like it did above hot pavement, yet she *felt* that phantom cock shuttling in and out, stretching her wide.

She pinched the pointed tip of his ear and hissed at his temple, "Harder—fuck me *harder*."

A growl erupted from Allarion, and suddenly his two fingers joined his magic. He pushed inside, giving her no quarter. His fingers and magic kept opposite rhythms, always retreating and thrusting, thrusting and retreating. Her hips rocked frantically, the pressure pinching her belly until—

With a yelp, Molly came apart again.

When she regained consciousness, sounds came back to her first. Her own breathing sawing in and out of her desperate lungs. Allarion's strange but enticing keening, the sound piercing as his fangs threatened to do at her throat.

Molly blinked up at the canopied ceiling.

Good gods, I could spend my life doing that.

Her focus narrowed when she felt the point of a fang pinch her skin. Molly's heart, trying to catch up, lurched—*is he going to bite me?*

She held still, waiting to see what he'd do—and wondering why she wasn't more repulsed by the idea. Molly liked a little pinching or spanking, but she wasn't fond of true pain, with sex or without. She tensed as she waited, Allarion a stiff, coiled thing above her.

"Allarion?" she called his name softly.

One by one, his muscles unlocked. It took several moments, but when he raised his head to look at her, it was her fae staring back at her, not a beast threatening to bite. She thought she saw a glimmer of shame in his eyes, but he was quickly rearranging her in the bed and throwing the covers over them.

"The goddesses have blessed me with you," he murmured, pressing a tender kiss to her temple.

Rolling onto her side to face him, Molly asked, "What about you?" Running her hand down his flank and hip, it took no effort to find the bulge straining the front of his trou. To say she was curious about him and what he had hidden under there was an understatement.

And while she was certainly still tired from the day and her two exquisite orgasms, Molly also wasn't a quitter.

Allarion groaned and wrapped a hand around her wrist. "There's no need," he insisted. "This was for you. I am content."

"Fuck that," she scoffed, tossing the coverlet aside to reveal him to the soft candlelight. "I want to see your fae cock."

A surprised laugh parted his lips as he watched her sit up. She could see he meant to argue again, so Molly employed one of her best methods to get her way. Swinging a leg over him to straddle his legs, she smiled to herself to see how his gaze riveted on her swaying breasts.

She arched her back and pushed them together slightly with her upper arms as she worked quickly on the ties of his trou. Despite himself, his hands drifted onto her legs, up to her flanks, and up to frame her waist.

When the ties loosened, Molly greedily sought her prize. His hot flesh nearly scalded her as she drew his cock from the waistband of the trou.

She cooed in appreciation at the sight of him. Long but not too long, thick but not terribly so, he had the most perfect cock she'd ever seen. Even if it was flushed a deep violet. And most interesting of all was the gleaming silver ball studded near the head.

Teasing her finger over the piercing, she grinned to see how he jumped and twitched at her touch.

"This will feel amazing inside me," she mused. "Did you get it just for me?"

"I didn't know it then, but yes," he breathed. "Everything's always been for you."

She hummed with pleasure. "I like that. I think I'll like this, too."

A richly dark chuckle reverberated from his throat, and Allarion lifted a hand to hold her chin between finger and thumb. That thumb pressed into the soft flesh of her bottom lip, his eyes watching rapturously as he eased it into her mouth. "The things that come out of this wicked little mouth . . ."

Molly smiled, catching his thumb with her teeth. "This all you want to do with my mouth?"

His nostrils flared.

Keeping his gaze as he had hers, Molly lowered herself over his lap. She *loved* his choked moan when she caught his cockhead on her tongue. As she rolled the piercing on her tongue, she gathered her breasts in either hand to capture the shaft between them.

"Molly . . ." he wheezed. She smiled around his flesh—he'd never wheezed before.

She set about seeing what other sounds she could have him make. His cockhead stretched her lips, and it took effort to take more of him inside her mouth, no matter how she wetted it on her tongue.

So she did what she could, delighting in his responses as she teased and kissed and nipped the head and piercing. He nearly jumped off the bed when she wrapped her lips around the silver stud and sucked.

Her breasts ached and her nipples hardened as she massaged them against him. Little by little, his hips began to buck, pushing the shaft through the pocket between her tits. Spend leaked down the head and shaft, easing his way.

"That's it," she murmured against the head, "give it all to me."

Allarion bared his fangs in a grimace of agonized pleasure, and Molly shuddered to see the razor-sharp teeth that'd sat at her throat. But it wasn't a shiver of fear she felt, oh no—a thrill of excitement pierced her in the belly, her cunt clutching on nothing.

Fates, did she *want* him to bite her?

She lost the thought as his magic teased around her hips. Molly gasped when it found her soaked entrance from behind and began to pool to cover all of her pink, swollen flesh. It rubbed at her clitoris as that phantom cock pushed inside.

Molly sealed her mouth around his purple cock and moaned.

Allarion threw his head back, his great chest heaving. Spend filled her mouth, salt and musk spilling from her lips. When she couldn't take more, she released him with a gasp, spend spurting to paint her chin and tits.

Another smaller orgasm rippled through her, that phantom cock unrelenting, and Molly pinched a nipple and his piercing to prolong everything.

She rode his shuddering, bucking body through both their orgasms, and when he settled, Molly slipped onto her side beside him, boneless.

They were both a sticky mess and had probably ruined his fine trou, but she really couldn't care. If this was what awaited her long life with him . . .

Happy days.

His hands came around her, and she let him pull her up his body to cover him like a blanket. Tucking her head against his chest, he kissed the crown of her head.

"My clever, beautiful mate," he sighed happily, and that was the last thing she heard before slipping into a deep, peaceful sleep.

20

Allarion tried to pay attention to Lady Aislinn and the council meeting, albeit not very hard. How could he, when his Molly looked so fetching in her new gown beside him? The soft red velvet clung to her generous breasts and nipped waist before draping over her rounded hips—in short, emphasizing every delectable curve and contour of her.

Between devouring her with his gaze and glaring at anyone else trying to do so too, he'd little attention to spare for the meeting.

Molly had grumbled and pouted over being pulled from bed at dawn, but Allarion had insisted. In the early hours, he tracked down Lady Aislinn's seneschal, a helpful, competent woman named Fia, who'd known of a dressmaker in the city who should be able to accommodate their needs. With Fia's directions, Allarion fetched his sleepy, sated *azai* and whisked her off into the city.

In truth, she'd looked so precious curled up in bed, a pillow hugged to her naked chest in lieu of him. Allarion had known few things more pleasurable than holding his mate while she slept. Not once did his mind wander or grow bored; he watched her gentle breathing, memorizing every lash and freckle. He mused over her dreams and fantasized over all he intended to do with her and her lush, giving body.

Goddesses, he nearly wept thinking about the perfection of her breasts. Many, *many* of his fantasies involved those generous globes. His cock stirred with the smallest memory of last night, how she'd cradled his cock with her breasts and claimed him on her tongue.

Sitting through an early morning fitting at the dressmaker's had been its own special agony.

Eyes still a bit bleary after being hustled out of bed, Molly was perhaps a bit more docile than she normally would have been as the dressmaker fluttered about the pedestal, slipping finished or almost-finished gowns over Molly's head and pinning.

They had been in luck, a cancellation sitting there waiting as if it'd been made for Molly. Granted, the dressmaker had two of her seamstresses fervently working to open the cups to accommodate his mate's bust as she took measurements for another three gowns, but within an hour, Molly slipped into the back, out of her shirt and trou, and emerged in the red gown.

Many emotions vied within Allarion at seeing her in that gown, but first among them was pride. The gown was simple but elegant, all clean lines that enhanced Molly's own beauty and figure. A few details had been added to the swooping neckline and cuffs, but otherwise, the focus was left on the wearer, just as it should be.

Her smile, almost shy but so, so happy, was worth its weight in gold to Allarion. He made sure to pay the dressmaker and seamstresses handsomely, arranging for the other dresses to be completed as quickly as possible and sent to the castle.

When they left the shop, Allarion swore Molly walked a little taller. A comely blush colored her cheeks when people stopped to look at her, but it was a flush of pleasure rather than embarrassment. She carried herself with poise as they ascended the castle steps, every bit the lady any other noblewoman here was, every bit the queen he knew her to be.

His pride at having such a mate swelled; although, he hadn't quite accounted for the jealousy. He'd never been the sort before, but now, after having finally had a taste of his beautiful *azai,* his fangs were ready to sink into anyone stupid enough to look at her too long. Like the aggressive unicorn stallions that guarded their mares during the summer heat, Allarion glared at all the other males in the council chamber, daring them to look at Molly with anything more than respectful admiration.

And even then, his jealousy snapped and snarled.

Honestly, it was disconcerting. So between that and stealing glances down Molly's bodice, Allarion hardly heard much of the meeting at all. Given the council itself had little reaction to Lady Aislinn's announcements, he was comfortable assuming nothing much of note was said beyond the usual harvest forecasts, news from the capital, and updates on ongoing projects.

It was a testament to Lady Aislinn's competent leadership that these meetings had grown mundane. His first few had been marked with strife and intrigue—exactly what he'd come to the Darrowlands to avoid. But with her grasping brother dead and her place as heiress secured, Lady Aislinn had assumed her role gracefully and capably.

The meeting adjourned near luncheon, and when Lady Aislinn declared their business closed, the landholders were quick to make for the dining hall. Allarion believed there would also be a banquet tonight and expected to sit again with the heiress and princess at the high table.

In the meantime, it was time for him to right a wrong.

Covering his mate's hand with his, where it was tucked into his elbow, Allarion leaned down to whisper, "May I take you somewhere?"

Those plush lips quirked up at him in a grin. "Is it back to bed?" she whispered back.

Allarion flushed with desire, fangs aching. The goddesses had truly blessed him.

"Once we return, and the moment dinner is done, you're *mine.*"

Molly didn't quite know if she was more disappointed or surprised that it wasn't to bed they went but back out into the city. She remembered Allarion saying he wished to procure several things for the house while they were in Dundúran, but she recognized their path soon after leaving the curtain wall, her neighborhood passing by as they swayed atop Bellarand's back.

Arriving at her uncle's tavern door felt like a dream. She didn't know what she expected to see from the plastered walls and heavy oak door, but it wasn't the place looking . . . exactly the same. Or perhaps a little worse. More cracks appeared in the off-white plaster, and more of the name, once scrolled in fancy lettering atop the door, had chipped away.

A candle burned in the front window, a sure sign that the tavern was open, but the street was fairly quiet, even for early afternoon.

Swinging a leg over Bellarand's hindquarters, Allarion smoothly dismounted. Molly slid from the unicorn's back into the waiting arms of her fae, but she hardly felt the descent, nor his gentle hands.

Chewing her lip, it was hard not to think of the last time she was here, packed onto Bellarand thinking she'd been sold off, the neighborhood watching on. Standing here now, beside her fae in their finery, poked at a soreness deep inside her.

Standing out on the street did garner a few curious stares, and more than one stumbled to a stop when they recognized her.

Molly flushed, looking down at her pretty new gown. She still couldn't quite believe Allarion had managed to do it all in a morning, but she was starting to suspect there was little her fae couldn't do. Although the tone of red had been different, and it lacked the frills of black lace, the similarity to the dress he purchased in Mullon for his mysterious friend wasn't lost on her. Slipping into something so wildly different from her usual garb had startled her—especially when she liked what she saw staring back in the mirror.

When they'd entered the council room to stand with the other non-noble landholders, more than a few pairs of eyes had taken note of her transformation. Her velvet armor had Molly brave enough to look Fiona Braithwaite in the eye and bob her head in greeting, but she didn't bother with more. In her gown, she could at least wrap her mind around, if not fully believe, that she stood there as an equal.

That she *belonged* there.

Standing in the street outside her uncle's tavern, in her new dress, Molly had the distinctly uncomfortable sensation of not belonging. It wasn't something she'd experienced with the tavern; despite Brom's insidious comments that she should be grateful for him taking her in, despite how rundown the place often was, Molly still felt attached to it. Like it was somehow *her* place.

She'd certainly worked hard enough for it to be.

Looking at it now . . . a prick of sadness stung her. For the state of the place. For ever leaving, yet for coming back, too.

Allarion seemed to know what she'd say even before she murmured, "I'd better go in by myself."

His mouth was an unhappy, downturned line, but after a moment, he nodded. "You're sure?"

"Yes. Do your shopping." She tried to smile through her apprehension. "You have my permission to buy any rug you see fit for the atrium and conservatory."

One of his brows ticked up, and he respected her attempt to avoid the tension by joking himself. "Now that is a concession. I won't abuse this trust."

"Just nothing too yellow. Or too pink."

A small smile, almost sad, touched his lips. "Of course, my love."

"Remember to haggle," she said, straightening the already perfect drape of his cloak. Knowing he was on the cusp of leaving her alone, just as she'd asked, had a desperate need to keep him there bubbling up. "They'll expect you to haggle. If you don't, they'll be insulted."

"I think they'll be happier for the full price in the end."

Molly opened her mouth to argue, but then Bellarand bobbed his head in impatience.

Come along, two-leggeds. If I stand here any longer, I'll start attracting pigeons.

She grinned despite herself, tipping her head back to receive Allarion's parting kiss. "I'll return by nightfall."

"All right," she breathed, and bit her cheek to keep from saying any more and keeping him. She tucked her hands into the folds of her gown to stop from clutching to him, too, just to be safe.

He regained his seat atop Bellarand, and with a final wave, the two of them headed off into the heart of the city—no doubt to the delight of every shopkeeper there.

Bellarand's clipping hoof-falls on the cobblestones had almost faded by the time Molly made herself turn and face the tavern.

Sucking in a breath, she put one foot in front of the other. The front door swung open with a small push, squeaking on its hinges just how it always did. The yeasty smell of beer hit her in the face, followed by the tang of stale, spilt ale and the spice of dripping candlewax.

Her nose twitched at the muzzy dustiness of the air, sunlight slanting in from the windows full of particles hanging lazily in the air.

Molly stood just inside, letting her eyes adjust to the dim murkiness of the tavern interior.

A gasp echoed through the space.

"It's Molly!"

She recognized the squeals and quickly threw her arms open wide. One little body, then two, ran into her waiting embrace, and Molly laughed and cried as she drew her cousins close and rocked them. Kisses fell on her cheeks as little hands grasped at her neck and shoulders.

"You're here!" Rory and Oona exclaimed.

They pulled her by the hands further into the tavern.

Brom stood stock still behind the bar, his overgrown beard twitching in surprise to see her. Nora was on the other side, portioning out some stew into a bowl for one of the handful of patrons wiling away their afternoon in the tavern. From out back came hurried feet, and Merry appeared, a smile cracking her usually dreamy face.

"Molly!"

Merry started for her, but then Nora's voice whipped across the tavern. "Merry, take this first. We've got customers."

Ducking her head, Merry went to Nora to collect the bowl and headed for the far side of the tavern. Molly watched with a frown as Merry, barely fourteen, deposited the bowl at the table of three rough-looking men. She scurried away as quickly as she could, hurrying for Molly and the girls.

It was then Molly noticed that Merry—all the girls, actually—wore aprons, some of them Molly's own old ones.

Merry threw her skinny arms around her, and while she hugged her tight, Molly's temper sparked in her chest.

What was going on?

Oona pulled at her velvet skirts. "This is *nice*," she marveled.

"It's too nice," noted Nora, drifting over but not embracing Molly. "Where'd you get it?"

Molly didn't answer, instead looking at all the girls in their aprons. Nora and Oona had their hair tucked behind linen caps, and all of their sleeves and skirts were stained. Rory had a clumsy patch on the elbow of her jacket, and Molly knew Oona wore hand-me-down socks from Merry because she'd darned them herself. Worse, they all seemed . . . if not quite gaunt, then skinny.

"Are you *all* working here?" she murmured. A pit of devastation sucked at the bottom of her stomach.

Nora's cheeks flamed, but she covered it with a scoff and roll of her eyes.

"Papa needed the help," said Merry in a little voice.

"Well," boomed Brom, finally coming out from behind the bar, "let's see you, then."

Molly didn't accept his greeting, neither going to embrace him nor shake his hand. She stood her ground, frowning up at the uncle who'd made her think Allarion was her buyer.

Brom planted his fist on his hip instead, using his other hand to throw a bar cloth over his shoulder and circle his meaty pointer finger through the air. "That fae keeps you looking nice. C'mon then, give us a twirl in your fancy dress."

She did no such thing. Her cheeks flushed so red, they probably matched her gown, as she took a good look at Brom and the tavern. Her uncle too seemed as though he'd lost some of the roundness to his cheeks. His beard had lost its shape, grown scraggly and wild, and his eyebrows were too long. Stains smirched his tunic, and she could smell the stale sweat on him from steps away.

It was the same bar behind him, the same tables and chairs. Nothing had been fixed or replaced. The tabletops had a greasy shine to them, and crumbs collected in the cracks of the floorboards. The only thing that'd changed was the layer of dust that'd accumulated where Molly had once been sure to clean.

"What *in all the hells* is going on here?" Molly seethed.

Brom shrugged and waved an arm at the nearly empty tavern. "You know it's never busy this time of day."

"No." Getting in close, she poked a finger into Brom's soft gut. "Where is that *fucking* money?"

Brom's face flushed red, but he made a show of trying to laugh. "Fates, all the fancy ladies talk like that or are you showin' them how?"

"Why are the girls in rags?" she hissed.

Nora's face darkened, and the younger girls looked away in embarrassment.

"Just because you're fine folk now," Nora sneered.

"That's awful poor of you, Moll. You come from here, same as them."

"Don't you dare!" she screeched. "Allarion's money was supposed to take care of the girls! Why are they working here? They should be in school."

Brom held up his hands, making Molly want to shriek again. He had a way of doing that, of making it seem like she was being the unreasonable one. The sight of his shrug, his feigned helplessness in the face of her supposed tirade, had her seeing red.

If he thought *this* was her in a tirade, he'd forgotten—

"Look, Moll, we're happy to see you, but we've got work to do. If you're going to stay, keep out of the way."

There were exactly four patrons in the tavern, all of whom were nursing their ales and stew while trying to pretend they weren't hanging on every word.

Brom lumbered back behind the bar, and Molly pursued him.

"You were supposed to use that money to fix the tavern. To send Merry to academy!"

Her uncle shot her a grumpy look as he began cleaning out a tankard. "Knighthoods are expensive, all right? We got Bryan sponsored—he went off to Gleanná a fortnight ago. I gave him what little was leftover. He'll need it in the capital."

Molly blinked, the believable explanation catching her off guard.

"You promised . . ."

"Money only goes so far, Moll. We've been doing the best we can without you."

With another glare, Nora went off to wipe down tables, abandoning Molly at the bar. Her deflated anger left the crust of her indignation to crumble.

Looking back at her littlest cousins, though, Molly couldn't quite believe the easy excuse. She was happy for Bryan—he'd wanted to train for a knighthood since he was a boy of three. Training and earning your spurs of course cost a good deal, which was why most knights were sponsored by their well-to-do families. It wouldn't be easy for a young man from the poor side of Dundúran, especially one considered old for squiring. But all of what Allarion had given Brom . . .?

Forcing a smile, Molly returned to the girls and drew them to the back, where the staircase up to the living quarters stood. Sitting on the steps, she pulled them in close to kiss each on the cheek.

"Enough of that," she said. "Tell me everything that's happened."

It took a bit of coaxing, but soon the girls were talking over each other, telling her all about their recent lessons in school, any neighborhood gossip they'd heard, and their more colorful experiences so far of working in the tavern.

Molly listened to it all, a gnawing fury eating at her gut. She herself had been young when Brom put her to work in the tavern, but that was different. *She* was different. Hearing of shy, brilliant Merry having to clean up after drunk men rather than studying, of boisterous Rory being yelled at by patrons to hurry up, of little Oona washing tankards in scalding hot water—it devastated her.

The girls covered their unhappiness well, but Molly saw the signs. They were tired, discouraged. They should have been studying at school in the day and playing with their friends from the neighborhood in the evening. Many others in the neighborhood worked hard to support their families, but all understood the importance of education. The late Lady Róisín Darrow had established schools throughout the city for all of Dundúran's children.

On quiet nights at Scarborough, Molly sometimes tried to better her reading and writing, making up for what she should've learned as a girl. That wasn't supposed to be her cousins' fates, too.

She spoke with the girls for over an hour but learned nothing specific that would shed light on where the money had truly gone. As the shadows lengthened with the afternoon, more patrons began to wander in, and Brom called for the girls to come help Nora.

Molly bit back her arguments, a sick feeling settling in her belly watching them get to work.

This is wrong. She had to do something. Allarion probably wouldn't like it, but she couldn't leave her cousins to fend for themselves like this.

A plan began to form in her mind, and when Nora next passed by, fetching something from the back, Molly tried to grab her. The girl was slippery and wriggled out of her grip.

"Don't," Nora hissed, "my *rags* might get you dirty."

Molly ignored the jab, even if it hit its target on the head, and reached to take Nora's hand. "Is it true, Nora? Is the money all gone?"

She rolled her eyes. "Papa drank an awful lot right after you left. Bought himself some nice boots and there were a lot of . . ." Her cheeks pinkened and her gaze skittered away. "A lot of *ladies* coming by at night."

Molly just held in the keening wail of anger that wanted to erupt from her throat. Brom had squandered the money on *whores* and *booze*. It was such an unimaginative, cliché thing, but Molly found it far more believable than all the money being used on Bryan.

Pulling out of Molly's grip, Nora sneered, "Maybe your fae man didn't pay as much for you as you thought."

Molly understood now that that was far from the case—Allarion truly would have paid any price. She'd seen the sack of coins with her own eyes.

She thought it would've been enough.

It *should have* been enough.

Molly waited to feel that familiar burn of temper—Brom certainly deserved the true heat of her ire for this. Yet, Nora's waspishness only threw sand on the bonfire of her anger. An aching sadness was all she could muster, for really, this was her own fault, too.

She'd left the girls. She should've known better—Brom couldn't be trusted to do what was best for them. He couldn't run the tavern on his own; that was painfully obvious by the state of it. The girls were far too young to be helping him, and this was a dangerous place for girls.

Molly still resented being exposed to it so young, but she'd done it so Nora and the others wouldn't have to.

That sacrifice had been for nothing. Her bride price had been for nothing.

"Ya know, if you really wanted to help your family, you could pitch in!" Brom called down the hall.

Stepping away, Nora said, "Just go. You've already left, anyway."

"Nora . . ."

Her cousin hurried back to the bar to take more orders.

It took Molly only another moment to decide. Pushing up from the steps, she walked into the main room to a cheer. People called out her name in surprise and pleasure, some of the regulars coming up to pat her arms and wish her well.

Soon, the front door was thrown open. "Hey, Molly's back!" someone shouted into the street, and more people, both regular patrons and curious neighbors, came to have a look.

Molly untied the too-big apron from Oona's waist and instead tied it round her own. She caught Rory and Merry, too, and told them, "Go on up and read. I'll take care of tonight."

"But you don't work here anymore," Rory reminded her.

"I know. But I haven't forgotten." She pinched Rory's nose, making the girl laugh.

She made sure all three had bowls of stew for their dinner before sending them up. Nora cut her unreadable glances, but Molly didn't approach her again. The damage was done, and she'd have to show Nora she meant to help.

As night fell, more and more people filled the tavern. Every table and chair boasted an occupant, straining the old floorboards. Having more people venturing inside—and therefore more coins changing hands—perked Brom up, and by evening time, he was a jollier version of himself, shedding the gloomy frown for a toothy grin as he poured drinks.

Molly loaded trays with drinks and wove through the tavern delivering them. Her body remembered just what to do, years of practice lending her confidence in her gait and balance.

The familiar cadence of a busy tavern, of dropping off full tankards and picking up empties, of smiling for the patrons and flirting for tips, was easy to slip into. For a while, it didn't feel like she'd been gone for months. For a while, she was the old Molly.

"It's never this full anymore," Nora remarked as they both stopped at the bar to hand over empty tankards. There wasn't too much malice in her voice this time, but her mouth pursed when Molly slid a handful of tipped coins across the bar to her.

She glared at them a moment before grabbing them up to squirrel away in her pocket.

Nora hurried off before Molly could say anything.

Then there wasn't time to say anything as more neighbors came with well-wishes. Between answering questions about her fae betrothed and his strange steed and taking orders, Molly hardly noticed the evening passing. Well, her feet started to notice, aching in that way they usually did by the end of the day.

And she was quickly reminded of the *charms* of working a tavern when a patron, already deep into his cups, stumbled, splashing Molly with ale. Her apron caught most of it, but a dark splotch bloomed across the red velvet near her hip.

Molly ground her back teeth, dabbing at the stain to reduce its spread, as the tavern tittered in amusement to see her fine gown besmirched. She was soon forgotten entirely when Brom led them in a rowdy rendition of a favorite shanty, and Molly was left to dodge more sloshing cups.

She was making her way carefully to the far side of the bar, watching her movements so carefully, that at first she didn't hear how the noise suddenly fell. Not until she next looked up did she realize that Allarion stood at the threshold of the tavern, all eyes turned toward him.

His dark gaze ran over Molly slowly before turning to regard the others. He entered slowly, his cloak sweeping the floor behind him.

As he approached, Molly angled her tray to hide the stain.

"Molly, what do you do?" he asked, and although his voice was low, everyone in the tavern heard.

"Just . . . helping out for the night."

A frown began to mar his brow, and his keen eyes shifted over her to lock onto the bar.

Molly laid her hand on his chest. "Let me just finish out the night."

When he lowered his gaze to her again, Molly tried to convey what she could in a look; although, she feared all he saw was her embarrassment at being caught playing barmaid.

"As you will." His acceptance came easily, but something about it had Molly's insides twisting with an oily sort of guilt.

She made him comfortable at his usual table, and the tavern resumed its chatter around them, although it never regained its full fervor. Under Allarion's cool gaze, everyone, including Molly, watched what they said and did.

Molly knew there'd be plenty of explaining to do soon enough.

21

Allarion entered the large front solar of Dundúran Castle with a frown on his face. He'd tried his best to smooth it on the walk over from the chamber he shared with Molly—it wouldn't do to meet the princess looking so sour.

Yet, he couldn't help it. He shouldn't be attending the meeting alone.

"She's only really requested you," Molly had reminded him that morning.

That didn't dissuade Allarion from wanting Molly to be there, but she insisted she needed to return to her uncle's tavern.

"They need me."

What her uncle needed was a swift kick to the posterior, but even Allarion understood that sentiment, while perhaps shared, wasn't helpful. Still, it'd been with sharp teeth that he held his tongue as they padded around an argument.

Allarion meant to make things right by bringing her back to her family—he'd taken her from them under questionable pretenses, and while Molly had chosen to stay with him, he suspected that, for his own peace of mind as well as the strength of their bond, she needed to make that choice again, outside of his sphere of influence. And what was more, he had to provide the situation for her to choose fairly.

None of that was particularly easy to swallow.

Walking into the tavern the previous night to find her serving drunk patrons, a scene all too familiar, had enraged him. Not because she didn't have to or even because he resented her family for taking her time. No, what Allarion hated was the vision of Molly without him.

Molly waiting tables in the tavern was one who hadn't had him in her life. It was *before*. And . . . as a small part of him feared, could be the future if she chose to remain in Dundúran.

He didn't truly believe she would, at least, not the rational part of him, nor even the sentimental part. Both had pressed his suit and claim in the late hours, feasting on her cunt until she couldn't bear it any longer. Crass as it was, he enjoyed a feral sort of pride knowing no other could make her feel so good. *He* was the owner of her pleasure.

In the light of day, though, doubts crept in. Again, his rational side knew that she would have to choose, and the odds were good she'd choose him. Her cousins were something that could be accommodated—even brought to Scarborough when he was sure it was safe, if she so wished.

It was the side of him that remembered how it felt to watch a friend die, to feel the stab of betrayal by the Queen he'd sworn loyalty to, that sparked his resentment most. It was an ugly feeling, especially to have at the expense of children, but it couldn't be helped. It was there. All Allarion could do was not let it rule him.

So he walked into the solar to meet Princess Isolde, alone and frowning a little.

If she noticed his tumultuous thoughts, the princess was too well mannered to show it. She rose from her seat on the sedan, a perfect smile adorning her lips. Her light brown hair, nearly auburn, had been brushed back behind a crescent cloth headdress that was fashionable with human women currently. For a princess, her gown appeared somewhat plain, a simple affair of dove gray and dusky pink, although up close, the subtle but exquisite embroidery and beading was evident. Much like its wearer, the simplicity of the gown belied its richness.

She'd grown a little from when Allarion saw her at the wedding of Lady Aislinn and Hakon. On the threshold between girlhood and womanhood, she was all long limbs and rounded cheeks. She reminded him very much of Ravenna at that age, a little too desperate to grow up.

"Your Grace," he greeted, taking the hand she offered and bowing to kiss the back.

"Good morning to you, master fae. Thank you for agreeing to meet with me."

"It's a fool who squanders an audience with the crown princess, and I am no fool."

The princess's smile widened. "No, but you are trained in flattery."

Allarion bobbed his head in assent. "Indeed, Your Grace. My house is an illustrious one, ancient as the highland cliffs. Manners are a requirement to my mother, the scion of our house."

"She sounds formidable," Princess Isolde quipped. "We have that in common, you see."

"Formidable mothers are a force unto themselves."

The princess hummed in agreement before gesturing at a chair positioned opposite the sedan. Once she'd resumed her place, Allarion sat gently on the edge of the cushion.

"I enjoy talking with you, master fae. I hope we may visit more while you're here in the city."

Allarion nodded, unsure quite where the princess led. "I enjoy speaking with you, too, Your Grace."

"I hope you continue to." Her smile faltered and, gaze dropping to her lap, the princess pulled a sealed letter from her pocket. "I asked for this meeting to convey a request from my father, King Marius."

Without meeting his eye, Princess Isolde held out the letter. Allarion considered it as he reached to take it from her. He quirked a brow in question, but the princess could only nod at the letter.

"Please read it."

Suspicion slithered through his veins as Allarion broke the wax seal. The symbol pressed into the red wax was of spread eagle wings set before a round oak shield, the symbols of Pyrros and Eirea, respectively. The paper was of the highest quality, soft between his fingers, and the writing itself was of a precise, meticulous hand. Even before reading, curiosity pricked Allarion to wonder if this was the king's own hand or the neater writing of a scribe.

It mattered less as Allarion read the king's *request*.

> *To Allarion Meringor,*
>
> *My daughter, Isolde Monaghan, has been granted authority to treat with you on the matter of your continued presence within Eirea and lordship of the Scarborough estate.*
>
> *I am desirous to know of your immediate plans for the estate. I understand that pledges have been made to the Darrows; however, further pledges of fealty to the crown will be most conducive to a friendly course between us.*
>
> *It is also imperative to determine your commitment to the safety of this kingdom. While I commend the Darrows' willingness to welcome all to their demesne, inclusion within Eirea must also come with the sacrifice to crown and country that any Eirean would be called upon to make. Should the safety of Eirea be threatened, the crown requires assurances that you will defend her.*
>
> *This, of course, would come with a hand of friendship to you. An esteemed fae such as yourself will be welcomed at court and shall receive the estate of Haldenbrück within the crown demesne of Loígas.*
>
> *Consider this carefully and convey your answer to the Crown Princess. I know you to be a wise man and look forward to your friendship and presence in Gleanná.*
>
> *And congratulations on your impending nuptials. I hope to soon*

meet you and your Eirean bride.
    With all respect,
    His Excellence
    King Marius Caellus of Eirea,
    Prince Prospect of Pyrros,
    Lord Protector of Gleanná,
    Liege Loígas

Allarion read it twice just to be sure he hadn't misunderstood anything. His grasp of written Eirean wasn't as strong as that of written Pyrrossi, but coming to the flourish of signatures and titles at the end again, he felt certain he understood.

"Your father is threatening me," he remarked.

The princess, the Twins bless her, choked.

Allarion waited patiently as the princess coughed as delicately as possible. Her color was still high when she finally regarded him with a pinched expression.

"My father wishes to ascertain if you will fight for Eirea, should the need arise," she said, the perfect little diplomat.

His answering smile was all teeth, and the princess's pulse visibly jumped in her throat. He didn't relish scaring the girl, but it seemed she and her family needed a reminder that he wasn't someone to threaten.

"My loyalty has been and shall remain to the Darrows, the ones who welcomed me and others here."

Princess Isolde nodded carefully. "And that's commendable, as is the work Lady Aislinn and her father are doing. It's only just—to be citizens here, to enjoy all the benefits of our beautiful kingdom, is it not reasonable to ask for the loyalty expected of all subjects?" Her nostrils flared, taking in a deep breath, and Allarion wondered how many times she'd practiced that line.

"My loyalty has been pledged and assured. Bellarand and I fought to secure Lady Aislinn's place as heiress. It would be foolish to think that I or any other folk who came to the Darrowlands seeking peace, would wish to make promises that should lead us into battle."

The princess raised her hands in supplication. "There is no battle to speak of. It is merely a formality. The Darrows pledge fealty to the crown, as do their nobles. As a landholder yourself, it isn't unexpected."

"And are other Eireans expected to journey to the capital and pledge their loyalty?"

He didn't need to see her flush to know they weren't.

"So it is me and my fellow otherly folk who would be asked to do so."

Princess Isolde tried to assure him again. "You are new to the kingdom. Any liege or ruler would want assurance from new actors. We have faith that you bring your best intentions to our kingdom, but again, it isn't unreasonable to want assurances."

"I and the others have lived here for months peacefully. We have made assurances to Liege Darrow. We have paid our taxes and fought on the battlefield." Leaning forward, he handed the princess the letter back. "Your kind tried to use otherlies to fight their battles before. Mark me, princess, the wounds are fresh enough in their minds. Your human war games won't be settled by otherly blood."

Her throat bobbed, and her fingers clutched the letter in her lap. "You would defy the king?"

Allarion's attention snagged on her last word. *King.*

"In what capacity does your father write this?"

The princess's lips pursed. "My father is king consort. He speaks for my mother when she is indisposed. Unfortunately, her health has been poor since last spring."

"But is this demand sent in her stead? Are these your mother's words?"

Princess Isolde's silence spoke far more than her careful answers. Allarion's disgust curdled in his gut. It was as he suspected from the precise wording of the letter; the king consort had sent his daughter, a youngling, to do business that was both unsanctioned and self-serving.

Allarion's lip curled. "It seems your father asks for that which isn't his to have. He is not the crown."

Her mouth fell open, to argue or reprimand, Allarion didn't know. She snapped it shut just as quickly, and he watched as her eyes went glassy and her expression brittle.

Standing, Princess Isolde thrust the letter at him, obliging Allarion to retake it.

"I have executed my duty, you have read the king's request. I anticipate your answer tomorrow." She bobbed in a small curtsey, staring around Allarion's shoulder. "I suggest you consider his offer."

With that, the princess left him.

Allarion sighed, turning the letter about in his fingers.

As his Molly might say, what a fucking mess.

Allarion's mood improved little throughout the day, but it had less to do with the king consort's demands and much more with Molly being gone past dark.

When he passed Lady Aislinn on his way down to the stables, he made their excuses.

"Is Miss Molly all right?" she asked, her fair brows knitted with concern.

"She is well—just visiting family. I go to fetch her now."

The heiress nodded, gaze straying to the door that led into the dining hall.

"Your absence wouldn't have anything to do with our special guest, would it?"

Allarion shook his head. "The princess is merely the messenger. I wouldn't punish anyone for that, especially not a girl."

Lady Aislinn stepped closer. "I don't mean to pry, but is this business between you something my father should know about?"

"The king asks for what you and your father already enjoy—fealty from me and the otherly folk. However, his methods are perhaps more heavy-handed."

"Ah. I see." A troubled look overcame her golden face. "The queen hasn't mentioned requiring such a thing in her letters. I don't presume to know all her thoughts, of course, but I'd assume she'd mention it if it was on her mind."

"I don't believe this comes from the queen, my lady."

Her brows arched in understanding. Looking at the entrance to the dining hall again, the heiress sighed. "Poor Isolde. She's caught in the middle between them."

Allarion hadn't poked his nose into the business of human politics terribly much in his time in the Darrowlands—yet, it was hard not to hear of how little love was lost between Queen Ygraine and her consort. Distant cousins from two feuding branches of the Eirean royal family, their union had ended years of bloody warfare between the sides that saw dozens of noble houses decimated. The kingdom emerged smaller, weaker, and divided.

It was why the orc clans had begun moving further into the western foothills and the Pyrrossi advancing from the south. Perhaps the fae too might have made a play for more territory, had Amaranthe's attention not been solely focused on herself.

The princess stood to inherit a multitude of problems with few allies, even from within her own family. If Allarion was charitable, perhaps the king sought to shore up alliances for his young daughter and heir. However, Allarion had lived far longer than the king and his whole family line. Many human royals had come and gone, too many for him to keep count. What they did, they did for their own interests.

The thought of King Marius and his possible motives only brought Allarion's thoughts back to Brom Dunne. It seemed, despite miles of distance and fathoms of difference, the men weren't so unalike.

"I will speak with you tomorrow, after I have met with the princess," Allarion told Lady Aislinn. Bowing, he took his leave. "Please excuse me while I fetch my bride."

"Of course. Good evening, Allarion."

He left the heiress, descending through the castle and out the main steps. Bellarand awaited him at the bottom, and Allarion lost no time swinging himself up onto the unicorn's back.

Off to get the human?

Yes. I don't wish her to walk in the dark.

Bellarand's great hooves clattered on the cobblestones through the city. Although not everywhere was as well lit as the castle and main thoroughfares, they needed no lights to guide them.

The city was lively at night, light and patrons spilling from various drinking establishments. However, it wasn't so busy in the part of the city where Brom's tavern sat. A few neighbors milled about in the pools of light burning from the tavern windows, and about a dozen patrons had packed inside, but nothing like the previous night.

When Allarion swung the door open, the space inside was far calmer. Molly was bringing two tankards from the bar to a pair of patrons, and she looked up with a smile when she saw the door opening.

That smile faltered, and Allarion *hated* it. Now that he knew what her true smile was, he never wanted to see the forced one again.

Rather than take a table as he had before, Allarion remained in the doorway, his message clear. They were leaving.

It may have been unfair, even callous of him, but he wanted his mate.

Molly noted his rigid stance, and he watched her sigh and turn back to the bar. Unknotting the apron from her waist, she placed it on the steps leading upstairs.

"I'm headed out," she called to her uncle.

"It's early yet," Brom argued. "And there are still customers. Don't make me get one of the girls."

Molly turned a spitting glare on her uncle. "Don't you dare wake the girls."

"Someone's got to—"

A thrust of magic boomed through the tavern, snuffing all the candles and lifting the blanket of dust off every surface. Several hats were knocked off heads, and Allarion's own cloak fluttered in the artificial gust.

"Leave," he growled.

The patrons stared through the dim before, as one, they slapped down coins and hurried past him out the door.

When the tavern was cleared out, Allarion held his hand out for Molly.

Her lips twitched. "An early night would do everyone good," she told her uncle as she strode to take Allarion's hand.

Together, they left the tavern. He helped Molly mount Bellarand before swinging up behind her. As the unicorn turned toward the castle, Molly leaned her body back into Allarion's.

He buried his nose in her hair and took a long, deep breath. His arms came around to hold her tighter to him, for the tighter he held, the looser the knot in his chest.

"I missed you," he breathed. "I don't like being parted from you."

"I know," she said quietly, her hands coming to lay over his. "I missed you, too."

The words pricked holes in his inflated anger, and Allarion sighed into her hair, most of the heat of his ire escaping him. Goddesses, the effort of staying irritated with her and the situation at the tavern had so little value next to having her.

Still, "I don't want you staying there so late. I worry about you."

"I don't want to serve there again, but I worry about the girls. If there's any money left, he's keeping it for himself."

Molly had told him, even through her exhaustion last night, of how Brom had squandered the money. Allarion burned with indignation to think of a father depriving his own children when it was in his power to change it. His own father had been aloof, but he always provided for all his children. Maxim's sacrifice for Ravenna was true fatherhood, and men like Brom Dunne cheapened it.

"I can provide for the girls, sweetling. That isn't a problem."

Molly rubbed the backs of his hands. "You're a good man, Allarion. But more money won't solve this—he'll just find a way to take it from them."

"Then what is to be done?" Dropping his mouth to her neck, he kissed the curve where her shoulder met her spine. "I won't give you back to him."

"I . . . I think I'm going to see the mayor tomorrow. He's intervened before, maybe he can help."

That means more time here, doesn't it? Bellarand grumped.

I'm afraid so.

The unicorn huffed. *The hay in the stables makes me itch.*

"We will see this issue of your cousins resolved, sweetling. This I promise you. But we cannot be away from Scarborough for much longer." Between the days already spent in Dundúran and being parted from Molly for much of it, the magic gathering inside him had begun to burgeon. If it was left to swell too much, he couldn't account for how volatile it could become when mixed with his temper.

Although Brom Dunne deserved whatever retribution Molly would allow, Allarion couldn't say the same of their neighbors.

Molly worried her lip between her teeth. "All right. I'll see what the mayor says tomorrow."

Another knot loosened inside him when she didn't insist she stay behind in Dundúran. He was still resolved to give her her choice, but he couldn't promise he'd abide by that resolve, when it came time to leave. The thought of returning to Scarborough without her stung like burrs against the skin, rubbing him raw.

Molly laid her head back on Allarion's shoulder to peer up at him. He didn't know how much she could see of him in the intermittent light of illuminated windows and lampposts, but he devoured the sight of her gentle face, lips curving into a small grin.

"I'm almost afraid to ask, but how was your day? What did the princess say?"

Allarion sighed, wishing he had better news to share. Molly listened carefully as he relayed what the princess said and the king's letter. As he spoke, a frown gathered at her brow, deepening with each revelation.

By the time they made the castle wall, she was outright scowling.

"I don't like it at all," she grumbled.

"Neither do I. But kings have a way of making demands and expecting them to be heeded."

Molly chewed her lip again as they crossed the courtyard, so Allarion laid his fingers on her throat, tipping her head back so he could take those poor abused lips for his own.

"Let me," he murmured into her mouth.

He tasted her laugh, and one of her hands reached back to grip his hair.

Ugh. Bellarand came to a stop and gave them a jostle. *Take it inside, I'm tired.*

Allarion dismounted before he could be thrown off, helping Molly down just as the unicorn turned for the stables.

"Thanks for the ride!" she called after him, getting only a flick of his tail in response.

"He doesn't like the hay," Allarion explained.

"He's a big baby is what he is."

I heard that.

"Then clop faster!"

An indignant huff echoed from the shadows.

Allarion took Molly's hand to tuck into his elbow. He was ready to lay down with his mate—hopefully after spending an hour worshipping her pretty pink cunt. Two nights and already Allarion knew he couldn't survive without them; he needed to have her on his tongue and he needed to hold her as she slept.

A growing desire to have her hold him as he slept had taken root in his mind, too.

Tiredness nipped at the edges of his mind, and it'd likely be wise to take a long sleep tomorrow, but there was simply too much that had to be done. And, he wouldn't leave Molly unguarded for so long.

He turned toward the castle steps but stopped when Molly tugged on his arm.

He found her expression once again troubled, those lovely brown eyes dark under her frown.

"I don't like being a vulnerability for you."

"Oh, sweetling, no." Gathering her close, he tucked her under his cloak to guard against the night chill and banded his arms around her. Pressing a kiss into the crown of her head, he said, "You are my greatest strength. Any who would think otherwise, or underestimate you, are fools—and you are no fool."

One sad little laugh vibrated against his chest, where she'd pressed her cheek. "I don't feel very strong most days." She wrapped her own arms around him and squeezed gently. "But . . . you make me feel like I am."

"One day soon, I hope you won't need my assurances, though you will always have them. That you will see what I do."

Molly tipped her head back, resting her chin on his chest. "What are you going to tell the princess?"

Allarion grumbled. "That's not so easy. To draw the ire, and worse the eye, of a man like King Marius . . . he could make things difficult if he so wished."

"Fuck him," Molly said, bold as could be.

He couldn't help a guffaw of surprise.

"You've already defied a queen far scarier than him," she reminded him. "What's a king to Amaranthe? A king *consort* at that."

Allarion folded himself around his precious *azai,* body shaking with the laughter he worked to hold in.

She smoothed her hands in soothing strokes up and down his back, whispering, "Don't let him force you to do something against your conscience."

He hummed in agreement. "Not diplomatic, but infinitely wise is my *azai.*"

"And don't you forget it.

22

Molly pulled in a breath to settle her stomach before walking into Town Hall. She was armed with a letter from Lady Aislinn herself, and a page had run ahead to let Mayor Doherty know she intended to come, but still, the weight of walking into the space settled on her shoulders.

It's time, was the first thought she awoke to that morning. *Time to fix this.*

Her cousins' situation at the tavern had become untenable. Molly liked to think she'd managed things well enough while in her uncle's house, but those days were done. No matter how Brom needled or Nora guilted her, Molly wasn't going back.

But that didn't mean she'd leave the girls behind.

Town Hall was an ancient building, even for a place as storied as Dundúran. It'd once been a longhouse, built for the first chieftain family of the demesne. A long time ago—that Allarion apparently remembered, though Molly tried not to think much about that—Eirea had been the name of the land, not a kingdom. Dozens of tribes and clans had lived throughout the continent, and it was only after threats by the orcs to the southwest and Pyrrossi to the southeast that they banded into a unified kingdom under a single ruler. Most of the chieftains retained some form of control over their ancestral lands, however, and here was where the first Darrows had lived.

Centuries ago, as the foundations of Dundúran Castle were laid, the Darrows had gifted the building to their people. It'd served as the mayoral residence and seat of city politics ever since. The majority of the first floor was made up of a basilica, a wide central nave laid with gray flagstones and lit by great iron braziers. Square wood columns lined either side in colonnades, carved in exquisitely intricate designs that, as they spiraled upward, told mythical stories of the demesne and city. Through the colonnades were narrower aisles on either side with doors into smaller rooms, most of which had become administrative offices over the years.

The second floor held more offices, including the mayor's and other leading city officials, and each of the guild-masters kept an office as well. The city public archive also resided on the second floor, containing many of Dundúran's founding and most important documents. The third floor was the mayoral residence, where Mayor Thom Doherty and his large family had lived since he was first elected some twenty years ago.

Molly spotted the man himself on the far side, near the apse of the building. Squaring her shoulders, she walked with purpose down the nave, passing beneath heavy iron chandeliers dripping wax and around groups of harried city workers, off on this project or that task.

Light filtered in from the second-story windows above, illuminating those walking around the railed gallery and pooling in narrow rectangles on the stone floor. Through one of these beams of light, Molly caught the mayor's eye.

After a word to the two people he'd been speaking with, Mayor Doherty stepped forward to greet Molly. His hand was dry and warm when she took it to shake, and the way he patted hers and offered a friendly smile settled some of her nerves.

"Well, good day, Miss Molly. It's a pleasure to see you in Dundúran again."

"Thank you, mayor. It's been good to visit."

Waving her along to follow him, Molly walked beside the mayor at his slow pace. Nearing seventy, Mayor Doherty was beloved throughout the city. Many of his ten children had grown up in the mayoral residence, and it was a widespread joke over the veritable army of grandchildren he had. A few political upstarts had run against him in the past two elections, but faith in Thom Doherty was unshakable.

"I received the message that you intended to come see me. I hope it's nothing to do with that fae man of yours." His bushy white brows rose as he peered at her over his shoulder.

"No, not at all," she assured him.

"He treats you well?"

"Very well, yes. I'm happy at Scarborough."

"Ah yes," he chuckled as he led her into a small office off the corner of the apse. "I should be addressing you as Lady Scarborough now."

Molly blushed as she took the seat he motioned her toward. He shuffled behind a desk, much too big for the cramped room.

"You absolutely don't need to," she insisted, then hurried to help retrieve papers he knocked over with his rounded middle as he scooted around the edge of the desk.

"Forgive the cramped quarters," said the mayor as Molly did her best to restack the papers and parchments. "These knees weren't what they used to be, and Margaret wanted me to stop climbing the stairs so much."

"They didn't have a bigger office for you?"

"I didn't want to displace anyone here. You'd be surprised what a bureaucratic nightmare it'd be to shuffle spaces about."

Molly joined the mayor in a laugh, but soon it was time to get to business. Trying not to chew her lip, she pulled Lady Aislinn's letter from her pocket and laid it on the table.

"Well well, this does look serious," said Doherty as he picked up the letter. "What's going on, my dear?"

"It's my cousins—the Dunne girls."

The mayor looked up from tearing open the seal, his eyes suddenly sharper. The steel glinting there was why Thom Doherty was so beloved—jolly and benevolent as he usually was, the picture of grandfatherly good nature, all of it was over a spine of steel. In his tenure, Doherty had improved sanitation in the poorest communities, campaigned for the rebuilding of tenement houses, established fire brigades, and got the guilds to pay into a fund to cleanse the Shanago River.

While Molly didn't like having to air out Dunne family laundry, she understood that she couldn't do this on her own. She needed an ally like Lady Aislinn herself, and hoped she could trust the mayor to see it through. Given that the girls were all of an age to Doherty's own grandchildren, she suspected her trust would be well placed.

"I've come to give evidence against my uncle. With Lady Aislinn's approval and your own, I want the girls taken out of Brom's care."

The words fell from her lips like stones into the river, splashing her before sinking down down down. She held her breath, fingers threaded together into one big clenched fist, as the mayor stared back at her. Although wizened, his hair a poof of white fluff, Doherty's eyes were still as sharply blue as ever, and they seemed to take her measure.

Finally, a grin cracked his face.

"Thank fates," he said. "I've been waiting a long while for you to say that to me, Miss Molly. Tell me what you need."

With Molly out on her mission, Allarion took it upon himself to stroll the grounds of the castle. It was an excellent meditative exercise, helping him order his thoughts, and if he just so happened to run into Princess Isolde, well then, all the better.

Strolling past Lady Aislinn's prize rose garden, he discovered the princess and her guards taking a turn about the larger castle gardens, near where the kitchen gardens grew food for the inhabitants. If the princess paled when she saw him coming, he pretended not to notice.

"Good day, Your Grace." Allarion bowed at the waist before folding his hands behind his back.

He thought the casual stance would put her guards at ease, but if anything, they twitched and stiffened to have his hands out of sight.

"Good day," the princess replied by rote. It wasn't just the sunshine in her eyes that made her face pinch, he suspected.

"I have thought on our conversation yesterday and come bearing my answer."

The girl nodded gravely, as if he meant to pass sentence on her.

"First, though, I would hear your honest opinion."

Princess Isolde's eyes went wide, but she quickly snapped them shut with the midday sun above them. Offering his arm, Allarion led them to a nice, shady alcove below a leafy maple tree. It had yet to shed all of its autumnal colors and offered a cool place to stand and talk politics, no doubt the alcove's precise purpose when it was designed.

Though out of the sun, the princess's color was still high as she peered up at him.

"You want to know my opinion? Why?"

Allarion shrugged artfully. "I haven't met your father—nor your mother. You are my only representative of your family, and you have proven yourself wise beyond your years. It is also you who will lead this kingdom one day. If anyone's opinion should matter, it should be yours."

Her eyes rounded with his speech. "That's not a sentiment shared by everyone even in my mother's court."

"Then it's fortuitous that you are here and not there. I understand that your father has brought some . . . new traditions with him, as well as several Pyrrossi cousins. However, the kingdom is not just Gleanná. There is much love for you and your mother within the Darrowlands."

A reluctant smile curled the princess's mouth. "I've noticed that. It's been wonderful visiting more of the land that will one day be mine, and the Darrows are gracious for hosting me all winter."

If Gleanná was anything like the fae capital of Fallorian, Allarion didn't doubt that a season away from it would do the princess immense good. Subterfuge and intrigue had a way of making its own little world, one that warped perspective and diluted priorities.

Taking a deep breath, the princess looked away to consider her next words.

Her voice dropped to a tentative softness when she finally said, "If I were you . . . I would refuse my father."

"Indeed?"

She nodded at the garden. "My father has many qualities, but unfortunately, he's a jealous man. His cousin is the Pyrrossi emperor. His wife is the Eirean queen. Nowhere is he ruler in his own right." Looking up at him, Princess Isolde said, "I've heard him speak of retaking Caledon, how it would bring glory to our name to reunite all of Eirea under one rule."

"And does the queen support such conquest?"

"No, of course not. Her health, though, is . . ." The princess bit her lips together, her eyes going glassy. "Her health isn't strong, and if she cannot keep a close eye, my father does whatever he wishes."

"I see. And he hopes, one day, to lead a conquering army into Caledon? One with otherly soldiers?"

She nodded gravely. "That's what I suspect, yes."

Grave, indeed.

Allarion sighed. This wasn't totally unexpected or unprecedented. Humans had always had a tenuous relationship with the other races.

Smaller and unable to wield magic, humans only had their numbers as an advantage in ancient battles against the dragons and orcs and manticores. It was their numbers that attracted otherly folk in times of peace, too, and there were far more halflings in the world than either orc or human or dragon cared to admit.

Not that humans were always the aggressors or villains in these stories, of course. There had been one Fae Queen, many ages past, who'd thought to subjugate the human realms in order to serve the fae. It took a united front of orcs and humans to repel the attacks, and many fae warriors and dread-mounts had been lost. The fae rarely ventured past their borders since.

Allarion supposed, in some small way, the king's demand made a sort of sense. Human memories were far shorter, yet they retained a sense of foreboding when it came to otherly folk. The rivers of their lands had flowed red many a time as everyone jockeyed for space and power, and humans were often slaughtered in the process.

If there were to be otherly folk in Eirea, best to make them loyal subjects, ones who would fight *for* you.

Yet, here again, the human memory was short. Humans had tried this not a century past, pitting harpy flocks against orcish mercenaries. The ensuing battles were so bloody, so horrific, that it wasn't just harpies and orcs who abandoned the human realms. Sirens left their coves for more peaceful waters; the dragons disappeared to their island strongholds; and the manticores disappeared into the deepest reaches of the grasslands.

"I recommend King Marius read his own histories," Allarion told the princess.

Her brows rose nearly to her hairline. "That's what you want me to tell him?"

"Yes." He thought he said that clearly enough. "And I hope he heeds my advice. Lives are not weapons to wield blithely, and I am not the only otherly who won't bleed for his conquest."

Princess Isolde regarded him gravely, her countenance far more serious than it should be for one her age. "I understand, Lord Allarion."

Taking her hand, Allarion bowed over it, touching his forehead to the back. "I'm glad to hear it, Your Grace. I won't fight your father's war, and my loyalty is to my own queen, my beloved *azai,* but I can offer my friendship to the crown of Eirea, Queen Ygraine, and her true heir."

A blush bloomed across the princess's cheeks, and her lips parted in shock.

"B–but you said . . .

"Your father is not the king he thinks he is, Your Grace. Ygraine is queen, as you will be one day. I hope to be a friend to you both."

The princess swallowed hard, but he enjoyed witnessing the look of determination that hardened her soft face. These were far more responsibilities and worries than a child should have to bear, but Allarion admired how ably she carried them nevertheless.

"Thank you, master fae," she said, breathless. "I hope to earn that friendship."

"I'm sure you will." Straightening, Allarion added, "And please also tell your father that threats to myself, my mate, my home, or the Darrows won't be tolerated."

Princess Isolde actually smiled when she said, "He won't like that very much."

"I suspect not, no." Offering her a smile and his arm, Allarion led them back out into the garden proper. "Now, would you care to take a turn about the gardens with me? I'm rather bored without my Molly and would appreciate your company."

23

Of the four girls, Rory was the most difficult to pack up and bundle off out of the tavern. She didn't throw a tantrum or lock herself away, but it took hours of coaxing to finally get her out of her room and into the care of Mayor Doherty's eldest daughter, Glenda.

Over the three days it took to get the girls sorted and settled, Molly cried every night, her heart breaking for what had to be done. Although their father and the tavern were often horrible, it was what the girls knew. Molly well understood that the most terrifying thing was the unknown—when she'd left her village at the age of ten, part of her had wanted to run back to the cottage she'd been trapped in with her deceased parents because it was all she knew. The prospect of going to a new place, a *city,* where the only person she knew was Brom had terrified her more than plague.

Ripping the girls away from the familiar was best for them, but Molly still had to remind herself of it almost minute by minute.

Bryan and Nora's mother hadn't been seen in Dundúran in years. After a few cursory visits to her children once she'd left Brom, the woman hadn't bothered coming back. Molly had requested that inquiries be made, but that was only really to let her know where Nora would end up. Her best guess was that the woman was in Gleanná and so sent messages along to Bryan, too, about what was happening.

Merry and Rory's mother had died of drink years ago, before poor Rory could really get to know her. Her sister, however, the girls' aunt, had always hung about on the periphery, contacting Molly a few times about the girls. Molly was sure to update their aunt to tell them where the girls would be and encouraging her that, without Brom's influence, the girls would likely welcome her.

Little Oona's mother had been trying to claim her for years, and Brom, with more means and friends, had delighted in keeping her away from the girl. She too was with the extended Doherty clan now, and the plan was to help get her established so that she could take all the girls, with the help of Merry and Rory's aunt.

It was hard to explain all this to the girls, that a community had rallied around them. Dozens of neighbors came to help. Meals, foodstuffs, and clothing flowed into Glenda's home to help support her new charges, and Molly took such relief in seeing them all fed, bathed, and clothed.

Getting the girls back into school helped in establishing routine, and as they attended lessons during the day, Molly worked with Glenda and the other women to ensure that all the records were secured, all the necessary documents signed, and all the notifications sent. Her wrist ached from all the documents she messily signed, including a long written account of her own life with Brom and everything she'd witnessed.

Detailing her life at the tavern wasn't painful, per se, but Molly didn't look upon the memories fondly. There had been bright spots, of course, as in any life, but there were also a multitude of times that Brom neglected her, abused her, or otherwise made her life more difficult. Writing them down, seeing how the list grew and grew, was devastating in a way that Molly had tried to avoid all her life. Sometimes the hardest thing to endure about brutality was the acknowledgement of it.

Indignation kept her going through it all, the heat of her anger hardening her to the girls' sadness. Unlike her normal temper that burst in bright flashes, this anger burned coldly, a blue flame of rage that rendered and sharpened her determination. The girls wouldn't have lists like hers.

For once, Allarion had been the one to explode with anger. She'd made the mistake of taking the document back with her in the evening to finish, and while she prepared for bed, he'd stolen a glance at it.

The flames in the hearth exploded, a burst of energy lifting the coverlet and every small item in the room. They all clattered to the floor as the fire sizzled and wheezed.

"Say the word, sweetling," he'd hissed in a deceptively low, calm tone, *"tell me yes, and I will obliterate him."*

Watching Allarion *seethe* for her, his magic whipping in unseen whirls around his head and filling the air with the smell of petrichor, had offered her her own kind of calm. One of a coiled snake, about to strike.

Padding to him, she'd taken his face in her hands. *"He's not worth it,"* she told him, *"not anymore."*

And for the most part, Molly meant it. Brom was, at his core, a coward. Dismantling his life, taking away any trappings of success or control, would hurt him most.

"Am I bad for enjoying it?" she whispered later, when the night was darkest and Allarion held her in the bed they shared.

"You're too kind. You would burn down his life, whereas I would incinerate the man himself. Let me bring you his cinders."

The vicious promise had finally lulled Molly to sleep, comforted in knowing that if she was bad for enjoying someone else's pain, at least she was bad with her fae.

Molly set out to do for her cousins what she wished someone had done for her. What could have taken months, if not years, was handled within days with the full weight of the Darrows' and mayor's support—and, perhaps most importantly, the support of the community, who knew the kind of man Brom Dunne was.

But there was one final thing she had to do on her own—even if her fae, the mayor, and his daughter all warned her against it. Well, all right, not entirely alone. She agreed to bring Bellarand before her fae had the closest she'd ever seen to an outright conniption.

The girls were in school and comfortable if still adjusting with Glenda. Every document and message had been signed and sent. There was nothing left for Molly to do but hand Brom his copies of all the writs and protective orders, declaring his limited rights to see the girls under supervision.

Molly walked into that tavern for the last time, a packet of papers filling one hand and her cold rage making her brave.

The space was quiet, every chair and table empty. Although the sun was high in the cold winter sky, little light penetrated inside, and only a few of the braziers had been lit near the bar. They illuminated the hulking form of Brom behind the bar, and even from across the room, Molly could smell the stale stench of him.

He looked up, eyes bleary and bloodshot, at the sound of the door opening. Seeing her, he sneered.

"Wha' you want?" he slurred.

Molly watched in disgust as he took a hearty swig from an open liquor bottle. It seemed, without customers, Brom had decided to drink the stock. One of the mayor's assistants, the acting city treasurer, had warned Molly that all this would likely mean the collapse of Brom's business. The tavern would go under.

"He'll lose everything," the treasurer had told her carefully.

Molly hadn't been moved.

"Perhaps if he hadn't lost his family, he wouldn't lose everything else."

But that would've required Brom Dunne to be a different man— and Molly had learned years ago to stop hoping for that. Her uncle had survived for far too long on his meager charms, handful of friends, and shameless bullying. Perhaps if he'd had consequences along the way, these interventions and the blow they dealt wouldn't have been so large, but that wasn't the way of it.

It was time for her uncle to face the hammer blow. What he did afterward with what he had left would decide the man he truly was.

Brom waved a meaty hand around, gesturing at the empty tavern. "Nothin' left for ya to take, s' don't darken my door. Get out."

Stiffening her spine, Molly strode across the tavern to lay the packet of papers on the bar. Brom scowled at it and didn't move to open or read it.

"What's that?" he sneered. "Snatching the deed from me? You selling me off? Or are they more of your stupid lies?"

"You'll find everything written here. It's all official," Molly said, working to keep her voice even. "Your first sanctioned visit with the girls is next week at Town Hall. It'll be supervised by the mayor himself, so I'd take a bath and look presentable."

Brom snorted derisively. "Don't need the mayor to see my own girls."

"You do now. That's what happens when you don't take care of your children." The venom in her voice was biting, and even Brom heard it through his belligerent drunkenness.

"They're *my* girls! You hear me! *Mine!*" he roared into her face.

Molly nearly choked on his rancid breath.

"Then do the right thing and be a better man," she growled. "That's the only way you'll be in their lives."

Having done what she came to do, Molly turned for the door.

She wasn't expecting, big and drunk as he was, for Brom to be faster than her. She sensed him before she heard him, turning so he caught her shoulder rather than her hair.

Brom jerked her around, grabbing hold of her arm and shaking her.

"This here's my tavern! I built it, I ran it—you're not taking it away!"

"Rot in it for all I care!" Molly yelled back, losing her grip on her temper.

The more she pulled to free her arm, the harder his grip became. Dragging her forward into his chest, Brom put his face right in hers.

"You ungrateful bitch. I took you in—fed you, clothed you. I should've buried you with your parents."

Molly's hand cracked across his face, palm stinging with the smack of skin. "Yeah, you should've," she hissed, and slapped him again.

A bestial growl vibrated from Brom's chest. She was ready for his fist when it slammed into her jaw, but the impact and pain of his punch sent her reeling. He jerked her back with the hold on her arm, grabbing both her hands in one of his. Like a fish on a hook, he reeled her back just to hit her again.

Brom was beyond words, his face so red it was nearly purple, glowing with rage. Molly's face smarted and ached with his strikes, but she just turned her face up to snarl and sneer. It hurt, but seeing him unhinged, seeing this animal, gave her such vicious pleasure, she didn't bother fearing for her own safety. It was stupid, and she could just hear her fae's hiss of horror, but she got her own unhinged kind of glee seeing Brom reveal just what kind of man he was—and now everyone would see.

They tussled across the tavern, Molly trying to pull herself free and make for the door. She pushed at him, getting him unbalanced, but his big, sweaty hands were always there, grasping and grabbing.

It was when true fear began to trickle past her bravado that the front door, which she'd left ajar, crashed open. The sound thundered through the empty tavern, startling Brom enough to make him look up.

The ominous clop of hooves echoed through the tavern.

You just couldn't keep things simple, Bellarand grumped. *You went and had to get me involved.*

Brom visibly quivered when the unicorn lowered his head, pointing that long, sharp horn square at his chest.

Let me do it, Bellarand whispered through her mind, voice almost coaxing, far softer than she'd ever heard before. *Let me finish him. His blood will be so warm on my horn.*

Molly stamped her foot on Brom's instep, and finally the brute let her go. She stumbled away, hurrying to stand beside the unicorn.

She spat out a mouthful of blood onto his dirty floor. "Abide by the terms, or else we'll be back."

Brom made a noise of disbelief but paled when Bellarand scraped his hoof across the floorboards.

"Goodbye, uncle."

Grabbing a handful of Bellarand's mane, she turned to leave.

The sun outside was overbright, and Molly stood in the courtyard blinking for a moment, letting her eyes adjust. She rubbed at them to ease the sting, definitely *not* to wipe away any tears that weren't there.

A warm muzzle snuffled at her shoulder.

Are you all right?

"Yeah." Molly put her hands on her hips and turned her face to the sky. "Thank you for coming to save me."

It was no trouble. You know how I enjoy inspiring terror.

She went to grin but remembered her bruised jaw. Groaning, she touched a hand to her face, some feeling returning. She definitely had a split lip, and her jaw was sore to the touch.

Bellarand lowered his big head to inspect, and a huffing horsey laugh puffed against her.

Oh, you're going to be in so much trouble.

24

Not only had Molly been in trouble, but she finally witnessed what could only be described as a true, full-blown fae conniption. There were dire threats against her uncle, there were long-winded scoldings and fierce *I told you so*'s, there were furious hand gestures and rogue bursts of magic. It'd taken hours and standing bodily in his way to stop Allarion from riding for the tavern to burn it down with her uncle, still alive, inside.

"It's what he deserves," her fae insisted.

"I agree, but you're still not going to."

Even though the sight of the tavern burning down may have been cathartic for Molly, she knew the girls weren't ready to fully say good-bye to the place and their father. Perhaps he could set himself up with its sale and actually change—although she doubted it. And, she didn't want to be the one who set the whole neighborhood alight.

She explained all these reasons, but her poor fae was beyond reason. Every time he saw her bruised jaw, he turned more purple than gray. She'd never seen him truly livid before. If she hadn't known it was on her behalf, it might have been terrifying, but since it was, she actually found his rage arousing.

Eventually, Molly was able to use her body in other ways to keep him in the castle with her. Although her jaw and face were too sore to take him in her mouth, she was more than happy to massage him between her tits, something that'd become a fast favorite for him. He found it difficult to keep arguing when she dropped to her knees and pulled down his trou to play with his cock.

"Molly . . ." he warned.

"I thought I got whatever I wanted," she said, laying on her pout a little thick. "I want to make you feel good—and then I want you to return the favor."

A growl rumbled through him, and Allarion let his head fall back, his starlight hair hanging to nearly his rounded, muscled backside.

"Twins save me from headstrong mates."

"I thought you'd prayed for a headstrong mate," she reminded him.

"I did. I might be regretting it."

"No, you're not." And to prove it, she took him in her hand and pumped, adding a twist of her wrist at the end.

Allarion choked on his argument.

To her delight, he quickly scooped her up and laid her gently back on the bed. Their clothes were soon gone, and Molly spent the evening lost in a series of orgasms that took her pain away. He took his aggression and frustration out with his tongue, lashing and spearing her with it, and Molly only wanted more.

He devoured her long into the night, until she cried off, but even then, when she woke in the morning, it was to his mouth sucking hard at her clitoris. Her fae was insatiable, and he rendered her lax, boneless, and drowsy before breakfast.

"Too tired to leave?" he said, revealing his scheme.

"Mmhmm. Do it again."

And so, as compromise, Molly stayed abed their last day, resting between shattering orgasms. She joked that at this rate, he'd have to carry her over his shoulder when they left the next day.

His purple eyes sparkled—he took it as a challenge.

It was late morning by the time they were ready to leave Dundúran. Molly had said her goodbyes to the girls already, leaving clear instructions with them, Glenda, and Mayor Doherty of how they could write to her at the estate. She'd managed to extract promises from all the girls except Nora to write her at least once a week, if only to practice their letters—and managed to save the worst of her tears for when she was packing up her things back in their room in the castle.

The day was a parade of nobles and yeomen in their finery marching out of the city, a grand processional sendoff, presided over by a patient Lady Aislinn. Though, if Molly wasn't mistaken, the heiress watched them all vacate her castle with no small amount of glee.

Clad in one of her new dresses, a dark aubergine with shocks of lilac and pink threads, Molly held onto Allarion's arm as they descended the castle steps. It was remarkable to think she'd ascended these same steps only a handful of days ago, unsure of her place beside her fae. She couldn't say she was any more comfortable with the attention of the other landholders, nor surer that she belonged beside the striking figure of Allarion, but these past days had proven to her at least that she was brave—and that counted for something.

Bellarand practically pranced where he stood in the courtyard, ready to be out of the city. He'd been needling them all morning about when they'd be ready to depart. Seeing them emerge from the castle, he headed for the stairs, not caring which pages or grooms or statesmen were in his way.

Unfortunately for him—and her and Allarion—they were joined on the bottom step by brother and sister Fiona and Dougal Braithwaite. The siblings turned to peer at them, eyebrows arching to see Molly and her fae.

Lord Dougal smiled half-heartedly. "We look forward to seeing you next season."

"Indeed. At least next time we'll have been introduced," said Allarion without bothering to look.

Molly hid her snickering behind her hand.

The sound drew Lady Fiona's attention, and she craned her neck to look around Allarion at Molly.

"It was delightful to make both of your acquaintances. Our new friendship made the dull journey to Dundúran exceedingly worthwhile."

Molly could feel Allarion's mind catching on her supposing there was friendship between them, but then the noblewoman uttered a gasp.

"Dear me," Lady Fiona tittered, "what is that on your face? Were you . . . in a bar fight?"

A guffawing laugh escaped Molly before she could stop it. She pulled back her lips to snarl a smile at the noblewoman, setting Fiona back a step in alarm.

But just as her temper flared, Allarion's arm came around her waist, and he neatly spun to deposit her on Bellarand's back.

Bowing the least amount possible, Allarion said, "Good day, my lady," and swung up to join Molly, leaving behind a blinking, baffled Lady Fiona.

"Let's leave the city with a fond memory of us, yes?"

Molly snorted. "I could take her."

"Oh, yes, I'm quite certain of that."

I say let them fight, Bellarand hooted in their heads.

Both of you behave, Allarion intoned in his most serious voice, *at least until we're out of the city.*

Of course, neither of them behaved at all. Allarion tried to be stern, but it was hard when he was endlessly amused by the arguments his mate and his mount got into. They bickered over the smallest, silliest things. It was only recently that he'd realized—they enjoyed poking at each other. It was their form of friendship and fondness.

Although, he was wise enough not to point this out to either of them.

They alternated between rude insults and even ruder jokes as the noonday sun shone overhead. It wasn't until they passed the pastoral village of Granach that Molly looked about her and realized, "This isn't the way to Scarborough."

"It's a circuitous route, I'll admit. I wish to speak with Balar and a few others to pass on this new demand from King Marius."

Molly nodded, before an evil glint sparkled in her eyes.

"I suppose this makes you a *messenger pony,*" she crowed at Bellarand.

The unicorn huffed and puffed, and the newest volley of insults lasted them to the outskirts of the otherly village. It'd been established not far from the Brádaigh estate where Allarion and many otherly folk had migrated to after hearing about the Darrowlands.

As they approached, Allarion easily spied all the progress they'd made since his last visit. Log cabins had been erected in neat rows, and something of a town square had been demarcated by logs and stones. Several people, including humans, milled about in the square or walked between cabins.

It was an idyllic picture, and Allarion looked proudly at how far the otherlies had come. From a disjointed camp of people unlike each other as much as they differed from humans, they had built a community to support themselves and their dreams of a peaceful existence within the Darrowlands.

Lady Aislinn and her father had nothing but praise for the village, and he was pleased to hear that Granach and several other villages surrounding Dundúran had welcomed the manticores, half-orcs, harpies, and dragons into their taverns, markets, and festivals. There was even talk of establishing a new school, headed by the half-dragon Briseis.

Molly's eyes rounded with wonder. A handful of villagers noticed their arrival; some came to greet them as others ran off to spread the news.

The first to approach was the formidable manticore Balar. The eldest of his pride of brothers, the tawny male was something of the village mayor. Allarion knew him to be a somewhat surly male, although level-headed compared to his brothers, but he was all smiles and shining golden mane and swishing tail as he came to greet them, his leonine eyes fixed on Molly.

"Well now," the manticore boomed, "it's about time you introduced us to your bride!"

Balar held up his paw—five fingers like human or fae, though the palm side was rounded with sensitive pads and each finger tipped in a wicked, if retracted, claw. His feline nose wrinkled as he smiled wide, revealing long upper fangs and sharp front teeth.

Allarion could feel how Molly's heart thudded in her chest, but she still gave over her hand for Balar to kiss with his bisected lips. He couldn't help scowling when the manticore tickled her with his whiskers, making her laugh—which only deepened when he remembered manticores spread their scent with their lips and tongue.

"And who are you, kitten?"

"Molly Dunne. Who are you, tom cat?"

Balar's golden eyes glittered up at them as he said, "She's lovely, Allarion. No wonder you stole her."

Molly hooted with laughter, Bellarand stomped and whinnied, and Allarion scowled as he grumbled, "He is Balar."

More gathered round to greet them—or at least get a look at Allarion's *azai*. He recognized all of Balar's fellow manticores, as well as several of the half-orcs and two of the harpies, Maritza, the eldest, and Andreen.

"Come, sit by our fire," said Balar, "share all your news."

"Next time, my friend. We are on our way home after days away, and we must return."

Balar nodded agreeably. "Come to tease us, I see."

"To warn you."

That caused a bit of a stir, a few stepping closer. Balar's rounded ears flattened against his mane.

"About?"

Allarion succinctly explained the letter from King Darius, as well as his answer to Princess Isolde. Balar and the others listened with grave expressions, mouths pulled down around fangs and tusks.

"I encourage you all to meet the princess, she is a clever child. I have hope for Eirea's future."

"It sounds like her father will be a problem," remarked Maritza. Her large violet eyes had gone haunted by the mention of possible war with Caledon. Many harpies had remained in the northern fjords even after others fled the human realms; they still had dealings with humans, but their allyship had cost them dearly in previous battles.

"Perhaps, perhaps not. He is far away yet." Allarion tried to reassure them, displeased with having to be the one to bring such ominous tidings. "Nothing may come of it, but I thought it pertinent for you to know. The king may circumvent the Darrows to reach out to your village. I thought you should be prepared."

Balar offered his paw and Allarion took it to shake firmly.

"We appreciate the warning, my friend."

"If you are ever in need, you have only to send word to Scarborough. You are always welcome there."

Balar and the others nodded in thanks.

His task done and burden relieved, Allarion found the worry inside him replaced with a new sort of pride. He was proud of the work accomplished to found this village, and though he'd never closely associated with any of those there, he still counted them as allies, friends. They had all fought alongside Lady Aislinn and Hakon when her brother threatened Dundúran, proving their loyalty and bravery.

When his work on the estate was complete, Allarion determined to extend his magic and reach south, toward their village. A line of communication would be useful, especially if the village was ever in need of him.

They exchanged a few more pleasantries, with a promise to come visit soon as well as for Balar and anyone else who wanted to, to come see the estate in spring. Allarion shook hands with Balar, his brothers, Maritza, and a few of the halflings before it was time to bid them farewell.

Balar waved them back toward the road. "Go on and get your pretty new bride home," he laughed, throwing Molly a lascivious wink. "Until next time, kitten."

Molly waved as Bellarand turned. "It was nice to meet you, tom cat!"

It wasn't Balar's flirting that kept Allarion hot under his high collar the rest of the ride to Scarborough, although he did have the uncharitable hope that when Balar found his own mate, he'd understand the agony of not simply hoarding her away but having to share her with others.

No, what kept Allarion painfully aware of everything around him—namely, Molly and her lush form pressed to him from groin to shoulder—was the implication of Balar's parting teasing.

They would return home soon. They would be alone.

Perhaps they . . . finally . . .

His arms tightened around his mate, even as he willed his cock to settle down. She'd thankfully grown used to feeling him press into the small of her back—it was a common occurrence by now, and she took it with good, oftentimes flirtatious humor.

Allarion was infinitely grateful to be welcomed into her bed. The nights he spent with her fed his soul in a way nothing had before. It was more than enjoying the pleasures of her body; laying beside her as she slept, holding what was most precious to him, listening to her heartbeat and soft little snores—it all filled him with a peace deeper than he'd ever known.

This is where I belong, he often thought to himself through the nights with her. He'd card his fingers idly through her hair or trace gentle patterns on her back. Part of him was impatient for her to wake and rejoin him, but another loved the quiet peace of it, of knowing she trusted him enough to sleep in his arms.

The hope of continuing this, of remaining beside her, was a living thing inside him. More than he wanted to finally feel the hot clasp of her cunt around his cock, he wanted to lay beside her each night.

Even if it was the sweetest torture, his fangs aching all through the night.

The dark desire had only grown with his love and devotion to her. Although no longer scared of the impulse, like an itching wound, it was hard to ignore. He wanted the feeling gone—or resolved.

He'd made no more sense of it than when he'd first felt it. Allarion bore a small fear that when he did finally slide inside his perfect mate and feel her holding him tight, he'd lose all control. There were even times when he lay lapping at her pretty cunt that he had to fight the desire to turn his head and sink his fangs into the plushness of her thigh. Fates, when she squeezed her thighs around his head as she came apart on his tongue, a hunger so *deep* took root that he—

Bellarand stopped in the middle of the road, ears flicking. Birds jumped from nearby trees into the air, cawing a warning.

There's something—

The ground beneath them began to roll. The earth shook and

quaked, and the air crackled as if a storm gathered over the horizon.

Bellarand lurched and staggered, trying to keep upright.

Molly yelped, her fingers digging into his forearm banded around her middle. Allarion clutched her close and held onto the reins. He squeezed his thighs and swayed with Bellarand as the unicorn fought to keep his footing.

Agonizingly slow moments ticked by, the ground rumbling angrily. Trees creaked, and the stones lining the road shook loose of their places.

Then, as suddenly as it'd started, it stopped.

The world went preternaturally quiet.

Bellarand stood with his four legs spread, heaving breaths panting into his big chest. His ears swiveled back and forth, trying to catch every sound.

"What *the fuck was that?*" Molly shrieked, voice shrill.

"This is awfully far north for an earthquake," Allarion said. Unsure of the cause or its implications, and unwilling to speculate with his mate so exposed, he patted Bellarand's shivering flank. "Home, as quickly as you can."

Yes. Bellarand shook out his mane and leapt forward, breaking into a gallop. Dirt flew from under his hooves, and Allarion leaned forward into Molly, bending them lower on the unicorn's back to ease his way.

Bellarand raced through the countryside, mouth hanging open to gulp air as he ran. The trees streamed by in green blurs, but Allarion peered through their darkness, searching for . . . anything.

Eirea had had earthquakes before, but they were incredibly rare in a northern demesne like the Darrowlands. Of course, the world was a wild place and impossible to predict. It could be a fluke, an anomaly. Anything else made little sense.

Yet it was that anything else that sent a prickle up Allarion's spine.

The tightness in his chest only relented a fraction when they made the border of the estate. They passed through the wards protecting the border, magic a warm wash over them.

Allarion felt the forest stirring, noticing their return. The trees shook out their limbs, and the ferns unfurled their fronds. The lampposts lining the drive burst to life even though it was the afternoon, casting a meager light.

When they rounded the bend leading up to the house, already he could hear the shingles rattling and shutters swinging on their hinges in greeting. The house waved them home, although Bellarand didn't stop until they'd made the side door to the kitchen.

He came skidding to a stop, dirt flying. Allarion quickly dismounted and helped Molly down. She darted to stand by Bellarand's head, careful of his horn, and laid her hand on his quivering neck.

"You were faster than the wind," she praised.

Of course—I was—always—am.

Allarion took their bags off Bellarand's back.

Thank you for bearing us so swiftly, my friend.

Depositing the bags just inside the kitchen door, Allarion touched a hand to the wall of the house. Casting his senses wide, Allarion searched for . . . *something*.

But the house had nothing of note to report. A few things had fallen over in the quake, but the foundations held firm, and the house hardly cared about the shaking, too excited that they were returned.

When Bellarand had caught his breath and Molly seemed less shaken, Allarion drew her into the kitchen. Already, the house had a kettle steaming for tea, and he pulled out the small sack of provisions he'd acquired for her until a fresh shipment of food could be delivered. Assured she was safe and provided for, Allarion gathered her hands in his.

"I must check the wards and borders. Earthquakes are rare, but they are powerful."

Molly nodded. "Of course. I'll start making myself some dinner—and tell the house all my gossip."

The shutters of the kitchen window flapped excitedly.

She smiled, but it didn't reach her eyes. Allarion didn't like to see the tightness of her expression and the worry that pulled it taut. Yet, the same concerns lurked in his own chest. Best then to ensure nothing was wrong. Then . . .

"I will check the forest and perimeter. Then . . ." Bringing her hands to his mouth, he kissed each knuckle. "May I come to you tonight?"

The worry bled from her face as her brows arched in surprise. Allarion watched, enchanted, as her pupils blew wide.

"I'll be waiting for you," she said, her voice a breathy siren's song.

Groaning, Allarion couldn't resist taking a kiss. It had to last him one more interminable afternoon.

olly kept herself busy throughout the intervening afternoon, putting away provisions they'd brought with them, including the purchases they'd made at the dressmaker's the morning of the council meeting. Hanging up her new gowns in the armoire came with an odd feeling.

She stepped back to look at her rather eclectic collection of clothing now stored in the armoire. Different pieces hung alongside one another, like her best serving dress and the embroidered one she'd made and a sumptuous creamy white gown from the dressmaker's. She enjoyed all the colors and textures and fabrics, and as she looked, Molly realized that, although different, each piece belonged in the armoire. Each gown and bodice and trou had its place and use.

They represented all the facets of her growing life, all the new flavors and dynamics.

Yes, she liked that very much.

Although, there was one piece she hadn't yet tried on. A special piece she'd whispered to the dressmaker about, so that even sensitive fae ears couldn't hear. The lilac silk and lace confection she laid carefully on the bed, pulse fluttering to think of finally wearing it for him. She loved all the little buttons down the back and how the hue nearly matched his fae coloring—and soon, he'd get to appreciate it, too.

She breezed through making her dinner, the house and Bellarand keeping her company. The house was a bit too enthusiastic to help cook, sending every pot to boiling too quickly and curdling the sauces, but Molly didn't mind so much.

Bellarand claimed to be weary from the trip and running with such heavy loads, although Molly thought he looked fine. Still, she spoiled him with carrot ends and turnip slices, grateful for the company.

The earthquake had rattled them worse than the dirt below, and Molly didn't want to be by herself. She'd heard of the phenomenon, of course, but earthquakes were something that happened in Pyrros, especially when its great fire mountain, the Lupatian Volcano, belched fire. Could the volcano have erupted and caused such a massive stir that they felt it even so far north?

Bellarand thought it possible, and it was the only thing they could think of that made any sense. Even so, they spent dinner debating increasingly more ridiculous reasons for the earthquake—her favorite being his thought that all the worms had come down with severe flatulence.

By the time dusk settled over the tree line, Molly made her excuses and hurried up to her bedchamber. Breathing gone rapid with a warm, flushed excitement, she made quick work of throwing off her day clothes to wiggle into the layers of frothy silk.

It took her longer than she cared to admit to figure out all the buttons and layers, but by the time the full darkness of night settled around the house, all the candles and lamps in the room flickered with soft light and she stood before the floor-length mirror admiring her work.

A thin negligee, airy as gossamer and cinched at her waist, fell in dramatic drapes to the floor. It just barely hid a satiny set of stays that lifted her tits to perfection and nipped her waist nicely. Garters attached the silk and lace stockings to the bottom hem, and Molly wiggled her toes just for the joy of feeling the softness against her skin.

She might never have considered such garments before, not with her spots and pockmarks peeking out between the stockings and stays or beneath the semi-transparent fabric. Yet, twirling in the mirror, she couldn't help the smile that overcame her. She looked and felt like a cloud, swirling with beauty and elegance. Perfect for seducing a certain fae.

Yes, she liked this part of her new life, very much.

She was grateful not to have been rushed off to bed, even after having discovered what a talented tongue Allarion had, but that didn't mean she wasn't achingly ready to finally make love to him.

Her heart leapt into her throat at the sound of three rapping knocks on her door. It swung open, revealing Allarion looming at her threshold. Those purple eyes caught the soft light of the candles, fixing on her silken form.

Molly didn't imagine how his chest expanded with surprise, and she felt his hungry gaze rake over her from head to stockinged toe.

"Come in," she murmured.

Allarion stalked into the room like the predator she sometimes saw lurking in his eyes. His stark features gave him a ranginess, shadows catching in the hollows of his cheeks and temples. He crossed to her in just a few steps, coming to tower above her, but he kept his hands folded at his back.

Licking her lips, Molly said, "House, we'd like to be alone tonight. No snooping."

The shutters rattled in good humor before falling silent.

One of his brows arched, but otherwise he held perfectly still.

"Everything looks all right? All the wards and borders and trees and—and whatnot?" Honestly, another quake could shake them all night and Molly didn't think she'd care, so long as she got her hands on her handsome fae.

"Everything is in order. The estate is perfectly safe."

"Good."

Heart racing, Molly couldn't seem to catch her breath, not with him looking down at her like that—like every promise he'd ever made was about to come true. Fates, if Molly had told herself when she first arrived here that she'd be aching to take Allarion to bed . . . well, she might've believed it. For all their differences and the way they'd ended up here, she'd always been drawn to him.

Maybe there was something to what he'd said about his goddesses finding perfect matches.

His throat bobbed and his lips parted, but it was a moment before words came, as if he wished not to utter them.

"When I asked to come to you . . . I wish to hold you as you sleep. I don't presume more."

"Well, I do." Molly closed that last step between them, running her hands up and down his front, feeling the soft glide of his fine tunic spread over the solid muscle of his chest. "I don't wear something like this for sleeping."

Both brows arched this time. His arms slid around her, hands unerringly finding their way to rest on the swells of her backside. "Oh? And what do you wear it for?"

Pulling on his tunic, he dutifully lowered his head so she could rise on her toes and deliver a nipping kiss.

"It's for being fucked senseless by my fae lover," she whispered against his lips.

A bestial sound ripped from his lips, vibrating his chest under Molly's hands. She gasped in delight when his arms went tight as vices, crushing her to him. His mouth greedily took hers, lips pressing searing promises into hers.

Molly clutched at his tunic, her world spinning. Her moans of pleasure echoed in his mouth as his hands kneaded her backside, tucking her pelvis firmly to his. She felt the rigid, burning bar of his cock caught between them, and her cunt clenched with an answering throb to feel how he pulsed beneath his trou.

Digging into his tunic, Molly battled the buttons, desperate to feel his skin under her hands. His kisses kept distracting her, at once a bruising punishment for making them both wait so long then nipping and teasing to soothe. When she gasped for a breath, he trailed his lips across her cheek to her jaw and down her neck.

He lingered at her throat, and Molly felt the unmistakable scrape of his fangs along her skin. Her pulse jumped there, and he shuddered in her arms.

She whimpered when he straightened out of her reach, his face gone pained.

"If we make love, I fear . . ." A great heaving breath rounded his shoulders, and Molly didn't like seeing him try to make himself smaller, as if he felt he needed to seem less.

"What?" she whispered. "Tell me, my love. I promise, it's all right."

His nostrils flared as he searched her gaze. Molly held still, hoping to convey whatever he needed to find there. She was more than a little desperate for him, for the passion of a moment before, but she could reassure him. Whatever troubled him now had been vexing him for a long while. Best to get it out of the way so they could focus on the better things.

"I don't want to scare you," he murmured.

Molly bit her cheek to keep in the giggle. "My darling, I've seen you being eaten by roots. I promise you won't scare me." Surprise, most likely. Maybe even a little alarming. But scared? No, not anymore.

"They weren't *eating* me, merely—"

She touched her finger to his lips. "Tell me."

Gathering her close again, he kissed her fingertip. "Since bringing you to Scarborough, I have wanted . . . to bite you."

It was Molly's turn to arch her brows. "Bite me? Is that all?" Perhaps in those first days, she might've found such a declaration terrifying; his fangs weren't small. She'd be lying if she said she didn't have a few twitches of trepidation over feeling the pain of it, yet it didn't seem too much to ask of her. Not now, when she knew exactly who she held in her arms.

Allarion choked. "Isn't that enough? I've never wanted to sink my fangs into another lover before."

"Well, now I feel special." She smiled up at him, although she didn't think her attempt at lightheartedness truly reassured him. Taking his face in her hands, Molly made sure to speak clearly so he understood her when she said, "Allarion, many people enjoy a little roughness with their lovemaking. If you want to bite me, you can."

The shock was evident in his eyes. "But . . . to take your blood . . ."

"It's all right. I don't particularly like pain in my bed play, but if you feel you need this . . . just be gentle—and make it up to me."

A shuddering breath exploded from him, and Allarion clutched her close, burying his nose in the hollow between neck and shoulder.

"My beautiful, generous mate," he crooned, "you are too good to me."

"Mm, that's probably not true. But you've been nothing but good to me. It's a small thing to ask in return."

That rumble cascaded through him again, but rather than the explosive cadence of before, it was almost like a purr, seductive and deep. His hands turned from almost clutching to caressing, fingers tracing up and down her curves.

"Oh, sweetling, I promise you, by the time I'm ready, you'll beg for my bite."

Molly hummed in interest, glad that the matter seemed settled. She happily eased back into receiving his fervent kisses, although their passion now was more measured, a building up rather than a frenzy.

She couldn't honestly say the idea of a bite—a true one that broke the skin, not just a love nip—didn't give her a smidge of trepidation. However, it was worth it. Allarion was worth it.

This had troubled him for weeks now, and if it was the only barrier remaining to their finally enjoying each other fully, well, the answer was simple.

His hands wove magic of their own around her, touching her everywhere he could reach, stoking the flames a little higher with every caress. He deftly spirited them across the room to her large bed without his mouth ever leaving her skin.

When he did lean up, it was to again admire her garments.

"You got this just for me?"

"Just for you," she agreed, popping the last button of his tunic.

"Have you been planning this? Your seduction?"

"It wasn't much of a plan other than putting it on, but yes."

With a finger and thumb, Allarion pulled loose the simple knot keeping the negligee closed. The slippery tie fell around her hips and the translucent robe fell open, revealing the partially transparent fabric beneath. Molly knew her nipples would be just visible through the stays, dark points begging for attention.

His searching fingers found one, tracing a teasing circle around the peak with the barest touch. Molly bit her lip, resisting the urge to press herself into his hand.

"I think these should all come off," she said, tugging at his open tunic.

A wicked smile curled his lips. "Anything you wish."

"Oh, I wish very much."

She stood back a step, doing some admiring of her own. Like in all things, his movements were efficient, economical, graceful, but he somehow managed to make them seductive. It was the way his gaze almost never left hers as his tunic slipped from his shoulders and his undershirt came unlaced. He toed off his boots and stepped out of his trou with the elegance of a dancer, and by the time he stood before her naked, Molly's mouth had run dry.

He stood before her proudly, letting her look at her leisure. She already knew he was a fine man, every muscle packed tight with strength, but seeing him stand there, his legs spread and stance firm, had her heart fluttering all over again. His ridged abdomen led down to narrow hips with a distinct vee, all pointing to the dark purple cock bobbing against his lower belly. That ball piercing reflected a pinprick of light, and the memories of how it'd felt catching against her tongue arrowed between her thighs.

When she moved to slip off the negligee, Allarion stopped her with a gentle hand.

"Oh, no, sweetling, this should stay on as long as possible."

He drew her back into him, taking handfuls of the silk and lace. Molly thrilled to feel every inch of naked flesh pressed to her. Having him totally naked while she still stood clothed—albeit scantily—had her hands and mouth growing greedy. She needed to taste and feel and have all of him. Now.

Feeling the lustiness in her touches, Allarion answered in kind, his tongue curling round hers and his hands sliding beneath the negligee to take great handfuls of her backside. His breath hissed against her lips as his cock rubbed against the silkiness of the stays.

Molly delighted in feeling every bit of him she could reach, running her hands from his broad shoulders down his strong, lithe arms. She traced down the furrow of his spine to his taut backside and dipped her fingers in the winging dimples just above it. Gooseflesh bloomed across his flanks as she scored them lightly with her nails.

Allarion groaned her name, pulling back to incite her with his amethyst gaze. That hungry smile teased the corners of his lips as he pulled her toward the bed.

But when Molly expected to climb in or even have him lift her up onto the blankets, Allarion sat himself on the edge and reached for her. Pulling her by the waist, he drew her between his legs, his hands greedily running up and down her curves.

Her only warning was his grin twitching wider, then she was spun around and pulled down into his lap. He neatly gathered the long drapes of the negligee to the side, and Molly gasped to feel the burning length of his cock nestle against the gusset of her underthings.

A pleased rumble teased Molly's back. She held her breath as he arranged her, drawing her back into his front. He hooked her knees with his, drawing her legs over his and spreading them wide. She moaned as cool air kissed her overheated skin.

Her whole body clenched with need to be so exposed, so opened. He spread her unmercifully wide, almost straining her legs, and she loved it. Reaching an arm behind her, Molly buried her hand in his starlight hair and held on.

Allarion hummed in approval, his hands coming round to claim a breast and delve between her quivering thighs. He made another pleased sound to find how easily the gusset covering her cunt unlaced.

Molly moaned again as his fingers found her slick, needy flesh. He hissed in her ear as he soaked his fingers. His other thumb strummed against her hardened nipple, using the fabric of the stays to create an extra spark of friction.

He held her like that, suspended and exposed, as his fingers worked her higher and higher. She had no real leverage like this, no way to roll her hips or bear down for more of that delicious pressure, and no matter how she whined for it, he wouldn't be rushed.

Allarion petted and stroked and rubbed, his rhythm unhurried. Molly quickly felt herself melting, coming apart at the seams. She clutched at his head and laid her other hand over the one at her breast, pressing them harder to her.

The unyielding pressure grew low in her belly, a million little sparks of pleasure cascading from her head to her toes. Molly leaned her head onto his shoulder, arching her back and trying again to find a little leverage.

"Give me your eyes, sweetling. I want you to watch."

With effort, Molly picked her head back up, not understanding what he meant.

He lifted the hand she held, and with a simple crook of his finger, the large gilt-framed mirror across the room slid over the floorboards. It stopped a few feet away, framing their images in gold.

Molly stared at the picture they made, her swollen lips falling open in aroused shock. She felt how wide and exposed he'd pulled her, but seeing herself spread so obscenely—her gaze snapped to movement along her pink core. Her flesh glistened in the candlelight, as did his fingers as they eased through her folds. His fingers spread her wide for their mirror selves, revealing where she *wept* for him.

His other hand returned to her breast, and she watched his fingers play and strum at her before they dug under the cup to pull her flesh free. She overspilled his hand, his fingers nearly swallowed by the plush give of her.

Molly stared at herself in the mirror, seeing how she'd gone swollen and pliant for him. She almost didn't recognize the person staring back, lips parted on moans of pleasure and eyes gone half-mast and bleary with desire. Reclined on her fae, swathed in transparent fabric, she looked like some offering to an old god, ready to be sacrificed to their wicked desires.

His talented fingers worked her clitoris in perfect circles, but that wasn't why Molly gasped. The tease of his magic crept up the insides of her thighs, an invisible weight that rolled like syrup up her skin. Molly shuddered as the magic pushed against her entrance, and she watched as she opened a little more for the unseen force.

His magic filled her up, and Molly couldn't help it—she arched in his lap, head falling back onto his shoulder.

Magic working her cunt like a cock, fingers playing with clitoris and nipple, Molly couldn't focus. Sensation crashed through her, a rip tide that pulled her under. She gasped for air but got none, her lungs squeezed tight as her body bowed, the pressure bordering on pain as it pulled tight.

Molly rolled her head to the side, wanting to watch.

She met her gaze in the mirror, and sharper than the crack of a whip, she came.

Allarion nuzzled her shoulder and then—sank his fangs into her neck.

Molly's blood spilled across Allarion's tongue, a metallic burst that punched through his senses and slid down his throat in a smooth glide. Bright and visceral, more potent than even magic, it pooled in his center.

It conquered his senses and focus, even as he felt the spend splash from his angry cock, even as Molly's slick soaked his hand. What had to be his stomach, never used before, clenched around the sweet invasion of her blood, and another orgasm lurched through him to have her taste on his tongue.

He held her in a merciless grip, his instincts needing to hold and claim and keep. She came apart in his arms so prettily, her body bowed to thrust her heavy breasts forward and her pink cunt down. She overspilled his hands, dripping onto the floor to join the pearlescent ropes of his spend.

Allarion lapped at the two punctures he'd made, sealing them before he took too much. He couldn't quite settle on any one emotion as she went lax in his arms, legs and arms gone boneless and her head falling back onto his shoulder. His own release left him shaking, but still he couldn't loosen his hold.

Nuzzling at her silky skin, what settled over him then was a bone-deep satisfaction, the craving that had dogged him for so long finally abated. He swallowed down every last drop of her he'd taken, amazed and so, so grateful for the gift he'd been given.

When he was sure she wouldn't bleed and his legs wouldn't give out, Allarion stood. Molly slumped neatly into his arms as he turned to place her reverently on the bed.

She looked up at him with soft, sultry eyes, her lips flushed and swollen.

Although he'd just had her blood and his own release, it wasn't enough. The sight of her there, spread out before him like a feast, only fed his hunger. He'd never forget the sight they made in the mirror, seeing how Molly came apart watching herself be pleasured. His satisfaction in seeing her witness how well he could please her, how her pleasure was *his,* was fierce and consuming.

Allarion gently unlaced and unbuttoned her pretty underthings, careful to place them neatly on the trunk at the foot of the bed. He wanted to see her in them many more times but knew he couldn't be trusted not to rip or soil them.

Molly lay back, docile and well-sated, a little smile playing at her lips. When he finally had her naked, Allarion crawled over her to claim that smile, to taste it for himself.

"Did you get what you needed?" she murmured against his mouth.

He eased himself down over her, settling into the cradle of her body. His breath stuttered to feel how perfectly they fit together, how her body welcomed his. Her thighs drew up to frame his hips, and her arms came round to blanket his shoulders. His back arched in delight when her nails gently scraped his scalp.

"That and more," he answered, claiming another kiss. "You are the most generous of mates."

"Maybe, but I'm also a greedy one."

Beneath him, she rolled her hips, canting them so the underside of his cock slid along her mons.

"Are you now . . ."

Allarion delved a hand between them, taking hold of his messy cock to glide it up and down the center of her cunt. Molly moaned, her fingernails scratching and scraping along his shoulders. The bite of her nails grew sharper the more he teased, and Allarion considered going until she drew blood. Let her leave her mark on him as he had her.

Goddesses knew, she'd already left her mark on him inside. There wasn't a single part of him that wasn't utterly hers, and to wear her red welts as proof gave him a fierce kind of pleasure.

Molly's heel pressed into the small of his back. "You're too good at teasing," she panted. "Come inside me. I want to feel you."

Rumbling with satisfaction, Allarion notched his cockhead at her weeping entrance. He watched his flesh disappear inside her, her body giving round his. A shudder bowed his spine, and he fell over her, claiming her mouth in a ferocious kiss as he pressed onward, not stopping until he'd found his way home.

Little mewls and whimpers caught in her throat, and Allarion drank them all down. He gave her no quarter, needing this, needing her with a pain that only she could soothe. So many years, so long a life, all leading to this, to her—it was almost too wonderful to believe.

Their hips met, flushed together as he sheathed himself inside her. Those fingers that had nearly clawed him turned gentle, the pads running up and down his back in feathery caresses that left gooseflesh in their wake.

Her cunt clenched around him, a silky hot grip that robbed him of thought and sense. Burying his nose at her throat, kissing the punctures he'd made, Allarion moved.

Molly choked, throwing her head back on the pillows. "Your piercing," she croaked.

Ah yes. He could feel it dragging along the upper wall of her channel, catching her in just the right places. He'd found them with his fingers, tongue, and magic, so he knew just how he needed to angle his hips so that he grazed that spot with every stroke.

He found a rhythm, hips shuttling against hers in a dance far older than the fae, the forests, and even magic. She gave him all of her so sweetly, her sounds and touches filling him up as surely as his cock filled her. She welcomed him on every thrust, milking and gripping him with every retreat, as if begging him not to go. But he always returned—he always would to her. His home. His queen. His Molly.

She moaned his name, head thrashing on the pillow, her hips rolling to try keeping time with his. Allarion picked himself up on his hands, changing the angle and offering more leverage. His pelvis smacked wetly against hers, their sounds and scent of lovemaking saturating the bedchamber.

Molly's plush lips drew back in a rictus of pleasure, her hands grasping at his forearms for something to hold onto. His magic wrapped round her thighs and he drew them as wide as they could go, allowing him just that little more.

As his rhythm stuttered into a frenetic frenzy, he watched rapturously as her breasts bounced with their rocking. He pooled his magic on her lower belly, where he could just see the faintest shadows of her muscles clenching around his length. One tendril he sent up her middle to circle round her breasts; it spiraled around the lush mounds before capping her pert nipples, plucking and rolling under the insubstantial weight. The other rippled down her mons, settling around her clitoris. He could just feel its warm touch as he thrust inside.

With his magic working in concert, Allarion let go. He drove his cock deep inside her, wishing to join them forever. Her body took and gave, and a silent scream rent her lips wide as she came apart. Slick gushed around his cock, and Allarion lost his mind.

Drunk on her feel and scent, he was nothing but motion. He ran her down and pinned her with his hips, a brutal orgasm ripping through the fabric of his being. His magic snapped around them, knotting them together in an explosion of sensation.

For a moment, his mind touched hers—a golden light that washed him in warmth.

It was a divine light, the soul of his very own goddess.

Their bond snicked into place as the magic spun around them in whirls of blue and white light. His belly full of blood burned inside him, a heaviness that anchored him to this place, to her. As he filled her up with the last of his spend, Allarion had just enough wherewithal to smile down at her.

Mine, he thought. *You're mine.*
And in that golden glow, he heard the echo of her mind, too.
Yours.

26

Molly woke with a start, eyes blearily searching the dimly lit room. A single brazier still burned in the far corner, its small sphere of light casting most of the room in an inky blue.

A groan rasped behind her, and Molly realized the body that'd been pressed to her when she fell asleep was gone, taking the blankets and all the warmth with him.

She rolled onto her other side, sleepy and confused, only to gasp in alarm.

Allarion lay in the center of the bed, tangled in the blankets, his skin bearing a gleam of sweat. Although his eyes were clenched shut, one of his hands fisted at his chest as if it pained him.

Another groan ripped from his throat, and Molly's heart gave an answering lurch. Clambering to her hands and knees, she crouched above him and shook his shoulders.

"Allarion. Allarion!"

His head lolled to the side, mouth pulled taut over his teeth in a grimace.

Molly shook him more violently, desperate to see his eyes. She knew he'd need a long sleep soon after returning home, but he hadn't said anything, and he'd been so good about warning her when it was time.

He always looked so serene in his long sleeps, too. They weren't supposed to pain him!

Bellarand! She called through her mind. *BELLARAND!*

What did I say about shouting?

Allarion won't wake up! Is he supposed to . . . is that supposed to happen after the fae have sex?

An agonizingly long pause awaited her. *No . . .*

Well he's—

Allarion jackknifed, sitting straight up in bed in one sudden motion. Molly yelped, rolling to her side with his momentum. His hair billowed around him, and although his eyes were open, he didn't seem to see her, his hand clutching again at his chest.

"Allarion!" she cried, snapping her fingers to get his attention.

He flinched before his eyes focused on her hand, then her face. The breath shuddered out of him, mouth dangling open as he panted.

Molly held perfectly still, unsure what to make of the wild look in his eyes. Those purple irises stared at her in utter shock, striking as they were framed in white.

"Molly . . ." he groaned.

He grabbed her hand and dragged her forward. Wriggling closer, she frowned when he pressed her palm to his chest. Another breath shuddered out of his great chest, his skin burning and clammy beneath her hand, and his heart beat a wild staccato—

She gasped, jumping to her knees to plant both hands on his chest.

"Your heart! You have a heartbeat!"

Allarion stared up at her, dumbstruck. "It . . . it thuds," he said.

Tears sprang to her eyes even as she smiled. "Yes, it does. Like a heart should. But I didn't know . . ."

She'd never heard him have a heartbeat or seen him with a pulse before. Yes, he breathed air like she did and so had lungs. He'd once in a while ingest something and so must have a stomach, too. And he certainly had blood, black blood that had to go somewhere; she just never considered where, as his chest had always been quiet.

In her wonder, Molly searched his face, trying to gauge how he felt. To never feel your heart beating, and then all of a sudden have one, it had to be alarming.

But as she looked . . .

"Hold still," she told him, leaning to her bedside table to pick up the lamp that sat there. "House?" The lamp in her hand lit, illuminating them in a soft yellow glow.

She brought the lamp closer to his face, lifting his chin with a crooked finger. Turning his face into the light, Molly saw why he'd seemed different.

The whites of his eyes were white—not black.

"Your eyes . . ."

Grabbing his hand, she turned it over to examine his wrist, where thick veins ran beneath his pale skin. Even in the dimness, she could see how the blackness had faded. It wasn't blue or green like hers, but it wasn't the dark spiderweb he'd gone to sleep with.

Allarion silently brought his wrist to his mouth, and before Molly could stop him, he scored it with the tip of a fang. Dark blood dribbled down his inner arm as Molly quickly put down the lamp and grabbed a kerchief.

She mopped up the trail of blood and pressed the cloth to his small wound.

"What's happening?" she whispered.

He gently took her hand and eased it off the wound. The kerchief came away stained with his blood—a dark claret red.

Molly pushed the cloth back when the wound welled with another bead of blood.

"Allarion?" she said, more forcefully.

"I didn't know how he did it," was what he finally said.

"Who did what?" Grasping his chin, she forced him to look at her. "Please talk to me. You're worrying me."

As suddenly as he'd sat up, a ridiculously wide smile broke across his face. He laughed, a wild sound, and gathered her up in his arms to sit her in his lap.

"Your blood—it must be your blood."

"Don't blame this on me," she grumbled.

"Oh, my wonderful *azai,* it's entirely your doing. I wondered how Maxim had begun to look so different but never imagined he'd imbibed her blood."

"Who's Maxim?"

The name sobered him, and Allarion's gaze dropped to regard her. Although she had his eyes, his gaze was far away on memories.

"It's time I told you, sweetling . . ."

Cuddling her close, Allarion told her a story, one of friendship, love, and sacrifice. He spoke of his dear friend Maxim, a fellow fae and warrior, in reverential tones, telling her how he'd stumbled upon his friend's deepest secret. A human mate and halfling child.

Everything might have been well—the child wasn't the first between a fae and human—were it not for the girl's gift of foresight. Hidden away as they were, still nothing might have happened, but as the girl grew, so did her powers. Her magic, wild and uncontained, touched the magic of the faelands, and there was almost nothing that happened in the fae realm that the Fae Queen didn't know.

Soon, whispers slithered through the trees, into the faelands. They permeated every street, every home. That a halfling girl had foreseen the death of Amaranthe.

Wanting it not to be so, desiring a child with such a gift, the Fae Queen began her hunt—and Allarion, Maxim, and Aine began to plan.

Allarion told her of Maxim and Aine's sacrifice in a quiet voice lacking much inflection. The memories were still raw inside him, and Molly wrapped her arms around him and wept with him as he spoke of his friends' deaths.

His story ended with a hurried escape from the faelands, to a bower built into a hill. In whispers he described how he'd helped Ravenna into the deep sleep to mute her powers, to await when it would be safe again.

His final words echoed in the bedchamber, a somber reminder of his promise to his friend.

Molly lifted her head from his shoulder. "The other bedchamber . . . Ravenna is the friend you've been expecting."

Allarion nodded, his face a mask of grief.

Molly ached for him—and for the girl, out there even now, sleeping in her bower, awaiting a brighter day. Her past jealousy over the girl shamed Molly; she knew what it was to be orphaned, and to leave everything she'd ever known.

"I hope the estate will be safe enough soon," he murmured.

"All this . . . it's been for her. For Maxim and Aine."

His lips lifted, but it wasn't quite a smile, for it was far too sad. Leaning his forehead on hers, he said, "At first, yes. But then I saw a woman at a well—and she changed everything."

Her heart ached in her chest, and for a moment, she wanted to weep all over again. She let herself have a moment of disappointment that this had all begun for someone else, but then forced herself on. She should have known his reasons for doing all this were noble and selfless, for that's just who he was—her fae was good to his core. Far too good for her, but it was too late for that now.

Even with how he'd gotten her here, Allarion had spent every moment proving to her that he was sincere. That unlike any man before, he meant what he said. He gave her space and time. He gave her choices. He gave her a home.

It didn't matter how this had all begun—nothing was perfect and life wasn't a fairy tale. What mattered was that they were here, together. By some divine intervention or cosmic force or utter coincidence—didn't matter. Nothing would part them now. Not a Fae Queen, not a belligerent uncle, not even her own stubbornness.

"I love you," she whispered.

Those beautiful eyes searched hers, so changed and yet so familiar. They were exactly the same hue, the same glittering jewels that saw straight through her, merely set in a different frame.

"I have loved you since I first saw you. I may not have known it, but I *knew* it." Taking her hand, he placed it on his chest, where his heart thudded steadily. "Holding you in my heart has been my greatest joy. And now, you are the beat of my heart. My life's blood."

Molly wished she was half as romantic with her words as he was, but all she could do was kiss him. Wrapping arms and legs around him, she clung tight to her fae, showing him in every touch and caress and kiss that he was the one for her. He saw what no one else did, cared when no one else did, was there when no one else was.

With him, Molly wasn't alone.

Allarion received her fierce love with all the patience and grace she knew he would, holding her tight as she carded her fingers through his hair and sucked his bottom lip. And although she was sore and sticky from their previous lovemaking, she began to roll her hips, another ache for him pulling at her belly.

Keeping his transformed gaze, Molly reached down between them to take hold of his hardening cock. After a few firm strokes, she guided the cockhead to her cunt and bore down gently. He glided inside, a small roll of his hips thrusting his cock deeper.

Arms around him, weight on her knees, Molly began to rock her hips, taking him that much more with every downstroke. That infernal piercing slid up and down, catching just the right spot with just enough pressure to make her shudder deliciously.

Dropping his head to her shoulder, Allarion kissed along the tender curve to her neck.

"You wonderful girl," he breathed, tickling her skin.

Molly laughed to hide how much the words pleased her. "I didn't do anything. Not really. You did all the biting."

He lifted his silvery head to pin her with a look as serious as a dirge. "You've done everything, my love. *Everything.*"

His words sank inside her, and in the soft darkness of their bedchamber, as they softly rocked together, Molly began to believe it.

27

Allarion had never seriously considered his own mortality, nor even truly his own health. As a fae, long-lived and a stranger to sickness, such things were often far from not only his mind, but the minds of all fae. It was a disconcerting realization that he was, however, dying.

That was, until his clever, wonderful, beautiful Molly brought him back to life.

Over the course of several days, Allarion witnessed something that was nothing short of miraculous. After a few more bites to sip a mouthful of her blood, his own completely reverted to a dark red, just like hers. His sclera went white, his gums and tongue pink. His skin lost some of its gray pallor, his hue taking on a more mild lilac coloring with a pinkish flush of health.

He couldn't help it—in those first days, he could often be found standing naked before a mirror, staring in amazement at the transformation taking hold.

An early winter morning shone brightly from the windows, illuminating his form from behind. Allarion flexed his hands and wiggled his toes, watching the tendons move beneath his purplish skin.

Goddesses, in some ways, he hardly recognized the male staring back at him in the mirror. It was the same face, the same hair, the same limbs. And yet . . . it wasn't.

Not only had Molly's blood rejuvenated his own, it'd awakened his appetites. No longer did he look upon food and drink apathetically. The aromas that wafted from the kitchen set his belly to rumbling—an alarming thing when it first happened. He'd put Molly's hands on his middle so she could feel, but it only sent her into a fit of giggles.

"You're hungry," she told him. *"Come here, I've made luncheon."*

And so Allarion tried everything and discovered a new favorite pastime. He devoured whatever Molly put in front of him whether he liked it or not. Most of it he liked, savoring the tastes and textures of food. He enjoyed wiling away an afternoon as he and Bellarand stood at the butcher block, tasting things Molly offered.

Bellarand was certainly right about carrots, they were fantastic. So were the potatoes Molly liked making, roasted in butter and garlic. And the sauteed green beans and squash. And the crusty bread she baked, and the sweet treats she called pie. And then to learn pies could be savory, filled with vegetables and fish—utterly amazing. And the drink, oh, the drink, he found wine enchanting and enjoyed mead as much as he thought he would, the taste reminding him a little of Molly's.

All this meant that, even just within a few days, his face wasn't quite the same. As he turned and twisted in the mirror, his ribs weren't so prominent, his spine not so pronounced. His cheekbones and jaw, while still more sharply contoured than a human visage, were filling out. He was beginning to put on meat, no longer rangy but . . . healthy.

It was an oddly thrilling thing to see in the mirror. He needed to look at himself to believe it, to witness not just how quickly he changed but how quickly he took to the change.

His magic still sparked inside him, was still connected in its partially formed bonds with the estate, but he could feel the weave of it changing. Molly had added her own weft to the pattern, transforming the very weave and texture of his magic. With their growing bond, he'd felt how his magic was shifting, but with her blood flowing in his veins, it was as if he'd ripped apart the last vestiges of his former life and world. They were threaded together now in the very fabric of the land and its inherent magic.

One day very soon, he would be strong enough to leave the estate and retrieve Ravenna.

And the reason for it slipped her arms around him from behind, splaying her hands along his middle. Molly's breath tickled at his shoulder as her fingers glided up and down the ridges of his abdomen, tracing arcane patterns along his skin.

"Look at how pretty you're getting," she said, peeking out from behind him. He caught only her eyes and the corner of that impish mouth reflected in the mirror.

"I've always been handsome," he told her, "I'm merely becoming more so."

Her smile pressed into his back. "I agree." In the mirror, he watched as those lithe hands trailed down his body, skating over the flat plane above his growing cock. "Whatever did I do to deserve such a handsome husband?" she crooned as she took him in her soft grip.

"Vixen," he said, attention riveted on the dual sensations of having her plush body pressed to his back yet her hands deftly fisting his eager cock. "We both know it's I who am the lucky one."

She made that delicious sighing hum, breath puffing along his spine as her hands worked in tandem up and down his shaft. He was no match for her attentions, especially not when he knew her to be especially amorous in the morning. She had him engorged and dripping in little time, her movements perfect and precise.

He admired the efficiency and couldn't help his amusement at how successfully she'd learned to work his body.

A hunger for food wasn't the only appetite he'd grown in the intervening days.

Oh, no. Much as he desired food, he craved his mate far more. She satiated him in a way nothing ever had, filling his now-beating heart with a need so dire, he never wanted to be more than a few paces from her. If he'd thought himself besotted or devoted before, it was nothing to the way he obsessed over her every feeling, thought, and whim.

He delighted in watching her play with him, but soon enough, it was time to gorge.

Taking her hands in his, he turned in the circle of her arms, grinning down to see the high color in her comely cheeks. Drawing her arms up around his shoulders, he stepped into her body, relishing the soft scrape of her nipples along his skin. They tracked twin lines up his body as he knelt and caught her behind the knees.

She jumped into his arms, the both of them now more than familiar with the move. Allarion found he was happiest with his mate in his arms, carrying her to bed.

He bore her down to the already tangled blankets, giving her some of his weight as their mouths joined in that perfect dance. It was just as thrilling as when they danced in the evenings in the solar, the harpsichord playing a merry jig. Their lips and tongues moved in concert, nipping and sucking until Allarion melted into her—just as he wanted to be.

When he rolled to his side and his hand began to slide down her soft body, Molly opened her legs for him. She bit his lower lip as his fingers found her warm, wet cunt, already throbbing and ready for him.

"Did you wake like this?" he asked her.

"Mmhmm," she hummed, hips rolling under his fingers. "Dreamt of you."

Allarion rumbled against her mouth, pleased to hear it. He dreamt of her in his long sleeps, too, always wanting to be near her.

Much as he'd poured into this estate, this house, it was his *azai,* his Molly who was his home now. It was with her he wanted to be. She was his home, his sustenance, his very heart.

His lips trailing down her neck, Molly turned her head, offering better access to her throat. Allarion laved the flat of his tongue over the scabbed punctures but moved on. The skin was too sore and red and needed time to heal.

She made a noise of confusion, then a sharp inhale as he dipped down to circle his tongue around her left breast. Her gaze seared him with its heat as he teased the tip of his fang over her peaked nipple.

Throat bobbing, Molly bit her lip before nodding.

"My sweet mate," he praised.

He filled his mouth with her breast as his magic gathered to dote on the other. His tongue flicked and worried the nipple in the opposite rhythm of his magic, and soon she was wriggling on the bed beneath him, hips snapping to find more pressure from his fingers.

The warmth of his magic pooled around his fingers, taking over as he moved to fill her with first two and then three fingers. He curled them slightly, seeking and finding that textured patch of skin on the upper wall.

Molly's back bowed, her legs falling open as she clenched around him. Her fingers dug into his hair, and Allarion needed no further prompting—he sank his fangs into the tender flesh of her breast, tongue still lashing her nipple.

A small stream of blood began to flow, and he sucked at it and the nipple, fierce pulls that made her groan and whimper. Her cunt seized around him again, a second orgasm cascading through her.

He'd never grow tired of her body. His Molly was a delight in every way—not least of which, that she could orgasm multiple times in quick succession. Goddesses, he was the luckiest fae alive, and it was his duty and pleasure to wring as many as possible from her before taking his own.

As he soothed his tongue over the punctures, his magic pooling over them to ensure the bleeding stopped, he replaced his fingers with his cock. He hissed through his bloodied fangs as he eased inside, aftershocks of her orgasm rippling through her.

Drawn deep, he pressed inexorably on until he was seated fully inside her. Surrounded by his Molly, Allarion dropped his head to claim those plush lips, catching her in soft kisses as he indulged in the bliss of her body. He'd stay like that all day if he could, buried inside his mate, kissing her softly as the sun crossed the sky.

He was the patient one of the two of them, however.

Eventually, her little heel dug into the small of his back. "Sometime today," she teased at his ear.

"Later, then," he whispered back, settling himself on his elbows.

Molly laughed, her eyes dancing with mirth and morning sunshine.

Biting her lip, Molly waggled her brows as she clenched her muscles around him. Goddesses, he was no match for her when she did that.

He held out for a while, brave fae warrior as he was, but the little rocks of her hips and rippling grip of her cunt were the victor.

Flexing his backside, Allarion began a gentle rhythm. Every thrust and retreat was a gift, every sound from her throat a boon. He took his precious mate lazily, greedily, for he knew as surely as he did that his heart beat for her that he would never tire of her. She was a hunger that could never be sated, a need that would never dull.

So even though she dug that heel into his back and growled naughty things at him, he took his time. He indulged. Every day, she brought him back to life, and he wanted to savor every moment.

Throughout his transformation, Allarion found himself caught in a bittersweet wish to speak once more to Maxim. He missed his friend, and the grief of his loss would be a burden Allarion carried for all his days—but now, even more than that, he felt himself bonded to his friend in a way he couldn't be to any other fae alive.

Maxim alone knew what it was to have a human mate. A heart beat.

And to sacrifice that for their child . . .

Allarion's respect for his friend only grew. To know now what it was to have an *azai,* to feel how deeply his love and devotion went for her, he didn't know if he could allow Molly to do what Aine had done. Even to save their child. Perhaps one day Allarion would know the profound joy of having his own daughter to cherish and protect, and perhaps then his perspective and opinion would change, but now, he didn't think there was anything in this world he valued more than the life of his Molly.

His precious mate lay reclined on his chest in their bath, and he couldn't help bending to kiss the crown of her head. Her wet, fragrant hair slid against his lips, a complement to her silky skin under his hands.

Afternoon light limned their arms in a white glow as they sat soaking in the great copper tub. A morning of lovemaking and then baking berry pies had left them sorely needing to cleanse, and there were few things he enjoyed more than bathing with his Molly.

Sitting with her between his legs, given the trust and privilege of washing her hair and back and limbs, it all filled him with an indelible sense of peace. The warm steam that floated around them, the feel of her supple limbs under his hands, the soft, pliant way she let him care for her soaked his soul in the kind of happiness that some could only dream of.

Washed and scrubbed, they lay together as their fingers and toes wrinkled, enjoying the last of the water's warmth. Outside, a clear but cold day shone through the windows, but inside, their haze of fragranced water and heady steam felt a world away.

He watched on as Molly gently traced a finger up the inside of his arm, following a thick vein to his wrist.

"Does it feel much different?" she mused quietly.

"Yes and no." He held his hand open as her smaller one explored the dips between his fingers. "So much changes and yet some things remain the same."

She hummed in consideration. "Just no growing taller. I like you this height."

Allarion chuckled, drawing his legs up to cuddle her closer. Yes, he thought he was the perfect height, too; perfect for tucking her under his chin when they lay together and for her to bury her face in his chest when they stood.

"I never thought . . ." He turned their hands together, marveling at the crystal droplets that caught along their skin and reflected pinpoints of afternoon sunlight. "I don't think the fae always had black blood."

"No?" She tilted her head back to peer at him. "You don't think it's a side effect of having a human for a wife?"

"Oh, it very much is," he said, kissing her temple. "Maxim too had lost the black in his blood after marrying Aine. I didn't know how, he wouldn't say. But . . . I don't think you and she transformed us—I think you've restored us."

"Wouldn't you remember having red blood and a heartbeat?"

Allarion thought so, but then again, his life had already been so very long. If he'd been this way as a child, he'd no memories of it. His mother and other fae older than her, though scarce, didn't speak of a time when the fae lived with heartbeats. There were a few mentions he could recall in ancient stories and texts, of fae feeling their hearts soar or pound, but he'd always thought it metaphorical, creative license.

"I don't. I'm not sure anyone alive remembers such a thing. But our hearts and stomachs must be more than just vestigial remnants. I think, as our bond to the faelands and its magic strengthened, we forgot how to live without magic."

Molly's brows and lips puckered with thought. "You think the blackness in your blood is magic?"

"Yes."

"But you still have your magic, right?"

"I do. It flows in me as it ever did, yet it feels . . . freed. It isn't my lifeblood, no, but still inherent."

She nodded slowly. "Your kind is the only one I've heard of that doesn't eat. Everything else has to at some point. I know your kind is unique, but it doesn't make sense for you to be so different, if that makes sense."

"It does," he assured her. "Feeling hunger . . . it is the natural state of all life. For whatever reason, I think my kind began to rely on magic too much. Perhaps it started slowly—using magic to stave off hunger in dire times, to keep the blood flowing during sickness. Magic can do so much, and there are few who'd resist the temptation to use it to save themselves, or someone they loved."

There was nothing he wouldn't do to keep Molly safe—magic or no. Countless fae before him likely felt the same about their *azai* and families.

"Perhaps they even used it to extend their lives," Allarion mused.

Molly stiffened in his arms. "Do you think without—?"

"I will be perfectly fine," he said, "I promise. We have always lived much longer than other beings. And, although magic may extend it, I think perhaps in the end, over so many lifetimes, it is killing us." It couldn't be natural to live so long without eating, without having a heartbeat. When he recalled how his face appeared just a few days ago, he seemed almost skeletal compared to his form now.

The fae were a lithe, willowy people, but perhaps they weren't supposed to be. At least not so much as they appeared. So many were painfully thin, ribs prominent and cheeks sunken. In the faelands, this was just what it was to be fae. But perhaps . . . over lifetimes, the fae were starving.

"Like Amaranthe," Molly whispered.

Allarion drew a long breath. "Yes." She used warped magic to extend her life, to break the cycle of queens—but perhaps she wasn't the first. Perhaps her actions merely exposed the rot that had been festering for so long.

Turning onto her front, Molly laid atop him, wrapping her arms around his middle. He drew his legs up, cradling her body with his.

The fae were ill, sickened by their own magic and a queen who refused to cede her place in the cycle. The enormity of the realization made him shudder, and he sank further down in the tub.

"Don't despair," Molly whispered against his neck, sensing where his thoughts went. "There's time yet for your people. One step at a time."

Allarion pulled in a deep breath, steadying himself.

Indeed, that was the only way. *One step at a time.* This hadn't happened in one cataclysmic event but over time in increments. Healing would have to be the same.

For now, it was enough to be here, healing in his mate's arms.

Their existence might have been perfect—were it not for the earthquakes. Allarion had heard of aftershocks, and he thought perhaps the region shook with them now. Although, each seemed stronger than the last.

The next quake happened in the middle of the night, while he was dozing and holding his sleeping mate. All the little items in the room began to wobble, and the undulating rumble shook the bed.

Allarion threw himself over Molly, tucking her body under his as the shaking went on and on. She yelped when items went clattering to the floor, and the house rattled its shutters with fear.

He sent his magic down into the earth, feeling the weft and warp of the native magic woven with his own. The forest trembled, uncertain and frightened by the shaking. All it knew was that the tremors came from the south.

When the shaking finally stopped, it took a little time to calm Molly, and then even longer to calm the house. The shingles clinked with agitation, and as Molly crooned to it, Allarion rearranged everything that had fallen, broken, or shifted.

He spent the next day searching the estate, but other than a few more felled trees and a disgruntled family of beavers whose dam had ruptured, there was little damage. That was something to be grateful for—and though he was, a shiver of suspicion crept up his neck.

The second shake came two days later, about an hour after luncheon.

Allarion stumbled as quickly as he could to the garden, losing his footing over the shaking earth. He found Molly on the ground, fallen on her backside and eyes wide in surprise.

He went to help her regain her feet, but she instead pulled him down to her. On the ground, they rode out the shaking.

Around them, birds cawed and tree limbs shook. Those that still had leaves to shed flung them off, and pinecones came toppling down like bristling projectiles.

A great crack rent the air, and they turned in time to see a great pine tree shudder before its roots gave, the force of the shaking too much for its trunk. It came down in a great crash, limbs tearing and sending a spray of dirt into the garden.

This shake lasted for an interminable count of twenty before finally relenting.

At first, he didn't quite discern it, his own body quaking.

Then the world went quiet.

Enough! Bellarand came stomping around the side of the house. He scraped the dirt with his horn and stamped his hooves. *Stop this shaking!*

Allarion agreed. Only, he didn't know how.

Just that the quakes were growing in intensity—and closer together.

"This never happens in the Darrowlands," said Molly, her face pale.

He *hated* the fear in her eyes.

And hated even more that he couldn't make it stop.

28

olly hustled down the drive, expectation a sharp wedge in her chest. Allarion had reminded her that the letters would work their way up to the house on their own, the trees helpfully passing them along, but she couldn't wait. And, with the recent rain, she didn't want them to get wet and smudged.

She'd made the girls promise to write, but two days had come and gone from when she'd asked them to send their first letters. Every day that passed made her that much more anxious, so even though the morning mist hadn't yet burned off, she was already in her sturdiest boots trekking for the estate border.

Of course, her darling fae hadn't let her leave without bundling up. Already she sweated under all the layers of knit and fur and oilskin cloak. From the way he'd fussed and dressed her, anyone else would think she meant to hike through miles of a blizzard, rather than follow the graveled drive a half mile to the eastern edge of the estate.

Still, when she rounded the bend in the road around a salient grove of trees, she wasn't prepared for the sight that met her.

A parade of furniture, barrels, and crates rolled slowly down the drive, balanced on wide wooden pallets. Most had been covered with tarpaulins, roped down to the pallets to stave off the worst of the damp air.

Molly blinked before a surprised laugh burst from her.

It seemed Allarion's shopping from Dundúran had arrived.

Chuckling to herself, she hurried down to meet the caravan. She kept pace with the slow-moving furniture, peeking under the tarpaulins. He'd told her he made a few purchases while she was at her uncle's tavern or in Town Hall with the mayor. She hadn't realized he'd bought the whole marketplace! No wonder a few people came to wave goodbye as they left the city.

Two grandfather clocks, velvet-cushioned chairs, dressers, a sedan, trunks, a marble-topped washboard, a foldaway desk, end tables, and empty gilt frames were just what she could see and recognize. More was stowed away in straw-stuffed crates and lidded barrels.

Molly jogged to catch up with the front of the caravan, marveling at all the goods. This was enough to furnish at least three more rooms—she recognized some of the pieces as possibilities they'd discussed for the formal dining room, the atrium, and conservatory. Others were surprises, and she looked forward to hearing his arguments about where he thought they should go.

On the first pallet sat a sturdy, dark-stained cabinet. Affixed to the top was a leather sheaf.

She plucked it out from under the ropes, unwinding the leather ties. Molly rifled through the papers inside; some looked like receipts and other correspondence from the merchants, but tucked there in the back were her prizes.

Smiling wide, Molly pulled out three letters.

Popping the wax seals, she wasn't surprised nor disheartened to see that Nora hadn't written, nor that Rory and Oona's letters were short. She treasured the words no matter how many.

Stepping out of the way of the pallet parade, Molly greedily read each of the letters quickly and then a second time, slower.

Oona, being the youngest and sweetest, had taken the easiest to the new arrangements. She enjoyed getting to spend more time with her mother and wrote that she liked getting to go to school more regularly.

Rory's letter was terser, an account of her new schedule and what she'd learned at school. She didn't like Glenda's cooking, nor the additional lessons Glenda had her in to catch her up with the other children her age. Molly might've worried, but the letter ended with a quick account of a ball game she'd won against some of Mayor Doherty's grandchildren. If Rory was playing and being competitive, Molly knew she'd be all right soon enough.

Merry's letter was longest, giving detailed accounts of Oona, Rory, and Nora. Molly was grateful for the news, reading what she could in the paragraph on Nora. The eldest Dunne girl would need the most time to heal, but Molly held hope that Nora was smart enough to take the opportunity she had now.

As for Merry herself, the second half of the letter was devoted to all the different books she'd been able to borrow from the mayor. Having access to his library obviously brought her great joy, and Molly laughed reading about titles and subjects she'd never heard of. Merry's happiness practically shouted from the page, and it gave Molly a little peace of mind.

This was the right thing.

She hoped next year to have the girls at the manor for summer, and perhaps holidays, but an isolated estate wasn't a place for them to grow up. They needed to be with others their age and go to school and stay near the familiar, as well as keep a routine.

Allarion was many things, but a slave to routine wasn't one of them. Every day was something a little different, a new task or project. She adored watching his mind at work, seeing how he puzzled out problems and made decisions.

She especially loved helping him try new things and discover his favorites. It was a good thing she was headed to Mullon soon for more supplies—he'd nearly eaten her out of house and home. He seemed determined to make up for a lifetime—a *fae* lifetime—of deprivation within a fortnight.

Molly wasn't complaining. She got to try out new recipes and ideas, and better, watch his reaction to them. And it wasn't just food he was hungry for.

A blush touched her cheeks, and it wasn't just from her many, many layers. Fates, she'd fucked him twice that morning and only been away from him less than an hour and she already missed him. If she wasn't so besotted with him, she might've found it pitiable.

Yes, it was best for the girls to stay near what family and friends they had—and away from the antics of their cousin and her fae lover. It wasn't that Molly necessarily meant to seduce or be seduced by Allarion in every room on every surface of the house, it just happened. And she didn't need to scandalize the girls.

Stowing the letters safely between her layers before they could get damper, Molly looked up. The caravan had left her behind, though it wouldn't take long to catch up, lumbering as it was.

Before she could start off again, something caught her eye.

Turning toward the trees, Molly squinted into the murkiness between their trunks.

Near where she thought the border was, a pair of red eyes, glowing like coals, peered out at her. They disappeared in a slow blink, but otherwise lingered in the gloom, unmoving.

Huffing, Molly planted her hands on her hips. "Well?" she called to the lurking unicorn. "Are you going to help?"

Another blink, those coals winking in and out.

When Bellarand didn't answer, she called with her mind, *What, you're going to make me walk back?*

It was a long moment before he replied, *No? You walked yourself out there, you can walk yourself back.*

Grumping, Molly rolled her eyes and turned back up the drive to follow the caravan.

Typical.

By the time she returned to the house, she'd far outpaced the caravan, wanting to get in out of the misting drizzle. Molly hurried into the kitchen, shaking condensation off her shoulders.

She looked up to find her handsome fae sharing a carrot with his overgrown pony. Literally, he took a bite and made sounds of rapture before holding the carrot out for Bellarand to take a hearty chomp from. Then took another bite *from the same carrot.*

Molly choked on her giggle before bending in half laughing. They stared at her, Bellarand reaching for the remaining nub with his horsey lips and Allarion looking charmingly confused. He was even more confused when Molly ducked out from his reach when he went to give her a kiss in greeting.

It was a long time before Molly caught her breath—so long she didn't even bother berating Bellarand for not only not bringing her back but also getting home before her.

Molly woke the following morning to the sound of rain pattering against the windowpanes. After stretching her limbs and popping her fingers and toes, she rolled over to admire her handsome, sleeping fae.

He looked utterly serene in his long sleep, as always.

Since taking her blood and rediscovering his heartbeat, Allarion had begun to keep slightly more human hours. He dozed in the night as he lay beside her—especially when she did her best to exert him with their bed play. He still needed his long sleeps, though, even if they weren't as long as before. A night and a morning usually.

At first, Allarion had moved back into his bedchamber to take his long sleep, not wanting to disturb her own rest. However, Molly had rolled around under the blankets, uncomfortable and unhappy. Taking her pillow with her, she'd climbed into bed beside him and settled to sleep.

Now, he tucked himself in for a long sleep in her bedchamber—or, what had become *their* bedchamber. He kept most of his attire in the other room, for he had more clothes than she did, but each night, it was in their room, in their bed that he lay.

Still sleeping soundly, Molly didn't worry about disturbing him as she curled up against his side. His chest rose and fell steadily, and she liked pressing her cheek to it to listen to the heartbeat there, the one that was just for her.

She smiled to herself, only a little smugly. It was the best, handsomest heartbeat there ever was, if she did say so herself.

Molly listened for a long while, lazing in bed. Heavy rain meant another day without going into Mullon, but she didn't worry so much, even with more mouths to feed. She had plenty for a hearty stew that would get them through the day—so long as Bellarand hadn't raided the pantry in the night.

He hadn't managed it yet, but that also hadn't stopped him from trying.

Grumbling to herself about big black horned house pests, Molly finally pulled herself out of bed. Slipping into one of her wool dresses for a little more warmth, she wrapped a soft shawl he'd bought her in Dundúran around her shoulders and middle before tying it at her back.

Before leaving him to his slumber, Molly leaned down to kiss his smooth cheek.

"Dream of me," she whispered, "and then come find me when you wake."

He was always affectionate, but especially so after a long sleep. Although they spent most of it together, snuggled in bed, he still found it a separation to make up for. Molly loved it.

Looking forward to their reunion and hearing about whatever wicked things they did in his dreams, Molly made for the kitchen.

It was a relief not to find Bellarand there already, big head rifling through the cold box—again. But it did make breakfast a little lonely, and she was quick to chop the leftover meat and vegetables for the stew so she could start her next task.

With the big pot simmering under the watchful eye of the house, Molly sang one of her favorite songs as she made her way to the front of the house.

Taking up most of the front atrium and some of the stairs sat the many items from the caravan. It'd taken them most of the day to finally roll up to the house, just making it inside before the worst of the rain started in the early evening.

Banked fires in the formal dining room and sitting room lent a little more heat, helping to dry out the lingering dampness. The tarpaulins had been unmoored and placed neatly to the side, and all the crates and barrels had been opened.

Molly peered inside each, amazed at everything he'd managed to buy over just a few days.

Blowing out a breath, she pointed at the easiest decisions. A long dining table, a dozen chairs, and two carpets stepped off the pallets to follow her into the dining room. After choosing which carpet she preferred, Molly directed the table and chairs then began bringing in other furniture to adorn the room.

She soon made a game of it, singing rhymes as the house set the chairs to dancing. The carpet slid across the floor, adjusting the table, while a curio cabinet and washboard trundled across the room in a clumsy jig. Molly laughed and clapped along, spinning in time to her song and to avoid zealous chairs, as she directed where the furniture should go.

It took all morning to arrange the dining room, and it seemed as though she'd hardly made a dent in the forest of furniture crowding the atrium. Savory smells wafted from the kitchen, her stew nearly done, meaning it was time for luncheon.

Molly stretched out her back, turning in little circles and rocking back and forth. She barely had to lift anything with the house's help, but still, making so many decisions before noon was a task!

Stepping up to one of the grand picture frame windows that lined one wall of the dining room, Molly looked out onto the front of the estate. The rain came down in sheets, gathering in the gutters to pour like a waterfall over the sides. She could hardly see anything through the wet mess of it, and yet . . .

Drawing closer, Molly squinted, not sure if she imagined movement out between the trees. Surely nothing would be out in this, and surely it was too far away to see, but still, the longer she stood there looking, the more she felt something . . . looking back.

This looks nice.

Molly jumped, whirling around to stare at the black form taking up the threshold.

Bellarand stood there, dripping water and mud, his mane plastered to his neck and a great puddle gathering around his hooves.

Molly squeaked in horror.

"Not on the carpets!"

Between the overgrown pony, her amorous fae, all the new furniture and goods to sort, and writing each of the girls a return letter, Molly forgot all about the strange little things around the estate. The strange shadow she thought she saw. The glowing eyes when she knew Bellarand to be in the kitchen. The occasional looming presence. Always there and gone again, none of it felt like more than the work of her imagination.

Molly even put the earthquakes from her mind—at least, until she heard Lorna, the dressmaker in Mullon, commiserate with another customer about them.

"I was lucky," said the dressmaker, "only a few toppled displays. Poor Mina and Renault, their brick oven cracked. With all the other damage around town, the masons haven't been able to get to them yet."

"I was wondering why they were still closed," said the other customer.

The two women chatted a little longer, and Molly waited in the wings, itching to speak with Lorna. Finally, willing the other woman to leave worked, and she bid her farewells.

Hurrying forward with the bolts and threads she wanted, Molly asked, "You felt the earthquakes here?"

"Oh yes," Lorna sighed, "we felt it all right. Couldn't believe it—I've never experienced one before. I think only Miss Hattie, you know, the dried herb woman down the way, has. She used to live near the old border with Pyrros. Said they'd get them sometimes, the earth would split open and all the houses would shake. Some would even collapse. I'm so glad it wasn't as bad here."

"I'm glad to hear there hasn't been too much damage," said Molly.

"Nothing serious, just frustrating. Some foundations cracked. The masons and bricklayers are having to call in help from the guilds in Dundúran to repair everything that needs fixing."

"Have the Darrows been notified about the damage?"

"I'm sure the mayor has said something."

Lorna didn't sound confident, so Molly made a note to herself to add a letter to Lady Aislinn with those she was sending along to the girls. It was a strange thought, knowing a letter from her would reach all the way to the heiress herself. One she still wasn't used to.

"I'm sure the aftershocks haven't helped," Molly remarked. "Were they able to stabilize the foundations before they hit?"

The dressmaker looked up from folding the fabrics Molly had purchased. Frowning, she said, "We only felt the one quake."

Molly went still. "Just one? But . . ." They'd felt at least three aftershocks at the estate.

"One was plenty. Should we have felt aftershocks?"

Shaking her head, Molly demurred, not wanting to frighten the woman. She was frightened enough for the both of them.

The conversation lapsed as Molly stared at the bolts behind the dressmaker, her mind spiraling with questions and suspicions. Why had they felt aftershocks but not Mullon? The town was two hours' ride away, but they should have at least *felt it,* even if not so strongly.

When the dressmaker finished wrapping up her purchases, Molly quickly thanked and paid her, not wanting to linger. She needed to find Allarion and tell him.

Something strange was happening—and it seemed to be just around Scarborough.

29

The moment Allarion heard Molly's news of the earthquake after-shocks being isolated to Scarborough, he bundled up his mate, put her on Bellarand's back, and they headed for home.

It was one thing to have witnessed a few strange idiosyncrasies himself—the rational part of his mind found ways to explain them away as the oversensitive paranoia of a mated male protecting his home and *azai*.

It was another to hear that the strangeness existed outside of his own mind. He took no chances with his Molly's safety—for home they rode, where he knew he could keep her safe. They hadn't acquired everything she wanted from Mullon, but good cheese and new kinds of wine for him to try could wait.

With one arm banded around Molly's middle and the other hand on the hilt of his sword, he cast his eyes about, as if enemies lurked behind every tree.

He couldn't say what agitated him so, only that this strangeness had lingered on the wind some days now. Ignoring it hadn't made it go away, and now, off of their land, away from their haven, their vulnerability gnawed at him.

If only there'd been more time. If only he'd begun extending his reach beyond the borders of Scarborough. South to the otherly village. Northeast to Mullon.

His inability to guarantee Molly's safety wedged between his ribs, stabbing at the heart that newly beat. It pained him, this distrust of the open. They'd made this journey many times now and never felt insecure, yet while the rolling landscape was familiar, he couldn't trust it.

Bellarand cantered down the road, and they met no one on their path. That wasn't unusual, few ventured out toward Scarborough, as there was a wider, well-traveled route that headed south to other towns on its way to Dundúran. Still, being alone on the road exacerbated his disquiet.

On that ride back to Scarborough, Allarion agonized over every mile. He'd thought isolating them was the best strategy, that the solitude afforded him more freedoms and opportunities to do what he needed with the land and magic. That may have been true, but on that ride, as the foreboding crept up his spine to agitate his warrior's senses, he understood that whatever this was, whatever shook the earth and lurked in the trees, he would have to meet it alone.

There were no allies—no warrior brothers-in-arms, none of his siblings, no Maxim, no one.

Old as he was, powerful as he was, there had rarely ever been a time that that truly mattered to him. He was confident he could handle himself and any enemy.

But he wasn't alone. Not now.

He held something far more precious than all the magic in all the world in his arms. Allarion could feel Molly's heart racing in his forearm, tucked beneath her breasts. She clung to him, her mouth set in a grim line.

Allarion was proud of the brave mate sat before him; she didn't tarry or worry or panic but sat straight, body moving with his and Bellarand's.

He was prepared to do anything for this woman.

So when not one but two fae knights burst from the trees behind them and another down the road, Allarion drew his sword.

Hold on! Bellarand whinnied, waving his horn in a threatening arc.

Rather than stop or slow, the dread-mount put on speed, horn clattering with the unicorn in their way. Allarion's sword sang through the air, catching the fae knight in his armor. It wouldn't wound, but he didn't need it to—just move the warrior and unicorn out of the way.

Molly grunted and curled down onto Bellarand's back, making herself small as Allarion swung again. The knight caught Allarion's sword with his own, the mounts circling as their blades clashed in a scream of metal.

"Stop!" another warrior shouted in faethling. "Stop in the name of the Queen!"

Allarion gave them no heed. As Bellarand battled with the other unicorn, horns swiping for vulnerable eyes and tender lips, Allarion used his blade and body to shield Molly.

It wasn't the lone warrior that worried him—it was being outnumbered by the other two hurrying to surround him.

Away, Bellarand!

Allarion caught the knight's sword with his own, swirling it out of the warrior's grip and sending it flying. Bellarand broke away as the foe unicorn lunged, and the fae knight and his dread-mount went toppling into the dirt.

Triads were famed for their dedication and devotion. The swore loyalty only to the Queen and each other. They gave up worldly bonds, even eschewing a mate and *azai,* in order to better serve the crown. Single-minded and lethal, a triad knew only duty and death.

They galloped down the road, dust flying behind them. Bellarand's black coat rippled as his great muscles catapulted them forward, but Allarion knew they would be pursued every step. A triad of fae knights gave no quarter and no surrender. It was success or death.

He bent low over Bellarand's withers, flattening Molly beneath him. He could feel her heart racing through her back, and her knuckles were white where they clung to Bellarand's mane.

Bursts of magic splattered the road around them, and Bellarand screamed in outrage, pivoting to avoid the craters left behind. The two knights in pursuit closed the distance as Bellarand regained his pace, their hands reaching out to grab at Allarion's cloak.

He unclasped the brooch holding it in place, the velvet sliding over his shoulders. With a flick of magic, he sent it billowing like a great sail into the face of one of the dread-mounts, blinding him.

When the other knight grabbed again for him, Allarion unknotted a saddlebag and threw it at the knight, catching him in the gut. The other saddlebag got left in the dust, lightening Bellarand's load.

The wind whipped their faces as Bellarand ran, but still the knights pursued. It was miles yet to the northern border of the estate. Too many miles.

I can make it, Bellarand declared.

Allarion had faith his mount indeed could; what he couldn't stomach was risking him and Molly both. This was Allarion's fight, one he'd promised to take up long ago, and he wouldn't allow that promise to threaten those dearest to him.

It hurt to do, but Allarion opened a new pathway in his bond with his mount, thrusting his magic into forging it. It was inelegant and tenuous, scraping across his mind like a blunted knife, but Molly couldn't hear it when he told Bellarand, *One rider is lighter than two.*

The unicorn huffed in reluctant agreement, and Allarion could feel Bellarand's unhappiness with his plan. That was all right; he could be unhappy, so long as he kept Molly safe. She was all that mattered.

They want me, not either of you.

You don't know that! Bellarand argued.

But he did. With the same surety he'd known that Molly was meant for him, that he picked Bellarand out from the herd as his dread-mount, that he'd stepped onto Scarborough and felt at home, he knew it was him the triad wanted. It was him who'd defied Amaranthe, and it was him who knew where Ravenna was hidden.

Allarion had promised Maxim that he would see this through, to whatever end. And as her mate, he had a duty to ensure the safety of his *azai*.

Take care of her, my friend.

You'd better live, grumbled Bellarand. *She'll be insufferable if you don't.*

I intend to.

Gathering the reins, he quickly looped them around Molly's wrists, cinching them together in a loose knot. She could get out of it easily, but it would stop her from trying to jump off until he was clear.

"What're you doing?" she screeched.

Allarion pressed a quick kiss into her cheek. "Run hard and don't look back."

"Allarion, *no*—!"

He vaulted from Bellarand's back, suspended in midair as the unicorn and Molly continued down the road. She screamed his name, her distress carrying on the wind, but he made himself deaf to it.

Allarion skidded through the dirt, coming to a stop in a cloud of dust. Drawing the dagger from his belt, he ran back the way they'd come, feet pounding the road to intercept the triad.

Let them come.

Let them see what it is to threaten Allarion Meringor.

"**B**ellarand! Bellarand, STOP! We have to go back!"

Tears streamed down Molly's face, made icy pinpricks by the wind that lashed her cheeks. She struggled against the leather knot of the reins, working a hand free, but no matter how she tugged and twisted, the unicorn wouldn't listen.

"*Bellarand!*"

No, was all he'd say.

Molly screamed and sobbed helplessly, her temper flaring alongside fear for her fae. "We have to help him!" She tugged on the reins again, but they did nothing but tangle in Bellarand's mane, streaming behind him like a banner as they flew across the countryside.

The wind beat at her cheeks and tore at her eyes, and a steady stream of tears poured down her face. Molly couldn't stop crying and pleading, but nothing worked. Even driving her heels into the unicorn's sides as she'd seen other riders do didn't stop him.

No, he said again—and Molly didn't imagine the twinge of sadness to his tone.

He didn't slow, even for corners, so there was nowhere she could safely jump off. She didn't know what she'd do when she did—tuck and roll and go from there. Allarion needed them, they couldn't run away!

Don't you dare! Bellarand thundered. *Just hang on.*

"We have to go back!" she sobbed more than said.

But Bellarand galloped on—and not to the estate.

Molly grunted when he leapt from the road, cutting through a meadow and up a hillock. Bellarand's hooves cut through the tall grass, the stalks hitting her like shards. Molly ducked to protect her face, burying it in his mane. Against her lips, she felt how his body shivered with exertion, his pace unforgiving.

Keep low, he commanded, just as Molly thought she heard another set of hooves.

Peeking under her arm, she caught sight of another large unicorn chest, chestnut brown and adorned with a gleaming gold breastplate.

Heart in her throat, Molly kept low over Bellarand's withers and gave him his head.

The countryside passed them in a blur of colors, almost indiscernible with their speed and Molly's tears. Her body ached as she was jostled and bounced, but she did her best to move with the unicorn and make herself as small as possible.

Bellarand wove through trees and bounded over roots and logs, kicking up decaying detritus. The air was noticeably damp and cool on her burning cheeks, and Molly shivered.

When they broke through the tree line, it was to catch another road, this one wider and marked on either side with paver stones. As his hooves clattered onto the cleared path, Molly realized where they were—the road south, to Dundúran.

No no no!

"We have to get to Scarborough!" she cried. She didn't know what she could do there, only that it was home—and where Allarion would go. Imbued with his magic, it was a stronghold. She and the house could—she didn't know, throw shingles and rotten floorboards, anything to help him!

But Bellarand didn't respond, not even to tell her no. He leapt forward with every stride, running faster than she'd ever known a beast could run.

Even the other unicorn and fae broke off, unable to keep pace with Bellarand's blistering gallop.

Molly knew it was no use, but for miles and then hours, she tried to make him turn back. She begged, she pleaded, she threatened.

As the landscape became more familiar, she began to worry about Bellarand, too. His sweat soaked her hands where she clutched to him, and his mane went stringy with it, thick droplets sluicing off as he ran. His black coat rippled under the wan winter sky, but no matter what she said, how she begged, he wouldn't stop.

The sun raced them, falling to the west as they galloped south. It just touched the tree line as they rounded the bend, Dundúran dominating the horizon.

Bellarand neither slowed nor stopped, barreling through the north city gate and into the cobblestone streets. His hooves clattered, sparks flying beneath them as he ran full tilt. City folk gawped and yelped, some having to dive out of the way of the mad unicorn.

They thundered through the city, everything and everyone jumping out of the way—people, carriages, carts, they all made way for Bellarand the Black.

As they charged through the castle gate, he let out a deafening scream. It echoed across the courtyard, curdling the blood of any who heard.

With one last heave, he crossed the courtyard to the wide steps leading up to the castle. At their foot was where, finally, he came to a skidding stop.

Molly slid off, body quaking with the hours-long ride. Her knees couldn't bear her weight, and she slumped onto the first step, one of her wrists still caught in the reins. She stared dumbly up at the unicorn, panting and shaking.

Bellarand stood with legs wide apart and locked, barely holding himself up. Foam ringed his lips, and a thick stalactite of saliva drooped from his lolling red tongue. Mane plastered to his neck from sweat, he dropped his great head, utterly exhausted.

She didn't know why, but the sight of him so drained, trembling after bringing her so far, to safety, had more tears leaking from her eyes. She didn't think she had any left, but she wept for Bellarand.

Despair rushed into the hollowness of her chest, and for a sickening moment, Molly didn't know what to do.

Get up.

It wasn't his voice, nor Allarion's, but her own.

You have to get up.

Allarion had sacrificed himself.

Bellarand had done his part.

It was time for her to do whatever she had to.

Gathering all the air she could into her lungs, Molly leaned back and screamed, "HELP! SOMEBODY HELP US!"

And she kept screaming, sometimes not even words, just the anguished sound of a woman terrified for her man. She screamed and screamed until hands came around her, bearing her up.

Those hands were green.

She looked up in surprise to see a worried Lord Hakon staring down at her. At his elbow stood Lady Aislinn, her face contorted with concern.

"Molly!" she cried. "What's happened?"

"Allarion—" Molly croaked.

30

By the time night fell across the forest, Allarion had successfully worked his way further toward the estate, although it hadn't been as much progress as he wished. Traveling through the treetops was slow, dangerous work, yet even away from Scarborough, Allarion found the trees worked to aid him.

They extended their limbs when the distance was too great to jump, and those still with their leaves shielded him from the keen sight of his foes. Logs rolled in their way, and roots lifted to trip their dread-mounts.

But still, the triad pursued him.

At first it was just the two he occupied on the road, but it was with some relief he noticed around dusk that they were three once again. From the snatches of faethling that echoed up to him, he was viciously pleased to hear that Bellarand and Molly had made their escape.

The triad turned their full focus on trying to catch him, and so he played an arduous cat-and-mouse game with them, working his way steadily southwest toward the border of the estate. He could feel it nearing, his magic a siren's call. Within the border, he could activate the wards. A protective shell of magic would keep out the warriors, and he could mount a proper defense.

Getting there was the sticky bit.

Hunger gnawed at his insides, his empty stomach complaining. Allarion didn't dare use magic to soothe it, either. That was likely how his ancestors had started all this, a little here, a little there, solving small things. Molly had broken the cycle for him, and he wasn't about to undo her gift. Even if it meant chewing on tree bark.

His wounds, though, were another matter.

Having lost his pursuers for the moment, Allarion found a sturdy branch to hunker down. Setting his back against the thick trunk, he gritted his teeth and prepared for the pain.

The broken arrow shaft sticking out of his shoulder screamed agony through him when he wrapped his hand round it. It'd be better to leave the arrowhead in, but he was losing strength in his left arm, strength he needed for climbing.

Best deal with it now.

In one swift motion, he pulled the shaft and head from his shoulder. His magic rushed in to fill the puncture left behind, stoppering the blood and soothing the edges of his broken skin. The magic dulled the worst of the pain as it got to work meshing him back together.

Allarion rested his head against the trunk, letting the magic do its work. Already, it'd healed numerous little cuts and scrapes on his hands, arms, and knees from clambering through the forest, as well as a deeper gash from one of the triad's blades. It was a lucky blow, one that still annoyed him hours later.

Had he been smarter, more cautious, he'd have worn his armor whenever he left the grounds of Scarborough. And fashioned Molly a set, too.

He didn't let the magic take away all of his pain, not when it kept him alert and . . . he felt he deserved some of it. He'd been negligent, complacent, in the one thing that mattered most—the safety of his mate. The only thing that soothed his wounded pride was knowing that she wasn't the target, that he could remedy the threat to her by leading their enemies off.

Twins take him, that didn't take much of the sting out of his shame, though. Life had been too good, too easy. The signs had been there. The earthquakes were strange, and he should have inquired in Mullon sooner. Too enraptured with Molly and his transformation, Allarion had let his defenses slip.

But he'd be damned if anyone other than him faced the consequences.

Placing his hand over the wound to add pressure, he took a little heart in knowing that Molly and Bellarand were safe. Much as he'd underestimated Amaranthe's reach and spite, even she wouldn't dare attack a large human stronghold.

She didn't want war—or Molly. She wanted Ravenna.

"She won't have her." Maxim's words rang in Allarion's ears. *"Promise me."*

"I swear it."

Anger, hotter than the blood that pooled at his wound, scorched through him. How dare Amaranthe destroy everything that was good? How dare she abuse what she was meant to protect? To corrupt her own people, slay her own family, desecrate her own line—all for what? Power? A few more centuries of debauchery? It all seemed so . . . cheap.

There would be no forgiveness for what she'd done to Maxim and Aine. For what she took away from Ravenna. And now, for her attack on his home.

No provocation, no justification. Her rotten fingers reached across the land searching for him like a plague—no wonder the native magic shuddered in horror to feel her putrid touch.

And yet, angry as this attack made him, that the triad was even here, that Amaranthe even bothered to search for him did offer a bit of relief. She hadn't discovered Ravenna. Coming after him, after years of nothing, boded ill for her efforts to find Ravenna herself. Knowing that Maxim's wards and plan had worked so well gave Allarion a spiteful kind of pleasure.

The twang of a bowstring pierced his ears, and a moment later, splinters burst across his thigh, an arrow glancing off the thick branch he sat upon.

Ah, there they were.

"Yield, sworn-sword!" called up one of the triad. "We know you are wounded."

"It will take more than pinpricks to bring me back to that hoary hag."

"You dare insult the Queen?"

Allarion laughed without mirth. "She is no Queen of mine." And she was nothing compared to the woman he worshipped. "You know in your hearts as well as I that she is nothing more than a usurper. She poisons our people with her rot."

"You defile her name and your own honor!"

"I assure you, my honor is hale and hearty." His pride a little less so, but that was for another day—one when he reunited with his mate and made his apologies through kisses and caresses. He knew that wicked mouth of hers would heal him more than any magic or tincture.

"Yield," they called again, "there is no honor in this."

"I agree, there is no honor in chasing a man and his mate and threatening his home."

"You are a fugitive, convicted in the rule of our law, by order of our Queen."

"Without trial, I suppose. And we aren't in the faelands; your Queen's laws mean nothing here." Leaning to his left, Allarion spied down to the forest floor below.

The knight he spoke with sat mounted near the base of his tree; the other two had fanned further afield. They were trying to box him in, a clever if uninspired tactic. Time to move.

Still, Allarion did try one last time to reason with them.

"You've seen my face, sworn-sword," he declared loudly, for all of them to hear. "You've seen the red of my blood. Do you not wonder at it? I have escaped the curse of our people. Amaranthe is killing us all with her corrosion."

"Being away from the faelands has clouded your mind, Meringor. You are sick."

A solitary bark of laughter escaped Allarion as he heaved himself back up onto his feet.

"I am *right,* sworn-sword. And you shall know it by your end. Now, shall we continue?"

Another arrow whizzed past where he'd just stood, but Allarion leapt to the next tree.

A great cracking filled the forest, and he turned to watch the branch he'd sat on go crashing down to the ground. The dread-mounts screamed and scattered as Allarion pushed on, his sights set on Scarborough.

Just a little farther. A little more. And then he would see her again.

Although given the room she'd shared with Allarion not long ago, Molly didn't sleep. She couldn't.

It was so strange being there without him. There was where he'd first undressed her. There was where he'd held her all night long. Here was where she'd sucked his cock and there was where he'd broken a lamp with his magic seeing her bruised jaw.

Really, though, everything about this was strange.

Molly paced the room, arms folded tightly around her middle—she needed something to keep herself from completely falling to pieces.

There was no hope of getting any sleep, not when all she could think of was where Allarion was, if he was safe, if he'd outrun those fae. She might've stayed in the stables with Bellarand if he hadn't sent her off with Lady Aislinn and Lord Hakon. Far more gently than he'd ever spoken to her, he'd said, *Make a good plan and then get some rest, titmouse. Try not to worry, Allarion can take care of himself.*

That the overgrown pony was trying to be sensitive only worried her more.

After hours of hasty plans, she'd scraped all the loose skin off her lips and bitten all her nails down to the quicks.

That Bellarand was being nice *and* they had a plan that wouldn't happen until morning kept Molly pacing. Lady Aislinn and Princess Isolde had tried to coax her into eating a small dinner, but she hadn't been able to stomach the thought of food.

Was Allarion hungry? They hadn't taken luncheon in Mullon like they'd planned before leaving. He was always hungry at dinnertime, but what could he eat out in the forest? He didn't know what plants were edible or poisonous. What if he was felled by a bad mushroom rather than a fae blade? What if—

A swift knock rapped against her door before Lady Aislinn's golden head poked inside. She offered a small smile that didn't reach her eyes.

Stepping quietly inside, she proffered a fine linen nightgown, laying it out on the bed. "This should fit nicely," she said, smoothing nonexistent wrinkles.

Molly's throat closed at the simple kindness. She wanted to thank Lady Aislinn. She wanted to tell her it didn't matter, she wouldn't sleep anyway. She wanted to demand they leave *now*.

What she managed to get past her clenched teeth was, "Everything's ready?"

Lady Aislinn nodded, her eyes heavy with sympathy as she gazed upon Molly. "Hakon just arrived back with Balar, Theron, and several others from the village. Captain Aodhan has already found a dozen volunteers to ride out with you tomorrow, too."

Molly swallowed hard, wishing the news would calm her roiling stomach. Nothing helped, of course, but she rationally knew this was all good news.

If she'd had her way, it'd be the entire castle garrison riding out, but Molly understood that all this put Lady Aislinn in a precarious position. They couldn't confirm it, but the fae knights had no doubt been sent by the Fae Queen. Doing battle with a foreign queen's warriors could be flirting with a declaration of war, which Lady Aislinn couldn't have. However, as she put it, *"The otherly folk are a different matter. As your Allarion has found, they inhabit a gray area of fealty. That includes my husband, and I of course won't send him off without proper protection."*

At first, she hadn't wanted to hear that they couldn't leave immediately with every available knight to help Allarion. It'd taken a good hour of calm, sensible arguments from Lady Aislinn and Lord Hakon—they had to gather their allies, they were losing the sun already, they couldn't walk into a dangerous unknown—to finally sway her.

"There's also been word . . ." Lady Aislinn delicately cleared her throat. "Mayor Doherty sent word that your cousins have asked after you. The city is already humming about your ride through the streets. I hope I haven't overstepped, but I sent word back that you are well and will send word when you can."

Chest seizing, Molly nodded. "Thank you," she murmured. "I don't want the girls to see me like this." She didn't mean to say it aloud, but it was the truth. Seeing the girls, feeling their alarm and worry, might break her.

Lady Aislinn bowed her head in understanding. The two women gazed at each other for a long moment, Molly sensing the heiress wished to say something else.

"I know this will feel like the longest night of your life," Lady Aislinn said softly, taking Molly by surprise, "but do try to rest. Allarion is strong and capable, I'm sure he will handle himself."

Another tear spilled down Molly's cheek. "Thank you," she croaked, "for all of this."

"Of course. Allarion is a friend. You both are. A threat to you is a threat to all of us." Offering another kind look, if not quite a smile, Lady Aislinn asked, "Do you wish to have company tonight or would you rather be alone?"

More tears welled, making Molly's nose burn. Her immediate instinct swung from wanting to be alone to desperately wanting distraction and back again.

"I'll be all right," she said, for her benefit as much as the heiress's, "but thank you."

Nodding, Lady Aislinn stepped toward the door. "All right, then. Try to rest. Hakon and the others will ride out with you at dawn."

Molly thanked her again and managed to hold in the tears until after the door shut softly behind her. The day, the ride, the plan, the kindness, all of it bore down on her in a wave of heartache.

So insulated in their little bubble of magic, the outside world seemed so far away. Allarion had sounded so sure that nothing fae could reach them here.

She was angry that he'd been wrong.

Angry at him.

Angry at Amaranthe, a nameless hag who meant to destroy the little life Molly was just beginning to build.

Well, she couldn't have it. It wasn't hers to take.

Molly would ride out with reinforcements tomorrow—and yell at Allarion good and proper when she had the chance. Because she *would* have the chance, she'd accept nothing else.

Molly didn't know what to do with all of her anger and heartache. There was nowhere for it to go, nothing for it to do. The hours of night stood in her way, and there was nothing to do but wait it out. It was an interminable task, and although she paced, although she plotted, nothing helped.

Were feelings supposed to be this big? This brutal? Her utter terror for him threatened to consume her from the inside out. With her lips abused and nails bleeding, all that was left was to start tearing at her hair, so Molly shoved her hands beneath the opposite arm. All this needed *out,* but there was nothing she could do—except accept it.

That taste sat bitter on her tongue.

Exhausted from her tears, heartsick with her worries, Molly finally unlaced her boots and climbed into bed. She didn't bother with the nightgown, wanting to be ready in a moment to leave.

Curling up in the first bed they'd shared, Molly imagined it retained a little of his scent, his presence. Clutching a pillow to her chest, she wrapped arms and legs around it. Behind the safety of closed eyes, she could pretend it was him.

"Just hold on," she murmured into the down. "Just hold on a little longer."

31

The weakest dawn light filtered into the courtyard and already, their party was mounting up, preparing to leave. Molly sat astride Bellarand, trying not to fidget. She'd already gotten one nip of reprimand for it and didn't want another. So she chewed her cheeks as she anxiously awaited the others to be ready to ride out.

A big paw reached out for her.

Molly startled, looking down into the golden, leonine face of Balar. He and all his brothers had come, along with the dragon Theron, Maritza and her harpy sisters, and a handful of half-orcs. Nearly the entire otherly village, it seemed.

The sight of them there, showing their support and solidarity, had more emotion clogging her nose.

"Don't despair, lovely," Balar told her gently. "We'll sort out your man before noon."

Molly forced a stiff smile. "Thank you."

She took the hand he offered, the rough pads of his paw rasping against her skin. His eyes were soft with sympathy and his expression sincere, but his golden wings fluttered and that scaled whip of a tail undulated behind him, giving away his excitement. Molly was sure he wanted to help, but he also looked forward to a good fight.

That didn't matter to her—so long as he fought off Allarion's enemies.

Finally, Lord Hakon climbed up into an uncovered cart full of other half-orcs, all bristling with weapons. "We make all haste for the Scarborough estate," said Hakon, "to render aid to our friend Allarion."

The captain of the castle guard, Aodhan, came alongside them on his horse. "There are three known fae combatants, all riding unicorn mounts," he announced to the gathered force, "so keep sharp and stay in formation."

And with a loud *Ho!* they lurched forward, leaving behind a waving Lady Aislinn and Princess Isolde on the castle steps.

You're sure you can make it? Molly asked Bellarand, not for the first time.

She didn't mean to pester him, for once—she just wouldn't soon forget the sight of him utterly spent yesterday, foaming and sweating and trembling. He'd looked about ready to keel over onto the cobblestones, and seeing the big unicorn so affected had rattled Molly terribly.

Yes, he grumbled back, *stop asking.*

Well, he couldn't be too poorly if he'd gotten his attitude back. It was a relief to walk into the stables to fetch him earlier and receive the gruff greeting of, *Where have you been? Let's go.*

Their party formed a neat column as they passed through the city at a more respectable trot than her and Bellarand's clattering flight yesterday. Despite the early hour, curious heads poked out of doors and windows to watch them go.

Once they'd passed under the north gate, the pace picked up into a canter. Molly pulled up the scarf she'd thrown over her shoulders, blocking the worst of the dust and cold.

They rode across the countryside in formation, the single riders on the flanks while two carts of warriors trundled along. Above swooped the manticores, harpies, and Theron, easily keeping pace. Molly had to bite her tongue to keep from urging them ahead, to get there as quickly as they could.

It wasn't fair—they didn't know what they raced toward, only that they intended to render aid. Molly was grateful for it, for all of them, but she couldn't help wanting to get to Allarion *faster*.

You've done your part, titmouse, Bellarand told her, *now let them do theirs.*

Quit being nice to me, it's unnerving.

I know, I don't like it, either.

Listening to Bellarand's grumpy tone in her head strangely soothed her, and so Molly did all she could—she put her head down and moved with the unicorn as he galloped.

Their journey took forever and no time at all, the trees narrowing her vision in a green blur. The path lay before them in a dusty, snaking line, but Molly sensed when they neared Scarborough. The hairs on her arms stood up, and she swore the trees began to bend toward them, as if to whisper their news.

Heart jumping into her throat, Molly leaned even further down on Bellarand's withers as the unicorn broke formation, thundering onto the estate. She heard someone calling out to them, probably Captain Aodhan reminding them to keep formation, but neither Molly nor Bellarand listened.

Gravel flew from under his black hooves as they pounded the ground, racing up the drive toward the house. Despite the cold but clear winter day, the lampposts all came blazing to life as they passed, burning with an eerie blue flame.

Bellarand flew into the front courtyard of the house, gravel spattering the steps up to the front doors. His nostrils flared as he heaved for breath, and he tossed his mane.

No Allarion to greet them.

He should be here.

Standing up in the stirrups, Molly pulled down her scarf, cupped her hands around her mouth, and shouted, "ALLARION!"

Her entreaty echoed through the quiet trees into the empty sky.

The house shuddered, its shingles clacking.

Soon, the sound of the others coming up behind them filled the silence, but Molly could hardly hear. She looked around desperately for her fae, as if he might materialize from the shadows or come strutting out the front door.

"Is Allarion here?" Molly called out to the house.

Nothing.

Her stomach dropped.

"Has he returned at all?"

Silence.

"Miss Molly, who do you talk to?" asked Lord Hakon.

"The house," she replied, not stopping to explain. There wasn't time. "Is he somewhere on the estate?"

The shingles clapped softly. Not a confident answer.

Do you feel him?

Molly frowned at the back of Bellarand's head, but before she could grumble that no, of course she didn't if he wasn't here, she stopped to really *feel*.

She drew in a deep breath, feeling the air around her, how it rustled through the pine needles and cedar leaves. The tree limbs swayed and the berry bushes rustled—all northward.

And Molly knew, as surely as she'd known anything, although not sure how but not really caring either, that *He's to the north.*

Bellarand shook out his mane, and Molly swore his horn began to glow purple. *That's what I thought. Hold on!*

She'd just enough time to grab onto his mane before he leapt back into motion.

"He's this way!" Molly called over her shoulder.

Bellarand led the charge around the house, catching the rutted footpath past the garden up into the wilderness of the northern part of the estate. Molly had seen it only once, hiking through trees and foliage with Allarion just for the sake of some exercise and seeing what all the corners of Scarborough looked like.

Densely populated with berry bushes and a gurgling stream, it was a pastoral area, full of big, established trees and crisscrossed with deer paths. It was the wildest part of the estate, and the darkest, and Allarion admitted even he didn't go there often.

The path leading north narrowed, and Molly thought she heard the carts screech to a stop. Shouts rang out, telling them to hold on, but Bellarand kept going. Neither sharp brambles nor fallen logs slowed or stopped the unicorn as he barreled through the forest, proving to one and all that he was its master.

She didn't imagine his horn glowing a faint purple through the murky dark of the deep forest. The crevices between the spiraling sections of the horn burned a molten amethyst, casting shapes onto the heavy limbs above.

Molly ducked and twisted to keep her seat and avoid the lower branches. Leaves and twigs scratched at her cheeks and caught in her hair, but she only urged the unicorn faster.

They flew through the air as Bellarand leapt over the stream. More light filtered through the trees ahead, where the edge of the estate lay.

It was where they finally found their fae.

A noise of shock caught in Molly's throat.

Allarion lay on the ground, his torso wrapped up in two coiling whips. Two mounted fae warriors held the other ends, pulling with all their might to drag Allarion back across the boundary. His fangs were bared in a flash of stark determination, hands reached out in front of him to claw and keep hold of the ground.

Roots strung around his forearms, holding on and pulling him back. The whips in one direction, the roots in the opposite—the strain made veins pop along his forehead and tendons push against his neck.

His clothes were torn and dirty, and the unmistakable stain of blood darkened his tunic, but that was all Molly could glean before Bellarand bore down on the enemy fae, a screaming whinny of rage on his lips.

Molly could only hold on as Bellarand's horn clattered with one of the other unicorns'. The sound rang hollower than steel, yet purple sparks burst from the contact. The other unicorns reared back in surprise, and Bellarand slashed his horn on the whips, cutting them both.

Allarion lurched forward with an *oof*.

The fae warriors shouted at each other, one leaping from his mount to fall on Allarion's legs.

She tried to call out—to Allarion, to Bellarand—but it took all her might to stay seated as the unicorn reared up on his hind legs, baring those horrifying pointed teeth. He came back down to the ground slashing and snarling, sharp hooves sending dirt flying.

The unicorns locked in a heated duel, their horns their blades as they parried and thrust. From her place plastered onto Bellarand's back, she met the eyes of the fae mounted on the other unicorn. He sneered at her, showing a fang. He said something in their language, something low and probably insulting.

Molly flipped him the rudest hand gesture she knew. "Get *the fuck* off my land!"

The unicorns both reared up, their fangs and horns clashing as they came back down.

Molly yelped, nails digging into Bellarand's coat.

She had to get out of the unicorn's way.

When Bellarand danced to the right, looking for an opening, Molly stood in the stirrups and jumped for a low branch. Pulling herself up, she climbed to the next, then the next when she felt a hand grasping at the toe of her boot.

Bent over a branch, Molly saw another mounted fae stand in his own stirrups to reach for her.

Molly kicked at his hand, scrambling to get her other leg under her.

A cracking sound made her freeze—but it wasn't a breaking limb. Her ankle stung as a whip lashed around it, and a heavy tug nearly brought her to the ground. A pained grunt punched from her chest as her vulnerable gut was squished into the branch.

"No!" she heard Allarion scream. "Molly!"

Sinking her nails into the tree bark, Molly held on for all she was worth, kicking and squirming to loosen the vice of the whip.

The fae pulled again, nearly wrenching her leg from its socket. Molly yelped in pain, clinging onto her branch.

It moved under her hands.

In awe, she watched as the limb curved upward, drawing her up with it. She felt the whip go taut, then from below, the heavy smack of bark hitting metal. After a deep grunt, she had slack and scrambled higher up, the whip falling away as she did.

Clambering onto a higher branch, Molly put her back against the trunk, breath heaving. She chanced a look down, only for her eyes to pop wide to see the fae who'd tried to grab her doing battle with the lower limbs.

He'd abandoned the whip for his sword, but all he could do was wave it blindly as branches bashed and battered him, their leaves scraping against his face. Roots sprung from the dirt, winding around his unicorn's legs. The mount reared in alarm, horn slashing at the branches, and its rider went toppling to the ground.

Pulling her legs up to fold in front of her, Molly tried to catch her breath—and sight of Allarion.

She spotted his silver head bobbing as the other two fae tried to get hold of him.

They want him alive, she realized. Only he knew where Ravenna hid.

The bottom of her stomach opened up as she watched from her perch. Allarion expertly disabled and dodged their blows and attacks, keeping clear of their grasping hands, but it was still two against one.

The other two unicorns had managed to herd Bellarand further away into the brambles, taking turns stabbing their horns at him.

Desperation clogged her throat, and Molly looked around frantically for something to throw. But there was nothing, not even pine-cones.

A whimper of frustration escaped her lips—just before the ground began to tremble.

Finally, reinforcements began hurtling over the stream. Balar and Theron led the charge, battle axes held high above their heads.

The small clearing filled with bodies and utter chaos. In the fray, Molly lost sight of her fae.

32

When he got the moment he needed, Allarion thumped his left shoulder against a tree, popping it back into socket. His groan of relief was profound; a few moments longer being pulled by whips and roots, he'd have split in half.

His body was littered with many littler, isolated pains, but they all converged to make him feel like one large, exposed nerve.

That didn't matter right now, though.

Getting his feet under him, Allarion turned back into the melee.

He didn't know how or why his land was suddenly swarming with half-orcs, manticores, harpies, and armored human knights, only that it was because of her. He tried to find her in the fray, the sharp dread that'd stabbed him when he saw her riding atop Bellarand straight for his fae attackers still smarting.

Another pang nearly leveled him when he saw Bellarand doing battle with two unicorns, riderless.

He caught the collar of the first person he could find.

Hakon. Excellent.

"Allarion!" the half-orc exclaimed. "Are you badly hurt?"

"Where is Molly?" he rumbled.

The halfling's green face paled.

There was little time to hiss at the lordling—the final fae still astride his mount came barreling toward them. Hakon raised his battle axe as the dread-mount lowered his horn.

Allarion didn't have time for halfling bravery nor this battle at all. He needed to find Molly.

With his good arm, he shoved Hakon away, out of the path of the charging unicorn, and caught the brunt of the attack himself. He grimaced, baring his fangs in agony as the horn punctured the meat of his left shoulder above his clavicle.

Grabbing the horn, Allarion stared down the dread-mount. Eyes as hot as burning coals seared him, and the horn prickled and sparked with heated magic against his palm.

Wrenching the horn from his flesh, he pulled the unicorn away. The dread-mount screamed in outrage, neck twisting painfully. Allarion kept hold, no matter how the horn burned or the unicorn hooves tried to paw at him. The fae knight swung his sword but Allarion was too close, pulling the unicorn around by the horn until he had no choice but to fall with his rider lest he break his neck.

The two went tumbling to the ground in a clatter of metal. A frenzy of tawny manticores fell upon them, fangs and claws flashing, and Allarion turned away.

He picked up a discarded blade, the perfect balance of it feeling right in his hand.

The border of the estate had fallen into chaos, pockets of fighting watering the tree roots with blood. The other two dread-mounts had gone back-to-back, fending off Bellarand's thrusts as harpies swooped from above. One fae knight had been caught in the middle of a circle of half-orcs and human knights, all trying to land a blow. So far, the warrior kept them at bay, but their numbers were too great. The last fae knight had managed to get a tree at his back as he fought the dragon Theron and three halflings.

Nowhere did Allarion see Molly.

It was time to put an end to this.

Although blood gushed and pain radiated down his side, Allarion charged the fae with his back to the tree. Cutting through the allies gathered there, he swung his blade. The warrior jerked just in time to avoid being pinned to the bark, the blade sinking into the tree just at his jaw.

"Yield," Allarion demanded in faethling.

"No," the warrior growled back. His hand darted for his belt, but Theron was quicker, kicking the dagger from his hand.

"Yield," Allarion said again. "You can be free of her—just lay down your weapons."

"You know we cannot."

"Enough," rumbled Theron, "we don't need to play with the food."

The fae warrior sneered up at the dragon. "I will squeeze your heart from the inside, scale-rot."

Allarion sensed the movement before it happened, saw the defiance in the eyes of his kin—but was too slow to stop it.

The warrior struck at Theron's knee, hobbling the dragon. The male loosed a thundering shout as he buckled, leaving his flank vulnerable. Grabbing the blade Allarion had sunk in the tree, the fae lurched forward, splinters flying as the blade wrenched free. It flashed in a perfect arc, down at Theron's head.

Allarion threw himself against his fellow fae, driving the knight back into the bark.

Face to face, the knight smiled sadly at him—before plunging a knife in his side.

Sadness passed between them, an understanding between kin. In another life, they may have fought beside each other, brothers in arms, bound by loyalty and honor. But that was not this life, where both had their duties to their queens.

Allarion felt no anger, no spite. He felt hardly anything when a green hand pulled him backward, out of the way of the enraged dragon.

Theron's red muzzle elongated in a partial shift, and he opened wide, baring every single sharp tooth as he roared in the fae's face. With vicious quickness, he raked his claws across the fae's face and throat, opening up four black lines in his flesh. Black blood spurted from the fae's neck, but before he could fall, another swipe from the other direction nearly decapitated him.

Allarion turned away, relieved at least that the knight was dead before the dragon descended on him in a bestial frenzy.

Someone said something, perhaps to him, but Allarion did not hear. Covering his slashed side with a hand, he felt the warm, sticky blood pooling there.

Damn, that stings.

He locked his knees to keep upright, viewing what remained of the battlefield.

The unicorns glistened with sweat and blood, claw marks scoring their backs and flanks. The other fae warrior had succumbed, slumped on his knees as the party gathered round him took turns delivering killing blows.

Numbness tried to blanket his senses, but it couldn't totally snuff the sick feeling in his gut.

"Orek, give us your hatchet—maybe it will cut through this damn horn."

Allarion turned to look at the manticores, the whole pride gathered round the slain unicorn and his rider. Paws and muzzles bloodied, one of the brothers stood with his foot on the unicorn's head, claws wrapped round the horn. A handful of blades lay scattered around him, bent or broken.

Allarion's upper lip peeled back from his fangs. "You will *not.*"

The hair on the manticores' shoulders lifted, their leonine eyes rounding at the ferocity of his tone.

Allarion met Balar's gaze and held it. Dread-mounts were *never* to be made trophies, only treated with the utmost respect. All of the triad may have been his enemies, but they still deserved honor in death.

Finally, Balar nodded. With a wave of his paw, his younger brother stepped back from the unicorn, letting the head fall to the ground.

When he was sure the manticores would heed him, Allarion turned back to the others.

"Enough," he called. "Enough!"

His shout rang through the trees, bringing a halt to every swing and blow, and even Theron paused, his face bloodied black.

"I thank you for your aid, my friends, but enough fae blood has been spilled today."

The harpies landed, and the halflings stepped back from the battered body of the remaining fae knight. With a bob of Bellarand's horn, the two unicorns, trembling and bloodied, got to their knees and then on the ground, laying their heads on the trampled dirt in submission.

"Where is my *azai?*"

A hand landed on his shoulder, and Allarion hissed in pain. His vision swam, and when he staggered, that hand caught his arm to keep him upright.

"Steady on," said Hakon gently.

"Where is Molly?"

You can come down now, titmouse, Bellarand called.

The sound of scrambling and breaking twigs echoed from across the battlefield, and Allarion managed to turn his head to see Molly clambering down from a tall linden tree.

My clever girl.

"Molly."

She jumped the final distance, racing across the strewn earth to him, her curls wild and her eyes flashing with tears.

"Allarion!" she yelped.

She flung her arms around him, and Allarion slumped into her embrace from the sheer relief. And blood loss.

Head feeling too heavy, he laid it on her shoulder as he tried to keep his legs under him.

"My Molly, I love you so," he murmured.

"Don't you dare!" she shrieked.

It took a moment of blinking to bring her dear face back into focus, and it troubled him to find it so afraid. He tried to wrap his arms around her, but he hadn't the strength to hold her as tightly as he wished.

"Why do you weep? We've won the day."

"You're *bleeding*," she cried, voice still unpleasantly shrill.

"Oh." He grimaced, remembering how his palm was full of his own blood. "Yes, that. I've had worse."

She snorted with disbelief, almost making him laugh. "You're losing so much blood. Too much blood." Pressing her lips to his ear, she whispered, "Take mine. Take as much as you need."

Her words roused him enough to shake his head. "I cannot. I won't. I need . . ." He sighed, thinking perhaps he should be worried he couldn't feel his hands or feet. "The meadow, take me there, sweetling."

Molly got her shoulder beneath Allarion's arm and braced her legs to stop him from going down. She yelped his name when his head lolled against her shoulder and a wordless moan buzzed against her skin.

But when Lord Hakon reached out to help, she swatted him away. "No! Don't touch him!"

"Miss Molly . . ."

"I just—I need to get him to the meadow. Bellarand. Where's Bellarand? Bellarand!"

Here I am. The unicorn trotted forward, ducking his head to get Allarion's other arm over his thick neck.

Although his eyes were closed, Allarion grimaced with pain.

Molly whimpered to see it. "Bellarand," she keened.

I know. We can heal this. Let's get him to the meadow. The forest will help.

She didn't know how it could, but Molly didn't really care right now. She knew it didn't make sense to keep Hakon and the others away and instead give the forest a chance, but she wasn't reasonable right now—not with her fae stabbed and slashed.

She'd only caught glimpses of it from across the makeshift battlefield, but Molly *felt* when her fae was wounded. It ripped at her soul, and only Bellarand's colorful threats kept her up in that tree.

"Miss Molly, we should see to his wounds at the house," Lord Hakon said.

"You all go back to the house," she told them as she and Bellarand got Allarion walking. "The house will take care of you. I'll be there soon. Just . . . just go to the house."

The others looked on in bafflement as she and Bellarand led their fae away, but she didn't care. After weeks and months with this fae and his grumpy unicorn, Molly was used to the strangeness. She was part of it now. They could all deal with it for an hour while she got Allarion to the meadow.

It was a slow, arduous walk. More than once, Molly begged him to mount Bellarand so the unicorn could take them, but Allarion insisted he could walk. The only reason she and Bellarand didn't force it was, without him helping her, it'd take too much time and effort to get him safely astride the unicorn.

The trees and ferns and brambles cleared a path for them, making the ground easier to tread. Limbs lifted out of their way, and roots sank so they wouldn't trip. Still, Molly watched every footfall, so closely that she didn't realize it at first when they made it to the meadow.

"Here," Allarion mumbled.

They set him down as carefully as they could. A bed of moss pushed up from the ground to cushion his way, and he settled comfortably on the earth.

Molly collapsed beside him, tears dripping down her cheeks.

"What now?" she asked. "What do you need?"

"Sleep," he said before going still.

A sound of alarm caught in her throat. "Allarion, wait—!"

Let him, Bellarand cautioned. *A long sleep will do him good.*

Molly tried to swallow her worry, but she didn't like seeing him preternaturally still. The long sleep took him away for a day, sometimes longer. Probably even longer with his wounds.

Another sound leapt up her throat when she saw roots and vines beginning to curl around his limbs.

"No!" she cried. "You can't take anything from him!"

Bellarand touched his soft muzzle to her arm. *It's all right, titmouse. Watch.*

With effort, Molly sat back on her haunches, watching through her tearful, blurry eyes. As the vines climbed over him, a soft glow emanated from their tips, a warm, golden light that reminded her of a summer sun. The foliage was careful not to directly touch his wounds, but as they crawled over him into a blanket, the blood staunched.

Allarion released a relieved sigh, the lines around his mouth smoothing.

Slumping back onto her rump, Molly witnessed nothing short of a miracle.

The forest gave back what Allarion had given. She didn't know how she knew, just that she watched it happen. It wasn't solely Allarion's magic, either. It was a combination, the threads of his magic and that of the land's woven together. It covered him in a soft halo of light, little sparkling threads, like spiderweb, cocooning him.

The warmth of the magic radiated from the fractals of light. Molly could feel it on her hands and cheeks, where it dried her tears.

The glow bathing him reflected in dozens of pinpoints around the meadow. Molly looked up in wonder as forest creatures began emerging from the trees. A herd of deer. A family of rabbits. Raccoons chittered on the branches, and moles came up from their holes. The rounded ears of a black bear twitched by a tree, although Molly didn't fear it.

From the forest, a red squirrel bounded up to them. Tail twitching, its liquid black eyes stared up at her for a moment before it laid an acorn beside Allarion. With a little chitter at Bellarand, the squirrel hurried back to the forest.

Only for another, and another to come, bearing acorns. The deer bore twigs, the raccoons pinecones. The black bear left a mouthful of late blackberries. One after the other, they left their gifts.

Molly's heart swelled. They were paying a sort of tribute. And more and more gathered at the edge of the meadow, watching over her fae.

Looking out at all of them, more tears began to run down her face. "Thank you," she murmured.

Beside her, Bellarand folded his legs under him to lay down. He let her lean back against his bulk, her body quivering as relief washed through her.

"The forest is healing him," she said, hardly believing the words as they left her lips.

It's helping him heal, Bellarand said.

Molly didn't care to parse out the difference. What mattered was that her fae would live.

Of course he'll live, snorted Bellarand. *The both of us are far harder to kill than with a few measly stabbings.*

She couldn't help wincing at his brusque attempt at reassurance. Molly never wanted to experience anything like today ever again.

"Just heal him," she begged the trees and the animals and the earth. "Bring him back to me."

33

Before the dark of night could fully take hold, Molly raided her bedchamber and Allarion's and even Ravenna's for the coverlets. The vast linen cupboards were stocked with some extras, and those she left for their guests, but for tonight . . . Molly wanted them to have their blankets.

The heavy fabric thrown over her shoulder weighed her down, and after nearly falling on her face twice, she heeded the house's unhappy creaks and watched her step.

When she reentered the kitchen, trailing coverlets behind her, she felt the weight of many eyes fall upon her.

It was such an odd feeling, having others in the house. They milled about the atrium, dining room, and conservatory. Several had found their way down into the kitchen, her biggest pots steaming with boiling water to cleanse wounds. They'd thankfully lost no one, but the fae attackers had certainly done damage before succumbing to superior numbers.

Hearing feet tread the floorboards and the muffled voices of over a dozen other people grated against her ears. It was nothing to the din of a full tavern, of course, but the house, the forest, were usually so quiet. Their peace had been uprooted, and although she was infinitely grateful for their help, having so many here at once, crowded in her spaces, itched under her skin.

All the more reason to hurry back to Allarion and Bellarand in the meadow.

Pulling the wet cloth from his bruised face, Balar stood when he spotted her from his unswollen eye.

"Here, kitten, let me carry those for you."

"No," she said, too quickly.

The manticore looked on her with sympathy, but it didn't soften her. Logically, she knew they were there to help. They already had. They meant Allarion no harm.

Yet, the idea of allowing them anywhere near him, to see him at his most vulnerable, made acidic bile burn the back of her throat.

Whatever he saw in her eyes, the manticore seemed to understand some of her feelings. Paws up, he approached slowly before dipping down to grab the trailing ends of the coverlets.

"Here, at least don't let them get wet."

Gently, he wound the coverlets over her other shoulder, making something of a bulky, unwieldy scarf.

"Thank you," she managed to say. She wasn't being a very good hostess, but then, she couldn't care less if they were comfortable. They weren't Allarion.

Stepping closer, Lord Hakon asked softly, "How is he, Miss Molly?"

Glowing. Covered in roots. Still asleep.

She blinked at him, throat bobbing as she swallowed the words—he probably didn't need to know all that.

"He's resting," she finally said, "and Bellarand thinks he will recover."

Of course, Bellarand was known to lie to her, but she didn't think he was this time.

Lord Hakon sighed in relief. "That's good to hear. We came here to aid him, only for him to take the worst blows." His green face drew tight with stark lines. "He saved me."

The need to get back to her fae pulsed through her veins, but Molly managed to nod at the lord consort. "He's insufferably noble. I love him for it, but he'll be getting an earful about it."

Lord Hakon offered a sad smile. "In his place, I would be too from my Aislinn. Please give him our best. We'll stay as long as you need. I've sent out scouts to ensure that no other threats remain on your land."

"Thank you," she said, truly meaning it and not just wanting to finish the conversation. That Lord Hakon and the others had so willingly and quickly rallied for Allarion, that they were still here now, just waiting to help more in some way, filled her with a gratitude sharp enough to pierce her numb panic.

Everything will be all right.

"We won't keep you. Just please know, our thoughts and hopes are with you and Allarion tonight."

Molly bit the inside of her cheek to keep back the tears, nodding brusquely to the half-orc's kind words.

"I'm sorry for not being much of a hostess. The house has everything you need, just ask for it."

His brows drew lower over his finely chiseled face. "I'd meant to ask—the house is . . .?"

"Alive, yes. The magic. It understands you when you speak." Raising her gaze and her voice, she called out, "House, help them with anything they need, all right? Everyone here is a friend."

The shutters of the kitchen window rattled, making several halflings jump. Even through the tawny fur, she thought Balar paled as he looked around at the rafters, the reality of a sentient house sinking in.

Having his answer didn't seem to fill Lord Hakon with confidence, but he shook his head when she asked whether they needed anything else.

"We'll manage. Be with your mate."

"I'll be back in the morning," she said, more to the house than anyone else.

She left to a chorus of farewells and chattering shingles. Girded with the coverlets, she headed straight into the forest, the shrubs and brambles curling out of her way. Although she could hardly see in the gloam, she put one foot in front of the other, trusting the forest to not let her fall.

By the time she made it back to the meadow, the darkness was thick and cold. Only a sliver of a moon hung in the sky, offering little light. Still, Molly had just enough to see the meadow opening up ahead.

The shadowy form of Bellarand was her landmark, and his dark head lifted as she neared. He watched her with those fathomless, liquid eyes as she shook out a coverlet and laid it out over Allarion—and all the glowing roots encasing him.

Next, she spread another coverlet over Bellarand. He said nothing, not even a little quip, until she'd crawled under her own blanket and settled beside Allarion.

Did you eat and drink at the house?

No. She'd completely forgotten in her haste.

He'll be displeased when he wakes to find out.

Well, I'm displeased he got stabbed, so we'll both have to be unhappy with each other for a bit.

Bellarand huffed a horsey laugh before laying his long head over both her and Allarion. The weight of him was solid and comforting, and the warmth from his great body seeped through the coverlets to keep out the worst of the night's chill.

Still, Molly couldn't help shivering.

"Did he wake up while I was gone?"

No. He won't wake for a while yet. The long sleep will take as long as it needs.

Peeking under the blanket covering Allarion, Molly watched the glow of the roots. Peeling back the tattered shoulder of his tunic revealed skin newly sealed back together. The scar was pink and raw, but his skin had already knitted well.

Before she could pull the coverlet further down to check the slash at his side, Bellarand slid his head up to pin her.

Go to sleep, titmouse, he advised. *The best thing for both of you is sleep.*

Molly didn't know how she could possibly sleep after today, yet as she lay in the little cocoon the three of them made, warm and beside her fae, her eyes grew heavier and heavier. The weight of the day, the worry over Allarion, somehow both lifted and bore down on her, heavier than Bellarand's head.

Burying her face against Allarion's arm, Molly took a long, deep breath.

You'll wake me if something happens?

I promise. I'll look after you both.

She meant to tell him not to try anything funny while she was asleep, like cover her in pinecones or steal her blanket, but Molly was already slipping away.

Wake up tomorrow, she whispered to her fae and to the magic that coursed through him.

When Molly woke, it was to find Allarion much the same. He looked as serene as he usually did in his long sleeps, so that at least was a little relief. No pain marred his brow, and the roots continued to glow.

She shook the dew off the coverlets as Bellarand disappeared between the trees to relieve himself. When he returned, Molly took her turn, picking berries to stave off the worst of her hunger and thirst along the way.

The morning began cloudy with a mild breeze that cut through her coat. Molly huddled back under the coverlet before tucking Allarion's tighter to him.

As she did, she noticed that the roots were slowly sliding back into the earth.

A noise of alarm caught in her throat. "Wait!" She tried to pull them back to cover him, but the roots kept retreating into the dirt.

The forest has done all it can.

Molly couldn't help her whimper as the roots disappeared entirely. She stared at Allarion's face, looking for any sign, but he remained still. Serene but still.

She covered him again, tucking him in so he wouldn't get cold.

Something close to an hour passed, and Molly couldn't contain her worry anymore.

"If the forest is done, shouldn't he wake up?"

Healing takes time, Bellarand reminded her. His calm, wise tone was starting to irritate her. *But . . . talking to him couldn't hurt.*

Molly couldn't think of anything to say—everything felt trite or unimportant. So, Molly began to sing. She sang him each of her favorite ballads and then all of his favorite songs. She sang him everything she knew except the dirges because they were too sad. Tears sometimes accompanied her singing, and sometimes Bellarand bobbed his head although he denied it, yet as the sun rose behind the clouds, Molly sang.

Her throat rubbed raw and her legs fell numb sitting there singing, but she didn't care.

She sang the morning away, and when she began the final song she knew, a low thrumming harmonized with her voice.

Molly yelped, the sound one of profound, desperate hope.

Allarion's brows wrinkled. "Why did you stop?" he muttered.

She crumpled at his side, hot tears washing her face and his as she sobbed with relief. Not daring to throw herself atop him, she wrapped him in her arms and pressed her damp face to his.

Molly sobbed his name and other nonsense, all her worry and relief and love pouring out of her. Arms came around her, pulling her down into his body. She resisted a moment, thinking of his healing wounds, but after another, she couldn't deny either of them.

"You're awake, you're awake, you're awake!"

A velveteen muzzle ruffled her hair and nipped at Allarion's face.

I told her not to worry, said Bellarand. *You're far too stubborn to die from one little stab.*

"Indeed," he agreed. "I've had far worse."

Molly groaned before a laugh bubbled up her throat. It was a mad sort of giggle, but it felt good—and so did their teasing, although she'd never admit it.

"Absolutely no more stabbings," she demanded, sitting up to glare at her fae. "I can't bear it again."

Allarion's dear face softened, those amethyst eyes glittering up at her. His hand, with those tapered fingers, cupped the side of her face, his thumb running a soft line across her lower lip.

"Forgive me, sweetling," he rasped. "I fear I've frightened you."

"You scared me to every hell and back!"

He chuckled to hear it, and she might've smacked his arm for it, if she hadn't seen him be stabbed the day before.

As he looked up at her from the forest floor, his expression faded into something more serious. Molly's insides clenched, and she reached out to smooth his brow.

Allarion caught her hand and kissed the palm.

"I truly must ask your forgiveness," he murmured into her hand. "I was careless. The triad should never have been allowed to ambush us. To get so close to you . . ."

"I'm not the one they wanted."

But Allarion shook his head against her logic. "You are my *azai,* my heart. Your safety is my greatest desire and duty." His brows drew together again, and Molly's heart lurched to see tears gathering along his fan of lashes. "I failed you."

"Never." Leaning down over him, Molly claimed his mouth, pressing a fierce kiss to his lips. "You couldn't fail me if you tried."

He made a noise of disagreement, so Molly shushed him with another kiss.

"I always get what I want, remember?" she said softly. "I don't want your guilt. I just want you."

"My sweet mate. You honor me."

Molly was convinced the honor was all hers. How a man like him, noble to his core and far kinder than he had any right to be, looked at her twice she'd never know, but she wasn't about to question it. No matter what he and Bellarand claimed, she'd come close to losing him. How close . . . well, that didn't warrant thinking about.

Whatever the future held, whatever else the Fae Queen might try, it didn't matter. What did was that he'd come back to her. Just as he'd promised he would.

"Can you stand?" she asked. The forest may have done its part, but she wanted to get him tucked into bed, where she could properly look after him herself.

"I'd like to try."

Molly pulled back the blankets, and Bellarand stooped to get one of Allarion's arms over his withers. Together, they helped Allarion to his feet.

Standing, he pulled a great lungful of air into his chest as Molly wrapped her arms around his middle. "Thank you," she said, to him, to the forest, to everything.

Allarion was fae, he was strange, and he was utterly hers. Molly would never take it, nor their extraordinary, magical life here, for granted.

He smiled softly at her before kissing her forehead. "You know I live to please you, sweetling."

34

Some Months Later

Molly woke to the warm press of small kisses against her cheek and a hot cock sliding against the curve of her backside. Grinning into her pillow, she pretended to sleep for a few moments longer, enjoying the gentle way her fae caressed and held her. This was her favorite way to be woken up—and his favorite way to do it.

She could feel how warm and wet she was between her legs already; he'd been at it awhile, apparently. Molly felt the magic sparkling along her skin beneath the covers, teasing at her inner thighs and mons. One of his hands gently plucked at her breast as his magic made soft passes just above her clitoris.

His lips buzzed against her bare shoulder as he rumbled. "Molly, are you awake?"

"Maybe."

Another rumble, far more pleased this time. "Did I wake you? Forgive me, sweetling."

She snorted a laugh. "You're not really sorry." Not when he did it most mornings and on purpose.

"No, I'm not."

His big hand reached under her to hold her head, and he turned her face up for his kiss. Molly sighed into his mouth, letting herself be moved and adjusted just so. His other hand hooked her behind the knee, lifting to secure it over his thigh. She sighed again at the delicious stretch in her thigh and back—and in her cunt as he pushed inside.

"Good morning, my darling," she whispered to him.

There wasn't a better sight in this world or the next than that of her handsome fae, purple eyes glittering down at her in the morning light. That determined, almost smug grin that teased at his lips fascinated her, and she traced it with her thumb as he pushed deep. His silvery hair spilled over his shoulder as he leaned down to kiss every freckle on her cheek.

"My sweet mate," he crooned, "the sun rises later and later for jealousy of seeing your beauty."

Molly, with her thighs spread under the blankets, might have laughed again had his magic not begun to swirl around her clitoris. A deep, satisfied moan worked up her throat, and Molly lay still, letting him do as he pleased—for what pleased him most was making her weep with pleasure.

His thrusts were lazy, a leisurely invasion and retreat, rocking them gently.

The morning passed by not in minutes but kisses, the soft light from the windows growing brighter as his hips began to gain momentum. He kept his measured pace, not to be hurried even when she became needy. Her hips rolled backwards to meet his, seeking that next level of friction as the pressure built low in her belly.

"Allarion . . ." she moaned, reaching a hand back to bury in his silky hair.

His mouth dropped to the sensitive curve between shoulder and neck, and he teased a fang there along her round scars.

He hadn't needed to drink her blood in a long while, but the memory of when he did, the unique ecstasy of his bite, had her clenching around his cock.

"Do you want my fangs?" he rasped against her ear. "I feel how you clutch at me, sweetling. Do you need my bite?"

A needy sound escaped her, nails digging against his scalp. "Next time," she said breathlessly. "When the guests are all gone."

In just a few hours, their first true guests to Scarborough would start arriving. Lady Aislinn and Lord Hakon and their retinue, Balar and his brothers, Maritza and her sisters, Orek and Sorcha Brádaigh and their clan, her little cousins and their families and guardians, Mayor Doherty and his family, friends from Dundúran, friends from Mullon, and more. She probably didn't need a new set of punctures to hide or explain over the next few days.

What she did need was for him to *move.*

Implacable as always, though, Allarion wouldn't be rushed. Not when she begged nor when she threatened. Snaking her hand under the blankets, she caught a handful of his taut backside and squeezed, but still he wouldn't increase his pace or power more than incrementally.

A big warm hand seized her breast and squeezed, making Molly whimper.

"I will have this, my love," he purred. "I have to make it last with so many guests over the next days."

Molly laughed, although it sounded more desperate than anything else. "They're not going to be in here with us."

"No, but they will be in the house. These are my last hours alone with you, and I mean to indulge."

He said that as if they didn't indulge every day. The only time they hadn't was the days immediately after his fight with the fae knights and during his recovery.

After more, shorter sleeps and staying abed for a few days, Allarion had declared himself healed. Molly still bullied him into staying in bed another day, although he'd only acquiesced when she joined him. She hadn't been convinced he was ready for anything, even if he insisted on at least using his hands and mouth to make up for time lost.

He tuckered himself out completely and took a two-day long sleep after that. So Molly had had her way, insisting he rest. For several weeks, he'd done little more than lay about or sit near, reading or watching her cook or playing the harpsichord.

His strength returned, his healing leaving just the faintest lilac scars on his chest. He'd had her touch them, to reassure herself that he was whole and hale, yet the sight of them still gave Molly pause. No matter what he or Bellarand said, those scars were proof he'd nearly been taken from her. If the Fae Queen had had her way, Allarion would either be a prisoner in the faelands or dead, and Molly hated her for that.

Months on, that hate still lived inside her, but she blanketed it with joy in the everyday. Slowly, life returned to their kind of normal. He resumed work on the house. Bellarand resumed his war with the squirrels, their temporary parley over. Molly resumed her projects and started new ones.

Winter had left and spring was beginning to warm into summer and, finally, not only was her fae back to himself, but the house was finished. Every shingle and every floorboard gleamed. Each room had been furnished to their tastes, new wallpapers and paints adding bursts of color to the walls.

Allowing the forest to help heal him had forged a bond between them, one that he'd never have had otherwise. He was this land and the land was him. With Molly's help, Allarion had little trouble tying the last knots to bond his magic with that of Scarborough.

Allarion was alive and healthy. The house was finished. The spring blooms were full and bright. It was time to celebrate.

Right after she got the orgasm she wanted.

His name was a hiss through her teeth this time as her hips rolled harder than the tide against the rocks. A rich, low chuckle echoed in his throat, inciting her, enflaming her.

"All right, sweetling," he murmured at her ear.

That talented hand replaced his magic between her thighs, the pads of two fingers finding her clitoris to make firm circles.

Molly's back bowed, a silent scream opening her mouth wide. She came apart, body quaking with all the burst tension he'd built over the morning. The pleasure scorched her like a sunburst, hot and intense. Her thighs clamped closed on his hand and cock as she ran down her pleasure, another wave cascading through her to feel him filling her up with spend.

Face buried in her hair, Allarion pumped inside her, their hips slapping together in a wet dance muffled by the bedding. His great chest shuddered at her back, his arms wrapping round to hold her tight.

The pleasure wiped all thought from Molly's mind, and she lay there for a long while, catching her breath. Her senses came back slowly, every sight and sound and smell of him.

So, so carefully, he lowered his leg to free hers, laying her supine in the bed. Molly rolled into him, welcoming him into the cradle of her body as they sank into more soft kisses.

They needed to get up.

Sure, the house could handle it, but as the new Lord and Lady Scarborough, they should really be good hosts at their first gathering.

But Molly couldn't help it, going for just a little more of him. A year before, she wouldn't have thought it possible to be with a person for so much of her time and still want more. They spent nearly every hour together, often just the two of them, and yet she never grew tired or bored of him. There was always something new or charming about him, something that kept her so utterly in love with her strange fae.

She couldn't quite say what it was about him—and really, she didn't want to know. The mystery was part of the charm. And, it wasn't just one thing. It was everything, every bit of him that made him Allarion.

She loved his compassion and kindness, she loved his dry sarcasm and cutting wit, she loved his grumpiness and surliness and bossiness. She loved that he took such care of her, and she loved taking care of him, too. Getting to hold him in her arms and her heart was the greatest honor of her life, and even if she struggled to put that into words for him, she knew he knew. She loved that, too.

Their stomachs rumbled for breakfast and they were sticky with this morning and last night's lovemaking and their guests would arrive in a few short hours, but none of that stopped Molly from pushing her fae to his back. Allarion went willingly, one of his fine brows arching in interest.

Swinging a leg over his hips, Molly mounted her handsome fae, taking his cock in her hand. Still wet with their spends, her hand glided up and down, up and down with ease.

Molly caught her bottom lip between her teeth and guided him inside. He held her hips for balance as she sank down, and they both groaned with relief to come together.

Setting her hands on his glorious chest, she began to move. He'd put meat on his bones over the past months, muscle and bulk from good food and hard work. No longer were his ribs prominent or his hipbones sharp. He'd always been beautiful, but like this, Allarion was magnificent. And he was hers.

Molly snapped her hips down on his, taking her fae for the ride she wanted, hard and brutal and delicious. He smiled that fierce smile, fangs flashing in the sunlight, long hair mussed and spread over the pillows.

He pulled her back down to him as she bounced on his cock, holding her there when she stopped to swirl her hips. The tendons in his neck popped against his throat, and Molly leaned down to lick the hot skin there. His big hands filled with her backside, and their rhythm turned frantic, brutal.

Molly loved every second.

She came in no time at all, spread thighs quivering as the pleasure rolled from head to toe and back again. He didn't give her time to come down, though, but held her by the waist, thrusting up from below. Their slick and spend dripped down onto his thighs, glistening in the morning light.

Molly held on for the ride of her life, a smile so wide on her face it almost hurt as she orgasmed again. Catching one of his hands, she pressed it against her breast and squeezed around his cock, wringing the pleasure from him in ropes of spend.

When she'd gotten every last drop and ounce and scrap of his pleasure and hers, Molly slumped onto his chest, ready for a nap. He bundled her into his arms and kissed her sweaty hair.

"My queen," he rumbled happily.

Allarion pinned his stiff collar in place before stepping back to look over his appearance in the mirror. Many of his clothes had needed adjusting over the intervening months, but his Molly was clever, especially with her needle.

His black tunic molded to his chest as it used to, the seams perfect, the cut flattering. Most of all he enjoyed the newly added embroidery to the sleeves and shoulders. Along with his family crests and warrior insignia, she'd added motifs from their estate; trees and deer and even several unicorns. All were done in glossy midnight blue thread, so that it was visible only when the light gleamed across the stitching.

Hair drawn back with a velvet ribbon and capelet thrown over his left shoulder, he looked every bit the fae aristocrat his mother had raised, ready to greet guests into his home. There was but one thing missing.

Stalking back through his old bedchamber and into the brighter one he now shared with Molly, he found her nearly ready. The gown she'd chosen was all soft lilacs and powdery blues. It was more feminine than her usual attire, although she'd added her own embroidering and modifications. She's told him she liked the color, as it reminded her of the color of his cheeks when he blushed.

Crossing the room to her, he said, "Let me."

Molly pouted at him over her shoulder. "Why they ever put the laces in the back is beyond me."

He rumbled in agreement, even if he quietly relished getting to tighten and tie her stays. There was something utterly alluring about lacing the strings and knotting the ends—especially knowing he'd get to untie them all that evening.

The back neckline swooped just below her shoulder blades, her freckles peeking out beneath her growing hair. Half fell down her back in soft waves while the other had been gathered elegantly atop her head.

When she tried to turn to face him, he placed a hand on her shoulder to keep her facing forward. From his pocket he pulled a white box.

Her hairstyle showed off the silver bobs in her ears, and Allarion took great pleasure in securing a matching necklace around her pretty throat. He heard her sharp breath when she felt the cool metal touch her skin, and she teased a fingertip over the pearls dangling from the silver chain as he secured the ribbons at her nape.

She glided to the tall mirror across the room, inspecting the necklace. It was a pretty thing, commissioned by one of his grandmothers. While not ostentatious, the silver filigree was exquisite and the pearls perfectly round.

Allarion grinned at her in the mirror when, rather than arguing it was too fine, Molly smiled at herself. His grin grew when she twirled, skirts fluttering as the dresser drawers opened and closed in applause. She giggled to herself as she came back to him, reaching to take the arm he offered her.

"Look at me, a proper lady," she said.

Her beaming smile lit him from within. Leaning down to kiss her cheek, he told her, "You are just as you should be."

A comely blush pinkened her cheeks. "I like being Lady Scarborough."

"There is none other who could be the mistress of Scarborough."

That earned him another smile, and he obliged when she leaned her head back for a kiss.

With his beautiful *azai* on his arm and her taste on his lips, Allarion led them down to await their guests.

The day turned into a pleasant one, just on the right side of warm with nary a cloud in the sky. Guests meandered the grounds and the first floor, admiring the newly finished rooms and partaking in the finger foods Molly had worked hard to prepare over the past days.

He was still learning about humans—and half-orcs, manticores, harpies, and dragons—but Allarion thought everyone was enjoying themselves. None more so than the house, which kept the small crowd of guests entertained with music and guided them to different rooms with cheery knocks of its shutters.

Even Bellarand and his small herd of unicorns—the two surviving dread-mounts of the triad, a dark chestnut bay named Achaiös and a dappled gray stallion named Tulare—had joined the festivities, allowing the children and women to fawn over them. The two unicorns were far more amiable than Bellarand, although all three enjoyed the admiration of those brave enough to draw near.

In another surprise, Molly had been able to bond with both unicorns, and through her bond with them, all the inhabitants of Scarborough estate were able to communicate. It made for a loud mind when there was a fresh shipment of carrots, but with practice, Allarion and Molly had learned to block the worst of the unicorns' quibbling.

Perhaps because she wasn't a female fae, Molly was able to forge the bond. Perhaps it was the uniqueness of Scarborough. Allarion wasn't entirely sure, although he suspected it was the first of many surprises to come as he too learned more about the ramifications of a lone fae weaving his magic into a new land and taking a human *azai*.

Achaiös and Tulare offered Bellarand company—and, honestly,

someone to lord over—and Molly protection. Overall, it pleased Allarion.

It was a small good to come of the triad's attack.

The scars on his body and the unicorns were the only proof that the attack had ever happened. Upon waking from his long sleep, he learned from Hakon that the other bodies had already disappeared, subsumed into the earth itself. It was a reminder that the forest was an inherently wild place, one that did not subscribe to human or fae morals. The forest gave and it could take, too.

While it may have given his honor peace to bury the triad in the traditional way, say rites over them and burn sweet sage to cleanse their spirits, Allarion understood that the forest had sacrificed to help heal him. It claimed the bodies and their magic for itself, and Allarion could only hope that, in some small way, it meant the fae and unicorn would live on, free of Amaranthe.

Something he hoped for all his kind one day.

And that day was closer now that the house was complete, the bond with the estate secure.

Today was about reintroducing Scarborough to their friends and allies. It was about Molly taking her place as the lady of the estate. Yet it was also for Allarion to finally decide on who he would ask to steward the estate while he and Molly were away.

He'd underestimated Amaranthe's reach and spite, only making him want to fulfill his promise to Maxim all the more. With the magic woven and the bond formed, Allarion felt it was time for Ravenna to come home. He had to hope that, despite no further signs or threats from the faelands, she was still safe in her bower. Allarion wouldn't leave it to chance much longer.

A heavy slap to the shoulder jarred him from his thoughts, and Allarion turned to look upon Balar, grinning at him in that leonine way of his. His tunic sleeves had been shorn short to show off his tawny, bulging arms, and the seams strained with how tightly it clung to his wide chest. His mane and wings had been groomed to a high shine, as were the scales of his tail and leather of his boots.

All the manticore pride swaggered around the estate, trying to catch the eye of every available female in attendance. When she'd seen them, Molly had just rolled her eyes. *"Just keep them away from the girls. Nora is at the right age to make wrong decisions."*

Thankfully, the manticores were gentle and friendly with the children, saving their lustier looks for any adult woman who crossed their paths—even the ones with graying hair.

Perhaps they should sleep outside, Allarion considered.

And have them stink up the forest with their pheromones? I think not, scoffed Bellarand.

"An excellent gathering, my friend," said Balar, slapping Allarion's shoulder again.

"Thank you for coming. It pleases me to have you visit finally."

Allarion had initially thought of Balar and his brothers to watch the estate, but now he was thinking Theron and his half-sister Briseis would be the safer option. He worried under the manticores, Scarborough would become little more than a den of iniquity.

Bellarand snorted. *As if you aren't up to plenty of iniquity yourselves. You're just jealous,* Molly quipped.

Allarion bit back a smile, soothed by the voice of his *azai.* Last he'd seen her, she'd been off to show her little cousins the library. Merry, the scholarly girl, had practically bounced as Molly led the way into the house.

"It's good to see you up and about," Balar continued. "You gave your female quite the scare."

"She takes good care of me."

Balar huffed in agreement. "Speaking of, how often have you been to this town of Mullon I keep hearing of? Are there many unmated females there?"

Allarion blinked, having to think about it. "I'm not sure . . ."

Somehow, the manticore roped him into providing an estimate, but thankfully, the conversation eventually moved to how the otherly village continued to grow. Balar spoke wistfully of how another two half-orcs had found themselves a human mate.

"Perhaps humans are more partial to the color green?" Balar wondered.

Allarion offered what advice he could, although he didn't know how helpful it could be. He didn't need Molly beside him to remember that stealing away or buying a human mate weren't viable options. Tempting and expedient as it might be, he would always remember how close he came to losing Molly entirely with a shudder of horror.

He listened to the manticore patiently, understanding that, under his bluster and boisterousness, Balar and his brothers were ultimately lonely. They'd fled a vicious pride war in the southern grasslands, wishing for peace and a good life—preferably one shared with a human mate. Allarion couldn't fault them for it, not when he met every day with an abiding gratitude to his goddesses for bringing him to his queen.

Slapping his hand on the manticore's beefy shoulder in return, Allarion said, "There are many beautiful human women in the Darrowlands. I'm sure one of them will make you a very happy man."

Balar laughed, his grin lopsided. "Well, I wish she'd hurry up about it!"

Allarion sensed his Molly before he saw her, turning his gaze in time to watch her emerge from the house. She had only one of her cousins in tow now, though the girl quickly scampered off to find more delights, leaving Molly to return to him.

His soul alighted to see her walking toward him, her eyes glittering and her smile beatific. Her hair had gone a little mussed over the day and her dress had wrinkled in a few places, but she was the picture of beauty and grace, every bit the lady she was meant to be.

He reached for her, needing to draw her closer that much sooner. Allarion tucked her into his side, his heart beating a little harder to have her beside him.

"Next time we're in Dundúran, you should find an excuse to be there, too. I'm sure I can make some introductions," Molly offered.

Balar's gaze gleamed with interest, so much so, he didn't seem to question or care why she knew their conversation already without having heard it. He listened intently as Molly offered her own advice, such as reining back some of the manticore intensity and not marking a woman's home as their territory before they had express confirmation that she was interested.

Allarion listened, too, charmed by the advice.

Is this how I should have courted you, sweetling?

Even as she spoke with Balar, she squeezed an arm around his waist.

You managed just fine, she thought, throwing him a little wink. *Even if your methods were . . . strange.*

Perhaps to her. To him, they were a mere fraction of what he'd been and was willing to do to have her. He could regret not speaking to her rather than her uncle, but he'd never be sorry for claiming what he knew was his.

For all his many days and long life, he would always remember the one that brought him to her. Every day with her made him that much more grateful for that day in Dundúran, when he heard a beautiful, laughing voice that drew his attention to a well. It had been like any other well, in any other city square. Yet, that day, that place had changed the course of his existence.

Slipping his hand to her waist, Allarion pulled her close to lay a kiss on the top of her head, her fragrant hair teasing his nose.

My heart.

She answered not with words but a wash of love, passed along the numerous threads of magic that bound them together. Her love rebounded down the weave of magic, reverberating in the weft and knit, declaring to every tree and beast connected to this land that she was bound, heart and soul, to him.

To know he held the love of such a woman was a force stronger than any magic, vaster than any ocean, and deeper than any mountain.

She was his *azai,* his pride, his life. She was the very beat of his heart. A surprise and a blessing, never to be taken for granted.

Allarion would do anything for such a love. Remake the world, dethrone a tyrant, cross land and sea unknown—even live a little life, obscure and happy. He didn't need fame or renown, honor or power. All he needed was her and her happiness.

And my *happiness,* said Bellarand.

Epilogue

One Month Later

For several days now, Allarion's hopes played tricks on his mind. As the landscape rolled around them, he convinced himself he recognized it, that a familiar hillock or stream meant Ravenna's bower was just a few moments away.

He did remember the path he and Bellarand had taken north when they first left her to the deep sleep. The stark memory was their guide south again, yet as each day passed without finally finding the bower, Allarion's fears only grew.

Molly was a balm to his agitated soul, soothing him that everything would be all right.

With their little herd of three unicorns, she was well protected, enough so that Allarion could stomach her coming with him. More than once, he'd considered leaving her behind in the safety of Scarborough. Yet, he couldn't bring himself to betray her trust.

And, he was more than certain she would have followed him on Achaiös and Tulare. So then he would have had her along *and* she'd be furious.

In the end, although he didn't take a long sleep and guarded his precious mate with the dread-mounts throughout every night, they'd met with little danger. A rushing river swollen with snowmelt and a cagey group of travelers scared off by Bellarand's horn had been the worst of their obstacles. Other than Molly having to sleep rough and live on rations, their journey was easy.

No earthquakes. No fae knights. Nothing.

It might have been comforting, had Allarion not already under-estimated Amaranthe once. The sooner they retrieved Ravenna and returned to the safety of Scarborough, the better for his peace of mind.

That day passed with more hazy memories and a dreadful sort of hope gripping his throat tightly. The surrealism of finally fulfilling his promise, of seeing the end of his mission, added another layer of ap-prehension. His mind couldn't quite believe that they approached the end, that for all Amaranthe's power, Maxim had outwitted her.

When the trees ahead began to look familiar, at first, Allarion dis-missed the feeling.

Then, Bellarand's ears perked.

I think . . .

Molly turned to look at him and then Bellarand. Atop Tulare, she peered ahead, worrying her lip between her teeth.

"Are we getting close?"

Allarion couldn't force words past his tight throat.

Yes, his heart and soul cried.

He knew these trees. And as they continued closer, the unmistak-able spark of magic burst in little pinpricks across his cheek.

A shudder of relief bowed his back as Allarion passed through Maxim's wards.

His heart lurched with joy, only for worry to clench it taut again when he looked over his shoulder to see Molly and the two unicorns left on the other side. Her head whipped about frantically, her eyes white-rimmed as they searched blindly for him.

She cannot see us, Bellarand realized.

"Where did you go?" Molly called, panic rising in her voice.

"Allarion?"

"Don't be frightened, sweetling," he told her, but she twisted in the saddle, her hands wringing the reins.

She cannot hear us, either.

I'm here, Molly.

She gasped, looking forward again.

"Where are you? I don't see you?" The shrill panic in her voice tore at him.

It's the wards. Maxim laid many to protect Ravenna in her sleep. I hadn't thought . . .

In his haste, he hadn't considered that Maxim would of course not have set the wards to allow a human inside, no matter who that human might be.

The sight of his worried mate upset him, and he'd nearly urged Bellarand back across the wards when he saw her take a long, deep breath.

You're all right? Not hurt? she asked, working to calm herself.

We're just fine, sweetling, I promise. The wards were meant to keep everyone else out, but not us.

Molly nodded shakily. *All right. All right. I'll stay here with the boys.*

A groan ripped from Allarion's throat. He didn't want to leave her; he never wanted Molly to be out of his sight, especially off the estate. Yet, his promise was a weight in his chest, and so close to completion . . .

You're sure? It may take some time to rouse Ravenna properly and get her ready for travel.

I'm sure. Molly nodded, casting a determined frown where she likely thought he and Bellarand stood. *You go get our girl.*

Goddesses, he didn't deserve her. His pride was a painful pleasure in his chest to hear her call Ravenna theirs. Although she'd never met her, Molly had spoken of Ravenna with nothing but compassion since learning of her plight. Allarion knew they would be fast friends, and that was just what Ravenna needed after her loss.

Thank you, Molly.

Go.

Bellarand turned for the grove of trees at a trot, bringing them deeper inside the wards. Maxim's magic hung over the grove like a thick fog, nearly choking. Inside, the air was preternaturally still, no breeze fluttering through the leaves. No birds or other small creatures jumped between branches, no noise from the nearby stream penetrated the wards.

Following the curve of the grove, they soon found themselves before the bower.

It was just as Allarion remembered it, a somber sight that brought every memory of his friend to the fore of his mind. The bower was blanketed in years of pine and leaf detritus, the sweet smell of decay the only scent.

The moss and grasses that had once covered the roof were brown and withered, dried out and dead. Nothing looked out of place, each of the barrels and pots still where he'd left them. Nothing had been disturbed, no footprints in the dirt nor sign of intruders.

Still . . .

"Something's wrong," he murmured to Bellarand.

The unicorn lowered his head, snuffling at the ground. *Where is Oberon and the herd? Their scents are faded and old.*

Allarion's throat closed around his terror, and he flung himself from Bellarand's back, bounding for the bower door.

The heavy oak door creaked on its unoiled hinges, revealing— nothing.

The bower sat empty, the bed unoccupied.

Allarion stared, not believing what he saw, mind unwilling to think what he didn't see. Numbness overtook his limbs as his hopes plummeted to the ground.

Ravenna was gone.

Glossary of People, Places, Pronunciations, Medieval Things, & Fae Words

Achaiös (ahk-kai-ohs)—a unicorn dread-mount

Aine (awn-yuh)—human mate of Maxim, mother of Ravenna

Allarion Meringor (ah-lar-ee-on mehr-in-gore)—a lone fae warrior, rider of Bellarand, our hero

Amaranthe (am-uh-ran-thee)—Fae Queen, a hag

Aislinn Darrow (ash-lihn)—future Liege Darrow, heiress of the Darrowlands, wife to Hakon Green-Fist

Andreen (ahn-dreen)—harpy living in the Darrowlands

Aodhan (ay-dawn, like Aiden)—captain of the guard for Dundúran Castle

azai (ah-zhigh)—*heartmate,* faethling for soulmate, fated mate

Balar (bah-lar)—manticore living in the Darrowlands

baron—in the book, a noble rank above earl and margrave but below liege lord

Bellarand (bell-uh-rand)—black unicorn, grumpy, lets Allarion ride him

Briseis (brih-zay-iss)—half-dragon living in the Darrowlands, half-sister of Theron

Brom Dunne—Molly's maternal uncle, runs a tavern

Bryan Dunne—Brom's oldest child and only son, Molly's cousin, a farrier's apprentice

Caledon (kal-ih-don)—northernmost kingdom of humans that split from Eirea hundreds of years ago

deep sleep—for the fae, a level of sleep like torpor, when bodily and magical function shuts almost completely down; can last for years

demesne (duh-mane)—similar in meaning and pronunciation to domain; historically, the land attached to a noble manor; in the book, means the regional lands overseen by liege lords (e.g., the Darrowlands)

dread-mount—a stallion unicorn bonded to a fae warrior

Dougal Braithwaite—an unwise nobleman, brother to Fiona, Earl of Longmere

Dundúran (dun-dure-un)—capital city of the Darrowlands; can mean the city or the castle itself

earl—in the book, a noble rank below liege lord and baron but above margrave

Eirea (eer-ee-uh)—central kingdom of humans, still recovering from brutal wars of succession

faelands—territory claimed and inhabited by the fae; imbued over millennia with their magic

faethling—native language of the fae

Fallorian—fae capital

Fia (fee-uh)—Aislinn's seneschal

Finn—Molly's ex-lover, a dead man walking according to Allarion

Fiona Braithwaite—a nosey noblewoman, sister of Lord Dougal

Gleanná (glay-ah-nah)—capital of Eirea

guild—an association of craftsmen or merchants that oversee the stages of production of their craft/product (e.g., stonemasons, bricklayers)

Hakon Green-Fist (hay-kon)—half-orc blacksmith at Dundúran Castle, future Lord Consort of the Darrowlands, husband to Lady Aislinn

Isolde Monaghan (ih-zolde mon-uh-han)—Crown Princess of Eirea

Jennet (gen-et)—Molly's friend, a fellow barmaid

liege lord—historically, a superior lord/authority to others; in the book, the highest rank of noble below the royal family, rules and oversees the entire demesne

long sleep—for the fae, a normal type of sleep taken every few days rather than a nightly rest; can last for a full day or more if the fae is recovering from injury

lord/lady—in the book, honorific of any noble person of any rank, usually attached to the person's given name

Lorna—a dressmaker in Mullon

margrave—historically, a noble rank that oversaw the lands along the borders of a kingdom; in the book, the lowest noble rank after liege lord, baron, and earl

Maritza (mar-ihtz-uh)—harpy living in the Darrowlands

Marius Caellus (mar-ee-us kay-luhs)—King Consort of Eirea, half-Pyrrossi

Maxim (max-ihm)—fae warrior, Allarion's oldest friend, mated to Aine, father to Ravenna

Merrick Darrow—Lord of the Darrowlands, father of Aislinn

Merry Dunne—Brom's third child, Molly's cousin, absolutely brilliant

Molly Dunne—human barmaid, orphan, our heroine

Mullon—a market town about two hours' ride from Scarborough

Nora Dunne—Brom's oldest daughter, Molly's cousin, a bit of a pill

Oberon (oh-burr-on)—Maxim's unicorn mount

Oona Dunne—Brom's youngest child, Molly's cousin, a certified cutie patootie

Orek Stone-Skin—half-orc hunter living in the Darrowlands, mated to Sorcha

Pyrros (peer-ohs)—southern kingdom of humans, has conquered other lands, countries, and tribes to the south

Ravenna—half-fae, half-human daughter of Maxim and Aine, gifted with foresight

Rory Dunne—Brom's fourth child, Molly's cousin, very good at riling her sister Nora

Scarborough—abandoned estate bought and overseen now by Allarion

seneschal (sen-uh-shull)—historically, the overseer of a manor or a high-ranking official; in the book, the direct assistant to the lord/lady

Sorcha Brádaigh (sor-sha brah-day)—horse trainer, mated to Orek, friend to Aislinn, eldest of many siblings

stone sleep—for the fae, a type of eternal sleep taken by elder fae when it is time for them to pass on to the afterworld; typically taken on the Twins

Theron (ther-ohn)—red dragon living in the Darrowlands, half-brother of Briseis

Tulare (too-lar)—a unicorn dread-mount

The Twins—the two fae goddesses that represent the sun and moon, life and death, war and love, and all duality, they are believed to bestow azai as a sign of favor; also associated with the two islands off the coast of the faelands

yeoman (yo-man)—historically, a free but not noble man who owned a landed estate; in the book, all non-noble landholders

Ygraine Monaghan (ee-grane mon-uh-han)—Queen of Eirea

Author's Note

Hello! Thank you so much for reading *Sweetling!* I hope you enjoyed Molly and Allarion's story and returning to the Monstrous World!

Once Allarion and Bellarand showed up on the page, I knew their story needed to be next. I also knew that their heroine needed to be a particular type of woman. I always thought it'd be fun to have a barmaid heroine, and I think Molly was the perfect counterpoint to Allarion. A woman has to be brave to have all that strangeness coming at her and take it like a champ!

Basing their story loosely on *Beauty and the Beast* was also so much fun! It was an enjoyable puzzle to decide what facets of the beloved fairy tale I would try to keep. Some fit so nicely into their story and helped move the plot along, so win win. I loved the idea of a pretty beast, as well as a sentient house. The house was a character unto itself, and it was so fun thinking about the noises and actions a house would do to emote.

Now, I know what you're thinking. What about Ravenna???

Her story is coming next! I've had this planned for a while, knowing that Allarion's story would be followed by Ravenna's. I know we have a lot of unfinished business in the faelands, and our girl has some serious revenge to take. Good thing her hero will be more than up to the task. (He's been name-dropped already, I look forward to your guesses ;).)

Ravenna's story will be called *Faeling*, and I can't wait to reveal more and start teasing her story. Keep on the lookout for art soon!

Before I get to her story, though, we're back to gargoyles! I'm looking forward to getting to June's story and back to the museum. We have lots more hunky gargoyles waiting for their heartsongs, so back we go! I'll be working on *Heartsworn* (War of the Underhill 3) the first few months of 2025. The rest of the series is still on submission, so I'm not entirely sure where it will be published initially.

Ravenna and *Faeling* will be coming summer 2025, either July or August. After that, I'm hoping to get to a fun spinoff of the WoU series.

So lots to do and look forward to!

Thank you so much for reading! If you enjoyed this story, I'd appreciate it if you'd consider leaving a review. Reviews are so important in helping spread the word about a book and getting it in front of more eyeballs. Thanks again!

Come say hi on social media or check out my website, www.sewendelauthor.com, for more on my stories and to explore awesome merch!

Thanks so much!

—S. E.

Acknowledgements

I'd also like to take a moment to thank some of the people who made this book possible!

A huge thank you to Mita and Abigail, my writing besties and the best beta readers out there!

Thank you to Leah, my awesome PA, who helped me go from hobbyist to big girl author with my own website and everything.

I'm also so grateful to my amazing ARC team, y'all are amazing!

And I have to mention too the amazing artists who helped bring Molly and Allarion to life. A huge thank you to Beth Gilbert, the stunningly talented artist who illustrated the cover. I also want to thank Milene, Marianna, Jylia, Jeannine, and more, you're all so amazing and I'm so grateful for the care you've taken with my book babies!

Other Works

A Time of War and Demons (House of the Rising Sun, Book 1), fantasy romance novel

Aerie (Broken Wings Duet, Book 1), fantasy romance novel
Haven (Broken Wings Duet, Book 2), fantasy romance novel

Stone Hearts (War of the Underhill, Book 0), historical monster/fantasy romance novella
Heartsong (War of the Underhill, Book 1), monster/paranormal romance novel, February 2026
Heartsworn (War of the Underhill, Book 2), monster/paranormal romance novel, October 2026

Halfling (Monstrous World, Book 1), monster/fantasy romance novel
Ironling (Monstrous World, Book 2), monster/fantasy romance novel
Sweetling (Monstrous World, Book 3), fae/fantasy romance novel
Faeling (Monstrous World, Book 4), monster/fae/fantasy romance novel
Changelings (Monstrous World, Book 5), monster/fantasy romance novella collection, Autumn 2025 + Spring 2026
Foundling (Monstrous World, Book 6), monster/fae/fantasy romance, Summer 2026

Stay in Touch

If you'd like to stay in touch, come on over to socials and say hi! I'm around on most platforms as se.wendel.author, and I'm most active on Instagram. Come check it out to find out about what I'm working on, get some reading recommendations, and get spammed with pictures of my cat. What's not to love?

You can also check out all my books, commissioned art, and book merch shop on my author website (www.sewendelauthor.com)! Lots of good stuff over there!

I've also started up a monthly newsletter. The first is out now and you can subscribe on my website to keep up with me and my news.

About the Author

S. E. is a California native who grew up with animals; her ginger tabby is her current writing partner and lets her know when it's time to take a break (by laying on her keyboard). She graduated from the University of California, Davis with a master's in creative writing and uses all her available time to build worlds, characters, and their stories. She enjoys animal rescue shows, almost everything in Trader Joe's, and all the beautiful landscapes of California.